LAKEFRONT BILLIONAIRES

LOVE REDESIGNED

LAUREN ASHER

Bloom *books*

Published by Bloom Books, an imprint of Sourcebooks
P.O. Box 4410, Naperville, Illinois 60567–4410
(630) 961-3900
sourcebooks.com

Cataloging-in-Publication Data is on file with the Library of Congress.

Printed and bound in the United States of America.

LSC 10 9 8 7 6 5 4

PLAYLISTS

▶

Love Redesigned by Lauren Asher

Scan to listen

+

Love Redesigned
Playlist

>

Fuck Love Songs
Playlist

>

Stressed and Depressed
Playlist

>

Get Hammered
Playlist

>

Duke Brass: Greatest Hits
Album - Duke Brass

>

To those whose love language is words of affirmation.
Your praise kink is safe with me (and Julian Lopez).

CONTENT WARNING

This love story contains explicit content and topics that may be sensitive to some readers. For a more detailed content warning list, please scan the QR code or visit laurenasher.com/lrcw.

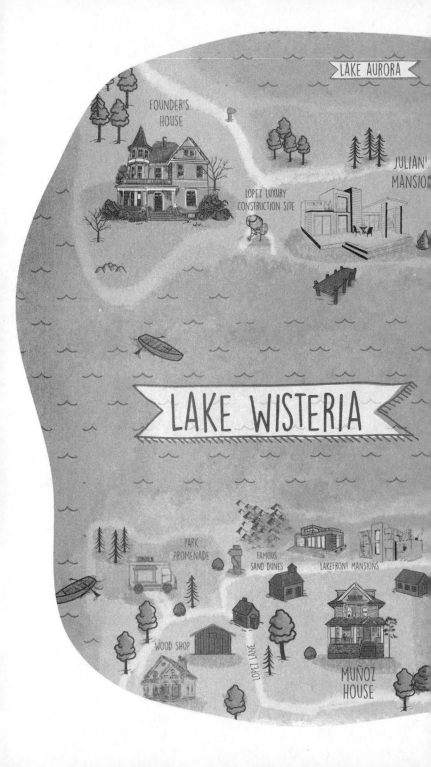

RAPHAEL'S FARM

HISTORIC DISTRICT

LAST CALL

MAIN STREET

SWEETS & TREATS

ANGRY ROOSTER CAFE

WISTERIA HIGH

FESTIVAL FAIRGROUNDS

CHAPTER ONE

Julian

I'm about ten seconds away from losing my goddamn mind, and I have the painfully slow driver clogging up the only road into town to blame.

The sun set twenty minutes ago, giving me nothing to focus on but the illuminated California license plate caught in my headlights. I resist the urge to flash my high beams and honk my horn, although I nearly give in when the black Mercedes-Benz sedan weaves slightly to the side before correcting itself.

Cálmate. You only have five more miles left before hitting Main Street.

While I'm tempted to cut around the other driver so I can make it in time for my godson's talent show, I don't want to risk damaging my new McLaren by going off-road. I didn't

Cálmate: Calm down.

spend the last few years of my life talking myself into buying my dream car only to ruin the suspension a week after having it delivered.

The blast of my phone's ringtone startles me as my cousin's name flashes across the screen. I take a deep breath before stabbing the button on my steering wheel.

"Where the hell are you?" The sound of Rafael's harsh whisper fills the car.

"I'll be there in ten minutes."

A disapproving hum follows. "But the show starts in five."

"Don't worry. I'll make it before Nico takes the stage."

"Not sure how that's possible when he's in the opening act."

Mierda. "I had no clue."

"The program schedule got switched at the last minute after a few kids came down with a bug. I texted you this morning about it." He doesn't bother hiding his annoyance.

My hands clutch the smooth leather wheel. "The meeting in Lake Aurora took a lot longer than expected."

"Of course it did."

"Things should slow down soon."

"Sure they will." His rough tone only fuels my irritation.

Before his wife filed for divorce two years ago, people called Rafael the easygoing Lopez cousin, with him constantly going out of his way to put a smile on everyone's face.

Rafael's deep sigh cuts through the silence. "It's fine. Nico will understand."

My godson might be a mature eight-year-old kid, but he

Mierda: Shit.

2

isn't *that* mature. And after everything he has been through with his parents' divorce, I refuse to add myself to his growing list of family disappointments.

"Your mom saved you a seat in the back of the auditorium in case you make it."

"Rafa, I'll be—"

He hangs up before hearing the rest of my sentence.

Pendejo.

Rafa and I have been butting heads more often than not lately, mostly due to his attitude and my busy schedule running my late father's construction company. While I try my hardest to balance my personal life and Lopez Luxury expanding beyond my father's wildest dreams, I keep falling short.

I scan the narrow space beside the road. The incline is muddy but still drivable for the handful of seconds I need to pass the car in front of me.

Stop overthinking and do it.

The rosary my mother hung from my rearview mirror spins as I turn my wheel toward the shoulder and slam my foot against the gas pedal. The engine revs as it switches gears, and my tires squeal.

My heart lodges itself in my throat as the other vehicle veers to the right and blocks my clear path.

Fuck. Fuck. Fuck!

Time seems to speed up as our two cars collide. My headlight shatters and metal crunches as the front of my car smashes into the rear bumper of the other. I'm propelled forward, only

Pendejo: Dick.

3

to be shoved in the opposite direction as my seat belt locks in place.

Thankfully, the airbags don't deploy, although my relief is short-lived as whatever spark of hope I had of making it to Nico's show fizzles out, leaving me with nothing but a desire to yell at the reckless driver.

Take five. The memory of my dad's voice pulls at the invisible strings wrapped around my heart until the tightness seems unbearable. I can picture him clearly as he helped me calm down from another night terror, one deep breath at a time.

I never thought I would be using the same strategy twenty-five years later, but here I am, with my eyes screwed shut as I force myself to count my breaths until the chest pain lessens and I'm no longer vibrating with rage.

I'm hit with an early October breeze as I walk toward the other car. The driver is hunched over the wheel, her dark, shoulder-length hair obstructing my view of her face.

I reach out to tap on the window, but a high-pitched shriek coming out of the car's speakers stops me. "Don't worry! I'm on my way!" The call cuts out after two beeps.

The woman's panicked breathing becomes more obvious with each rapid rise and fall of her back.

"Hey." I knock my fist against the window when she doesn't acknowledge me. "Are you okay?"

She lifts a trembling finger to the glass while keeping her head down. "One second." Her voice wavers.

My stomach muscles clench. "Do you need an ambulance?"

"No! I'm fine!" Her head snaps in my direction.

Vete a la chingada.

"*Julian?*" My name leaves Dahlia Muñoz's parted pink lips in a hoarse whisper.

It's been years since I heard Dahlia say my name in that soft voice of hers, and it hits harder than a sledgehammer to the chest.

The last time I saw her was at Nico's baptism eight years ago when we became his godparents. We both put on a happy face for our families, but the tension and awkward silence between us nearly choked me, especially since we hadn't spoken since my dad's funeral a year and a half prior.

She stayed at Stanford all year round, including the summer break, while I kept my distance because I was a coward.

A coward who was blindsided when she showed up with Oliver, my ex-roommate and her new boyfriend. I didn't think they would become friends, let alone a couple, although it makes sense given Oliver's jabs about my crush on Dahlia and the way he looked at her despite knowing how I felt.

Since the baptism, we have both done an outstanding job of avoiding each other—or at least we *had* until she ruined all our efforts with tonight's surprise visit.

"Dahlia." An intense need to escape overwhelms me as her eyes slide over me.

I hide my shock as she exits the car with her head held high despite the mascara running down her cheeks and the slight trembling of her chin. Dahlia has only cried twice in the thirty years I've known her—once when she broke her arm trying to

---

Vete a la chingada: Get the fuck out of here.

beat me in a tree-climbing contest and the other while at her father's funeral.

Like the tide with the moon, I'm unable to resist Dahlia's gravitational pull as my gaze follows the length of her body.

The plain white T-shirt she wears complements her golden skin and wavy brown hair, while her ripped jeans appear more fashionable than functional with how her knees pop out of the large, gaping holes. Her curves perfectly balance out her sharp cheekbones and pointed chin, creating the best combination of soft and sultry.

The base of my neck tingles, and I look up to find Dahlia's red, puffy eyes narrowed at me. Her ruined makeup doesn't detract from her beauty, although the dark circles underneath her eyes have me speaking before my brain catches up.

"Your face is a mess."

Pinche estúpido. Unlike my mom and cousin, I'm not a people person, and it clearly shows.

Dahlia's golden rings glint in the moonlight as she wipes at her cheeks with a frown. "I had something in my eye."

"Both of them?" I widen my stance as I cross my arms.

She dabs at the corners of her eyes with her two middle fingers. "A decent person wouldn't call me out on that lie."

"Since when are we decent to one another?"

"It's never too late to start."

Because of our slight height difference, she is forced to tilt her head back to get a good look at me. Her walnut-colored eyes remind me of long-ago late nights spent in the woodshop,

Pinche estúpido: Fucking idiot.

meticulously obsessing over staining my latest carpentry project.

Whatever resolve I had quickly crumbles when she *sniffles*.

"Allergies." Her defensive tone, paired with her twitching nose, makes my chest constrict in an act of ultimate betrayal.

What the hell is going on here, and how do I get it to stop?

I keep my facial expression neutral despite the rapid thumping of my heart against my rib cage. She doesn't last long under my scrutiny before slumping against the door with a sigh.

I'm struck with a compulsion to say something, but words fail me.

My ringtone shatters the moment. "Shit!"

Her brows shoot toward her hairline. "What's wrong?"

You. Always you.

Blaring sirens drown out my response. Every muscle in my body goes rigid as a rush of vehicles makes its way around the bend in a single-file line. A fire truck and ambulance lead the safety brigade, followed by the sheriff, his deputies, and the Lake Wisteria trolley.

You've got to be kidding me.

Dahlia curses up to the stars. *"Dios, dame paciencia con mi mamá."*

My gaze cuts into her. "That's who you were talking to?"

"Unfortunately."

Leave it to Lake Wisteria to turn a fender bender into a community crisis.

Dios, dame paciencia con mi mamá: God, give me patience with my mom.

It's not the cars they're concerned about. It's her.

Dahlia is more than my childhood rival. She's Lake Wisteria's Strawberry Sweetheart who is finally returning home after years spent away living out her California dream.

And you're the cabrón *who nearly drove her into a ditch.*

I rub at my throbbing temple.

"Do you think we can escape before they get here?" Dahlia's gaze flicks from me to my car.

"This is all your fault." The words slip out.

A few minutes in Dahlia's presence already have me slipping back into the bad habit of speaking without thinking.

Add it to the long list of reasons you should avoid her.

She pops a hand on her hip. "*My fault?* We wouldn't be in this mess if you hadn't tried to cut me off."

"I had somewhere to be."

She throws her arms up. "Well, I was..."

Usually I crave silence, but something about Dahlia shutting down at the first sign of opposition frustrates me.

Bright flashing lights cast us in shades of red, white, and blue as a few of the firefighters hop out of the truck to assess the scene while two medics quickly determine both Dahlia and I are fine.

The older fire chief pulls Dahlia in for a hug. "Your mom made it sound like you were dying."

Her eyes roll. "You know how overprotective she can be."

The fire chief ruffles Dahlia's hair. "She comes from a good place."

Cabrón: Bastard.

"Lucifer said the same thing about hell." Dahlia fixes her appearance with a pinched expression.

"Dahlia!" Rosa hops out of the trolley and runs toward her daughter with a rosary clutched in one hand and a bottle of holy water in the other. My own mom exits the trolley with a group of people trailing behind her, turning our car accident into a town reunion.

"*Mami.*" Dahlia checks out the crowd forming behind the deputy's line. "Did you need to involve everyone?"

"Don't start with me. *¿Qué pasó?*" Rosa scans her daughter from head to toe before ripping the cap off the holy water.

For the first time tonight, Dahlia's eyes twinkle brighter than the stars above us. "Julian crashed into me."

That little brat.

Rosa stares at me as if I committed a felony.

I bristle at my mom's voice as she storms over to us. "Julian? Tell me that's not true."

"Ma."

She snatches the bottle of holy water from Rosa's hands and gives me a swift blessing before sprinkling me with it. "What were you thinking by trying to run Dahlia off the road?"

"That it's a shame I failed."

The fire chief covers up his laugh with a cough.

Dahlia's heated glare threatens to burn a hole in the side of my face. "Don't tell me you've spent all these years plotting my murder only to fail now?"

"Trust me. I won't make the same mistake again."

¿Qué pasó?: What happened.

She flips me off.

"Dahlia Isabella Muñoz!" Rosa tugs at her daughter's hand while my mother whisper-shouts, "Luis Julian Lopez Junior!"

My mom only uses my official first name on rare—and very pissed-off—occasions, so I better rein myself in before she loses her cool.

Dahlia and I sigh at the same time, and our gazes collide, scattering my thoughts until I'm left with only one.

Her.

The sheriff approaches the scene, saving me from embarrassing myself any further. Thankfully, the deputy with a personal vendetta against me stays far away, a blessing in itself given my bad luck today.

Knowing Dahlia, she would befriend him to spite me.

The older sheriff drags Dahlia into a quick bear hug. "So, what happened here?"

"You should arrest Julian for attempted murder." Dahlia's wicked grin sets off a blaring alarm in my head. Memories I spent years erasing surge to the forefront of my mind, flashing before me like a haunted movie reel.

The way her smile grew wider whenever I got flustered and spoke out of turn.

Her sparkling eyes looking up at me as we—no, *I* stiffly moved us around the dance floor during her quinceañera.

How she had a similar expression during her valedictorian speech as she thanked me, the salutatorian, for putting up a good fight throughout high school.

It's pathetic how one smile from her can stir up countless

memories, all of which are best left in the past, along with any feelings I once had for her.

Truth is, I'm not sure why Dahlia Muñoz is back, but nothing good can come of it.

Nothing good at all.

CHAPTER TWO

Dahlia

If I had known my return to Lake Wisteria would include a panic attack, a car accident, and a trolley full of townspeople waiting to greet me, I would have stayed in San Francisco. Turns out my plan to run away from my problems had a few major flaws, starting with the man who has spent the better part of his life making mine impossible.

Emergency lights flash across Julian's tan, angular face, casting a red glow over him like a devilish halo as he speaks with the sheriff.

I was so caught up in avoiding Julian over the years that I failed to notice how much he had matured during that time.

Failed to notice? More like was intent on ignoring.

Red, flashing lights draw my eyes toward his sharp jawline, only for them to steal my attention again as they highlight his soft lips and five o'clock shadow.

Based on my eye for luxury clothes and nose for real Italian leather, I can tell Julian's outfit tonight has to easily cost ten thousand dollars, a shocking assessment in itself. But despite his pristine suit, perfectly trimmed dark hair, and fancy designer loafers, bits and pieces of the rugged Julian I knew peek through.

The slight bump in his nose after I accidentally broke it with my elbow.

A thin, white scar running across his stubbled cheek from when we thought it was a good idea to compete for who could jump the highest from a swing set.

The firm press of his lips whenever someone speaks to him—a habit he picked up when we were kids to stop himself from talking out of turn.

As if he senses me staring at him, Julian looks in my direction. The dismissive pass of his rich brown eyes over my body should annoy me more than anything, but the goose bumps scattering across my skin show it has the opposite effect.

I turn away from Julian in a rush of self-preservation and allow his mom, Josefina, and mine to fuss over me. The two best friends both have brown hair and eyes, but their different heights, facial features, and personalities set them apart from each other.

Although our mothers became best friends growing up together in Mexico, Julian and I most definitely are not. At best, we're family friends, while at worst, we're childhood rivals who turn everything into a competition.

"You've lost weight. Are you sure you've been eating enough?" Mom pinches my cheeks with a dark, furrowed brow. "What do you think?" She turns me toward Josefina.

Her sour expression confirms my mom's observation. "It's nothing some good food can't fix. You know, *panza llena*—"

"*Corazón contento*," my mom finishes.

Too bad home-cooked food will only fill the empty pit in my stomach, not the one in my chest.

Mom inspects my shoulder-length hair. "*¿Y qué pasó con tu pelo?*"

"I cut it."

"But why?" she moans.

I can only muster up a long, exaggerated sigh.

"I love it, especially because of why you did it." Josefina winks.

A haircut was what the doctor ordered after my heartbreak, along with a bottle of Zoloft to keep the sadness at bay.

Mom grips my shoulders as she scans me from head to toe. "I'm happy you're home. The rest we can deal with later."

"Me too." My voice cracks. There was nothing I wanted more than my mom's hugs and her unwavering belief that Vicks VapoRub will cure everything, including a broken heart.

Josefina places her hands on my shoulders and squeezes. "Don't you worry. We'll make it all better, starting with some of my *pozole*."

Where my mom is a worrier, Josefina is a fixer like her son.

If only Julian had inherited her empathy too.

Panza llena, corazón contento: Full stomach, happy heart.

¿Y qué pasó con tu pelo?: And what happened to your hair?

The sheriff interrupts our reunion by clearing his throat. "Dahlia."

"Yes?"

"Julian wants to keep this off the record and pay for both repairs himself."

"So he's not going to get a ticket or mandatory community service for hitting me?"

The sheriff chuckles. "Do you want him to?"

"Only if you can promise he gets the kind that requires him to pick up trash on the side of the road for hours." I snap my fingers. "Scratch that. *Days*."

"*Mija*," Mom warns as Josefina laughs.

"How else is he supposed to learn his lesson? Someone could have gotten badly hurt."

The sheriff spares me a knowing look. "To be fair, you should have pulled over if you were having car trouble rather than continuing to drive like you did."

My brows scrunch together. "Car trouble?"

"Julian explained everything already. If you ever struggle with the engine again, pull over and call for help."

Why would Julian Lopez make up a cover story instead of telling the sheriff I was too busy crying to properly drive?

Perhaps because he plans on blackmailing you later.

My mom gives my hand a knowing squeeze, and the tension in my muscles bleeds away. "I'll do that."

The sheriff tips his hat. "Now that it's all settled, I'd better get everyone back to the school auditorium for the talent show.

Mija: My daughter.

15

Some of these folks should be in bed before their meds kick in at ten p.m." He whistles and points to the trolley. "Let's clear out!"

"We'll hitch a ride with our kids instead." Josefina waves the sheriff away.

The deputies wrangle the protesting crowd into the trolley while the first responders head to town, leaving the Muñoz and Lopez families alone.

"What talent show is he talking about?" I ask.

"The one the elementary school puts on each fall." Josefina passes the bottle of holy water back to my mom. "About that, it would be so nice if you joined us! Nico would love to see you, and then we can all go out to dinner afterward."

My throat dries up. As much as I want to see my godson and give him the biggest hug, dinner with those who know me best sounds like another panic-inducing situation I'd rather avoid tonight.

"I'm sure Dahlia is tired," Julian says in that bored tone of his.

Either I look as shitty as I feel, or Julian is making it known that he doesn't want me there.

I'll go with the latter.

I consider attending the talent show to prove him wrong, but then I think about what that would entail.

Are you ready to see everyone in town?

Nope. Definitely not. It was a small blessing to be spared from the welcome party this evening, so I better not push my luck.

After two years away, I will have to face everyone eventually, but today is not that day.

"Julian is right." The words slide across my tongue like daggers, and the bastard has the audacity to stand taller at the admission. "I'm pretty shaken up with everything that happened, and after spending the whole day driving, all I want to do is get some rest."

"Oh." Josefina's smile dies, earning me another scowl from her son.

"What if Julian takes you home on his way to the show and Josefina and I can drive your car to the auditorium?" Mom suggests.

My right eye twitches. If this woman hadn't spent my whole life raising me, I would never speak to her again. She knows Julian is my sworn enemy, right up there with midnight snacking on pan dulce and driving in California rush-hour traffic.

"But..." My protest dies when my mom shoots me a look. "All right."

Julian's eyes narrow as he pulls out his keys. "Let's go. I don't want to be late for Nico's performance."

Josefina's fingers fly across her cell phone screen. "No worries. I'm texting the principal now and asking them to switch Nico's spot."

Julian's head swings in his mother's direction. "You couldn't have done that before I got into an accident trying to rush over there?"

His mother shrugs while typing away. "You didn't ask."

I bite down on my tongue to stop myself from laughing. I'm positive Julian would rather die than ask anyone for help, including his mother. It's a chronic condition he inherited from his late father.

I grab my purse from my mom's hand and give her and Josefina each a kiss on the cheek before heading over to Julian's car. It resembles a spaceship with all the sharp lines and chrome detailing, and I'm sure it flies like one too when given a little gas.

I have a hard time processing how the guy who considered buying a new video game a luxury became the billionaire in front of me who owns an electric blue McLaren. My mom swears Julian has never let money get to his head, but I bet he struggles with an insufferable ego and a god complex.

While I had huge success with my interior design company and home renovation show, Julian struck gold after he helped his genius cousin and computer coder Rafa create Dwelling, the most popular real estate search engine around, at the ages of twenty-three and twenty-five, respectively.

The idea might have started out as another one of Rafa's crazy, unsuccessful attempts at creating the next best app, but then it evolved into a billion-dollar company with investors, a board of directors, and the Lopez cousins securing a spot on the coveted *Forbes* 30 Under 30 List.

Julian and I reach for the passenger door. His hand brushes across the back of mine, and a spark of recognition flares to life.

The smell of his cologne—clean and expensive—invades my nose. It twitches before a sneeze shoots out of me. I jolt, and my butt brushes against Julian's front.

Oh God.

He yanks the door open. "*Salud.*"

"What a gentleman," I reply in a dry voice.

His grip on the door tightens until his golden skin turns

white. "Can't have your mother thinking I'm anything but chivalrous."

"No need to try so hard. She thinks you're the first person since Jesus to walk on water."

His deep chuckle, soft and barely audible over a gust of wind, has an unacceptable amount of influence over the pace of my heart.

I throw myself into the passenger seat and bang my elbow on the stick shift in the process of avoiding him, making me wince.

"*Nos vemos allá*," my mom calls out before taking off down the road while blasting "Mi Primer Millón," one of my dad's favorite songs.

I sink into the soft leather seat once Julian shuts my door. The vibration makes something rattle near the hood of the car, so he walks around the front and kneels.

He glares at the bumper for what seems like an eternity before entering the car with a thunderous expression and stiff posture. Neither of us says anything as he pulls back onto the road and presses his foot against the gas.

In the past, I would fill the silence with questions to annoy Julian, but tonight, I draw back into myself.

Just another way you changed because of Oliver and his family.

Silence eats at me as we catch up to my car, and I take in the damage from the crash. Besides my bumper resembling a

Salud: Bless you.

Nos vemos allá: We'll see you there.

19

crushed pop can and the taillight being knocked out of place, the rest of the car appears fine.

Your therapist would be proud of you for noticing the positives.

After losing my wedding venue deposit and my new agent informing me that the media learned about my broken engagement today, I need all the wins I can get.

"You're too quiet." Julian's rough voice cuts through my thoughts a few minutes later.

My fingernails press into my palms from how hard I clench them. "Shouldn't that make you happy after all those times you begged me to stop talking?"

That silences him, although the quiet only lasts a minute before he speaks up *again*.

"You always knew how to make an entrance." His gaze remains fixated on the road.

Maybe I hit my head after all, because I must be hallucinating. Julian just attempted to start a conversation *twice* without being influenced by alcohol or his mother.

I sink deeper into the seat. "Believe it or not, I wanted to lie low for a bit."

"That's impossible."

After tonight, I'm worried he might be right. If I could avoid everyone for a few weeks while I gather my bearings, it would be a miracle.

"It's not like I enjoy all this attention." All I want to do is disappear and pretend my life in California isn't falling apart.

"Says the woman who has her own television show and décor brand in stores all across America." He loosens his chokehold on the wheel.

I fake gasp. "Julian Lopez, are you a secret fan of my show?"

His face remains unreadable. "I have better things to do with my time."

Ouch. "I'm sure spending every night with your mother takes up a lot of it."

Whatever drove Julian to attempt speaking with me dies as my shitty shot hits its mark.

A couple of minutes later, we pass the strawberry-themed *Welcome to Lake Wisteria* sign that boasts about our famous Strawberry Festival and a new tagline that states *Home of Dahlia Muñoz, celebrity interior designer and reality TV sensation.*

I drop my head into my hands with a groan.

So much for lying low.

The neon Early Bird Diner sign shines like the North Star, guiding me home as we hit the corner of Main Street. From the cheery fall display in the center of Town Square to the lamp pole banners promoting the upcoming Harvest Festival in November, everything about Lake Wisteria is warm and welcoming.

It's understandable why our small town has grown in popularity, both among summer tourists visiting our beach and wealthy Chicago residents who want a weekend getaway. The unique Victorian-era seaside charm can transport anyone to the late 1800s, and our spotty cell service will sure make them feel like it too.

After spending two years away, I should be overwhelmed by excitement and nostalgia, especially with all the Halloween décor, but my entire body is numb as we drive by the pumpkin photo-op area, the ginormous strawberry fountain lit by orange and purple lights, and the park where my dad always took my sister and me.

Julian turns away from the modernized Main Street and heads south. The southernmost part of town, where both our families grew up, doesn't have million-dollar lakefront properties and an elite private school like the upper south side or the modern buildings and amenities on Main Street and the eastern quadrant. Nor do we have the rich history associated with the northern Historic District, but we do have the best pizza spot in town, so who needs a fancy mansion or an up-to-date apartment with a gym when I can get You Want a Pizza Me delivered in ten minutes or less?

The one stoplight standing in our way of getting to my mom's home flashes from yellow to red. As time ticks by, I'm left with the grim reminder of how tortuously tense things are between Julian and me.

Once upon a time, we were friends with a healthy competitive drive. Then puberty hit during middle school, and a new rivalry was formed, driven by hormones and immaturity.

But now, we're nothing but strangers.

An invisible hand wraps itself around my throat and squeezes until I'm breathless. I struggle against the heaviness threatening to consume me, only to fail as I spare a glance at the first man who broke my heart. It took him nineteen years to earn it and only six words to obliterate it.

And I don't plan on forgetting that.

CHAPTER THREE

Julian

Dahlia gawks at the street sign. "Lopez Lane?"

I stay quiet as I drive past the street I grew up on before turning onto hers.

"Why would they name a street after you?"

Dahlia's reaction is exactly why I protested against the mayor wanting to publicly honor my monetary contributions. While I don't regret my ten-million-dollar donation, I do wish I had gone about it anonymously.

Dahlia unbuckles her seat belt as I pull up to her childhood ranch-style house. It holds many memories for our families, including my dad and I working on remodeling it together when I was a teen. While the flowers and decorations change depending on the season, the light blue paint and white trim have remained the same since the redesign.

The house might be a far cry from my current projects, but

it still represents everything I love about construction. It was during the Muñoz renovation project that I realized how, like my parents, I have a passion for fixing things.

Houses. Problems. *People.*

It's a character flaw I've spent years trying to eradicate, only to have it resurface at the most inconvenient times.

Like now.

My inability to ignore Dahlia's unusual silence is the only reasonable explanation for why I took a stab at having a conversation with her *twice.*

And look how well that went.

I pull on the parking brake with enough force to make it tremble.

The tightness in Dahlia's muscles matches mine as she reaches for the door handle. "Thanks for the ride." Her chest rises and falls with a long exhale. "And I'm sorry about your car." The small scrunch of her nose has me biting back a snarky reply. "I should have pulled over and waited things out."

"Is everything okay?" The earlier edge in my voice is gone, replaced by something far worse.

She shakes her head. "Just tired."

"Keeping up false pretenses must be exhausting."

"Do you have something else you want to ask me?"

A beam of light from the porch bounces off her monstrosity of an engagement ring, nearly blinding me.

How's Oliver? I want to ask with every ounce of vitriol I have toward my ex-roommate.

Have you picked a wedding date yet since you've been engaged for two years already?

Out of curiosity, did he admit to stabbing me in the back by pursuing you?

Questions linger on the tip of my tongue like poison arrows. "Nope."

"Perfect. Now if you don't mind, I have a date with *The Silver Vixens* and don't want to be late."

The Silver Vixens?

Shit. Things must be worse than I thought. Dahlia only saves binge marathons of *The Silver Vixens* for the shittiest occasions, like when her dad died or when that asshole football player she liked called her a prude bitch when she didn't have sex with him after their first date.

Before she has a chance to open the door, I grab her hand. The physical contact makes my palm tingle, so I drop it like a stick of burning dynamite.

We both speak at the same time.

"Umm, I should—"

"You need to—"

"I better get going so you don't miss Nico's performance." She rushes to get the words out before bolting from my car.

I help remove her luggage from the trunk. With a grumbled "thank you," she takes off toward her house, her designer suitcase kicking up dust behind her.

I'm not sure what possesses me to speak again, yet I can't help myself as I ask, "See you around?" My heart hammers against my rib cage while I wait for her reply.

She stops at the stairs leading up to the porch. "Why?"

"I'm curious."

"I hope you're not planning all the ways you can torture me already." Her half-hearted tease lacks any oomph.

"Torturing you is my favorite pastime."

A spark flashes in her eyes before it is snuffed out like a fire in the middle of a snowstorm. "Have you ever explored your need to turn everything into a competition to make up for your massive inferiority complex?"

Dahlia makes me feel more exposed in a custom-tailored suit than I have while naked, because where most people see a reserved guy one bad interaction away from becoming the town asshole, she sees me.

The real me.

The self-conscious me.

The me I have spent the last ten years loathing because he represents everything I hate about myself. He was weak, shy, and too damn prideful to do anything but suffer in silence while he fumbled his way through life.

It's best I remember that she knows everything about me, including the parts of myself that I've spent a decade erasing.

Effective immediately.

♛

Fall-themed bulletin boards blur as I rush past the dark classrooms of my youth and head inside the newly renovated auditorium.

Somehow, I make it in time to see Nico walk out in a tailcoat tuxedo and a pair of his most colorful prescription glasses. The crowd claps loud enough to drown out my cousin's huff as I settle into the empty chair between him and my mom.

With Rafa's overgrown hair, worn-out jeans, and wrinkled button-down shirt, I wouldn't guess the man is filthy rich. He still drives the same pickup truck from high school and refuses to upgrade his outdated cell phone, despite being a tech geek. He only splurges on Nico, but even that has a hard limit because he doesn't want to spoil him rotten.

All the tension in Rafa's body bleeds away once Nico takes his seat in front of the grand piano and runs his hands over the ivory keys. I'm not one to brag, but my godson is going to be up there with all the most renowned musicians one day. The kid is only eight years old and can already play three different instruments, one of which he learned by watching YouTube tutorials all on his own.

A standing ovation follows Nico's performance, and my cousin flashes a rare smile as he whistles and shouts his son's name.

I expect Rafa's good mood to disappear once the curtains close, but it remains after the lights turn on and my mom disappears into the crowd to search for Nico.

"I'm glad you could finally grace us with your presence, given your busy work schedule and all." Rafa gives my shoulder a squeeze.

"Aren't you the same guy who spends all day every day in front of a computer, coding until his eyes cross?"

He shrugs. "Not anymore. Unlike you, now I make time for other things beside work."

It's not like I *want* to spend most of my days working, but what else am I supposed to do with my free time? Go on dates my mom sets up?

No, thanks. Been there, done that, and made an enemy out of a town deputy in the process after my mom's last matchmaking attempt with his ex.

We rise from our seats, and my cousin nudges me toward the exit. "Remember when we got drunk at that cabin in Lake Aurora?"

"Which time?"

His smile only grows wider. "The weekend Dahlia got engaged."

Somehow my strides remain steady. "I'm struggling to recall."

He pokes me in the back. "That's probably because of all the alcohol you consumed."

"A good cousin would have gotten drunk with me."

"And risk you dying in your sleep after choking on your own vomit? No way. Your mother would have never forgiven me."

"I'm sure you would've been happy stepping in as my replacement."

His dark brown eyes roll. "Anyway, I'll never forget what you said that night."

My lungs stall.

He clasps my shoulder. "You wouldn't shut up about how if you got a second chance with Dahlia, you'd do things differently."

It takes everything in me to keep my voice neutral as I say, "I was drunk."

"*And?*"

"She's engaged."

"According to your mother, not anymore."

Mierda. "How did she find out?"

"How else? Rosa told her."

"And so the *chisme* begins." I don't expect anything less from the two best friends who have been attached at the hip since kindergarten.

His scowl deepens. "It's hard to keep it a secret when it's all over social media tonight. Dahlia has her own trending hashtag and everything."

My stomach churns as questions bounce around my head, making it impossible to come up with a reply.

Why did they break up?

Is there any chance they will get back together?

Was Oliver the reason Dahlia was crying earlier today before I crashed into her?

Rafa shoots me a look. "No."

I blink. "What?"

"Whatever you're thinking, don't."

"You're the one who brought her up."

"Because I wanted to be the one to break the news before your mom started whispering in your ear about how now is your chance."

"My mom whispers a lot of things into my ear about who I should date, yet you don't see me giving in to her."

Mierda: Shit.

Chisme: Gossip.

"Dahlia is different, and you know it."

"Doesn't matter anymore, because whatever feelings I had for Dahlia are no longer relevant." Something twists in my chest.

Rafa's reply is cut off by Nico's shout.

"*Papi!*" Nico abandons my mom and runs down the hall.

My cousin gets down on his knees in time for Nico to launch himself into his open arms.

"I'm so proud of you." Rafa fixes Nico's glasses so they sit right.

Nico's forehead wrinkles from his frown. "But didn't you hear me mess up?"

Rafa scoffs. "You were perfect like always."

Nico, who must have inherited his perfectionistic tendencies from me, attempts to recount his slipup, only to be stopped by Rafa tickling him.

"No!" Nico wiggles in his father's embrace.

"Sorry. I can't hear you. What were you saying?" Rafa reaches for the spot under Nico's arm, making him squeal and squirm.

While Rafa might be closed off to the rest of the world, he is nothing but warm with his son. The way he acts with my godson despite all his issues gives me hope my cousin will heal one day.

I might have experienced nothing close to what Rafa has gone through, but I know it isn't easy to get over someone. Dahlia taught me that lesson a long time ago, and it's one I don't plan on forgetting anytime soon.

CHAPTER FOUR

Dahlia

My first official day back in town was quiet, most likely because I never went into town at all. With my mom and sister, Liliana, busy working at the floral shop, I did nothing but stare at the ceiling.

It's strange going from not having enough time to eat lunch and use the restroom to barely leaving my room unless absolutely necessary. My suitcase packed with expensive, trendy outfits sits untouched on my floor, a warning sign in itself.

While I've always had anxiety and perfectionistic tendencies since high school, depression is a newer struggle for me and a lonely battle I fought for months before getting help.

My therapist, Dr. Martin, is a wonderful woman who charges a small fortune for each session. While money isn't an issue for me anymore, I was hesitant about the emotional commitment, but she was highly recommended by my agent, so I took a chance eight weeks ago and have no regrets.

I'm not sure where I would be without Dr. Martin. She has endless patience, the calmest voice, and ends every session with a Jamaican proverb I don't understand until I look it up afterward.

Today, she barely speaks for the first half of our tele-health session, allowing me to go off about my mistakes and shortcomings.

She clasps her hands together, making her gold Cartier bracelets jangle against her deep brown skin. "What made you stay with Oliver for so long?"

Her never-ending patience is put to the test as I sit and think. I've been asked this question before, but at the time, my view on life was tainted by bitterness, self-loathing, and a thick cloud of depression.

"Things were good for a long time." *Which made the loss that much harder.*

Her tiny nod gives me courage.

It takes me another sixty seconds to come up with five words. "He made me feel special."

He never deserved you. Oliver pulled me into a hug after I broke out in tears while packing up Julian's dorm room, for which I never received even a simple thank-you text.

I like you…a lot more than any friend should, Oliver told me right before the holiday break during our junior year after we spent a year keeping things platonic.

Before that, it was easy to put him in the friend zone after Julian hurt me, but his blue eyes, blond hair, and effortless smile grew on me.

You're so talented, and you deserve to be appreciated. He encouraged me to post my first photo on the Designs by Dahlia social media page. It was a grainy image of my first apartment, and one I have kept pinned at the top of the page to this day because of everything it represents.

I was vulnerable and searching for reassurance in all the wrong places, including Oliver's family, who became immersed in my business once they started helping produce our TV show.

"Was it always like that?" Dr. Martin probes.

"Before we got engaged, we had seven years of typical relationship stuff. There were plenty of good moments mixed with some bad ones. He made it seem like he was the misunderstood black sheep of his family, only for me to realize he was actually the wolf."

If Dr. Martin is surprised, she doesn't show it.

"He made it seem like we could do anything together, but when we were finally put to the test, we failed."

I failed. Instead of valuing myself enough to walk away, I stayed because I stupidly didn't want to quit a relationship that I had invested so much time into. But it didn't matter anyway because little by little, Oliver pulled away, leaving me to grapple with my grief over never having a child of my own.

I pick at my cuticles. "Things took a turn for the worse after the prenup and the medical test, although I put on a brave face and shelved my pain while the cameras were rolling because I love my job and the people I work with, and the last thing I wanted to do was give it all up because of him."

Yet you lost it all anyway.

I have no show, no friends besides a few crew members,

and no hope that someone will want me after I was dumped because I "wasn't the woman he wanted."

Oliver might as well have admitted I didn't have the *womb* he wanted, but I digress.

Dr. Martin bows her head in understanding. "It's human nature to avoid anything that will cause us pain."

"It was so easy to throw myself into work, but while my business thrived, a part of my soul died."

The skin beside her eyes softens.

I'll tell my parents you're not coming. Again, Oliver emphasized with a huff before taking off for the Creswells' mansion, leaving me to blankly stare at a wall for hours until I cried myself to sleep.

It's not too late to break things off and find someone more suited for your future, Oliver's mother had whispered to him while she thought I was still in the restroom.

Thankfully, someone will carry on the Creswells' name, Oliver's dad said as his wife passed their daughter's ultrasound photos around the dinner table.

After my test, it felt like our relationship had taken a gunshot wound to the heart, and I was the only one trying to fix it.

Dr. Martin ends our session with another Jamaican proverb I don't recognize, and I spend the next ten minutes researching *Rockstone a riva bottom nuh know sun hat* instead of crying myself to sleep, which is a win.

> **Rockstone a riva bottom nuh know sun hat:**
> Sheltered people don't know hardship.

My second day in town goes about the same, although my psychiatry appointment put me through another emotional wringer. Hopefully the increased dosage of my antidepressants and my new commitment to engaging in more enjoyable activities will help boost my mood, although I'm still a bit skeptical since I barely want to leave the house, let alone decorate one.

I expect my third day back in Lake Wisteria to follow the same pattern of being left alone, but when I finally crawl out of bed at two p.m. in search of food, I'm startled to find the Lopez family spread around our house for our families' Sunday get-together.

My sister taps at her phone like the screen personally offended her while my mom and Josefina busy themselves chopping vegetables in the kitchen. Rafa completely ignores *"Robarte un Beso"* blasting from the portable speaker beside him as he watches a Mexican League soccer game on the TV.

"¿Madrina?" Nico notices me first and takes off running in my direction. It's been a couple of years since I last saw him, except for video calls, and he has grown about two feet.

"You're back!" Nico throws his arms around my legs.

"Hi." I didn't realize how much I needed one of Nico's bone-crushing hugs until now.

My godson peeks up at me with his big brown eyes. "I've missed you."

Madrina: Godmother.

"I've missed you too." I fight the darkness threatening to creep back in. "How's my favorite godson doing?"

He giggles. "I'm your only godson."

"For now."

"No! You're not allowed." He squeezes my legs harder, and a soft laugh escapes me as he lets go of me in a rush.

"I've been playing the drums you got me for my birthday! They're the best!" Nico smashes the air with an invisible set of drumsticks.

"Yeah, thanks for that one." Rafa shoots me a look.

"Maybe I'll have to get him an electric guitar and an amp for Christmas."

Rafa's eye twitches while Nico throws his fist in the air with a "Yes!"

Spoiling my godson comes naturally, although my last gifts have been delivered by courier rather than personally handed over. I know an expensive drum set or pricey guitar won't make up for my absence, but Nico deserves the best regardless, especially after everything he and Rafa have been through.

I didn't know Rafa's ex-wife well, and not for lack of trying on my part, but I do know she didn't make an effort to integrate with our family.

Rafa gets up from the couch and pulls me into a hug. "We've all missed you."

My first attempt at an honest reply fails, so I stick to humor. "At least your manners didn't disappear along with your fashion sense."

My comment earns an eye roll from the surly man dressed in a flannel shirt, faded blue jeans, and a worn ball cap. On anyone else, I'd find the lumberjack-inspired outfit hideous, but on Rafa, it works, thanks to his good looks and muscle mass.

Rafa is basically my older brother, so I'd rather suffer through a stomach flu before calling him attractive, but that doesn't stop all the women in town from stating it loudly.

He releases me from his hold. "How long do you plan on sticking around this time?"

"Not sure. Depends on a few things with work and stuff."

"You'll have to stop by our house and check out Nico's drum set."

Nico beams. "Yeah! You can watch me play them, and then we can build that special Lego set you got me—oh! You can meet Ellie too. She's so nice, and pretty, and the coolest."

"Who's Ellie?" The crack in my voice betrays my emotions. As much as I *want* to spend time with my godson, I don't feel remotely ready. Because being around Nico always made me yearn for my own family one day, and now...

"She's my best friend!" Nico's eyes light up.

"She's his *nanny*." Something dark passes over Rafa's face before he schools his features.

Mom said Rafa has changed since his divorce and Nico's retinitis pigmentosa diagnosis, and the truth couldn't be any more obvious given Rafa's stern expression and haunted eyes.

Nico grins at me in a way that reminds me so much of his father, missing teeth aside. "Yeah, sure. Anyway, do you want to play a game with me and *Tío*?"

Tío: Uncle.

I'm hit straight in the chest with a burst of anxiety. "Uh…"

"Please!" He presses his hands together.

"Well—" I choke on my reply.

Rafa's head tilts.

Nico tugs on my hand. "Come on. We need another person since my dad doesn't want to play with us."

Rafa ruffles Nico's hair. "Only because Julian always wins."

Nico drags me toward the unopened Monopoly box waiting at the kitchen breakfast table while his dad returns to watching the game. My godson pulls out my chair like a gentleman and waits.

When I don't move, he pats the seat with a furrowed brow. "Sit."

His request widens the crack in my chest until I find it difficult to breathe.

"I can't." The pain in my heart intensifies with each beat.

Nico's brows crinkle. "Why not? It'll be fun!"

I wrap my arms around myself and take a long step back.

The puzzled look on his face adds to his charm and my distress. "Are you okay? You seem sad." His bottom lip wobbles.

Rafa glances over his shoulder. "You good?"

"I need to use the restroom." I bolt toward the hallway with blurred vision. I'm disoriented as I pass my bedroom and rush down the hall toward the guest bathroom my sister and I share.

So much for the antidepressants doing their job.

Tears fall in a frustrating act of betrayal. I went from suffering with never-ending numbness two months ago to feeling too much all at once now and crying more in the last few days than in my whole life.

Be patient with yourself and trust the process.

Screw the process. I don't plan on leaving my room until—

Someone yanks on my elbow, and I gasp as I'm pulled backward.

"You better have a good reason for upsetting my kid." Rafa's rough voice startles me.

I recoil. "What?"

"Are you…crying?" He squints with a frown, throwing me back into the past.

I'm so sick of you feeling sorry for yourself. Oliver's lips curled with disgust.

You can fake it for the cameras just fine, but when it comes to me, you can't be bothered to do the bare minimum. His words were venomous, flooding my system with paralyzing self-loathing and hopelessness.

Call me when the Dahlia I fell in love with is back, he texted me later that night, only to come back a week later to let me know we were done.

"*Dahlia.*" Rafa's rough voice tethers me to the present.

I wipe my face with the sleeve of my sweater. "I'm sorry for upsetting Nico. You know I would never do that on purpose."

Rafa's harshness melts away. "What's wrong?"

I'm not sure what possesses me to open up to Rafa of all people, but I can't let him think I made Nico upset for no good reason.

"I… You see…" *Shit.* "I've avoided being around kids since I found out I will never have any."

He blinks a few times. "And then you saw Nico…"

I nod, unable to finish his sentence, mainly due to the

tightness in my throat. "It's only been a few months since I got the news—" I'm cut off by my sob.

Rafa yanks me into his arms like my dad did whenever I got hurt or was sick. "I'm sorry."

I didn't realize how much I needed to hear those two words until the tears start rolling down my cheeks. I'm not sure how long Rafa holds me there while I cry, but he doesn't let go until my breathing evens out and my tears no longer soak his shirt.

"Can you…" I sniffle. "Will you please keep this between us?"

He pulls away with a frown. "No one knows?"

I shake my head. "Only Oliver and his family."

"Your secret is safe with me."

My shoulders slump. "Thank you."

With one last parting glance over his shoulder, Rafa leaves me standing alone in the hall.

I head to the bathroom, and the deafening click of the door shutting adds to the emptiness growing inside me.

It's been two months, and I'm no better off than I was the day Oliver pulled the plug on our nine-year relationship. He didn't care about our show or the life we made together. Shit. He didn't care about anything except what *he* wanted. The perfect wife. A picturesque house overlooking the bay. Two kids and a dog all playing together behind a white picket fence, like some '50s sitcom.

It was a future expected of him and one I threatened to ruin.

Unlike the grief I struggled with after I lost my dad, this is different.

I am different.

I grip the edge of the porcelain sink and force myself to face the person I've become.

Disheveled. Damaged. *Depressed.*

It's difficult to acknowledge how far I've let myself go over the last few months. The broken person I've become is a far cry from the woman who woke up every morning full of energy, excited about choosing her outfit and doing her makeup regardless of whether she had plans to be on camera or not.

I miss the person I was. I miss her so damn much that I'm willing to put in the work to bring her back, even if it means attending extra therapy sessions and following through on difficult homework I'd rather avoid.

"You can bounce back." My cracked whisper fills the silence. "You can prove to him and everyone else that they didn't break you." I speak with a stronger voice this time, letting the words sink in. "And you can fight this battle against yourself and come out stronger because of it," I add with a sense of finality as I roll my shoulders back, fix my posture, and run my fingers through my messy hair.

From now on, I'm going to start living again. I only need to remember *how.*

CHAPTER FIVE

Julian

Nice of you to show up an hour late," my mom whispers as she corners me in the empty dining room.

I should have known her request for me to help set the table was a trap. "I was finishing up something for work."

"On a Sunday?"

I stay quiet as I arrange the cutlery.

She rocks back and forth. "I've been meaning to ask you…"

"You lasted a minute longer than I expected." I tap the face of my million-dollar watch. It's the most expensive thing I own, all because I bet against Rafa, who believed we would become billionaires after our Dwelling app was listed on the New York Stock Exchange.

I'm glad Rafa was right all along, although I nearly cried after buying us matching watches worth more than my current house and car combined.

Ma's lips purse. "*Mijo*."

"Yes?"

"I wanted to talk to you about Dahlia."

"What about her?" My voice lacks any inflection.

"I know you have your differences, but can you set those aside and be nice to her while she is getting back on her feet? She's in a fragile place right now."

"So I've noticed." It's obvious to anyone with eyes that Dahlia is one comment away from falling apart, but I want to know *why*. Oliver was a pretentious ass, but he seemed to respect Dahlia, according to my mom, so why call off a successful relationship after nine years?

Ma's voice drops as she says, "Rosa wants Dahlia to stay for a while."

I shut my eyes.

She continues, "I'm thinking it would be nice for you to team up on a project to help get her mind off everything."

I shake my head. "Dahlia and I don't work well together." Whatever the activity, we were sure to take opposing sides. Field days. Debate club. Model United Nations. If there was an opportunity to go up against each other, we rose to the occasion and duked it out every single time.

"Please think about it." Ma presses her palms together.

I pause for three seconds. "Done. Still going to be a no." Having Dahlia around again is hard enough after years spent avoiding her. Working with her would open myself up to a whole list of problems I have no interest revisiting in this lifetime.

She tucks her arms into her chest. "*Mijo*."

"I'm not trying to be difficult, but we have completely different mindsets when it comes to design."

"So? I think shaking things up will be good for her. Rosa says Dahlia has been in a creative rut for the last two months, so maybe taking on a different kind of job will inspire her," she pushes.

"Except you seem to have forgotten the time Dahlia called one of my projects an ugly gray box."

Ma makes a sour face. "To be fair, she wasn't exactly wrong."

It's my turn to glare. "You told me you liked it."

"I did because you made it, *mi amor*. As your mother, it's impossible not to love everything you do." She pats my cheek with bright eyes.

I make a noise in the back of my throat.

"Imagine what could happen if you put your two brilliant minds together for once."

There is only one woman in my life I would do anything to please, and she happens to be looking at me like I can single-handedly save the world if I go along with her request.

"Please?" she asks in that hopeful voice of hers.

I shake my head, hoping to knock some sense back into my brain in the process.

Her shoulders fall. "Oh."

You could use her request to your advantage…

Mijo: My son.

Mi amor: Motherly term of endearment.

44

A plan falls into place. "Actually, I'll consider it under one condition."

Her mood instantly perks up. "What?"

"I want you to stop trying to set me up with all your friends' daughters."

"How else do you expect to meet someone special with the crazy hours you work?"

"That's my problem."

"I thought you were interested in getting married and starting a family?"

I hold my tongue.

She frowns. "Don't tell me Rafa scared you away from marriage."

"He didn't." Shocking, given his current view on life and all.

"I'd like you to have a child while I'm still young enough to chase after them."

"About that…" While marriage is a part of my plan, having a kid is not—a fact that scared away half the women I dated.

Growing up with parents who struggled with years of infertility had a huge impact on me, and I don't expect a lot of people to understand what it was like to watch my father silently suffer while my mom went through depression, miscarriages, and a stillbirth that had her flatlining on an operating table.

Since my mom nearly died in the process of giving me a sibling, I don't plan on having children unless the woman I marry is willing to adopt.

My mom sucks in a breath. "*Qué?*"

I rub the back of my neck. "You know I'm not a kid person."

"But what about Nico?" Her pitch rises.

"An exception to the rule."

"Is this because of what I—"

"*No.*"

Her glassy gaze passes over my face before she looks away. "Okay. I'll respect your wishes."

A heavy weight pressing against my chest lifts.

She gnaws on her bottom lip. "I'll agree to your request, but you need to promise me one thing."

"What?"

"Please make this process enjoyable for Dahlia. You might not be interested in making me a mother-in-law anytime soon, but Dahlia—and Lily too—are the closest people I have to daughters, and I won't stand for you upsetting her when she is already down."

My mom manages to make me feel two inches tall despite me towering over her.

I tuck my chin in shame. "I won't."

She brings her hands together with a loud clap. "Great! Now, be sure to make it seem like this was all your big idea when you approach Dahlia about it."

"*Ma.*"

"I better go check on Rosa before she burns down the house. *¡Te quiero!*" She kisses my cheek before dashing toward the kitchen.

Te quiero: I love you.

Sundays at the Muñoz house haven't changed since I was born, although a few people have come and gone over the years, like Mr. Muñoz and my dad, who both passed away within a few years of each other. Rafa became a permanent member at the table after he was unofficially adopted by my mom when we were younger, once my dad's brother died.

My godson does a good job of keeping the conversation going with stories about his upcoming Halloween costume and his friend's birthday. Lily, Dahlia's twenty-seven-year-old sister, follows along with Nico's tales, while the rest of us easily become distracted by the empty chair and plate of untouched food beside me.

At one point, Lily takes a tray to Dahlia's room, only to come back fifteen minutes later with most of it left behind.

"She wasn't hungry?" Rosa stands and takes the tray from Lily's hands.

Lily shakes her head. "She ate some of it."

Everyone stares at the leftovers like a critical piece of evidence. Dahlia grew up like the rest of us, following three main rules: don't lie, don't cheat, and don't leave any food on your plate.

Ma kicks my chair. *Go talk to her*, she mouths.

I rise from my chair. "I'll be back."

The wrinkles etched into Rosa's face smooth out as I comb through my mental list of pros and cons.

Pro: You're doing the right thing.

Con: It doesn't exactly feel that way.

The quick shake of Rafa's head and his fierce scowl has me questioning myself.

Pro: Your mom will no longer set you up on dates.

Con: You'll be stuck working with Dahlia.

I tell myself to shut up and take a deep breath.

Thank you, Ma says by lifting her two thumbs in the air.

Before I lose my nerve, I walk away. The sound of my heart pounding fills my ears as I stop in front of Dahlia's door. I lift my fist to knock, only to hover above a hand-painted flower.

To describe Dahlia as talented would be insulting. She has a God-given gift to turn the most mundane objects into works of art, although I never stepped out of my comfort zone and praised her for it.

Once I lift my fist to knock, her door flies open.

"Julian?" Dahlia gapes at me with puffy eyes and a red nose.

I tuck my clenched hands into my pockets. "Hey."

"Is there a reason you're lurking around outside my room?" She checks the empty hall.

"I need to talk to you."

She squints. "Since when do you willingly want to speak?"

"Since my mother asked me to."

Her hollow laugh is chilling. "Still doing everything your mom asks? No wonder you're still single."

"I knew coming over here was a mistake," I grumble to myself. Dahlia will never agree to the idea of working on a project together if I come out and ask her.

My trap forms quicker than my mouth can move.

"Feel free to get lost." She reaches for the door.

I stop it from slamming shut with my hand. "Wait."

A wrinkle runs down the center of her forehead. "What?"

"Oliver and you are done?"

Her eyes turn into slits. "Are you only asking me so you can gloat?"

"No." Although her false accusation makes me want to.

Don't be petty, Julian.

She breaks eye contact first. "Yeah. We're done."

"Might want to get rid of that ring, then." I can't help but glare at the tacky piece of jewelry with a frown.

"I've tried." Her hand forms a shaky fist.

"Clearly not hard enough."

Something flashes behind her eyes. "I've been waiting to hear back from the Creswells' lawyer first before I got rid of it."

Rich people and their lawyers. While I might be one of them now, I'd never have one handle my personal business like that. My parents taught me people who want respect need to earn it first, and nothing says spineless quite like depending on a lawyer to do my dirty work.

"And what did this lawyer say?" I ask before I think better of it.

"I got the news an hour ago that I can do whatever I want with it."

"How convenient." My voice remains flat, although my words hits their target.

Her nostrils flare. "Are you insinuating that I'm lying?"

The silence following her question answers for me.

"You know what? I'm in the mood to prove you wrong."

Some things never change.

While I'm busy remembering the countless times she tried to do that, she catches me off guard as she slides the ring up her finger and holds it out for me. "Here."

I take a long step back. "What am I supposed to do with that?"

"Heck if I know, but I'm sure you'd be more than happy to get rid of the ring given how often you glare at it."

Fuck. While I was busy cataloging her next move, she was busy doing the same.

Checkmate.

I reach for the ring without the slightest tremble, although my heart beats wildly as our fingers graze.

I pluck the ring from her grasp and assess the tacky display of wealth that fits anyone but the woman in front of me. Although Dahlia loves jewelry—that much is obvious based on her endless rotation of rings, earrings, and necklaces—she hates gaudy wedding rings that can be found at any local jewelry shop.

I want a vintage ring like Mom's, she said once to her sister while they gawked over a cousin's engagement ring during a birthday party.

No way! I want a ring like the mayor's wife has. Lily beamed.

But it's so basic. Dahlia's nose scrunched.

Who cares so long as it's big, Lily snorted.

Dahlia clears her throat, yanking me away from the memory.

"You want me to get rid of it?" I ask.

She nods.

I'd like nothing more. Although…

An idea hits me. A terrible, stupid idea that has me acting first and thinking about regrets later.

"Fine, so long as you join me in the process." Getting her out of the house would probably do her some good. My dad always pushed my mom to do the same whenever she was deep in one of her depressions, so I know it works.

Plus, I have a feeling she will be more willing to agree to a working relationship if I play my cards right.

Her gaze bounces between me and the paused TV screen in her room. "I don't know. I'm a bit busy at the moment."

"Oh, my bad. Feel free to carry on with your pity party." I make a show of glancing at the mess on her bed. The purple comforter can barely be seen beneath the mountain of used tissues and discarded chocolate wrappers.

Her eyes widen. "Excuse me?"

I tuck the ring into my pocket. "I'll send you a video of what I end up doing with it. Hopefully you can make time to watch it in between binge-watching episodes of *The Silver Vixens* and crying your eyes out."

"I am *not* crying my eyes out."

My eyes flicker over her face for an extra beat before I turn around.

"You're a real asshole sometimes," she calls out.

"See you next Sunday. Or not. I'm sure you'll be real busy and everything." I don't bother looking back, although I throw her one last goodbye wave from over my shoulder.

She mutters something inaudible before saying, "You know what? I'm going with you."

Gotcha.

I kill my smile before turning around. "What happened to being busy?"

"Consider my calendar cleared."

I hope this doesn't blow up in my face.

Famous last words.

"You redid the interior." Dahlia runs her hand across the leather dashboard of my dad's old truck.

"Mm-hmm." I place my hand on her headrest and reverse down the Muñozes' driveway.

My dad was my hero, best friend, and future business partner, so I had no clue what to do with my grief when he passed. Restoring my dad's truck was eventually was one of the best ways to process his loss, although it came a few years too late.

She brushes her palm down the smooth leather bench. "How many times did he say he was going to do it? A hundred?"

Maybe a thousand, but he never lived long enough to see it through.

My dad had many dreams in his short life, including fixing up his truck, but he died before he could make them come true.

The same dull ache in my chest reappears, like a wound that never fully healed. Thankfully, Dahlia stops talking about my dad, giving me room to think without his memory distracting me.

Unfortunately, all good things must come to an end, including her silence after five minutes.

"Wait! Stop!" Dahlia nearly yanks my hand away from the steering wheel.

"No." I continue driving past the *nieve de garrafa* food truck located near the Lake Wisteria Park Promenade. Helping her get rid of the ring is one thing, but stopping for *nieve* along the way? Absolutely not happening.

"Please?" She actually presses her hands together. "I haven't had Cisco's in years!"

"It's October."

"So? There could be a blizzard outside, and I'd still want it."

My muscles tense even more. "This wasn't part of the plan."

"So help me God, I will literally jump out of this car right now if you don't pull over."

"At least let me speed up first to make it worth the trouble of another police report." I press the accelerator harder. Unlike my McLaren, my dad's old truck whines as it switches gears.

Her glare quickly devolves into the worst kind of weapon she carries in her artillery.

Puppy eyes.

"Please, Julian. I'm not above begging you for Cisco's."

Fuck me. Every cell in my body lights up at the sound of my name in that voice.

"I'll do anything. *Please.*"

Good luck saying no to her when she looks and sounds like that.

"Let's start with shutting up." I slow down and make a U-turn at the next median.

"Yes!" She does a little victory fist pump.

Nieve de garrafa: Handmade ice cream native to Mexico

I squash the urge to smile as I drive back toward the park and stop in front of Cisco's. A few families sit on the benches while some kids run around, probably enjoying the last few weeks of decent weather.

"Make it fast." I pull out my phone and begin reading through the thirty emails I've received in the short amount of time since I last checked.

She reaches for the door handle, only to hesitate. "Actually, you're right. It's too cold for Cisco's."

I stop my scrolling. "Are you serious?"

"Yes. Let's just keep going." She motions toward the steering wheel while scanning the park. The tension in her shoulders combined with her darting eyes gives her nerves away.

While Dahlia has always struggled with anxiety since we were younger, this feels different.

She is different.

With a sigh, I open my door.

"Where are you going?" Panic bleeds into her voice.

To do something stupidly nice. "I'm in the mood for Cisco's."

I walk away before I come to my senses and remember all the reasons why Dahlia is bad news.

CHAPTER SIX

Dahlia

Step one of my plan to get over my ex-fiancé includes mango-flavored *nieve de garrafa* from Cisco's, also known as the best food truck around. I devour my dessert while Julian taps away at his phone, doing whatever important things billionaires do on a Sunday night. At one point, he steps out of the truck to answer a call, leaving his lemon-flavored *nieve* unsupervised and available for the taking.

I can't be held responsible for my actions. If anything, I'm doing Julian's abs a favor by taking his dessert off his hands.

Once I finish both cups, he tosses them out before we drive away from the park with Morat on full blast. While Julian and I are very different, we share the same great taste in music, a fact I would never admit to his face.

Unlike my first night here, I take in the town and how much it has grown in my time away. While some businesses shut down during the slow winter season since not many people want to hang out by the lake when it's cold outside, most have remained open all year since they were first founded in the late 1800s.

Some of my favorite shops, like Hole in the Wall Hardware, Holy Smokes BBQ, and the Surf & Turf Meat Market, have been passed down for generations, while a few newer shops, like the Sweets & Treats Bake Shop, catch my eye.

"Where are we going?" I ask after a minute.

He lowers the volume. "One of my construction sites."

"I swear I'll haunt you forever if I end up being buried beneath six feet of concrete tonight."

"I'm flattered you want to hang around me for all eternity." His eyes sparkle.

Mine narrow into slits.

He raises his right hand. "No need to worry. So long as my mother loves you, I'll let you live."

"I'm not sure whether to be horrified by the threat or impressed you're willing to put up with me solely because your mother loves me."

He answers my question by increasing the volume of the music.

Cabrón.

When Julian suggested getting rid of my ring, visiting a construction site was not what I had in mind.

"Come on. Let's go." Julian switches his sneakers for worn

construction boots before forcing me into a hideous pair of large plastic ones that squeak with every step I take toward the fence.

He grabs a white hard hat from behind the barrier and places it on my head.

My nose scrunches. "Seriously?"

"Safety first." He turns my headlamp on before setting up his own.

Screw guys in backward ball caps and gray sweatpants. Men in hard hats and work boots are my new kink, thanks to Construction Ken standing in front of me with muscular arms and killer cheekbones.

I already know my therapist is going to dive right into this topic during next week's session.

"You good?" Julian's voice startles me.

"Yup," I manage to get out.

He opens the gate and leads the way toward the backyard of the semi-finished house. I follow behind him while watching out for tools and supplies scattered around.

Julian stops beside an empty concrete mixer near the exterior back wall overlooking the lake.

"You're joking." Of all the things Julian could have suggested, I would have never guessed this.

"Do you have a better idea?"

"No, but this feels criminal."

He keeps quiet while gathering supplies. His white T-shirt quickly loses its crisp color as construction dust clings to the material. His jeans suffer a similar fate, with the blue color turning gray when he pours the dry mixture inside the machine.

Though Julian probably hasn't touched a shovel since he broke ground on his fancy office at the corner of Main Street, he exudes confidence as he works.

If only his dad could see him now.

It was difficult to tear those two away from each other, especially when they were boots-deep in a project together. But then Luis Senior suddenly passed away from a heart attack, leaving a twenty-year-old Julian to grapple with a family business and his mourning mother.

I might dislike Julian for a hundred different reasons, but I will always respect the hell out of him and the sacrifices he made for his family, including dropping out of Stanford.

Julian curses to himself for the second time as he glares at the electrical panel.

"Are you sure you know what you're doing?" I ask.

"Just because I don't work on-site anymore doesn't mean I'm incompetent."

"Could have fooled me with how you kicked the machine when you thought I wasn't paying attention."

He scratches his nose with his middle finger, spreading gray dust all over the bridge. I reach out and wipe it away without a second thought.

He stares up at me like one does the sun—in equal parts pain and wonder.

I take one long step back and tuck my hands behind my back. "So, what's the point of being a billionaire if you don't have people at your beck and call ready to handle messy tasks like these?"

"Who says I don't?"

"Then why not call someone to come help us with this master plan of yours?"

His eyes narrow. "Because if my dad were still around, he would kick my ass if I asked for help making concrete. He taught me this stuff when I was Nico's age."

A pain echoes through my chest at his casual mention of his father. How many times did I beg Julian to open up to me after his dad passed away? Tens? Hundreds? He erected a wall around himself to effectively keep everyone out, including me.

He stabs at the power button, only to curse when nothing happens.

"Need any help?"

His back tenses. "I got it."

We fall into a comfortable silence as he takes apart the machinery. I become distracted by the stars twinkling off the surface of the lake while Julian reads through the user manual on his phone.

"¡*Chingada!*"

My head snaps in his direction. "What happened?"

He drops the cable like a live snake. "Nothing."

"Please tell me you didn't forget to check if it was plugged in."

"Of course I checked." The moon above us highlights the faint blush creeping up his neck.

The idea of Julian obsessively checking everything *but* whether or not the machine was plugged in has me curling over and laughing until my lungs hurt.

Chingada: Oh, fuck.

59

"This is the last time I do something nice for you." He grumbles something else under his breath.

"I'm sorry!" My voice comes out wheezy.

"No, you're not."

"Forgive me? Please?" I bat my lashes.

He glowers. "Only if you don't repeat this story to anyone. *Especially* Rafa."

"Cross my heart." I draw an invisible X over the spot.

"Tell anyone and I'll share that boxed wine video I have of you."

My eyes widen. "You kept it?"

"Blackmail has no expiration date."

The idea of him keeping funny videos of us from our time at Stanford shouldn't make me feel all warm and fuzzy, especially when it's Julian, yet my stomach does this betraying flip at the notion.

I keep my voice detached as I say, "Never fear. Your moment of incompetence is safe with me."

He leaves in a huff with the extension cord and a promise to be back in a minute.

Without Julian here to distract me, I'm left to grapple with my messy emotions. I rub at the faint white line on my ring finger like one would a stain, wishing it would disappear along with the pain about my relationship.

Former relationship.

In order for me to move on, I need to start letting go of the past and anything that reminds me of my broken engagement, starting with the ring.

It's everything I wanted and more, I lied as I held up my

shaky hand for the camera crew hired by the Creswells to film our publicized engagement.

A lot of women would be appreciative of a ring like that, Oliver said when he caught me not wearing the eyesore once after working out.

"Having second thoughts?" Julian's deep voice has me turning around.

"Are you sure an ability to mindread wasn't added during your last software update?"

His glare lacks its usual punch. "You've always been expressive."

"Not all of us were born with the ability not to feel anything."

"I feel things," he scoffs.

"Like what?"

"Excitement." He pulls my ring out of his pocket with an unhinged smile I've only seen on two other occasions—when I asked Julian to prom as punishment for him scoring higher than me on the ACT, and when the school's linebacker, who called me a prude bitch, was caught in a cheating scandal.

I never asked Julian about it, but I suspected he had something to do with the football player being busted and permanently benched from the team for the rest of the year.

"You good?" he asks in the same soft voice he saves for his mother.

My boots squeak together as I rock back. "What if this is a bad idea?"

"Do you plan on getting back together with him?"

"No. Definitely not."

"Do you want to sell it?"

I consider the option for a few seconds before shaking my head. "And pass that negative energy on to someone else? No."

"I could buy it off you."

I choke on my gasp. "What?"

He assesses the ring. "It's hideous, so I wouldn't pay more than a hundred for it."

"Bucks? But it's worth—"

He interrupts me. "Hundred *thousand*."

My eyes bulge. "That's a lot of money."

He *shrugs*.

Asshole. Unlike him, I still remember the days before he was a billionaire, back when our families ordering pizza with extra toppings was considered a luxury.

He casually spins the ring around his pinkie finger.

Sweat clings to my brow. "But…"

Hustling him out of a hundred thousand dollars does sound nice—

"The offer expires in three…"

Wait a minute. Why does he want to buy the ring in the first place?

"Two…"

Who cares? Take it!

"Fine!" I shout.

"You accept?"

"Sure."

"Great. Now with that settled…" He tosses the ring into the concrete mixer. The diamond gets swallowed up by the thick mixture as the machine spins round and round.

"Julian!" I jump to hit the red emergency button, but he yanks me away before I have a chance. All the air is knocked from my lungs as I slam into his body.

Our hard hats bang into each other, and mine falls off and lands at our feet during my fight to get loose. He wraps his other arm around my waist and tightens his hold, making any escape impossible.

"What are you doing?" I hiss like a wounded animal.

"Saving you from yourself." He hauls me farther away without my feet touching the ground.

"Are you serious? What was the point of offering to pay all that money for a ring you planned on throwing away?" I screech as I shove at the steel band of muscle locked around my body.

"It'll be worth every penny."

"But—" My reply gets lost somewhere in the chaos of my mind.

"You didn't like your ring."

I rear back. "What?"

"I bet you hated it from the moment Oliver got down on one knee and popped open that cliché Cartier box."

A two-by-four to the face would be less surprising than his comment.

My pulse quickens. "Why would you think that?"

"Because, like him, it was stuffy, obnoxious, and represented everything he and his pretentious, cookie-cutter family stand for." Julian's words hit hard enough to make my legs shake beneath me.

Julian saw Oliver and his family for exactly what they were.

A fancy façade.

I was comfortable going along with it because Oliver made it seem like he was different, but in reality, he was another Creswell clone desperate for an inheritance and his parents' approval.

And I was the woman standing in the way of that.

Julian lets me go when the fight drains from my body, and my mind drifts as the machine spins.

The demise of my relationship started with a prenup, and things quickly devolved from there as I was pummeled with tasks like premarital counseling and health screenings.

It's standard protocol for people like us, Oliver said as he passed me a stack of prenuptial paperwork thicker than my thigh. While I expected one given the Creswells' financial situation, its contents shocked me.

A genetic health screening? I asked with a frown, only for Oliver to wave away my concern. *It's a formality.* He grabbed my hand and gave it a squeeze. *Think of it as a protective measure*, he added.

I winced. *Protective measure against what?*

It's boilerplate language. He quickly moved on to the next section, dictating how I would be paid per child I gave birth to. Bonus cash if I breastfed.

God, I should have run after that meeting, but instead, I trusted him.

My throat tightens until I'm gasping for air.

"*Mírame*," Julian orders.

Mírame: Look at me.

I can't. At least not when I feel like *this*.

"I'll meet you back at the truck."

"If you want the ring, I'll pull it out." He speaks to my back.

I shake my head hard enough to rattle my already-scattered brain. "No." Tears pool near the bottoms of my eyes, about one second away from falling.

You better not cry in front of Julian, so pull yourself together and get the hell out of here.

"Come find me when it's finished." I fight the impulse to curl into myself as I accept that part of my life is over.

"Okay."

My lungs deflate from my heavy exhale as I turn. Every step away from the mixer feels like a small victory, and I'm proud of myself for making it to the truck without shedding a single tear, although the widening hole in my chest threatens to consume me.

But unlike before, I fight back. I don't want to cry anymore over a man who discarded me like trash.

I *refuse* to.

Starting now.

CHAPTER SEVEN

Dahlia

A flash of something red and white catches my eye. "Stop the truck!"

He slams on the brakes, and we both go shooting forward. I groan as the seat belt locks into place and crushes my chest.

"What's wrong?" His eyes dart across my face.

I press a hand against my chest. "Besides the fact that you nearly gave me a heart attack?"

"You asked me to stop."

"Not like that!"

"Sorry."

"It's fine. Give me a second." I unbuckle my seat belt.

"Where are you going? It's pitch-black outside."

"I want to see something." I climb out of the truck and walk back to the spot that caught my attention.

The *For Sale* sign posted in front of the gate feels illegal, and I'm tempted to steal it to prevent someone else from making an offer on the house of my dreams.

Lampposts lining the driveway illuminate the Queen Anne-style mansion sitting at the top of the small hill. Despite the warped wood and lack of upkeep, the house that once belonged to one of our town's founders is beautiful with its elegant craftsmanship, unrivaled view of the lake, and historic connection to the town.

Not just any Founder's house, but the one I dreamed of renovating one day. Ever since I was a little kid, I used to say that if I had three wishes, one of them would be to own this particular blue house.

Now you have the money and opportunity to make it happen.

The sudden rush of excitement sends my head spinning, making me feel drunk on the idea of restoring a house like this.

I'd be foolish not to take advantage of this rare opportunity. I've been obsessed with the Founders' houses long before I pursued a career in interior design. Their backstory, aesthetics, and view of Lake Wisteria and the forest beyond made them easy to fall in love with and impossible to forget.

A house isn't going to save you from your depression. The voice of reason speaks out.

No, but my therapist said I should engage in activities that make me happy, and this house would be a good start.

"Is this for real?" I flick the sign to be sure.

"Seems like it." Julian stops beside me and pulls out his phone.

"What are you doing?"

"I want to know how much they're asking for it."

"No!" I steal his phone.

"You can't stop me from being curious."

"You're not allowed to touch this one." The five original Founders' houses rarely go up for sale, so no way in hell am I letting Julian buy it.

"Is your name on the deed?"

"Not yet." I'll be damned if I let this project slip away from me. It's the exact kind of house that could help spark my creativity again while pushing me to take the necessary steps my therapist has been recommending for months.

Julian pries his phone out of my crushing grip. "Then it's fair game."

"Fair game? How is that possible when you're our local Monopoly Man?"

"I'm flattered by the rare compliment." His dry voice doesn't match the words.

"Ugh. *Lo juro por Dios*—"

He taps at his screen before placing it against his ear. "Sam. Hey. Sorry about the late call, but this is important. First thing tomorrow morning, I need you to contact a seller—"

I snatch his phone back and take off in the opposite direction. "Hi, Sam. It's Dahlia Muñoz. How are you?"

"I—uh—I'm sorry, did you say *Dahlia Muñoz*?" A male voice wheezes toward the end of his question.

"Yes."

"As in Dahlia Muñoz, founder of Designs by Dahlia?"

Lo juro por Dios: I swear to God.

"That's me."

"Holy shit," Sam whispers to himself.

I stick my tongue out at Julian while hitting the speaker button.

"I'm your biggest fan!" Sam shouts. "Wait. What are *you* doing with Julian?"

"Sadly, we know each other."

Julian shoots daggers at me.

"I can't believe Julian never said anything. He knows how obsessed I am with your…everything!"

"Oh, you are?" I ask.

"Of course I am! Ask Julian. He always gets pissed when I watch your show at my desk during my lunch break."

"Why do you think that is?"

Sam scoffs. "Beats me."

I laugh.

"It's not like he couldn't learn a thing or two from you. Seriously. I love what you did last season with the Mayhem Manor. It's one of my favorite designs, and the one I keep coming back to anytime I need some inspiration."

"With Julian's designs, that must be often."

Sam barks out a laugh while Julian glares at me.

I turn away and take Sam off speaker. "Sam, listen. I hate to cut you off, but I have a special request and not a lot of time."

"Name it." Sam speaks with conviction.

"Whatever Julian tells you to do, don't. At least not with the Founder's house."

"But he's my boss."

"Are you up for a new job? Because I'll hire you—"

"That's enough." Julian snatches the phone from my hand. "Sam, I'll call you back tomorrow. Sorry again about bothering you this late."

"But—" Sam's panicked voice disappears as Julian hangs up.

"Sweet guy. Out of curiosity, how much do you pay him?"

His eyes narrow. "You're not stealing my assistant."

"I mean, is it considered stealing if he wants to leave?"

Julian's frown deepens. "If you like the house, then you'll have to put in a competitive offer."

"But you're a billionaire."

"So?"

"*So* how the hell am I supposed to outbid you?"

He strokes his chin like an evil villain. "I see your point."

"Great. Now if you'll do me a solid and pretend you never saw the house, I'll be forever indebted to you."

"Forever indebted to me?" His voice lowers, awakening hundreds of butterflies from their cocoons.

Hell. Freaking. No.

I tilt my head back. "Let me have this one. *Please*."

"I'm not in the charity business."

"Excuse me?" I enunciate each syllable.

"It's nothing personal. I need land, and this place has it. One of these properties could fit ten of my houses easily."

I throw my hands in the air. "See! That reason alone is exactly why *I* should be the buyer."

"Because you don't want to capitalize on an opportunity? That's stupidity, not validity."

My fists ball at my sides. "It's not stupid to value a home's history."

"I value the financial kind more."

"And you think I don't? A historic home can make as much money as a new build if you fix it up the right way."

"I'm not saying it can't, but the math will always be in my favor, no matter how hard you try."

I groan. "How much do you sell one of your homes for?"

"Three mill, give or take."

My eyes widen. "Three. Million. Dollars?" Houses around the lake used to be worth less than a quarter million back when I was a kid.

He breaks eye contact first. "Yeah."

"And how many houses have you demolished?"

"Enough."

"Fifty?" He remains quiet. "A hundred?" I ask, earning nothing more than a blink. "Two hundred?"

He stays silent.

I shake my head. "Wow. At this rate, you'll be out of houses within the next few years."

"Exactly why I need a property like this to solve our supply-demand issue."

Time to switch strategies.

"Do you want me to beg?" My voice drops.

I bite down on my cheek to stop myself from grinning when he blinks twice. While Julian and I have engaged in many psychological warfare tactics over the years, seduction has never been one of them. But hell, if it means securing my dream house, I'm willing to flirt my way into a deal with the devil.

"No." His jaw tightens.

"I'm not above getting down on my knees."

His eyes drop to my lips before he glances away. "Shut. Up."

I clasp his chin and force him to look at me. "What do you want?"

He jerks his head free from my grasp and takes a step back. "Whatever the fuck is the opposite of this."

"I'll leave you alone if you walk away from this house." I brush my finger down the center of his chest.

He jolts. "I knew working with you was a mistake."

"What?"

"Nothing." His gaze flickers between the property and me for a whole minute before he speaks again. "What if we go fifty-fifty instead?"

"I'm sorry?"

"You want the house, and I want the land. I'm sure we can work together to get what we both want."

"Who says the town would let you build another house here?"

"That's my issue."

"You want us to go all in together, hoping to rezone the property and build a few extra houses on it?"

"Correct."

I shake my head. "That will never work."

His frown lines return with a vengeance. "Why not?"

"Because only one of us has style, and hint, it's not you." Unlike Julian's commitment to mid-century modern designs, my modern rustic design style is the complete opposite. I enter each home with the same goal of emphasizing its original architecture while combining different interior design styles.

One of the biggest reasons I started gaining popularity was that my approach was unlike everyone else's. I wasn't afraid of blending different styles, including Julian's beloved mid-century modern, which helped me stand out.

He pinches the bridge of his nose hard enough to leave a mark. "You're testing my patience."

"I'm surprised you still have any left when it comes to me."

He grumbles to himself before speaking again. "You can have full creative control of the house."

"Really?"

"Yes."

"And what if city hall denies your request?"

"Then we will need to flip the property and resell it for a price worthy of investing my time and resources," he says.

"What resources?"

"If you plan on restoring that house within the next three years, you'll need my company to get the job done."

"Why is that?"

"The only other construction company in town has a year-long waitlist because they're busy fixing up the motel."

Shit. I don't want to wait a year when this is the perfect project to help get me out of my design rut.

Still, despite my excitement, I worry about partnering with Julian. We have only worked on one project together in college, and it ended with me setting myself up for unrealistic expectations.

I can vividly picture Julian destroying the house to build his ideal neighborhood of white-and-gray houses made of equal parts concrete and glass. The history of the property would be erased and replaced with cold, sharp lines to match the man in front of me.

I shake the image away with a shiver.

No matter how much I dislike the idea of working with Julian, I despise the thought of him demolishing this house more.

I speak before I have a chance to talk myself out of the opportunity. "I'm in."

CHAPTER EIGHT

Julian

R afa and I walk to the unoccupied leather armchairs at the back of the Angry Rooster Café. It's been weeks since we last spent time together by ourselves. With him managing the Dwelling app and me working through growing pains as Lopez Luxury expands to new neighboring lake towns, we have been busy.

There are some days I want to turn back the clock and relive the times when I woke up at five a.m. to work on a build with my dad, not drive to an office. Those were some of my happiest days, and the ones I think about more often lately.

I'm not cut from the same corporate cloth as my competitors, and it shows in every interaction I have. The desire to hire someone else to run the corporate side of the business rides me harder than ever lately, but I don't have anyone I can trust with that kind of responsibility.

Rafa sinks into the leather chair. "I saw something interesting today on my drive into town."

"What?"

"Someone listed one of the Founders' houses."

"Hm." I take a sip of my iced coffee with extra caramel, caramel drizzle, and a splash of cream. The warm, sugary goodness hits my tongue, instantly elevating my mood despite the glaring man sitting across from me.

His head tilts. "It's the same one you were looking into a few years ago."

"It is."

"Well…are you going to buy it this time?"

The sweet coffee slides down my throat like acid. "Why?"

His eyes narrow. "Because you're not the type to let an opportunity like that go to waste. The land alone makes it one of the most valuable properties around."

My stomach churns. "I'm teaming up with Dahlia on it."

He raises a condescending brow. "And you thought that was a good idea *because*?"

"My mom asked me to."

"Of course she did. She's been planning your wedding since you both were in the womb."

The plastic cup beneath my fingers bends from the pressure. "She's worried about Dahlia."

"So are the rest of us." His scowl softens. "But that doesn't mean you need to be her knight with a shining tool belt."

"If a tool belt is shiny, it's clearly for looks."

"That's not my point, and you know it."

My shoulders stiffen. "I do, but that's not going to be an issue."

"What are you thinking, buying a house with her and fixing it up together like she did all those times with Oliver?"

Tension ripples through my body. "This isn't like that."

He stares.

"Do you have something you want to get off your chest?" My question comes out sharp.

"You're making a mistake," he grumbles.

"I don't expect you to understand." No one can, no matter how much they try.

Dahlia and I have a complicated history of antagonizing each other into being the best—and sometimes worst—versions of ourselves. That kind of connection doesn't go away no matter how many years I spend wishing it had.

"I understand enough to recommend you don't go teaming up with the woman you once were in love with."

I rub at my stubbled cheek. "I know what I'm doing."

"I know what you *intend* to do, but life has a funny way of fucking over our best-laid plans." He dismisses me with a flick of his gaze.

"We're working on a project together, not falling in love."

Dahlia made sure that wasn't possible once she began dating my ex-roommate after I dropped out of Stanford.

He snorts. "Because working together went so well the last time."

My teeth grind together as I remember the one and only time Dahlia and I teamed up: on a college psychology project. It was a decision made out of jealousy and became the first in a long list of mistakes I made when it came to her. Flirting. Kissing. Pushing her away because I didn't have the skills to process my fear of losing someone else I loved after my father's death.

"That right there is what I'm worried about." Rafa points at me.

I blink a couple of times. "What?"

"That look on your face."

"What are you talking about?"

He replicates an expression that sure as hell can't be mine. I toss a crumpled napkin at him. "*No mames*."

"I thought you were over her."

"I am. I was just…"

"Reminiscing?"

"*Thinking*," I correct.

"Please consider doing more of that, because clearly you haven't been lately."

"Helping Dahlia get over Oliver is the right thing to do." After all, I'm the one who introduced them to each other.

You'll be back soon, right? Oliver asked in the middle of me panic-buying a plane ticket home after I heard about my dad's heart attack.

Dahlia came over to help me pack up your stuff and ship it since you're too busy to answer a single text, he messaged me a month after I dropped out of Stanford. *And thanks for letting us know you weren't coming back, dickface. So much for us being friends*, he added.

Next thing I knew, Dahlia was in a relationship with the

No mames: Stop messing around.

asshole who had his head stuck so far up his ass, I'm surprised he hadn't suffocated yet.

Not a single week goes by when I don't regret becoming friends with Oliver and the mistakes I made that pushed him and Dahlia together in the first place.

♔

My fingers cramp from how long I've spent tapping them against the conference room table. It's hard not to feel antsy after a day full of meetings with project managers, architects, engineers, and interior designers.

My general manager, Mario, shuffles a few papers in front of him. "All submitted permits for our projects have been paused due to the person in charge going on paternity leave."

I frown. "And no one else can take over for the time being?"

"No. The same thing happened two years ago when Abbie was having her twins."

I release a frustrated exhale. If I worked in a bigger city like Detroit or Chicago, I wouldn't run into these kinds of issues. My life would be much less stressful if daily operations didn't cease because a few people caught the flu or one person was out having a baby.

And lonelier. The idea of moving away from my family again has me shutting down that thought.

I speak up. "Readjust schedules so all our guys have consistent work for the next few weeks. It shouldn't be too hard since city hall approved our permits for the townhouses." I turn to Ryder. "Any updates?"

Ryder, my project manager, quits tapping his pen against the clipboard. He's been working with me for seven years already and worked his way up to his current position before turning thirty-eight. Thanks to him, I can sleep easier at night knowing he can manage my crew like a disciplined drill sergeant.

He leans back and tucks his hands behind his dark head of hair. "I think we no longer need to worry about Mr. Vittori."

My fingers stop tapping. "How so?"

"He withdrew all his offers on the available houses in the area."

"Why?"

"I'm not sure. According to city hall, he hasn't purchased any properties or lots, so maybe he moved on to another town. It's not like you gave him much of a choice." His dark brown eyes light up.

"I don't like it." *Or him.*

I've been wary of Lorenzo Vittori since he randomly returned to Lake Wisteria twenty-three years after his parents died, and it isn't because of him bidding against me on lakefront properties or the gossip spreading around town about him wanting to run for mayor.

The town might have welcomed him back, but I don't trust him or his fake acts of altruism. It doesn't matter how many times he attends Sunday Mass or how many hours he spends volunteering at the animal shelter. For all I know, he is funneling his uncle's dirty money through different businesses and charities, all under the guise of being a good Samaritan who wants to make a difference.

He might have spent the first ten years of his life here, but a lot has happened in the years since then.

My twenty-five-year-old assistant, Sam, waltzes into the conference room armed with his headset, tablet, and a bright smile that reaches his brown eyes. "The architect team is waiting in conference room B to review the plans for the townhouses. I also set up the design team in room C, so once you're done there, head on in so they can present their ideas for the cul-de-sac."

"Great."

He readjusts his headpiece over his dark blond hair. "Oh, and then, when you have some free time, call Lake Aurora's mayor. He had a few questions about the town's infrastructure and wanted to run an idea by you."

"Thanks." I rub my eyes. Despite getting eight hours of sleep last night, I still feel tired.

When the Dwelling shares were listed on the New York Stock Exchange and our company went public a few years ago, I was invigorated by my newfound billionaire status and the prospect of turning my father's struggling construction company into Lopez Luxury. But now that I've accomplished everything my father dreamed of and more, I'm uninspired, exhausted, and growing resentful of every project I take on.

I've considered different options to reignite my passion, such as taking on an individual project again or changing up my team of designers, but I never seem to follow through. Part of me is afraid that I'll never return to the office once I remember what it feels like to invest my blood, sweat, and tears into a project.

Last night proved that. Dahlia wasn't the only one who had a spark in her eye at the prospect of fixing up the Founder's house.

I did too.

After a long day full of meetings, I'm relieved to return to my isolated mansion on the northern shore of the lake, located far away from the restaurants, parks, and couples who remind me of what I want but don't have.

I've had three other houses in the last four years which were in the southern part of town. While the sand dunes and beachfront were far nicer than the smaller, rockier northern shore, I couldn't stand being surrounded by tourists, couples, and families.

I dump my keys and wallet in the glass dish beside the front door before taking a hard left toward the chef's kitchen with windows facing the Historic District, although I'm quickly distracted from the panoramic views by my growling stomach.

Neat rows of premade meals line the middle shelf of my refrigerator, courtesy of my housekeeper. I microwave the first one within reach and take a seat at the kitchen island before connecting my phone to the speaker system.

Even with the music blasting around the house, the scraping of my utensils against the plate sounds worse than firing up a concrete saw at midnight.

I don't enjoy silence as much as people think I do. In fact, I've grown to hate it over the years because it reminds me of what I lack.

A home rather than a house.

A wife to love, cherish, and support.

A reason to wake up every morning that isn't my job or the people who rely on me for a steady paycheck.

Money might buy me a lot of things, but it can't cure the gaping hole in my chest that only deepens with every passing year. What used to fulfill me barely scratches the incessant itch anymore. Overworking myself. Casual dates that never lead to anything more. Spending all my free time with family while ignoring the wish to start my own.

None of it has the same appeal, and I'm getting worried.

Mejor solo que mal acompañado, my dad said in that deep, rumbling voice of his after I caught my group of friends making fun of me behind my back.

Pain slices through my chest. When I was younger, I would roll my eyes and ask what website my dad stole his latest quote from, but now I have an appreciation for how he had the right saying for every situation.

God, I've lost count of how many times I wished he were here, dropping proverbs whenever I needed them.

When the right person comes around, you'll know it, I tell myself.

But what if the right person has been there all along and I screwed it all up because I was a stupid twenty-year-old who didn't know any better?

That question has kept me awake since Dahlia returned last week, along with the what-if scenarios that could have happened if I had processed my grief the right way instead of isolating myself.

Mejor solo que mal acompañado: Better to be alone than with bad company.

CHAPTER NINE

Dahlia

D o you get cell service in that little hometown of yours?" my
agent, Jamie, asks as soon as I answer the phone.

I wince. "Sorry about not returning your calls."

Avoiding Jamie was easy after listening to her first voicemail, when she asked me how my planning was going for my
next décor launch, but dodging my other friends' texts and calls
has been more challenging. Reina, Hannah, and Arthur—the
three TV crew members I befriended on *Bay Area Flip*—send
messages in our group chat daily despite me only sharing an
occasional *I'm still alive* text.

While that statement is true, I'm not exactly *living*, so until
I am, I plan on keeping away from everyone.

Jamie makes a soft chuffing noise. "I'm only teasing you.
How's the R and R going?"

Seeing that I got out of bed before noon, took a morning

walk around the neighborhood, and helped my mom make breakfast, I'd count today as a win despite it only being ten a.m.

Look at you finding the bright side.

"Good. I needed the break," I reply.

"After wrapping up that last season, I don't blame you."

"Yeah."

"How are you doing mentally?"

I loosen my tight grip on my phone. "Some days are good, and some days are…"

"Absolute shit?" she finishes for me.

"Exactly."

"I know life sucks right now, but things will get better. I promise you that."

The ball in my throat grows larger. "I hope so."

She speaks after a brief pause. "I hate to be the bringer of bad news, but a reporter reached out with questions about your breakup."

My body turns to stone. "Oh."

"My team gave them the response we approved together."

Stomach acid bubbles, rising in my tight throat. "Right." Besides Oliver and his family, Jamie is the one and only person who knows the real reason why my engagement failed, and I hope to keep it that way, regardless of how many times Lily and my mom try to pry the answers out of me.

"I re-sent the signed NDA to Oliver and your ex-agent just in case."

My laugh comes out hollow. "You're the best."

"You might not be saying that in a minute."

I swallow back my fear. "What's going on?"

"I'm not the kind of agent who wants to bother you while you're on a much-needed break, but the team at Curated Living has been asking a bunch of questions about the plans for next fall's collection, and I can only deflect so many times."

My breathing quickens. "Right."

"They reported record-breaking numbers for your last launch, so they're excited to start planning your next one."

"Of course." I clench my hands to stop them from shaking.

"The team wants to know when you will be sending the preliminary sketches for it. If you want to launch by September and capitalize on your momentum, they'll need to start production before the end of February."

I haven't made it through this fall, let alone started thinking about the next, but no big deal.

Liar.

Panic swells in my chest. Every time I open my tablet to begin sketching, my energy levels tank, making me feel defeated before I have a chance to start.

"If you need to pull back for a season—"

"No," I blurt out. I've been working with Curated Living for the last few years, and I refuse to lose the last partnership I have left. "I'll get them the initial sketches before the end of the year, so you can go ahead and schedule our meetings for January."

"Are you sure?"

"Yup." I rub my pulsing temple.

"Great! I'll let them know."

"Awesome." My heart pounds against my rib cage as I ask, "By the way, do you have any pitch updates for the new show?"

While I was originally optioned to film another season of *Bay Area Flip* with Oliver, our broken engagement ruined any chance of that happening, so I'm hoping Jamie can secure me a new network contract. I love my job, and not a day goes by when I don't miss it and the people I helped.

"No, I haven't heard back yet, but it's only a matter of time before I call you with a new TV deal." Her voice seems uncharacteristically chipper.

"Oh." I fall back onto my bed. "Do you think no one is interested because the pitch is different from my last show?"

I appreciated the Creswells and their connections, which helped me land a show to begin with, but their tight grip on the production process left me wanting for more.

More control over the show's narrative. More clients from *all* socioeconomic backgrounds. And more freedom to discuss topics like grief, loss, and big life changes such as divorce.

While I didn't expect production companies to drop everything to sign with me, it's been a few weeks already without any follow-up meetings.

What do you expect when your personal life has become an internet meme?

My eyes sting, but I blink away the tears.

After Jamie hangs up, I'm tempted to crawl back under my covers and fall asleep, but instead, I make a conscious choice to get up, unzip my luggage, and search for my makeup bag.

Un Muñoz nunca se rinde, my dad always said.

And it's time I remember how to live like that.

I don't *want* to leave the house, but I choose to do it anyway because my mom and sister need my help with a large order of wedding centerpieces.

My mom's shop, Rose & Thorn, is located in the famous Historic District on the north side of town. The area was adequately named after the brick-and-mortar buildings and surrounding cottage-style neighborhood dating back to when the town was first founded in the late 1800s.

The Historic District makes up the heart of Lake Wisteria. A majority of the original buildings are located within the five blocks, including the library, bank, town hall, post office that once used carrier pigeons, and a tiny schoolhouse the size of a shoebox. We weren't wealthy enough to grow up there, but my mom was able to open up a tiny flower shop thirty-five years ago when my grandparents moved here because of a job.

It would be hard to miss Rose & Thorn with the pink paint covering the exterior brick walls and the fall window display full of red, orange, and yellow flowers of all shapes and sizes.

You can do this, I chant to myself as I exit the car and walk toward the sidewalk.

At least you look good, I add. In honor of getting my shit together, I picked out my best outfit, hoping the pop of color and dash of accessories would boost my mood.

You don't need to seek everyone's attention all the time; that old comment made by Oliver's mother about my clothing rears its ugly, unwelcome head.

I nearly twist my ankle at the memory.

One day I hope you feel comfortable enough in your own skin to stop covering it up, she said before handing me a bottle of anti-aging cream.

You should stop—

"Dahlia? Is that you?" a woman calls out behind me.

My mom stops next to me and turns with a smile.

Nope. Can't do this. Screw the meds and my therapist's advice to get out of the house. Helping my family with flowers is one thing, but having to face people is a whole different issue I'm not ready to tackle now that the news has broken about my failed engagement.

Mom grabs my shoulders to stop me from escaping. "It'll be good for you to catch up with old friends."

Except I don't have any friends at Lake Wisteria anymore. The two close ones I made in elementary school live in different states now, and although we call one another to catch up every now and then, I haven't been able to talk much since I found out about my genetic test. They're both pregnant and excited about having babies, which leaves me feeling like the odd woman out.

Mom turns me around before I have a chance to bolt for the store. *"Nos vemos adentro."* She kisses my forehead before locking the door to the shop behind her.

"I knew it was you! Only you could turn Main Street into your own fashion runway." Alana Castillo, one of my high school classmates, waves.

Of all the people from my past I could have run into, Alana is the best option. Not only is she nice, but we actually

Nos vemos adentro: We'll see you inside.

got along pretty well in high school despite being part of different friend groups.

Her dark hair shines under the sun, bringing out the different brown tones. A tall, handsome, blond man beside her whispers something in her ear before taking off toward the Pink Tutu with her daughter, who is dressed in a leotard, neon green ballet skirt, and combat boots.

I fight the usual oppressive sadness as I force out a casual "Hey."

You can at least try to sound excited to see her.

Alana wraps her arms around me and presses her cheek against mine. "How are you?"

"Fine."

She pins me in place with a single, knowing look. "I see."

I kick an invisible rock with the toe of my boot. "I've seen some better days."

"Is that why you're back in town?"

"That and my mom's cooking."

Ugh. I regret the words as soon as I say them. While I wasn't able to make it to the funeral service the town had for Alana's mom because of my filming schedule, I should have known better than to bring up mothers and cooking.

Her warm smile lessens my anxiety. "Not a single day goes by when I don't crave my mom's *pandebonos*, so I get it."

"Those were the best! My mom still kicks herself for never asking your mom for the recipe."

"If you want, I can teach you both one of these days."

My brows rise. "Really?"

After living in San Francisco, I forgot what it was like to

be surrounded by people who care. I was lucky if my barista spelled my name right, let alone asked me how I was doing because they genuinely wanted to know.

Alana's melodic laugh could warm the coldest of hearts. "Of course. Anyone is welcome in my kitchen, so long as they're not Missy."

"Don't tell me she's still trying to steal your recipes after all this time."

She lets out a huff of air. "That girl has been trouble since high school. She has good intentions and all, but she won't rest until she wins a Fourth of July Bake-Off."

"Dahlia!" Lily pops her head out of the shop. "We need your help in here!"

I offer Alana an apologetic look. "Sorry. I better get going."

"No worries. I should get back to Cal and Cami before they get themselves into trouble."

"Does that happen often?"

"Only when I leave them alone together for more than five minutes." Her eyes sparkle.

I pull her into a hug. "It was nice seeing you."

"Likewise. And remember that you're welcome to come hang out and cook with me any day."

"I might have to take you up on that."

🏆

After an inventory count gone wrong, my mom ran to Lake Aurora's flower farm, leaving Lily and me alone to finish up as many centerpieces as we can with the flowers we have.

"So…" my sister interrupts my mission to get through today's tasks without thinking or talking.

I look up from my half-assembled bouquet. Lily's eyes remind me of our dad, with the brown color nearly blending into her pupils. While I take after Mom with my shorter, curvier frame, lighter brown eyes, and softer features, Lily inherited her height, sharpness, and short temper from our dad. With genes like hers, she could have graced the covers of magazines had she not wanted to spend her entire life in Lake Wisteria, running the flower shop.

Lily continues when I don't speak. "I noticed something interesting."

"What?"

"You're not wearing your engagement ring anymore."

I swallow the thick lump in my throat. "No."

"Where is it?"

"You'd have to ask Julian."

"Excuse me?" she screeches.

"I have no idea what he did with it after he threw it in the concrete mixer."

Her gaze flicks over the faint white line on my finger. "A concrete mixer?"

I can't help laughing. "Yup."

"Wow."

"I know. Crazy, right?"

"Most definitely. But it's nice Julian helped you get rid of it."

"Don't tell me you're calling him *nice* now."

She raises her hands. "To be fair, he's matured a lot since you were both in college."

I press my fingers against my ears. "I can't hear you."

Her eyes roll. "You're a child."

"What happened to the sister who helped me with recon missions to score some blackmail on him?"

"She grew up."

I shoot her a look that she serves right back.

"Seriously. Why is he the enemy? And don't give me some lame excuse about you two having a rivalry since childhood because I know it goes beyond that."

I jerk back. "What?"

"I might act oblivious, but that doesn't make me stupid. Something happened between you two while you were at college, so what was it?"

"Nothing."

"You're such a bad liar."

I focus on the centerpiece. "I don't want to talk about it."

"You know you can tell me anything. I'm like Fort Knox."

A whole minute goes by before I speak again. "We kissed."

She squeals like a damn kid at Dreamland. "I knew it!"

I glare.

"What else? Tell me more!"

My entire face feels like it might burst into flames. "No."

Her eyes bulge. "You guys had sex, didn't you?"

A flower stem snaps between my fingers. "Lily!"

She throws her hands in the air. "Come on! I've waited *years* to ask you about this. At least take pity on me and entertain a few of my questions."

"Why didn't you ask me about this before?"

"You were avoiding him for some reason, so I wasn't about to bring him up."

"Yeah."

"So what happened? I have my suspicions and everything, but I'm not sure."

My gaze drops. "It's complicated."

"When did you realize you liked him?"

"Probably toward the end of our freshman year of college." Homesickness and a psychology project forced us to rely on each other like never before, and little by little, the two of us became friends.

"And then what?" my sister asks.

I kissed him a few weeks before everything in his life went to shit.

My shoulders drop. "His dad died."

"Oh."

"*Yup.*"

"Makes sense. I assumed the sex was bad or something—"

I choke on a laugh, and Lily gasps.

"Ahh! It was good?"

I can feel the heat blooming across my cheeks.

"Great?" she squeaks.

"I refuse to talk about this with you." Mainly because there is nothing *to* talk about. Julian made sure of that during a five-minute call that destroyed any hope of us having a future together.

You're a distraction I don't need, he told me over the phone after I offered to put the semester on hold and come back to Lake Wisteria after his dad died.

It was only a kiss, he spoke with a flat tone, making me feel like the dumbest girl in the world after I wanted to help him with his dad's company because I was passionate about design too.

I'm sorry I don't feel the same way, he said once I poured out my heart and admitted I cared about him in a real, raw, and scary kind of way.

I need time, he replied before ending the call.

It was the last time I spoke to him over the phone. All my other calls went to voicemail, even after I helped Oliver pack up his dorm.

Funny how confidence can take years to build and only a few interactions to destroy.

My sister cuts through the memories by speaking up. "Fine. I can respect your wishes. I'm just happy the two of you can be in a room together again."

"Me too," I admit.

"Josefina and Mom never said anything, but I know they missed having everyone under one roof. Things were never the same once you—" She catches herself.

"Moved to San Francisco?" I finish the thought for her.

She flinches. "Yeah."

"I thought you liked spending holidays there?"

"I did, but I won't lie. Nothing beats all of us getting together for Christmas, and no number of big-city holidays could replace how it feels to be home."

My head drops. "I'm sorry."

She walks around the table and pulls me into a tight hug. "I'm glad you're back. For now, at least."

"Likewise."

My mom and sister drop me off near the cemetery with a promise to come back in thirty minutes. The three of us have visited this dreary corner of town plenty of times over the years, although it's been a while since I last stopped by.

The bouquet of yellow roses trembles in my hands as I walk past the main gate.

Few people love yellow roses as much as my father did, and anyone who knew him heard the story of how he met my mom while searching Rose & Thorn for flowers before his date with another woman.

His memory makes my heart heavy with sorrow. Losing a parent is never easy, but being present at the young age of sixteen when mine flat-lined in an ambulance was devastating.

Luckily, I had a school counselor who cared enough to help me through the grieving process, and I poured the rest of my energy into getting a full ride to college like my dad and I always talked about.

I bend down and place the bouquet in front of his tombstone.

Hector Muñoz. Devoted husband. Proud father. Beloved friend.

"*Hola, Papi.*" My chin trembles. "*Ha pasado un tiempo desde la última vez que hablamos.*"

Birds chirp in the distance as a gust of wind hits me. I zip my jacket all the way to the top before taking a seat on the ground. "I wish you were here more than ever."

> **Ha pasado un tiempo desde la última vez que hablamos:**
> Some time has passed since the last time we spoke

I pluck a blade of grass and wrap it around my finger. "Although maybe it's for the best that you're not around. I would've hated for you to overreact about the broken engagement and get thrown into jail for assault charges because of Oliver." My laugh comes out all wrong thanks to the tightness in my throat.

A few leaves in the distance get picked up by another breeze.

"I made a big mistake." My voice cracks. "I was so stupid, *Papi.*" Tears flood my eyes, although I fight to make sure they don't fall. "I knew it too, but I still kept trying to make things work *porque un Muñoz nunca se rinde.*"

My father raised us to follow his motto of *ser fiel a ti mismo*—stay true to yourself—and I tried my hardest to stick to his values.

Yet you failed anyway.

"But the problem was that while trying to keep my relationship intact, I forgot myself. I gave up all the things that made me special because I thought it was the right thing to do to make the person who supposedly loved me happy." The tightness in my chest becomes unbearable.

"I realize now that the only person I was letting down was myself. I stopped trusting myself and the gut instinct that told me I deserved better." My head hangs.

"I'm sorry I haven't been around much in the last few years. Between us, I was kind of lost." I tear the blade of glass to shreds before ripping another off the ground. "I'm going to find myself, though. Because Muñozes never quit—not even on ourselves."

And by the time I leave Lake Wisteria after the holidays, I hope my soul will be fully healed.

CHAPTER TEN

Dahlia

I try my best to ignore my phone pinging, but after the eighth time, I give up. The Lopez-Muñoz family group chat continues to go off before I have a chance to read the first message.

I scroll to the start of the new messages.

JOSEFINA

Why am I finding out from someone who isn't my son that he and Dahlia are renovating a house together?

MAMI

What? OUR Julian and Dahlia?

Not difficult to conclude, seeing as we're the only two

people in town with those names—for now at least. Lake Wisteria's census last year reported record-breaking numbers, given our lakeside beach, massive sand dunes, and the rising demand for Julian's services and his frequent media exposure.

No wonder he wants to maximize opportunities and rezone properties to account for more houses, seeing as he turned our town into his own Monopoly game.

JOSEFINA

> Yes. Everyone in town is talking about how they're buying a house together.

I send a mental thumbs-up emoji.

RAFA

> Was Julian held at gunpoint?

LILY

> Or was it blackmail?

SECOND BEST

> ...

Julian's name on my phone has my lips curling.

Porque un Muñoz nunca se rinde: A Muñoz never quits.

JOSEFINA

To think I spent twenty-seven hours
in labor for this kind of disrespect.

RAFA

This is why I'm the favorite son.

Rafa dropping a joke? Maybe I should buy a lottery ticket today.

LILY

Debatable since Julian bought
your mom a house.

RAFA

Only because he beat me to it after
saying we could split the cost.

LILY

You're telling me Julian was caught being
shady as shit again? Consider me shocked.

MAMI

LILIANA!

All of us grew up without much money, so to go from

struggling to pay the mortgage some months to paying it off with a single check has me reeling.

It's still hard to wrap my head around the fact that Rafa and Julian are billionaires. While I have enough money to buy whatever my family and I want without feeling guilty, I'll never achieve their level of success.

I pick up my phone and think of a reply.

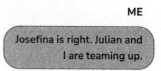

ME

Josefina is right. Julian and I are teaming up.

JOSEFINA

Yay!

MAMI

Power couple!

I let my mom's last text slide because I don't think she understands the label. She said the same thing about my sister and me when we redecorated her flower shop together a few years ago.

LILY

Am I the only one who's scared at the idea of those two putting down the sharp objects and working together?

RAFA

Nope.

My phone vibrates with a private text from Julian.

SECOND BEST

The house is ours if you want it.

My mouth drops open. It hasn't even been two weeks since we agreed to the plan.

ME

For how much?

SECOND BEST

1.2 million

SECOND BEST

We need to decide now because there's another offer.

ME

Who?

SECOND BEST

Some asshole from Chicago. He is willing to pay more, but I have a good relationship with the seller.

ME

Exploiting others for personal gain? Nice.

SECOND BEST

...

ME

Just curious. Do I know the other buyer?

SECOND BEST

Declan Kane.

My fingers fly across the screen.

ME

WHAT?

SECOND BEST

You know him?

ME

I know OF him. His family is the biggest name in the entertainment industry.

SECOND BEST

Well, the only thing he is entertaining tonight is a bruised ego.

My cheeks hurt from how long I've been smiling.

Snap out of it. This is Julian!

I throw my phone to the opposite side of the bed.

Reserved Julian I can handle. Even competitive Julian can be frustratingly funny at times, although I wouldn't tell him that solely because his ego doesn't need any more boosting.

But a *joking* Julian? I'm not sure I would stand a chance against this kind of behavior. Last thing I need is to stir up old feelings just because he makes me genuinely smile for the first time in months with a few quips.

God help you if your standards for men have fallen that low.

My phone vibrates with another text from Julian. Because I suffer from an inquisitive mind and a lack of self-restraint, I reach for it and read his latest message.

SECOND BEST

Do we have a deal?

ME

Yes.

My heart races as the three dots appear and disappear four different times before the next text comes through.

SECOND BEST

House is ours. I'll text you the details about scheduling a walk-through once I deal with all the paperwork.

ME

Shouldn't I be there for that?

SECOND BEST

Do you have a lawyer on retainer who can review all the contracts before tomorrow?

We both know the obvious answer.

ME

On second thought, I'll sit this one out.

SECOND BEST

I'll have Sam send you a standard company agreement that will honor your percentage after we sell the house.

I press my phone against my chest and stare at my childhood dream board. Although my design style has changed over the years and I no longer have an obsession with floral prints, my passion for historic homes has never wavered.

Lots of properties in Lake Wisteria have caught my attention, but the Founders' houses stole my heart the first day my dad drove me past them. There is something about the stunning views, isolated properties, and view of the lake and nearby Historic District that calls to me.

It feels like I've spent years waiting for an opportunity like this, and I plan on taking advantage of everything Julian and his company have to offer once I sign on the dotted line.

My sister barrels into my room an hour later wearing a pink cowboy hat and a dress with far too many sparkles. "Grab your comfiest heels and your favorite tube of lipstick because the Muñoz sisters are going out."

I pause my TV show and sit up in bed. "What? Since when?"

"There's a costume party at Last Call, and our attendance is required."

"I don't know…" While my mood has been improving thanks to my antidepressants and therapy sessions, I don't want to push myself too hard since there is a fine line between stepping out of my comfort zone and getting sucked into a black hole of panic.

"It'll be good for you to go out, even if it's for a little bit." My sister rummages through my luggage, throwing expensive designer clothes everywhere in the process. Where I am organized to a fault, Lily is the human equivalent of an F5 tornado, wrecking my system of packing cubes and color-coded outfits within a few seconds.

Honestly, it's impressive given how long it took me to pack everything.

Lily peeks over her shoulder. "What are you doing sitting there? Get out of bed and go work on your hair and makeup." She claps her hands together and yells, "Chop chop!"

I wrap a throw blanket around my shoulders. "I don't want to see people from town yet."

She frowns. "Why not?"

I stay quiet.

She rolls her eyes. "You care way too much about what other people think of you."

"No, I don't." My tone comes off annoyingly defensive.

"Then why else would you have spent the last week holed up in here, finding every excuse to avoid going into town?"

I scratch my nose with my middle finger.

Lily chuckles as she tosses a jacket on my bed. "It's okay. Little sister is here to save the day."

"How?"

She holds up a sparkly dress in the air, scrunches her nose, and tosses it on top of the growing pile beside her. "Consider tonight your first lesson in the subtle art of not giving a fuck."

"But—"

Lily holds up her hand. "Give me thirty minutes. If you hate it, then you can come home."

"What's the second option?"

She cracks her knuckles. "I will change the Wi-Fi and streaming passwords, hide your collection of *Silver Vixen* DVDs, and steal your entire overpriced skincare routine."

"You wouldn't dare."

"Are you willing to bet your Dyson Airwrap on it?"

"And people think big sisters are the bullies in the relationship." I stick out my tongue.

She tugs on the blanket until it slips from my hold and lands on the floor. "Come on. Tonight will be fun, I swear. Plus, ladies drink for free."

I fidget with one of my rings. "I shouldn't really be drinking with my medication."

"I won't tell anyone you're sipping mocktails if you don't." She winks.

As much as I want to say no, my sister's excitement won't allow me to. "Okay. Fine. But only for one drink."

"Sure. Yeah. Whatever." She pulls out a red dress from the bottom of my luggage. "Yes! This is perfect."

"And what am I supposed to be?"

She pulls a triangular piece of paper from her jacket pocket and pins it to the strap of the dress. "I'd rather you be surprised by whoever guesses it right." She throws the dress at me.

"Lily!"

She rushes out of my room, yelling, "You've got fifteen minutes to get ready, so get to it!"

CHAPTER ELEVEN

Dahlia

Last Call hasn't changed since I last left, although it currently features cheap Halloween décor to celebrate the holiday. The crowd has grown since we first arrived, most likely because parents and children are no longer wandering the streets collecting candy.

At first, I was sweaty and borderline panicked at the idea of speaking to anyone, but no one brings up the news of my broken engagement or Oliver, proving Lily's theory correct.

I *do* care too much about what others think. Whether about my makeup, clothes, or life choices, I let the Creswells' opinions rule my life, turning me into a version of myself I grew to resent.

You're a part of our family now, so you should dress accordingly, Oliver's mother said as she gifted me a beautiful designer gown two sizes too small.

No one likes a show-off. His sister shot me the fakest smile after I beat everyone during a family trivia night.

Couldn't even let me win that, Oliver whispered in my ear before kissing my cheek for our audience after I won the award for Best TV Host in the reality television category.

"I'm back." Lily yanks me away from the memory as she passes me another nonalcoholic strawberry daiquiri. While it isn't my drink of choice, I suck it up because Last Call isn't known for its world-class mixologists.

I grab the plastic cup and take a sip. "Am I Jessica Rabbit?"

"Who?" Her face scrunches.

I shake my head. "Never mind. What about Julia Roberts in *Pretty Woman*?"

She laughs before knocking back her shot. "Good guess, but no. Your dress is too short, and you're missing the iconic gloves. Now, let's go dance!"

Lily grabs my hand and pulls me toward the dance floor packed with people. After a few line-dancing songs, my worries fade away as I let loose and have fun.

I always loved dancing, all because of my parents and their habit of turning our living room into a dance floor whenever their favorite songs popped up. As a kid, it was embarrassing at family parties, but now I yearn for that kind of relationship.

As Lily spins me around with a laugh, the back of my neck prickles. I turn on the heels of my boots to find Julian staring at me.

No. Not staring.

Devouring.

Goose bumps spread across my arms as his dark eyes drag

from my body to my face. I raise a brow when his burning gaze connects with mine, and he looks away with a clenched jaw and a tight fist pressing against his thigh.

I take advantage of his shyness and check him out. From the tasteful amount of exposed forearm to the pair of jeans showcasing his muscular legs, Julian is one hundred percent my type.

Hell, he single-handedly *redefined* my type in college, and I did everything humanly possible to avoid the truth.

Julian is hot. Like *really* freaking hot in a look-but-don't-touch kind of way.

My fingers tingle at the idea, and I clasp them together and squeeze until they go numb.

You need an emergency therapy session.

I turn to get Lily's attention, hoping she can save me from my thoughts, but I find her busy dancing with a guy wearing one of those creepy light-up masks.

Great.

I drain the rest of my drink and head to the bar, picking a spot out of Julian's direct line of sight. Before I have a chance to raise my hand for a bartender, someone taps on my shoulder.

"Dahlia? Is that you?" A deep voice has me spinning in my heels.

"Evan!" I grin at the former high school prom king, beloved swim team captain, and the first person I kissed. Nothing happened after our game of spin the bottle at a lakeside bonfire, but I distinctly remember being on cloud nine for a few weeks after.

"Surprised you still remember me."

"It would be impossible not to after you sweet-talked

your way into borrowing my chemistry homework throughout sophomore year." Evan was one of the best-looking guys in our grade, and everyone, including me, was obsessed with him and his whole boy-next-door personality when he transferred to Wisteria High.

Yet fast-forward ten years later, and I don't feel the slightest buzz.

I fight my disappointment as I ask, "How are you?"

"Much better now that I found you."

The strange sensation of being watched has me glancing over my shoulder. I expected to find Julian glaring at me, but instead, he is shooting daggers at the man standing in front of me.

"So, how have you been?" Evan's question snatches my attention back.

"Good now that I'm back home."

His green eyes trace the shape of my face, making me feel absolutely nothing. "Did you like San Francisco?"

"Yeah, although it's a lot different than here."

"I bet. There aren't many places like Lake Wisteria."

"And how have *you* been?"

He leans against the bar top. "Never been better. Took over my parents' general store, which has a shelving unit dedicated to your décor line, by the way. We can't keep it stocked for longer than a week."

Blood rushes to my cheeks. "Really?"

He nods. "Locals and tourists love the idea of purchasing your goods from your hometown, so keep them coming." He winks.

I feel nothing but dread and that same choking feeling when I'm reminded of my responsibilities. "Yup. Will do."

Evan's eyes blaze a trail down my body, but my heart doesn't miss a beat, which tells me all I need to know.

"Listen—" I'm cut off as something firm and warm presses against my back. I turn to find Julian looming behind me with flared nostrils that look two seconds away from spouting smoke.

"Evan." Julian's deep, raspy voice sends a shiver down my spine.

"Julian." Evan tips his chin.

"How are you doing?" The vein above Julian's right eye pulses.

Evan's eyes lock on to mine. "Better now that I found out Dahlia is here."

"Why?" Julian's brittle voice makes me wince.

Why? I stomp on the tip of Julian's shoe with the sharp point of my heel. The asshole doesn't flinch, most likely because he is made of ice.

Evan's eyes glimmer. "Because I always thought she was cute."

Ugh. Cute?

Julian scoffs. "Right."

Evan's pinched expression probably matches mine.

"How's your brother doing, by the way?" Julian's question comes out of nowhere.

Evan's head tilts. "He's good."

They share a look I can't decipher.

"What happened to your brother?" I interject.

Evan checks our surroundings. "He was hanging around the wrong crowd while he lived in New York, but he's back on track and getting the help he needs."

I press my hand over my heart. "That's good to hear."

Julian pauses his death-stare contest to spare me an unreadable look, only to break eye contact first. "Is he adjusting to his new job all right?"

"Yes. Thank you for helping him get back on his feet. It was hard for him to find a job again with a record, and you were the first company willing to give him a chance."

"I'm glad I could help." Julian closes the gap between us until I'm not sure where my body ends and his begins.

I take a small step forward, which Julian matches with one of his own. When I raise my foot to stomp on his again, Julian clamps his hand around my hip, stopping me.

The heat of his palm singes my skin. Evan's eyes bounce from Julian to me before landing back on the mercurial man behind me.

"Well, Dahlia, it was nice catching up with you, but I should probably head out. Got an early morning tomorrow."

"No problem. Nice seeing you." I tamp down my annoyance with a smile.

Julian tenses behind me. Evan doesn't spare me another glance as he disappears into the crowd.

I escape Julian's hold and turn toward him. "What the hell was that about?"

Julian ignores me as he drains the rest of his whiskey.

"I asked you a question." I poke at his chest.

"He's not your type."

"And how would you know that?" I blurt out.

"I just know."

"Feel free to share, since clearly I don't." Julian being so acutely aware of my needs rubs me the wrong way.

Julian's nose scrunches with distaste. "He's too nice."

"I'm sure that seems like a negative trait to you, but to the rest of us, nice is good. Actually, it's the freaking bare minimum."

His eyes flicker over my face for an extra beat. While Evan's perusal didn't even make me blink twice, Julian's has my body temperature spiking.

"You'd get bored within a month."

"How would you know? You've never been in a relationship."

"That might be true, but I know *you*."

My lungs stall. "Oh, is that right?"

He remains quiet as he raises his empty glass toward the bartender. I'm not sure what makes me bolder—the annoyance pumping through my system or my insatiable need to peek behind the curtain of Julian's mind.

"Maybe I need a man like Evan," I say. "Someone kind and caring and willing to treat me well."

"That's fine, but you also want someone to challenge you, and Evan—the town's biggest people-pleaser—isn't it."

Shock is quickly replaced by horror.

Oh God. Did Julian and I screw each other up so badly that we can't find happiness with others because we're always looking for a fight?

I shake my head. "I'm not looking for a confrontational partner."

"That's not what I said."

"Then what?"

He pauses for a few moments before speaking again. "There's a difference between someone challenging you to be the best version of yourself because they *care*"—he sneers— "and someone looking for a fight."

I hold my breath.

He clears his throat. "Face it. You'd walk all over the guy in your glittery red-bottom boots, and he'd probably thank you for it."

"Damn right he should. These babies are beautiful and expensive." I knock my heels together.

"That comment alone makes you worthy of your costume because only a walking, talking red flag would smile like *that*."

I yank myself free of his gravitational pull. "Excuse me?"

"Your costume." His gaze slowly travels down my body, emphasizing his point.

"*La voy a matar*," I whisper to myself.

"You didn't know?" Julian traces the tip of the triangular piece of paper.

"No. Lily put it together." I sharply inhale as the tip of his finger teases the sensitive spot between my dress strap and my shoulder.

"Hm." He pulls away all too quickly, his hand flexing before it tightens into a fist.

A shiver wracks through me despite the warm air clinging to my skin.

La voy a matar: I'm going to kill her.

Fuck. How can a single swipe of his finger against my skin feel this good?

I'm grateful for the lack of lighting or else he would have noticed how much his touch affected me.

A bartender places a full glass of whiskey in front of Julian, and I snatch it before he has a chance to take a sip. I manage a single swallow before handing it back to him with a cough. "That's disgusting."

That's what you get for stealing Julian's drink.

"To you." Julian places his mouth right over the stain my lipstick left behind and takes a sip.

My stomach muscles clench as he smears half the mark in the process. It's the closest his lips have been to mine since college, and it makes my body buzz in the same way.

I wouldn't be surprised if the gutter started charging me rent with how often my mind hangs out there.

I drag my eyes toward his. "Since when do you drink whiskey?"

"Since I can afford the expensive kind."

"How much did you pay for that?"

"Enough to appreciate every last drop." He takes another sip, sending a zing down my spine in the process as he watches me with hawklike fascination.

Screw the gutter. I'm going straight to hell for the way I press my thighs together.

"Please tell me you didn't pay more than a hundred bucks for that."

He frowns.

"Two hundred?"

My question is met with the pounding music around us.

"A thousand?" My voice breaks at the end.

"I don't expect someone who orders strawberry daiquiris to understand."

I bat my lashes. "You know, maybe if you spent less time watching me and more time actively finding a girlfriend, you wouldn't be chronically single and working eighty hours a week to fill the empty void of your existence."

His frown reveals far too much. "Last time I checked, both of us were single."

"I'm the one who dated a toxic, controlling man for too many years. What's your excuse?"

I take his blank expression as a challenge.

"Are you unable to make a woman come?" I tease.

His eyes narrow into two slits.

"Maybe you're a one-minute man?"

His deep breath says more than any words can.

"They have coaches and medicine for that kind of thing, so no need to have it stop you from finding love."

Julian flips the script on me as he places his hand on my hip and squeezes. Before I have a chance to comment, his palm travels up the side of my body, brushing across my rib cage.

I stop breathing as his hand wraps around the back of my neck. The firm way he holds me isn't uncomfortable, but I squirm in place regardless.

"What are you doing?" I push against his chest to no avail.

His fingers tense, applying the smallest amount of pressure against my pulse point as he leans in and whispers in my ear, "Just because I'm selective about who I date doesn't mean that I don't know how to fuck."

"Am I supposed to take your word for it?"

His fingers squeeze harder, cutting off my airflow for a second. "Would you rather I demonstrate?"

"Are you suggesting I have sex with you?"

"Absolutely not. Sex with you would be…"

Every inch of my body tingles at the snapshot of him hovering above me, his heated gaze burning into me right as his mouth comes closer to mine—

I shake my head, and he frowns. "No need to look so horrified by the idea."

"Nauseated is more like it."

His thumb traces over my racing pulse point. "*Mentirosa*."

"Keep telling yourself that."

He glares at my lips with every ounce of hate he can muster. "I still remember the time when you begged me to kiss you."

Julian and I say a lot of messed-up things to each other, but bringing up that topic feels like the lowest of lows, and frankly, he should know better.

I rip myself free from his hold. "I also begged Oliver to do the same, so don't let it get to your head. And honestly, he was much better at it anyway."

My words hit their mark, obliterating whatever was brewing between us.

Should I have taken the high road and been the bigger person? Maybe.

Mentirosa: Liar.

Do I regret my choice to do the complete opposite? Absolutely not.

Julian knew what he was doing when he used our kiss as a weapon. Maybe next time he will think twice before bringing up the one weakness I have.

Him.

CHAPTER TWELVE

Julian

After Thursday's run-in with Dahlia at Last Call, I knew Sunday would be unpleasant. When I tried to get out of dinner plans, my mother wouldn't accept my excuse, claiming Rosa needed help fixing something in the kitchen.

Dahlia declares war the moment I step over the Muñoz threshold. Instead of acting like a mature thirty-year-old man and deescalating the situation, I match her snide remarks with my own throughout the afternoon and into family dinner.

Our families watch our exchanges like a tennis championship, their heads swiveling back and forth with every calculated barb.

At some point, our parents take over the conversation, only for my mom to turn toward me with *that* look in her eyes. "I was talking to Annabelle's mom the other day."

My body tenses, drawing Dahlia's eyes to my hiked shoulders.

Fuck.

"Ma," I warn. We had a deal about her matchmaking, and if she breaks it, then all bets are off for helping Dahlia with the house.

Is that such a bad thing?

On second thought, I hope my mom breaks her word. That way, I have the perfect excuse to pull out of the remodeling plan and leave Dahlia to fend for herself.

Would serve her right after today's hostility.

Don't be petty, Julian. You're the one who brought up the kiss.

At first, I felt validated in my decision to antagonize her, especially once she made her comment about kissing Oliver strictly to get under my skin. But the longer I consider Dahlia's reaction, the more guilty I feel about our conversation at Last Call and how I have acted today.

Because a hurt Dahlia is a mean Dahlia, and I was too pissed off to see her reaction for what it was.

A way to shield her vulnerability.

She is obviously struggling with overwhelming sadness, and I'm not helping matters by treating her the way I have.

It's not too late to apologize for what you said.

My mom waves me off. "I know. I know. Never mind."

"Who's Annabelle?" Dahlia can't hide that special glint in her eyes.

"She is someone newer to town whose family moved here from Chicago. Julian dated her a couple of months ago, although their relationship ended rather abruptly."

"You don't say," Dahlia dryly replies.

"Annabelle Meyers?" Lily frowns. "I had no idea you dated her." The expression of distaste on her face probably matches mine.

I pull at my collar. "She wasn't worth mentioning."

"Julian!" my mom calls out.

"How long did they date?" Dahlia asks with the softest, fakest voice.

My mom clasps her hand against her chest. "Not long, although that didn't stop my son from breaking her heart."

"Surprised she found him worthy of it to begin with." Dahlia smirks.

She didn't. I bite down on my tongue in an admirable display of self-restraint.

"Don't start, *mija*," Rosa warns her daughter.

"Sorry, *Mami*."

My mom shakes her head. "It's okay. I should have warned her mother before they started dating."

"Warned her about what?" Dahlia perks up.

"Julian leaves a trail of sad women behind him."

"No, I don't." I don't know why I feel the need to defend myself, but I stupidly continue. "And I didn't break Annabelle's heart." She would need to possess one to begin with, and our exchange proved otherwise.

"How would you know?" Lily asks.

"Because we only went on three dates." All of which ended with me politely escorting her to the door each night and giving her a kiss on the cheek.

There was no buzz. No chemistry. No special spark that had my blood rushing and my head spinning.

It was hard to find her attractive in the first place with how she mistreated those around her, including servers and those she deemed below her status.

Despite Annabelle's shortcomings, I know the problem lies within myself rather than with the women I'm set up with. They expect a charismatic billionaire who will wine and dine them around the world, but I'm not that guy. I prefer listening rather than speaking, quiet actions instead of elaborate displays of affection, and working hard to share my money with others rather than finding a way to spend it all on myself.

And while some were willing to accept that about me at first, all of them had the same reaction when I told them I wasn't interested in having kids—at least not in the way they wanted.

My mom frowns. "Her mother said Annabelle felt something special between you two."

"Better wife her up before she comes to her senses," Dahlia adds.

I glare at her. "She wasn't thinking clearly."

"Obviously not if she thought you two were special."

Remember that apology you practiced? Forget it.

"Dahlia!" Rosa chides.

She winces. "What?"

Her mom shoots her a look. "You know *what.*"

"*Perdón.*" She sinks deeper into the dining chair.

I fight back a smile.

Perdón: Sorry.

Dahlia scratches the tip of her nose with her middle finger.

"That's it." Rosa throws her napkin on the table and points a finger at her daughter. "You're in charge of dishes."

"But I got my nails done yesterday." She holds up her hands, showing off her intricate nail art.

"Wear my rubber gloves, then."

"Here you go." I place my plate on top of Dahlia's cleared one, making her scowl.

My mom throws her napkin on the table with a dramatic sigh. "Since you're in the mood to be helpful, you can do the dishes too."

"What?"

"Dahlia wouldn't be in trouble if you didn't keep bothering her all day."

"She's the one who started it."

"And I'm ending it. Go."

I scoot my chair out and stand with a scowl. "Fine."

Dahlia and I silently collect everyone's dishes before entering the kitchen.

"You wash and I dry?" she asks as the door swings shut behind her.

"You don't have a dishwasher?"

"It broke last night."

Great. "I'll take a look at it once we're done." I place the dirty dishes in the sink before rolling up my sleeves.

Dahlia tracks my every move with heated fascination, making my stomach clench.

Shit. "Do you have gloves?" I ask.

She snaps out of whatever trance my arms had her in. "Um,

yeah." She digs through the cabinet beneath the sink and pulls out a large pair of pink gloves.

I grab them from her, ignoring the tingle of her fingers brushing across mine. Both of us pull away a little too fast. I put the gloves on with too much force, nearly ripping one of them.

Dahlia searches the laundry room for a clean towel while I busy myself with the dishes.

She returns, only to pause midstride so she can snap a photo of me washing a plate. "Aw. The color of the gloves really brings out your cheeks."

"Delete that."

"Nope." She tucks her phone into her back pocket and leans against the counter beside me.

I drop the dish in the dirty water. Soap suds and water droplets fly from the big splash, landing on both of us.

"Hey!" She wipes a few drops off her face.

I take advantage of her distraction to steal the phone from her back pocket.

"Give that back!" Dahlia reaches for her phone, but I hold it above her head.

I struggle to rip one of the rubber gloves off thanks to the soap covering it, but somehow manage to bite down on the tip of one finger and pull.

"Julian!" She claws at my arm with her freshly manicured nails.

I can vaguely overhear Rosa speaking from the other room, asking if she should go check on us, only for my mother to assure her that everything is fine.

"What's your password?" I ask while attempting a few number combinations myself.

"Screw you." She turns her attention toward the spot between my ribs that has me jolting.

"Give it back." She tickles me again, and my grip on the phone slips.

Oh fuck.

Her phone falls into the sink full of water and lands at the bottom with a sickening thud.

"Oh my fucking God! I'm going to kill you!" She dives for the phone and pulls it out. Water drips everywhere as she does everything in her power to turn it back on.

I rip the other glove off and run my fingers through my hair. "Shit. I'm so sorry."

She scowls hard enough to make me take a step back. "You're sorry?"

"It slipped."

"It wouldn't have been in your hands had you not accosted me."

"Accosted? A bit dramatic, don't you think?" A small laugh escapes me.

My reaction seems to fuel the fire behind her eyes. "I'll show you dramatic."

With a burst of impressive speed, she grabs my phone from my back pocket and tosses it like a football into the sink. The glass screen hits the side of a heavy metal pot before plunging to the bottom of the sink.

Both of our mouths drop open as the cracked screen flickers once before going black.

"I can't believe I did that." She stares up at me with wide eyes.

"I can." I seethe.

Five deep breaths.

Except five doesn't exactly cut it. Twenty breaths later, I'm still fighting the urge to snap at the woman beside me.

El que se enoja pierde, my dad's go-to proverb, echoes through my head, easing some of my irritation.

"I'm so freaking sorry. I don't know what I was thinking." She rubs at her eyes.

"You're sorry?" I ask with a cool voice.

"Yes."

I can't explain what possesses me to react the way I do, but I grab the side hose and spray Dahlia like we did countless times as kids.

"Julian!" She holds up her hands, making the water splash everywhere.

I ignore her cry as I blast her face with cold water, ruining her makeup and hair in the process. A mix of mascara, eyeliner, and blush runs down her cheeks.

I drop the hose. "I accept your apology now." My gaze flickers toward her soaked T-shirt. The black fabric clings to the curves of her breasts like a second skin, emphasizing the—

"What the hell?" I sputter while choking on water.

"You look like you need to cool down." Dahlia sprays me with enough water to soak my hair, white button-down shirt, and the front of my pants. The water feels cool on my skin, but

---

El que se enoja pierde: Who gets angry loses.

a blast of warmth pours through me as her gaze follows as it trickles down my arms.

Her tongue traces her bottom lip as she focuses on my abs pressing against the wet fabric.

I follow her gaze. "Like what you see?"

"Consider me unimpressed." Although the faint blush creeping up her neck gives her away.

I grab my shirt by the soaked hem and lift it to wipe my dripping face. Dahlia's eyes widen as she is given a full view of what lies beneath the drenched fabric.

"What are you doing?" she hisses.

"Cleaning up the mess you made."

Her gaze flickers over my abs before following the angled muscles that disappear beneath the band of my jeans.

"Still unimpressed?"

She squints. "Even more so now that I got a better look."

"You've always been a lousy liar."

"And you've always been a terrible flirt."

"You've got something..." I swipe at the corner of her mouth with the pad of my thumb. Her sharp inhale is loud enough to be heard over the rapid beat of my heart.

She tilts her head back, giving me a better look at her hooded eyes.

My fingers tingle as I clasp her chin and lean in until our lips hover a few centimeters apart. "For someone intent on acting like she doesn't find me attractive, you desperately look like you want to be kissed."

Her eyes snap open as she shoves me away. "God! I can't stand you."

"The feeling is mutual."

She tosses a dish towel at me. I catch it a second before it lands in the puddle forming by our feet.

"I'm going to grab a bag of rice to soak our phones, and the mop to clean up this mess," she announces with flushed cheeks.

"That's a good idea after how you drooled all over the floor." I smirk.

You're playing with fire, my head warns.

Wrong. I'm playing with something far more dangerous.

Dahlia Isabella Muñoz.

CHAPTER THIRTEEN

Dahlia

When Julian texted me a few days ago to schedule a walk-through of the Founder's house, I thought he meant I would be meeting with his team to check out the work that needed to be done and compile a list of all our pending tasks.

Instead, I'm surprised to find Luis Senior's old pickup truck parked in the driveway and Julian standing on the ornate wrap-around porch. He leans against one of the intricately carved beams that support the fish-scale shingled ceiling above his head.

"I thought the McLaren was fixed?" I ask.

"It is, but there is no way I'm driving that car during the winter, especially not after our little incident." He tucks his hands into the front pockets of his slacks.

I am quickly distracted by the mansion. It looks so much grander in the daylight, with turrets shooting toward the sky and a west-wing tower that is so tall, it casts a large shadow across the lawn. The stained-glass window above the door and the colorful yet faded paint scheme add a personal touch.

The home is stunning, regardless of the obvious neglect and lack of upkeep. I'm overwhelmed by ideas of how I could update the exterior—

"Dahlia."

I look up to find Julian staring at me with a strange expression. "Where's the rest of the team?"

"Ryder and the crew are dealing with a septic tank that burst at one of our sites."

My nose twitches. "Gross."

"For once, I'm glad it's not me." His eyes run up the length of my body. "You look...interesting."

My hands ball up against my sides. "I see why you don't compliment others often."

His brows scrunch. "Why?"

"You genuinely suck at it."

He frowns as a faint blush creeps up his neck. "I was trying to be nice."

"Why?"

"Because I'm stupid," he grumbles.

"It only took you thirty years to finally admit what I've been trying to prove all along."

He frowns hard enough to reveal a few wrinkles.

I have an extra bounce in my step as I walk up to the house in my non-industrial booties.

His phone rings before he has a chance to say something. He checks the screen before showing me the caller ID. "Do you mind if I take this?"

"Tell your mom I say hi."

Julian does what I ask. Whatever his mom says has him turning away from me. I'm nosy, so it kills me to only catch bits and pieces of the conversation, especially when his mom makes him laugh.

Good God. Julian's laughs don't come often, but when they do, my whole world stops for a few seconds so I can process the sound.

His affection for his mother is not only genuine but frustratingly endearing. My stomach dips as he laughs and promises to stop by his mom's place after work because she is having issues with her leaking kitchen faucet.

Julian has more money than he could possibly spend in this lifetime and a roster of people who could fix a faucet in ten minutes flat, yet he offers to help instead.

Are you surprised after he spent an hour fixing your dishwasher because he refused to give up and call for help?

"Bye, Ma. *Nos vemos luego.*" Julian hangs up before walking down the creaking stairs. "Hey. Sorry about that."

"Everything okay?"

He tucks his phone into the inside pocket of his gray suit. "Besides the sink, yeah. She couldn't resist going over a few things about the Harvest Festival too."

"Oh? Is that coming up soon?" I feign ignorance.

His brows pull together. "You've been gone for a while, but not that long."

"Hm."

Nos vemos luego: See you later.

Lake Wisteria has four huge events each year to celebrate the different seasons: fall's Harvest Festival; the Lake Wistmas Holiday Extravaganza; spring's Food, Wine, and Flowers Weekend; and the famous summer Strawberry Festival. The entire town pitches in to help throw each event, and people from all over the state come and visit.

I've tried my hardest to block the upcoming Harvest Festival from my mind, but my days of ignorant bliss will soon come to an end since it's only a matter of time before my mom asks me to help with the Muñoz booth.

Everyone so far has been nothing but welcoming.

Doesn't mean all the visitors from neighboring towns will be.

His gaze narrows.

I move around him and head toward the front steps. Julian unlocks the door, and the hinges groan as it swings open and bangs against the wall, sending dust flying everywhere.

Julian and I break out into a coughing fit.

I wave my hand in the air and gasp. "Do we need masks or something?"

"Let me check to see if I have a couple lying around." Julian rushes to the truck bed.

Beams of light cut through the dust cloud, drawing my eyes toward the source.

"Oh my God." I walk inside, ignoring Julian's protest from behind me.

The dual staircase leading up to the second floor looks like something out of a movie. Intricately carved wood balusters and the elaborate hand-embroidered carpet running up the length of the stairs blow me away with the amount of detail crammed into a single statement piece. Whoever designed the entrance had an eye for detail and luxury.

"What the hell, Dahlia? You should have waited for me." Julian doesn't give me a chance to grab the mask from him. Instead, he covers the lower half of my face before fixing the straps in the back so my hair doesn't poof up.

To think I said romance is dead.

"Are you seeing this?" I wave toward the stairs with a muffled voice.

"I'm sure smelling it."

"Where's your mask?"

"I only had one left." His nose scrunches again before he sneezes.

I reach for my mask, only for Julian to push my hands down. The graze of his fingers against my knuckles sends a pleasant zing down my spine.

Oh Dahlia. You're a lost cause.

"I'm fine," he says with a sniffle.

"No need to act chivalrous without an audience."

He shoots me a look before walking toward the foyer beneath the stairs. "First impression of the place?"

"I'm in love."

His right brow rises. "Just like that, huh?"

"Just like that," I repeat as I note the detailed wood moldings throughout the space. "I mean, look at all the details."

"Whatever carpenter they hired did a great job. Termite damage aside, the craftsmanship is impeccable." He runs a hand over the baluster.

"Think you could replicate it?" I ask without thinking much of it.

His hand freezes. "I don't do carpentry anymore."

"What? Since when?"

With the way he becomes engrossed with a light switch, one might believe he was born before electricity was invented. "A while."

"Why?" My high-pitched voice echoes around us. Julian had the talent to turn a block of wood into a work of art with nothing but a few tools and a single idea.

To think he stopped…

He shrugs. "I got busy."

"I refuse to believe this."

He checks his watch. "I have a meeting in thirty, so let's keep going."

My eyes narrow. "We're not done with this conversation."

"All right. Make sure to bring it up again when you're ready to talk about why you and Oliver broke up," he snaps.

I jerk back.

His eyes shut. "Shit. Sorry, Dahlia. That was unfair of me."

The iciness in my chest that seems to vanish in Julian's presence returns with the strength of a blizzard.

"No worries. I've dealt with worse comments." I walk around Julian, ignoring the spark that flares between us when his skin brushes against mine as I head toward the next room.

"Wait!" He yanks on my arm.

"What are you doing?" I shake him off.

He tightens his hold, making my stomach dive in the process. "You almost walked into a spiderweb."

I look up from his arm wrapped around my middle to the massive web hanging like a curtain under the archway.

"Oh God." I shudder.

I freaking *hate* spiders.

Julian releases me, taking his warmth with him. "I'll take the lead."

I wave a shaky hand toward the spiderweb. "Go ahead."

"You could at least try to put up a fight about wanting to be in charge."

"Sorry. The feminism left my body the moment you mentioned spiders."

His lips curve at the corners. "Some things never change."

It only takes a single smile from him to make me forget I was mad in the first place.

He used your relationship with Oliver as a weapon. Act like it!

I kill whatever buzz I felt as Julian leads the way.

Julian and I make our way through the entire house, cataloging each room and all the work that needs to be done. He writes diligent notes on his phone while I take photos of every room.

Tension between us builds with every pass of the measuring tape, leaving me cranky and desperate to go home as we get to the seventh bedroom. When I hold my hand out in a silent request, Julian holds the tape hostage.

"What?" I grind out.

"I've been thinking."

"Should we mark this special occasion?"

A wrinkle cuts across his forehead from how hard he frowns. "I'm sorry for what I said downstairs."

"Fine."

Do I forgive him for losing his cool? Yeah.

Does that mean I'm not pissed about what he said? No, seeing as this is the second time he has used my failed relationship as a weapon against me.

I bite down on my tongue hard enough to taste blood. "Tape, please."

He doesn't make a move to pass it, so I lift my hand and wiggle my fingers.

His deep sigh of resignation echoes off the high ceiling. "I haven't been able to go into my dad's woodshop since he passed away."

My arm drops like a dead weight.

Julian continues, "I'm not sure why I'm telling you this." He pauses for a brief second. "I mean, I know *why*. I feel shitty for snapping at you earlier, and this is my way of making up for it."

"I appreciate the thought, but please feel free to stop sharing at any time." I keep my voice flat despite my rising heart rate. Julian confessing his deepest feelings isn't part of our arrangement.

Neither is you feeling sorry for him in light of it.

The crease between his brows disappears. "So I'm forgiven?"

"I forgave you after you stopped me from walking into a spiderweb, so yeah, we're good so long as you don't do it again."

"Deal. Now, will you explain what you said earlier?"

"About opening up the kitchen so more natural light can come through?"

He scowls. "*Déjate de tonterías*. What did you mean about hearing worse comments?"

"Oh. Pass."

He makes a noise in the back of his throat. "Don't make me resort to extreme measures to get the information out of you."

I scoff. "Nothing you say or do will get me to open up to you about that part of my life."

"Wanna bet?"

It's funny how two words can open a floodgate of memories I banished. From money to bragging rights, Julian and I spent years wagering bets.

Julian's phone rings. He looks down at the screen before cursing to himself. "I need to take this."

I wave him away. "No problem. I can finish up the last room on my own and lock up after."

"You sure?"

I fight the dryness in my throat as I nod. "Yup."

He ignores his annoying ringtone. "I'll give Sam your information, and he can coordinate the meetings."

"You're willing to let me speak to your assistant after last time?"

"Of course. I had him sign a new contract with a nice pay increase and a promise to never work for you so long as he lives."

Déjate de tonterías: Stop fooling around.

"I hate how you're always one step ahead of me."

He laughs for a second time today, throwing me off. "There's a reason I always kicked your ass at chess."

I flip him off, and he says goodbye with a smile on his face that remains with me long after he leaves.

CHAPTER FOURTEEN

Dahlia

Although I planned on heading home after finishing up with the final bedroom, I quickly changed my mind once I found a set of stairs leading up to the attic.

I love exploring attics, although not many people understand, thanks to their bad rep for being creepy and haunted. There is something special about appreciating a home's history, whether it be old diaries, letters to a lover, or a discarded trunk full of worldly treasures.

"Wow." I take a look out the round porthole window facing the valley and lake beyond. The sheer size of the attic itself is incredible, with enough space to create a whole in-law suite if I wanted.

Wood planks creak beneath me as I search all the nooks and crannies for anything worth salvaging. Unfortunately, I find nothing of value during my sweep.

"Huh." I turn in a circle. Usually, I find something—even a random journal or a forgotten Christmas present gathering dust.

The loud chime of my cell phone echoes off the high ceiling. A photo of Julian holding his Second Best trophy on graduation day covers the lit screen, along with his nickname in bold beneath.

I slide my thumb across the screen and answer. "Julian."

"Did you lock up?" he asks while a door shuts in the background.

I snort. "You can't trust me to do that right?"

It's not difficult to imagine him glaring as he answers, "You Muñozes can't be bothered to lock your front door at night, so forgive me for making sure."

"I've been locking doors since college, so never fear. I'll do so when I'm done."

"You're still there?"

"Yeah. Is that a problem?"

His silence only lasts a beat. "What are you doing?"

"Exploring."

"Couldn't that have waited until Ryder is there tomorrow?"

The wooden floorboards groan from all my pacing. "There are some things I like to do alone."

He pauses. "Like what?"

"You're going to think it's stupid." At least that's what the producers thought whenever I dragged a film crew around during my searches.

"What's stupid is you making assumptions about me without asking."

"Umm." When did Julian become so assertive, and why am I finding it kind of hot?

He huffs something to himself before speaking louder this time. "Be careful."

Two little words have my thoughts reeling and my pulse skyrocketing.

Shit. I'm not equipped to handle feelings right now. In fact, I wish I could replace my heart with a motor that runs on iced coffee and paint fumes while I work through my issues.

I fight the tightness in my throat. "When did we start caring about each other's well-being?"

"Since you're not covered under my liability insurance."

I fake a sniffle. "For a second, I thought you had feelings for me."

"Only the negative type."

"Please stop now before I swoon."

His chuff of air could be interpreted as a laugh. "Jokes aside—" He is interrupted by someone in the background calling out his name. "Sorry. I gotta go."

"It's fine. I should get going anyway."

"Dah—"

"I'll be careful. Bye!" I hang up before Julian has a chance to expand upon whatever he wanted to say.

It's for the best. I sigh at the ceiling.

And blink.

Is that…

I rub my eyes to make sure they're not deceiving me.

My heart thunders as I take off downstairs in search of the ladder Julian left behind for me. I teeter and nearly lose my footing twice while hauling the heavy thing up the flight of stairs, but I power through and make it up to the attic without any slipups.

I set the ladder beneath the wood beam and climb the steps toward the rolls of paper tucked between two support beams.

Gotcha. I swoop in and grab them before making my way down the first few steps.

A faint tickling sensation on my right hand has me looking up to find a gray spider crawling toward my elbow.

"Ah!" I scream as my foot slips. The rolls of paper go flying, along with the spider, as I do everything in my power to catch myself.

Wrong move.

My arms flail in a wasted attempt to secure my balance. I fall with a gasp, only for all the air to be knocked from my lungs as I crash against the floor on top of my left arm.

I nearly pass out from the sharp pain that shoots up. The idea of rolling onto my back so I can check out the damage seems impossible, especially once shock kicks in and my body goes numb.

You need to call for help.

My vision blurs and my body trembles as I pat my pocket with my right arm, only to remember I placed my now-fixed phone on the window ledge before I went to retrieve the ladder.

"Fuck." A tear slips out. Anxiety builds within me like a nuclear bomb waiting to detonate.

Please don't have a panic attack right now.

My brain ignores my plea as questions pummel through my last bits of sanity.

How am I supposed to call for help when I don't have my phone?
How many hours will it take for someone to notice I'm missing?
Will they know where to find me?

With every unanswered question, my anxiety grows. Black spots fill my vision, and my deep breaths do little to stop the panic clawing at my chest like a wild beast.

Think.

That's the thing. I *can't* think when I feel like this. I'm taken hostage by my thoughts, and there is nothing I can do but wish for this feeling to end soon.

Try grounding yourself.

I start the exercise my therapist taught me, but I'm interrupted by my obnoxious ringtone. How the hell can I reach the damn thing to call for help when I can barely move?

Think. Think. Think.

"Hey, Siri. Answer the call." I copy the way my mother talks into her phone whenever her hands are occupied at the shop.

"Help! I'm hurt and can't get to my phone to call anyone. Call Julian and tell him I'm stuck in the Founder's attic. He knows where it is." I repeat the number I know by heart twice in hopes that the other person gets it.

While I can't receive any confirmation from the other person, I know they'll figure it out or call someone who will.

I refuse to believe otherwise.

CHAPTER FIFTEEN

Julian

I didn't think when I ran out of my office.

Or when I broke five different road rules in my panic to make it back to the Founder's house.

In fact, my body is running on pure adrenaline and a single brain cell as I rush into the house, shouting Dahlia's name while searching for the attic.

She cries out from one side of the house, and I rush to the stairs. My shoes slap against the wood, matching the staccato beat of my heart as I hurry up the steps.

The sight of Dahlia cradling her left arm to her chest nearly brings me to my knees.

This is all your fault.

"What happened?" I do my best to tamp down the edge in my voice.

"Oh, thank God you came alone. I don't think I could

deal with my mom or sister hyperventilating and praying the pain away right now." Dahlia's voice cracks, betraying the calm mask she's fighting to keep.

My gaze bounces between her, the ladder, and the rolls of paper a few feet away. "What the hell were you thinking?"

"Can you help me first, lecture me later? I'm pretty sure I broke my arm." She points at her limp limb.

"I'm going to call for an ambulance." I kneel beside her and fumble for my phone.

"No!"

"Why not?"

"No need for that whole production."

I check out her arm again. "We could make everything worse by moving you."

"The thought of being in an ambulance…" Her voice shakes.

Shit. In my panic, I nearly forgot about how Dahlia had a front-row seat to her dad dying in the back of an ambulance from a stroke.

"Will you drive? *Please.*" She attempts to sit up.

I hold her down by pressing her shoulders while assessing the situation. "I'm going to have to carry you."

"I can walk! Watch. But help me stand up first." She attempts to sit up with a hiss.

"Stop moving or I'm calling an ambulance."

"Wait! Can you get my phone first? It's on the windowsill."

"Fine." I grab her phone and tuck it into my back pocket.

I kneel and slide my arms beneath her. Her eyes water as I hold her against my chest and rise, doing my best to avoid aggravating her injury.

My hands tighten around her. "You good?"

"Never been better." Her overly cheery voice grates on my frayed nerves.

When she answered the phone, my mind jumped to the worst conclusion based on Dahlia's muffled, panicked voice. I couldn't stop the graphic images from playing in my head after years spent working in construction.

Cracked skull.

Broken spine.

Paralysis.

You've seen it all, yet you never reacted like this *before.*

I shake the thought away, only to have it return with a vengeance as Dahlia hides her face against my shirt, dampening the material with her tears.

You still care about her.

Mierda.

I'm not given more than a second to process the thought before Dahlia speaks up again.

She sniffles. "This is all so stupid."

I stalk toward the exit. "What is?"

"Breaking my arm like this."

"How did it happen?" I walk toward the stairwell while doing my best to keep her steady.

"I had a run-in with a spider."

"A spider?"

"I know what you're thinking. But that beast was the size of a tarantula and had a set of fangs like a snake." She trembles against me when I take the first step down the stairs.

You should have been here.

I knew leaving Dahlia behind to finish what we started wasn't polite, but I had a phone call I needed to take and a meeting I couldn't miss.

Couldn't or wouldn't?

The best part of my day was doing the walk-through with her—an anomaly in itself—and the last thing I wanted to do was head back to the office.

The artery in my neck pulses with each annoying thump of my heart.

I missed a part of Dahlia's ramblings, but it's easy to catch on as she continues. "The creature was a thing of nightmares. I'm lucky to be alive right now to tell the tale."

Dahlia only talks to me like this when she is anxious or in pain. So to keep her occupied, I entertain her with conversation while walking through the mansion.

"Should I contact pest control?" I ask.

"Pest control? No way. You need the Department of Natural Resources to come out here and drop fumigation bombs because I have a feeling that creature was one of many."

"You think there are more?"

"Of course. Perhaps hundreds." She glances toward the ceiling. "Actually, no. *Thousands.* Make sure the DNR knows all of this when you give them a call tomorrow. When it comes to the government, you need to exaggerate matters to get any-one's attention."

"But by the time they get around to the case, the property will be overrun with spiders the size of people."

She tucks her face against my chest in a poor attempt to

hide her smile, only to pull back after a sniffle. "What happened to your cologne?"

I nearly trip over my own feet. "What?"

"The one you wore on the day of the car accident?"

Of all the questions to ask...

"Oh, yeah. I ran out." *Good job putting that one brain cell to work.*

"Hm." She falls quiet.

"I have an idea." I speak a little too fast.

"What?"

"What if we burn down the house?"

She clutches the fabric of my shirt with her good hand. "No!"

"But we could be saving the world from super-spiders."

"And anger the ghosts who live here? Hell no! I've seen enough horror movies to know better."

My brows crinkle. "What ghosts?"

"Didn't you research the house before you signed the paperwork?"

I'm not sure I was entirely thinking straight when I bought the house, let alone researching the past owners.

She looks around before whispering, "You didn't think to ask why a treasure of a house like this would be put up for sale?"

"Easy answer. It's a pain in the ass to fix." Based on the century-old electrical wiring, ancient drainpipes, and faulty foundation, the repairs would cost anyone hundreds of thousands of dollars.

Her eyes shut, whether out of pain or frustration, I'm not too sure. "I'm surprised you didn't hear about the ghosts. Everyone in town knows about them."

"Probably because I don't believe in ghosts to begin with."

She shushes me. "You're going to make them angry."

"*They* don't exist."

"All right." Except everything about her tone suggests the complete opposite.

The soft slap of my shoes against the wood floor fills the silence between us. In a stupid move to open the front door, I end up jostling her. "Sorry."

Her chin trembles, making me feel even shittier. "Anyway, we can't burn down the house. If you do, I will never forgive you."

"Should I add it to the list of reasons?"

She cuts into me with a single glare. "*Julian*."

An uncustomary fluttering sensation erupts in my stomach. I kick the front door harder than intended, making both Dahlia and the glass windowpane shudder as it closes.

Shit.

She stares up at me with glassy eyes. "Perhaps we can call a truce with the spider. It's not like it tried to bite me or anything, which it could have. I'm the one who went into its territory."

"Is the attic off-limits then?"

"Sure, so long as you go back for the rolls of paper I dropped."

"Of course, you want *me* to go in there."

"You'll be my hero. I'll get you a custom medal and everything." Her eyes brighten despite the tears pooling near the bottom lashes.

I help Dahlia get into the truck with only a couple of hisses before I slide into the driver's seat and start the engine. "I'm taking you to Lake Aurora."

"Why?" she cries. "Doc's is down the road."

"Absolutely not."

She huffs. "What do you have against Doc? He's been fixing broken arms since before our time."

"*Exactly.* I'm pretty sure the man worked the front lines during the last World War."

"Since when is being experienced a crime?"

"Since said experience means still using paper charts and a head mirror." I glare at her out of the corner of my eye.

"Not everyone knows how to use electronic medical charts."

"I plan on not stopping until I find you someone who does. End of discussion."

She grumbles something under her breath as I drive down the gravel driveway toward the main road. The uneven path pushes her around, which only pisses me off more.

"Can you play some music?" Her voice cuts through my noisy breathing.

"Sure." I pull out my phone and hit shuffle on my favorite playlist.

Dahlia goes quiet as I drive us away from the house and out of Lake Wisteria. The tension in her shoulders fades away with each song. I check on her a few times during the thirty-minute drive to Lake Aurora, but she remains in the same position with her eyes closed and her head leaned against the glass.

Despite my hesitation to wake her, I park my truck in the emergency bay and open her door. "Come on."

She raises a single sassy brow. "I'm going to need you to move out of the way first."

"I'd rather carry you."

Her eyes widen. "What for?"

"You broke your arm."

She frowns. "Funny. I didn't know I needed one to walk."

I resist the temptation to pinch the bridge of my nose. "I'd rather you not trip and fall, seeing as you couldn't even stand up earlier."

"I'm surprised you care about that."

"Only under certain circumstances."

Her eyes sparkle. "Like when I'm about to sue your company for damages?"

"I'd expect nothing less. Should I give my lawyer a courtesy call?"

"Sure. I heard from a good source you have a nice liability insurance policy."

I bite back a laugh. "Stop stalling, and let's go."

"Wai—"

I swoop in and pick her up before she can argue her way out of this one.

She stays quiet as I walk us into the waiting room and set her down before heading to the nurses' station. After a quick assessment, Dahlia is taken away for triage.

I spend the next twenty minutes on the phone with Dahlia's mother, reassuring Rosa that Dahlia is safe and receiving medical attention. Rosa offers to drive over, but I recommend against it.

"We should be done soon." At worst, Dahlia needs surgery, although I doubt her injury is anything a cast can't fix.

"Thank God you were there to help her," her mom says.

My fingers dig into my thighs. Thing is, I *should* have been there earlier so this never happened in the first place.

My phone buzzes repeatedly from our family group chat checking in on Dahlia. It hasn't stopped since I told them about her hospital visit, although Dahlia has remained silent until now.

LILY

How's it going?

S.S.

Never been better.

Dahlia attaches a photo of her broken arm that makes my stomach churn.

ROSA

Dahlia!

LILY

Add a content warning next time, freak.

She adds three green-faced emojis after.

MAMI

How are you texting right now?

S.S.

One-handed.

LILY

The talent.

S.S.

More like boredom.

RAFA

Nico wants to know if he can draw something on your cast this Sunday.

S.S.

Sure.

The night goes by painstakingly slow as I wait for Dahlia, giving me plenty of time to mull over my selfish decision to leave her all alone.

I told myself a hundred different times that I don't care about Dahlia—that any romantic feelings I had toward her died long ago—yet here I am, making myself sick over how she got hurt because of me.

Truth is, I *do* care about Dahlia, regardless of whether I want to or not.

Caring about someone isn't the end of the world, I tell myself.

Except Dahlia isn't someone.

She is so much *more*.

The thought has me jumping out of my chair. Instead of sitting around and stewing in my thoughts, I end up raiding the vending machine and purchasing a few wraps from the cafeteria. I like being useful, and everything about today has me feeling the complete opposite.

After another hour, Dahlia walks out of the two doors with her left arm wrapped in a purple cast and a reminder card for an appointment booked four weeks from now.

Relief hits me instantly like a wrecking ball to the chest.

She's okay.

Of course she's okay, you dumbass. It's a broken arm, not open-heart surgery.

"Hey." She fidgets with a loose thread on her sling.

"Nice color."

"It's my favorite."

I know. I grab the plastic bag off the floor and offer it to her.

"What's that?" She stares at the offering like an armed bomb.

"Food." My right eye twitching speaks louder than any words.

She sifts through the bag. "Why would you get me—Mini M&M's!" The childish squeal that comes out of her makes my mission to find it totally worth it. "I haven't had these in years."

"Why not?" I can't imagine her going a week without some, let alone *years.*

Her cheeks flush. "Filming diet and all that fun stuff."

"That's stupid." Based on the weight she has lost, she could use all the M&M's money can buy.

Her eyes roll. "I wouldn't expect you to understand." She attempts to rip at the plastic wrapper covering the tube. Despite her struggles, she refuses to ask me for any help, so I pluck the container from her hand.

"Give it back!" She tries to swipe it back with her good arm.

I hold it up above her head and tear the plastic off. To spite her for being difficult, I pop open the cap and pour some into my mouth before passing the container back.

She peers inside the tube. "You ate almost half of them!"

I reach inside the bag and pull out the second tube hidden beneath the turkey wrap and a bag of chips.

Her gasp of surprise feels like a victory. "You got me two? Why?"

"They were on sale." The lie comes out easily.

"If you keep doing things like this, I might end up thinking you're a nice guy or something."

"We can't have that." I reach for the bag, only for her to sidestep me.

"Never mind. Your reputation as an asshole is alive and well."

"And don't you forget it." I turn and head toward the exit while shielding my smile from the one woman who always finds a way to bring it out, whether she knows it or not.

CHAPTER SIXTEEN

Julian

I park my truck beside Rafa's beat-up one and hop out. Unlike me, my cousin doesn't live on the lake. Instead, after his divorce, he chose to purchase land at the top of the farthest hill away from town, where he could have a fresh start away from any prying eyes.

My mom used to say people do weird things once they make a lot of money, and I never understood what she meant until Rafa started fostering unwanted farm animals and being one with the land after Hillary left.

I swear, the man is one step away from signing up for one of those competitive wilderness shows.

"Fina told me you took Dahlia to the hospital yesterday." Rafa cuts to the chase as soon as I walk through his front door.

"Did you invite me over here to hang out or for an interrogation?"

"A mix of both." He tucks his hands in his front pockets.

"At least you're honest."

He shoots me a look before walking away.

The style of his house is completely different from mine—it feels warm and lived-in, with its oak floors and Nico's artwork hanging on every wall. The paint colors were chosen by Nico, with each room matching a different pair of my godson's glasses.

Not my cousin's smartest design choice, but one made out of love nonetheless.

I follow behind him, only to take a detour toward the classical music playing from the conservatory. Nico sits at the piano with his nanny and music teacher, Ellie. They play in tandem, perfectly in sync as their fingers fly across the keys.

Ellie's body sways to the music, making her blonde hair shift with the melody.

"Did you get lost on your way to the kitchen?" Rafa says.

Ellie hits the keys all wrong, making the most horrific noise.

"I wanted to say hi to Nico."

"*Tío!*" Nico slides off the bench and runs toward me. His coordination is a bit off because of his eye condition, but he jumps into my arms with all the momentum he can muster.

"Hey, you." I ruffle his hair before tipping my chin toward Ellie. "Nice to see you again."

She rises from her seat. "Likewise."

"Is Rafa making you work on Saturdays now?"

"Not usually, but he *inconveniently* forgot to tell me he needed my help today." She doesn't bother hiding her annoyance.

Ellie never gets flustered. I've watched her be thrown up on by a sick Nico, get kicked in the stomach by one of Rafa's goats, and twist her ankle during a hike, but I've never seen her look like this.

I spare my cousin a glance, only to find him glaring at Ellie. I'm not sure what's wrong with him, but he needs to figure his shit out and get himself under control before he scares her away like he did all previous nannies. Whether by playing instruments together or learning to read braille, Ellie stands apart from the others with how she goes out of her way to help Nico and support him with his retinitis pigmentosa diagnosis.

Nico still values his independence like every normal eight-year-old kid, but sadly, it is only a matter of time before he completely loses his sight, a reality that has been stressing Rafa out as my godson's vision worsens.

"Sorry you had to cancel your date." Rafa's face might be blank, but his eyes remind me of two burning coals.

Ellie smiles. "No worries. We rescheduled for tomorrow."

My cousin makes the most inhuman noise.

Her hazel eyes narrow. "Still struggling with that sore throat of yours?"

"You're sick?" I ask my cousin.

"Sick of Eleanor's bullshit is more like it," he mutters under his breath before turning back toward the hall.

I fight a laugh. "*Eleanor?*"

"Don't you dare call me that." She points a finger at me.

"What's up with him?" I ask once Rafa is out of hearing distance.

"He's been like that all week because of the *weather*." Ellie's gaze swings from me to Nico.

There is nothing worse than Hurricane Hillary influencing my cousin's mood long after their divorce.

I step toward the hall. "I better go before he comes searching for me."

"Bye, *Tío*!" Nico gives me one last hug before reaching out for Ellie's hand. They return to the piano and restart the song.

I find Rafa sitting at the kitchen island, staring at his coffee like it might reveal his fortune.

"You good?" I grab the iced coffee he made me. Rafa might be an irritable dick most of the time now, but he still goes out of his way to do sweet things because he can't help himself.

He runs his hands through his hair, making a mess of the already-disheveled strands. "Hillary called."

"Hm."

His shoulders droop. "She's flying into Detroit and wants to see Nico."

"When?"

"The weekend of the Harvest Festival."

My brows rise. "Is she coming?"

"No."

"Shocker." Once the divorce papers were signed, she booked a one-way flight back to Oregon to be with her family and never came back to Lake Wisteria. If it wasn't for Rafa flying out there so Nico could see his mom, I'm not sure she would have seen him until now.

"Nico's excited to see her." His fingers tighten around his mug.

"It's been what? Four months since he last saw her?"

"Five," he grunts under his breath.

"I forgot she missed his birthday."

"I sure didn't." His voice reeks of self-loathing.

"You've got to stop beating yourself up over her poor decisions."

"I'm the one who got her pregnant. Who else is there to blame *but* me?"

"You were barely an adult when all that happened. It's not like you could have predicted things would turn out this way."

"No, but that doesn't stop me from feeling like a stupid fool."

I shake my head. "You're too hard on yourself."

"I've been thinking…"

"Stop now while you're ahead."

"You're not going to like this."

The empty pit in my stomach widens as I say, "Then let's call it a loss and move on to better subjects, like betting on tomorrow's soccer game. I've got a few of my paver guys—"

"*Julian.*"

"What's the problem?"

He stares out the window facing his barn. "I've been thinking about moving."

I blink twice. "What did you say?"

"With Hillary living so far away, I've been wondering if it's in Nico's best interest for him to live closer to his mom."

"Is that in *your* best interest?" Rafa has spent his whole life within the small border of Lake Wisteria, so for him to move…

He rubs his eyes with the heels of his palms. "Forget I said anything."

A wave of nausea forces me to push my coffee away. "You're seriously thinking about moving across the country?"

"Only occasionally."

Losing Rafa and Nico would be devastating for our family. Besides my mom, they're the only loved ones I have left, so I selfishly don't want them to move away.

You could find a way to convince Hillary to move somewhere within driving distance, like Chicago or Detroi—

"Don't mention anything to your mom right now," he says, stopping me mid-spiral.

"But what if she moves back—"

"*Stop.*"

"What?" I blink away my confusion.

"This isn't a problem you can solve."

"Who said—"

He shuts me up with a single look.

I hold my hands up. "Fine. But talk to me before you make any big decisions."

"Fair enough." He scrubs at his cheek. "Anyway, I'm sorry to leave you alone to work the booth without me."

My mom takes a lot of pride in sharing her grandmother's *champurrado* recipe during the Harvest Festival. And ever since we were old enough to be trusted with the responsibility, Rafa and I have teamed up to run the Lopez booth together to make Ma happy and share our Mexican hot chocolate with the visitors.

"Josefina told me you could handle it. She reassured me that your booth will be next to the Muñoz one this year so that you can have someone to talk to."

"How thoughtful of her," I reply with a brittle tone.

"I told her the same thing before asking her to switch it."

"And?"

"She says it would be dumb to separate their *buñuelos* booth from our *champurrado* one."

I sigh. "It's fine."

"Maybe if you talked to her about how you're not interested in Dahlia like that, she would let up on her attempts at matchmaking."

"Knowing her, she will only see it as a challenge."

"I blame her obsession with those telenovelas." He takes a sip of his drink.

"I'm hoping Ma will realize Dahlia and I aren't meant to be once she finally leaves town for good."

His head tilts. "And when is that?"

"I have no clue."

"You really think she's done with Oliver?"

"I'd say yes based on how she sold me her wedding ring before I encased it in a concrete tomb."

His mouth falls open.

Shit. "It's not that big of a deal."

"You, the billionaire who considers eating out at a steakhouse a wasteful luxury, bought Dahlia's engagement ring just so you could bury it in concrete?"

"One, I think steakhouses are overrated when I can cook the same thing at my house for half the price; and two, it was worth it."

Rafa drops his head into his hands. "I don't know what to say to that."

"Nothing is preferable."

"How much did you pay for it?"

I don't answer him.

"Julian."

"A hundred."

"Thousand?"

I rub the back of my neck. "Yeah."

"Why?"

"I wanted to bury it in concrete."

"I'm struggling to believe you're the same guy who spent five years hyping himself up into buying a McLaren for double the cost of what you paid Dahlia for a cheap thrill."

When he puts it that way, it sounds bad. I don't act irrationally, especially when money is involved.

"Well, I always hated that ring." The excuse sounds weak to my own ears.

Rafa's deep sigh makes my stomach churn.

"What?"

"You say you're over her, but your actions say the complete opposite."

"Because I bought her ring?"

"Because of *why* you bought her ring."

My frown stretches. "I was doing her a favor."

"Keep telling yourself that."

CHAPTER SEVENTEEN

Dahlia

'm so happy you'll be here for the Harvest Festival this year," Josefina says. "It's changed a lot since you were last here." Julian's mom has been the town's event coordinator for two decades, and while I know she doesn't have favorites, the Harvest Festival remains one of her top contenders.

"How so?" I ask.

"Everything is different and in the best way possible—the food, the activities, the *rides*. And this year, we booked the same company that does the firework shows for Dreamland!"

I blink a couple of times. "Isn't that...expensive?"

Josefina laughs. "*Claro que si*, but Julian is our main sponsor."

"By main, she means *only*," Lily teases.

Claro que si: Of course.

My eyes bulge. Everyone knows Julian is disgustingly rich, but sponsoring every event seems excessive.

"He only donates that much because of how happy it makes you to plan everything without having a tight budget," my mom says.

"I'm not going to complain." Josefina shrugs.

We continue cooking and talking until the doorbell chiming interrupts Josefina's story about the latest event-planning mishap with the corn maze.

"That must be Julian or Rafa." She swipes her flour-covered hands across her apron.

"Dahlia, can you get it?" Mom looks up from her Michigan-shaped cutting board and points at the door with the tip of her knife.

"Sure. Would hate for Lily to get off her butt and do something useful today." I hop off the bar stool.

My sister sticks her tongue out at me before returning to whomever she can't stop texting.

I readjust my sling before opening the door. Julian stands on the other side with a roll of papers tucked underneath his arm and his phone placed against his ear.

"What do you mean—" Julian's voice cuts out as his eyes blaze a trail down my body. He blinks twice, which is Julian code for *fuck*.

Julian appreciating my efforts to look good feels like a victory I didn't know I needed after spending years squeezing myself into a mold for someone else.

I tuck my hair behind my ear before fidgeting with my dangling acrylic earring.

"Yes, I'm still here." His deep baritone voice has far too much power over my heart rate.

Here, Julian mouths as he passes me the papers from the attic. He could have easily passed the job off to anyone else, yet he went through the trouble of going back before today's lunch and retrieving them himself.

I try not to look too much into the gesture, but I lose the battle once he carefully places the papers in the crook of my good arm. The scowl he directs toward my broken arm makes my knees tremble.

"My buyer can't wait another month for the countertops." His muscles tense as he runs his hand through his hair, drawing my eyes toward the thick vein running up the side of his arm. Julian might spend most of his days in an office now, but he could still bench-press me *and* a bag of cement mix on his worst day.

His gaze flicks over to me, catching me in the act. His right brow rises in a silent taunt that makes my stomach flip.

If finding Julian attractive is a crime, consider me guilty as charged.

Haven't you learned anything after the last time you fell for his looks?

Julian didn't hurt me when we were in college because he rejected me. Sure, it injured my pride and made me feel like the biggest loser after the passionate kiss we shared, but my dislike toward him is so much more than that. He crushed my spirit when he cut me out of his life like I never existed in the first place.

I thought we had something special after spending a year

at Stanford together, with our relationship transforming from friends into something else entirely, but it was all a lie.

While I'd love nothing more than to eavesdrop on Julian's conversation, I shut the door behind me, although it does a shitty job at keeping out the sound of his soft laugh. My heart does this weird squeeze in response, which only serves to further piss me off.

Instead of heading back to the kitchen, I veer toward the empty dining room and place the three rolls of paper on the tabletop before reaching for the largest one. With one arm out of commission, the task of removing the rubber band wrapped around it proves more difficult than anticipated, so I secure it between my thighs for leverage.

"What are you doing?" Julian's gruff voice breaks through the quiet.

"What does it look like?" I push the rubber band toward the top of the roll.

"Crushing the paper." He doesn't wait before grabbing it.

Paper brushes against the inside of my thighs before sliding over a spot that tingles. Okay, fine, I haven't had sex in a while, but still…what the hell?

I take a long step back, although the heat in my lower belly remains as Julian's gaze flickers between me and the roll of paper.

He shakes his head before removing the rubber band and spreading out the blueprint for both of us to see.

"How cool is this?" I lean over the table to get a better look at the blueprint, which dates back to the early twentieth century.

Julian checks out the illegible scribble near the bottom of the drawing. "These are original copies."

"Gerald Baker." I tap the architect's name. "Do you recognize his name?"

Julian nods. "He signed off on a majority of the original houses here."

"You mean the ones you tore down?"

His hands briefly clench.

"It still looks exactly the same." I trace over the lines dividing the various rooms.

Julian removes the rubber band from a second roll before opening it up. "Hm."

"What?"

"Looks like you'll get to tear down that wall between the kitchen and dining room like you wanted after all." He points at the structural paperwork.

I rub my hands together with a big, goofy smile. "Nothing gets me buzzing quite like finding out walls aren't load-bearing."

His gaze flickers from my eyes to my lips.

"What?"

"You looked…" He shakes his head. "Never mind."

"Alrighty then." I reach for the smallest roll, only to have Julian swipe it from my hand. Our fingers graze, and a tiny spark of recognition flares to life.

With an annoyingly blank face that gives away absolutely nothing, Julian carefully opens the final roll. This one is different from the others, with the yellowed paper looking thin enough to shred at the slightest wrong move.

"This is stunning." Whoever drew the gazebo thought of

every detail. From the roses carved into the fret spindles, to the intricate posts meant to support the roof, it's a work of art. The artist behind the drawing created a vision, with a view of Lake Wisteria predating Town Square, Main Street, and all the mansions lining the beach.

I lean in closer to get a better look at the illegible scribble at the bottom of the page. A shadow catches my eye, and I flip the paper over.

"Oh my God."

"What?" Julian's hot breath hits my neck, making me shiver.

"It's a letter." I fight back a squeal.

I waffle between reading and not reading the paper addressed to someone else, but curiosity wins. *"My darling, Francesca.* Aw! Stop! He calls her 'darling.'" The secret romantic in me is already buzzing with anticipation, and I've only read three words.

"Let me have that." He steals the paper straight from my hands.

"Hey!"

"At your current pace, we'll be here all day while you swoon over ink on paper."

"Excuse me for having a heart." I attempt to snatch the letter back, only to have Julian trap my hand.

His heartbeat quickens beneath my palm, and I look up to find his eyes locked on our hands. They slowly drag away, stopping to linger on my lips before finally reaching my eyes.

His hand tightens around mine before he drops it altogether. I'm too stunned by everything to do much but listen as he picks up where I left off.

"*It's been three years since I last saw you, and while so much has changed, my love for you has never wavered. Our monthly letters keep me going despite the trials and tribulations I have been through to help turn this town into a suitable home for you.*"

My bottom lip trembles.

Julian spares me a sideways glance before focusing back on the letter. "*I have been working hard to earn your hand in marriage, although the path has not been the easiest. Building an entire town from nothing takes time, and I am afraid I am running out of it now that your father has started discussing marrying you off to another.*"

I gasp. "What? How could the dad do that?"

"Because feminism wasn't exactly a thing yet."

"Ugh." I shake my head hard enough to make my earrings rattle.

Julian keeps going. "*I thought I had more time before he began entertaining other suitors, but I am fearful that he might make a decision before I have a chance to fight for your hand.*"

I tap on the page. "What are you doing? Keep reading!"

His gaze flicks back over the paper. "*I will stop at nothing to make you mine.*"

The back of my neck tingles as his eyes lock on mine. We hold each other's gaze for the briefest second, yet it feels like an eternity has passed before we break away.

"*Once he sees all that I have done to make Lake Wisteria a town suitable for you, he will agree to my proposal. I am certain of it.*"

"Couldn't women get married without their father's permission back then?" I ask.

"Probably not without serious repercussions." Julian

continues, *"Our home is nearly complete. Although the process has taken me longer than I would have liked, my final plan is in motion."*

"The gazebo?" My voice hits a higher pitch than usual.

Julian nods. *"You always dreamed of getting married below a gazebo similar to the one we met under, and I have plans to do that."*

My hand clenches around the material of my shirt, right above my aching heart. "He wanted to build her a gazebo."

"Are you seriously going to cry over people you don't know?"

"Of course not," I sputter.

Julian mutters something to himself before wrapping up the final paragraph.

"I shall return for you in six months, once my affairs are in order and the house is complete. Until then, I ask that you do everything within your power to prevent your father from marrying you off to another man."

I rub at my itchy eyes. "Why didn't she run away with him?"

"And risk losing everything and everyone she cared about?"

"Sometimes people are worth the risk."

He scoffs.

Ugh. Este hombre. "I don't expect you to understand."

He crosses his arms. "What's that supposed to mean?"

"You're the most risk-averse person I know, so it's not like you're going to be making decisions solely based on fuzzy feelings and your gut." Which is exactly why he pushed me away and called me a distraction rather than acknowledge the truth.

His brows scrunch together. "I'm not risk-averse."

"You obsess over probability statistics and make pro-and-con lists for everything."

"That's called making an informed decision. Perhaps you should try it sometime, given the current state of your life."

"Screw you," I hiss as I reach for the rolls. Berating myself over my life choices is one thing, but having Julian do the same feels like taking a knife to the chest.

His eyes widen. "Dahlia."

"What?"

"I was joking, but clearly it wasn't funny."

I frown. Julian rarely admits when he is wrong, so to say I'm shocked is an understatement.

Groundbreaking.

I glare. He scowls. A tale as old as time.

He speaks first, which in itself is abnormal. "You're right."

"I'm sorry. Can you repeat that? I think my brain malfunctioned for a split second."

His frown deepens. "Don't let this get to your head."

"Are you kidding? I might get the words and today's date tattooed across my forehead solely so you're stuck staring at the reminder."

He wipes a hand down his face. "I can't believe I said anything."

That makes two of us.

He rambles on without his usual inhibition. "I'm not a risk-taker. Never have been and probably never will be, but that doesn't mean I have a right to judge people who are."

"Then why do you?" The question slips out before I have a chance to think better of it.

"I'm jealous."

I can't find words to answer that in any language, so I lean against the table for support.

He runs his hands through his hair, ruffling the strands. "I wish I could be the type of person who doesn't give a damn about probability statistics and worst-case scenarios, but that's not who I am."

My head tilts, along with my whole world. Julian and I don't do feelings. Hell, we don't do much talking either.

Arguing? Yes.

Teasing? Of course.

But sincere admissions? Abso-freaking-lutely not.

To be honest, it might be unnatural, but it is also kind of… nice?

Fuck me. My heart feels like Julian wrapped his ginormous hand around it and crushed it.

"As much fun as this has been…" I reach for the rolls again with shaky fingers, only for Julian to clasp his hand around my wrist.

"Wait."

Blood pounding in my ears makes me second-guess what I heard. "What?"

"I'm sorry."

I'm not sure how I keep my voice neutral as I ask, "Two apologies in one week? Are you dying or something?"

"Feels like it," he grumbles.

"Well, figure out if that shit is contagious before you pass it on to someone else." I attempt to pull my wrist free from his grasp, but his hold tightens.

"Apologies aren't contagious, Dahlia."

No, but feelings are, and I sure as hell don't know what to expect if Julian keeps stepping up to be a decent man. I can deal with him being angry after spending most of our lives slinging insults at each other. But him maturely apologizing after hurting my feelings and admitting when he is wrong?

I'm better off not getting to know *this* Julian, for both of our sakes.

Nico devours his lunch at a disturbingly fast rate before taking off for the living room to watch his favorite show, leaving the adults alone.

"How's the house going?" Josefina takes a sip of her water.

"Dahlia and I are meeting with the team on Monday," Julian speaks up.

"Which Founder's house did you buy again?" Lily asks.

I turn to my sister. "The blue one."

"Oh." Her gaze drops.

"What?"

The skin between her brows scrunches from how hard she frowns. "I heard that place is haunted."

"Same," Rafa says.

Julian glares at his cousin. "Not you too."

He shrugs. "I said I heard about it. Not that I actually believe it."

I throw my good arm in the air. "See! I told you everyone knows about the ghosts there!"

Julian's eyes roll in a way that *almost* makes him appear human.

"Dear Lord. Is it too late to sell the place?" My mom makes the sign of the cross while Josefina laughs.

"People say there's a reason it gets put back up for sale." Lily props her elbows on the table.

"It's true." Josefina nods.

"Tell us everything you know." I motion for her to continue.

My sister's voice drops as she says, "Flickering lights—"

Julian cuts her off. "Faulty electricity is normal with a house this old."

"If you're going to give me a hard time, I won't say anything," my sister huffs.

With my uninjured arm, I elbow Julian hard enough to make him grunt. "Let her finish."

He glares at me out of the corner of his eye.

Lily stares Julian down for a few seconds before focusing back on me. *"Anyway*, during high school, a few people from my class spent the night there on a dare."

"And?"

Rafa and Julian share a look from across the table.

Lily ignores them. "Supposedly one of them still sleeps with the lights on to this day. The other one moved away and became a priest."

My eyes widen. "You're joking."

"Nope. His mother begged for the town to demolish the house so her son could move back, but obviously that didn't happen."

Julian's eyes shine brighter than a neon warning sign. "Perhaps we should make the town happy and tear it down."

"I thought you didn't believe in ghosts." My molars grind together.

"Maybe I can be convinced after all."

Asshole. I stomp on his foot. At the speed of a viper, his hand wraps around my thigh and squeezes hard enough to have me choking on my breath.

"Are you okay?" Mom asks.

"Yup. Got a piece of steak in my throat."

"Here." Julian's hand abandons my thigh before shoving my glass of water toward my good hand.

I take a slow sip while staring him down. Once I'm done, I trace my bottom lip with the tip of my tongue to wipe away any remaining droplets.

He breaks eye contact, although the way he thickly swallows gives him away.

Men.

Lily's eyes ping-pong between us before landing on me. "You can ask anyone in town about the house, and they'll all have a different story to tell."

I turn to face the nonbeliever. "Do you think it's Gerald?"

"No. It's probably old plumbing, outdated electrical wiring, and materials rubbing together at night while the house cools."

Lily's eyes roll. "Of course you'd say that."

"Either way, I've dealt with a haunted property or two in San Francisco, so I'm not afraid of a few ghosts," I say.

She laughs. "What are you going to do? Hire a priest or something?"

"Or something."

Julian peeks over at me through his thick lashes. "What are you planning?"

"Nothing you need to worry yourself with." *Yet.*

CHAPTER EIGHTEEN

Dahlia

After one lengthy game of Monopoly that ended before a winner could be crowned, Rafa and Nico say goodbye. Josefina and Julian follow their lead five minutes later, so I decide to head out with them and ask Josefina to drop me off at the library.

"Where are you going?" my mom asks as I'm struggling to put on my sneakers.

"I want to stop by the library before they close."

Mom fidgets with her gold cross necklace. "Do you need to go now? It's going to get dark soon."

"It's five p.m.," I grunt as I attempt to slide on my sneaker and fail. Julian, in the ultimate fake display of gentlemanly behavior, gets down on one knee to help me.

Mom *aw*s while Josefina has the biggest set of heart eyes. Neither of them can see the way he obnoxiously smirks at me.

Julian has been pulling these stunts since we were teens, with both of our moms doting on him like a prince carrying a glass slipper.

The only princely thing about him is that he is a royal pain in my ass.

He carefully helps me into my sneaker before tying the laces. The slightest graze of his fingers over my ankle sends goose bumps scattering across my skin, earning a deep frown from me.

"Thanks." The word comes out rushed as he rises to his feet.

I ignore my racing pulse and turn toward Josefina. "Do you mind dropping me off at the library on your way home?"

She frowns. "I would love to, but I have to drive out to the Smiths' farm to check on a few things for the festival."

"No worries."

Her whole face lights up. "But Julian can drive you into town instead."

"Thanks, but I think I'd rather walk. It'll be nice to get some fresh air after spending the day inside." I pull Josefina in for a one-armed hug.

Josefina waves me away. "Nonsense. The library is on Julian's way home."

"Hell is already a long enough drive as it is. No need to add another stop along the way."

Julian chuffs while my mom's eyes narrow.

"Dahlia," she chides in that hair-raising voice of hers.

"I'm trying to be polite."

"I'm not sure you know the meaning of the word," Julian grumbles under his breath for only me to hear.

"I'm sorry. I didn't quite catch that." I lay it on thick, going as far as batting my lashes.

He frowns.

"Julian doesn't mind doing me that little favor. Right, *mijo*?" Josefina reaches out to give his bicep a squeeze.

"Anything for you, Ma." Julian kisses the top of his mother's head and my mom's cheek before looking over at me. "I'll be in the truck."

Mom waits until Julian shuts the door to speak. "Will you two ever get along?"

"Rosa," Josefina warns.

"What? I thought they would grow out of this…"

"Animosity?" I throw it out there.

"*Immaturity*," my mom finishes.

Ouch. "We can be mature."

Both her and Josefina's eyebrows rise.

"When we want to be," I tack on.

They share a look.

"Whatever. He's the one who usually starts it."

Josefina's eyes lighten. "Nico uses the same logic."

Being described as immature is one thing, but to be compared to an eight-year-old kid?

My nose twitches in distaste. "I get your point."

Being around Julian after nearly a decade apart brings out the worst in me. Things between him and me have always been strained, and it only got worse once we went to college and were introduced to a different kind of issue.

Sexual tension.

Mom tucks my hair behind my ears and straightens my necklace. "I hate to see you two bickering."

Sometimes I do too. There are brief moments when I wish we could go back to the time right before everything changed.

Before our kiss.

Before he destroyed my heart and any hope for us.

Before he dropped out of Stanford and cut himself out of my life, leaving me to grapple with not only losing Luis Senior but his son too.

My chest tightens.

I never told Julian how much it hurt to be kicked to the curb like I didn't matter.

And you never will.

The car ride to the Historic District is short, with Julian's playlist filling the silence. It's not until he pulls up in front of the library that he finally speaks.

"What's going on?"

I unbuckle my seat belt. "Don't worry about it."

"Impossible wherever you're concerned."

My stomach flutters again.

"What are you up to?" he asks after a beat of silence.

"I'm going to go find out more about the Founder's house. Maybe I can learn about Gerald and Francesca and why the place is haunted."

His jaw clenches. "There's no such thing as ghosts."

"Didn't you sleep with a night-light until you were twelve?"

"Only because I had to get up a lot during the night to use the bathroom." His heated glare has the opposite effect on me.

"Right! I forgot you used to wet the bed too!"

With a frustrated grunt, Julian continues down the road.

"Where are you going?" The library grows smaller in my sideview mirror.

He turns down the next road. "I'm going to park in the lot behind the library."

"*Why?*"

"Because I don't want anyone to witness your murder."

"You'll be changing your opinion on ghosts real quick if you kill me today."

His face remains blank as he makes a right turn and pulls into a parking space.

I hop out of the truck before he has a chance to say something and head inside the library. The faint smell of old books and recently brewed coffee lingers in the air as I make my way over to Beth, the librarian, who sits behind the help desk.

I'm so focused on my mission to get the special key to access old newspapers that I don't have a chance to become anxious about seeing her.

Look at that progress.

"Hi, Beth." I lean against the counter with a hesitant smile. Beth has been working here since I was a kid, with hair the size of Texas and a wardrobe straight out of the 1950s.

"Dahlia! I heard you were back!" She drops a stack of books before running around the desk with her arms wide open.

I hold up my cast to stop her from pulling me into a hug.

She frowns. "What happened?"

"Fell off a ladder. How are *you*?"

She holds me at arm's length and assesses. "Better now that you stopped by to visit. It's been a good while since I last saw you."

"I know." Staying away was easy compared to the alternative.

Facing the fractured person I have become.

"If I had known you were stopping by, I would have brought my copy of your design book."

"You bought one?"

She beams. "Of course!"

Something in my chest swells.

"I've kept up with all the latest and greatest things you've been up to. Team Dahlia forever, am I right?" She holds her hand out for me to slap.

"Right." I barely manage to hide my flinch as I high-five her.

"Do you plan on sticking around forever now that you and that Olive broke up?"

Beth is the first person in town to address my ex—albeit incorrectly—yet instead of panic, I'm hit with a burst of laughter.

"I'm not sure about that. I doubt Julian and I can last more than a few months in the same place without killing each other, so I'll be heading back to San Francisco by the new year."

Beth looks over my head with a raised brow. "Julian Lopez? What are you doing here?"

My muscles go rigid as I turn to find Julian glaring at me.

"I'm with her."

"Why?" I blurt out.

The vein in his cheek flexes as he ignores my question.

"Do I need to remind you two about the rules?" She nods toward the plaque behind the desk. A majority of the library rules were added after a few incidents between Julian and me over the years with lighters, air horns, and Nerf guns.

"No, ma'am," we both say at the same time.

"Well, what can I help you with?" Beth returns to her post behind the counter.

"I'm looking to check out some old newspaper clippings."

Beth opens up a drawer and pulls out a set of keys. "Anything in particular you're searching for?"

"Anything on the blue Founder's house."

"*Oh.*"

"You've heard about it?"

"You'd be hard-pressed to find someone who hasn't." She holds out the key ring for me. "Clippings should be organized in chronological order based on year, and the projector is located in the room beside the bathroom if you need it."

"Thank you!" I snatch the keys.

"Library closes in an hour," she adds.

"You got it!" I head toward the filing cabinets at the back.

Julian remains quiet as I sift through the first drawer of *Wisteria Weekly* newspapers dating back to when the town was founded in the late 1890s. I scan the headlines, searching for any information that might be helpful.

My eyes blur after the first fifty clippings. At this painstakingly slow rate, I'm only going to make it through four years of *Wisteria Weeklies* before the library closes.

The incessant tapping of Julian's fingers against the screen of his phone doesn't help matters, and I find myself scowling at him.

"I know it's a hard ask, but will you at least *try* to make yourself useful?"

"You didn't ask."

Who is he to talk? I'm pretty sure if Julian were on fire, he would do everything possible to put himself out before asking anyone for help because he is *that* stubborn.

Doesn't mean you have to be. "Will you *please* help me?"

"I love it when you say *please*." His deep baritone voice does things to my lower half that should be deemed illegal.

I shut the drawer hard enough to make the cabinet shake. "Asshole."

"*Sweetheart.*" He throws the old nickname in my face. Once upon a time, back when I won a beauty pageant after he bet I couldn't place in the top three, *sweetheart* was Julian's favorite nickname for me.

He hasn't called me that since college, right after he kissed me senseless.

A kiss he regretted instantly.

Screw him.

I tug open the first drawer within grabbing distance and point at the file in front. "Scan the pages for anything related to the house, Gerald Baker, or someone named Francesca."

"I think I found something." Julian's eyes flick over the clipping in his hand.

"What?" After thirty minutes of scanning newspapers, I can't contain the excitement in my voice.

"Follow me." Julian leads us toward a nearby table.

He pulls my chair out and waits. I slide in, and the tips of his fingers brush across my shoulder blades as he pushes me closer to the table. Thankfully, my harsh inhale isn't heard over the scraping of the chair legs against the floor.

Julian's arm brushes up against mine as he points to the headline. My body leans into his touch before I snap out of whatever spell he has me under.

"Gerald died before the house was fully completed."

I blink. "No!"

"Look." He shoves the article toward me before scooting his chair away.

I read the article with a frown. According to the reporter, Gerald died from a bacterial infection and was survived by his two dogs. Town sources close to Gerald mentioned how he refused to go to the hospital because he wanted to die in the comfort of his half-finished home.

My eyes itch. "That's so freaking sad."

"Stories like this make me glad I was born after penicillin was invented."

I check out the grainy image of Gerald holding a shovel in front of a plot of land. "He never lived long enough to see his house get completed."

"It appears not."

"Or marry his true love."

"Not many do." There is a slight edge to his voice.

"She must have been heartbroken when she got the news about his death."

"Why?"

I rear back. "What do you mean *why*? Because they were in love."

"If she truly loved him, she would have stuck by his side from the beginning."

"He was the one who told her not to come until the town was finished."

"Then it was her mistake to listen to him."

I can't help feeling defensive over Francesca and her choices, especially when I see a bit of her in myself. "She waited for him, wrote him letters, and held on to a dream that one day they would get married despite the odds stacked against them. That's what people do when they're in love."

"So you say."

The audacity of this man. "For someone who has never been in love, you sure have a lot of opinions on the matter."

The vein in his neck pulses with each erratic beat of his heart.

I continue, "What if *he* was the one who didn't want to take the risk on *her*? What if she begged to join him, but he shut her down time and time again? He could have asked her to marry him at any time, and perhaps her father would have agreed because he wanted what was best for his daughter."

"That's a lot of assumptions."

"You're the one jumping to conclusions here by judging *her* for not being brave enough to join him, when maybe *he* was the one too afraid of the risks. Maybe he should have built a life with her rather than erecting a wall to keep her out."

Shit. Shit. Shit!

His fist clenches and unclenches against the table. "Dahlia—"

My gaze dips back to the newspaper in the worst attempt to hide my flushed face. "Anyway, Gerald is probably the ghost, so the case is solved."

"I never judged you." Despite his whispering, he might as well have shouted the words.

"I was talking about Francesca." I stand.

He does the same. "Funny, because for a moment, it felt like you were talking about *us*."

My throat feels like he wrapped both hands around it and squeezed. "That's quite the narcissistic assumption of you."

"*No mames. Háblame.*"

I drag my eyes away from his balled-up fists. "You're about ten years too late for that conversation, don't you think?"

"Clearly this is a big mistake."

"Wouldn't be the first time you said that."

He opens his mouth, only to slam it shut.

Truth is, I can give Julian a hundred different chances to explain his choice to push me away, but it won't change the truth he made painfully obvious.

He didn't want me.

A bitter laugh claws its way up my throat. "It's fine."

"I never meant to hurt you." He exposes my insecurities with a single sentence.

"You didn't," I lie.

"What I did…" He loses his voice, along with whatever nerve he had found in the first place.

Good. I prefer it that way.

Háblame: Talk to me.

"Things happen the way they're meant to," I say.

He folds and unfolds the newspaper, only to refold it again. "I never expected you to go into design too."

He would have if he had given me a chance to explain my hopes and fears instead of assuming he knew what was best for me by pushing me to stay at Stanford to finish a political science degree I never wanted.

I was always interested in design—that much became obvious when my parents were remodeling our house and relied on me to choose most of the finishes and furniture—but I never vocalized it since they were set on me getting some kind of professional degree.

"I took a class or two before you left." Plus, I joined a club and got a mentor from the interior design program because I wanted to learn more without switching majors.

His brows rise. "I had no idea."

"Nobody did." I spent the better part of my life swearing I would become a badass lawyer, in part because my parents wanted me to have a stable, well-paying job, so the last thing I wanted to do was disappoint them by blowing a full ride to Stanford on a career that wasn't guaranteed to be successful.

Fans think my *political science major–turned–interior designer* story is endearing, but it really represents my lifetime struggle with the fear of failing.

He stays quiet while he seems to work through the mental puzzle of our memories. "When you made the offer to come and work with me at the company…"

"No need to dredge up the past. It's not like we can go back and change anything."

"Sometimes, I wish I could."

Breathing becomes a laborious task with how much my lungs ache.

He breaks eye contact. "I always regretted how I went about things with us. I didn't—" His reply is cut off by Beth popping out from behind a bookcase.

"Library is closing, kids! You'll have to wrap this up and come back tomorrow because I've got a date with a pint of ice cream that can't be postponed."

"Thanks, Beth." I ignore Julian's pinched expression as I hand her the keys and head back to the filing cabinet with the newspaper.

Julian doesn't say anything else. Not when we climb into his truck. Not during the drive back to my house, and certainly not before I escape inside with a small shred of dignity intact.

I slipped up earlier. Being around Julian again after all this time is like opening up an old wound, and instead of remaining level-headed, I let my emotions get the best of me.

Despite my efforts to forget the conversation we had, I'm stuck replaying the whole exchange after I crawl into bed for the night.

What was he about to say before Beth interrupted us?

Did he mean what he said about not judging me? Because it seems impossible after I ended up dating his roommate, whom he once considered a friend.

And what would have happened if I had confessed that he isn't the only one who regrets his actions, because I do too?

CHAPTER NINETEEN

Julian

The thought of going back to my empty house is about as enticing as a root canal without anesthesia, so I head toward Last Call after dropping Dahlia off at her house. The bar is pretty empty, with only a few Sunday stragglers taking up the stools and surrounding high-top tables. I nod toward a few locals before picking my usual spot at the end of the bar.

"Modelo?" Henry, the older bartender, places a napkin in front of me. I nod, and he sets down a bottle of my favorite beer.

"Open a tab for me." I throw my Amex on the counter and chug half of my drink in one go.

"Rough day?" A guy a few stools down from me speaks up.

"You could say that." I try to make out his face, but his ball cap casts a dark shadow.

"Work problems?"

I silently take another sip.

"Family issues."

My eyes remain focused on the shelf of alcohol in front of me.

"Woman trouble."

My fingers tighten around the bottle.

"Ahh. I see." He looks up at me with those dark, beady eyes I would recognize anywhere.

Lorenzo Vittori.

He takes a long sip from his highball glass before placing it on the bar top. "Julian Lopez, right?"

My muscles tighten beneath my shirt. "Yes."

"I'd say it's nice to finally see the man who has made the last year incredibly difficult for me, but then I'd be lying."

I remain silent. Competing against Lorenzo's house offers was easy, especially with my deep connections to everyone in town.

People in town might dislike that I'm buying up older properties only to tear them down, but they trust me more than Lorenzo, who only lived here until his parents died.

His grin doesn't reach his dead eyes. "Not much of a talker?"

I take a long sip of my beer instead. Most people in town consider me shy. Reserved. *Quiet.* What was once a weakness has become my biggest strength, especially when dealing with antagonistic tools like Lorenzo.

He lets out a long, exaggerated sigh. "Are you typically a bore, or do you save the quiet, stoic stereotype for me?"

Henry snorts.

I glare.

Lorenzo holds up his empty glass with a smirk. "How about another round for my friend and me here?"

"We're not friends." I keep my voice detached despite my annoyance.

"You're spending your Sunday night drinking in a bar with me of all people. If you have any friends, clearly they're shitty ones."

He hit my weakness on the head. Besides Rafa, I don't have any friends since half the men in town work for me while the other half are double my age.

Expanding my dad's business came with sacrifices, and my social life happened to be one of them.

But not the biggest.

Dahlia's words from earlier haunt me.

Maybe he was the one too afraid of the risks. Maybe he should have built a life with her rather than erecting a wall to keep her out.

Thing is, when my dad died, I struggled with a long list of issues—fear being only one of them. Pride. Anger. *Grief.* Everything in my life turned to shit, and my personality along with it.

Things I had wanted—like a degree from Stanford and a shot at something special with Dahlia—were no longer possible after my life drastically changed overnight.

I was barely an adult when I made the decision to push Dahlia away, and it led to my immature choice to cut her out of my life after becoming friends during our freshman year. It was insensitive and unfair of me, so she had every right to find someone who made her feel secure in a way I couldn't as a twenty-year-old guy battling grief while saving his dad's failing business.

A memory I kept locked away resurfaces, dragging me back to my time at Stanford.

"When do you plan on telling Dahlia that you like her?" Oliver asked me once Dahlia left our dorm room after our late-night study session.

"Who said I like her?" I kept my tone nonchalant despite my rising blood pressure.

"You smiled when you came back from the bathroom and caught her snooping around your desk."

I held my tongue. Rafa was the only person I felt comfortable enough with to talk to about my crush, and I planned on keeping it that way.

He shrugged. "You better tell her soon before someone else makes a move on her."

I'm yanked out of the past by a sharp pain shooting through my heart. No matter how many times I tell myself that I couldn't have known Oliver was an asshole, I still feel partially responsible for introducing Dahlia to him.

If you hadn't pushed her away, she would have never gotten close to him.

I take a sip of my beer, hoping to wash away the sour taste.

No amount of alcohol will change the fact that you care about her enough to resent yourself.

Fuck. I wipe a hand down my face. Drinking at a bar was supposed to give me a break from thinking about Dahlia.

I chug the rest of my beer and stand. "Henry, can I get the check, please?"

"Where are you going?" Lorenzo's smile quickly transforms into a frown.

I ignore the man who can't seem to take a hint. Henry is quick with charging my card and passing me the receipt to sign.

"I thought we were going to have a real bonding moment here." The ice in Lorenzo's glass rattles from his long sip.

"How much will it cost me to get you out of this town?"

"I have no interest in making any more money."

I pause for a beat. "Then what do you want?"

"Only friends get to know that." He raises his glass in a mock toast before knocking back the rest of the contents.

I add a decent tip and sign the bottom of my check before exiting the bar. My relief at escaping Lorenzo's incessant talking is short-lived when I remember the dull ache that hasn't left me since the library.

I rub the spot over my heart and wish for it to go away.

Good luck with that.

The only way to get rid of the constant throbbing is to remove the person causing it in the first place.

Dahlia Muñoz.

I spend the rest of my night devising a way to get rid of Dahlia. Simply put, if I find a way to speed up the renovation, then her creative spark will be reignited, thus restoring her faith in design. She can return to her life in San Francisco, leaving me to go about my life as usual.

The plan is foolproof. I only need to make sure Ryder and the rest of the team are on board for the changes, seeing as we will have to postpone a project to take this one on.

So, despite my reservations, I show up Monday morning at the Founder's house to speak with Ryder personally.

"Hey, boss. Didn't expect you to be joining us today." He shuts the back of his truck.

"There's been a few changes to the original plan."

The sun reflects off his brown eyes. "Like what?"

"We need this project done within the next three months."

His brows rise toward the edge of his hard hat. "What?"

"Do you think it can be completed by the end of January?"

Ryder's gaze bounces between the decrepit house and me. "Depends on what we find on the inside."

"We can modify schedules and postpone other projects if it means getting this one done faster. I want all hands on deck here."

"If you don't mind me asking, what's the rush?" he asks.

The answer to his question drives up to the house, blasting Ozuna loud enough to be heard through the sealed windows.

Dahlia climbs out of her sister's car in a pair of leather boots, a thin sweater that can't do much to fight the late October chill, and a designer skirt custom-made to drive me crazy.

God give me the strength to make it through this meeting with my team while fighting a hard-on.

A flicker of hesitation crosses her face before she props her sunglasses on her head and holds her hand out for Ryder to grab. "Hi, I'm Dahlia."

"Ryder. I'm the project manager." His gaze doesn't drop from her face.

Dahlia introduces herself to the engineer and architect next, both of whom check her out.

Are you seriously going to get jealous of your own employees?

With the way Dahlia looks up at them with her big brown eyes and wide smile, hell yeah I am.

"Let's start," I lash out, wanting to get this walk-through over with before I fire someone.

At first, Dahlia was hesitant to speak up, allowing me to take the lead, but after ten minutes, she warmed up to my team and started acting like her typical self.

I find myself at a loss for words as I watch her collaborate with my team like she's spent years working with them rather than an hour. I'm impressed with her wealth of knowledge, and Ryder seems equally blown away by her experience with Victorian homes.

He scribbles something down on his clipboard. "With the changes you want, I feel like we could definitely have this thing done within the three months Julian requested."

"Three months?" Dahlia glances over her shoulder. "I thought you said it could take six to eight."

I tip my chin. "Change of plans."

Her eyes narrow. "How fortunate."

Except since Dahlia crashed back into my life, I've felt anything but.

She carries on, and my men do everything they can to support her. I take a step away from the team to answer a call, only to come back to the crew laughing at something she said.

"What's going on?"

Ryder grins. "Dahlia was telling us a story about the difference between real-life home renos and the ones she did on TV."

"And?"

"Turns out production filmed another construction worker's hands for certain scenes since her fiancé had no idea what he was doing."

"*Ex*-fiancé." I have no idea why I choose to clarify, but I regret it the moment I say the word.

Dahlia's hands clench by her sides. "Julian. A word?"

My stomach drops as she storms off toward the kitchen, leaving me alone with my crew.

Ryder winces. "Damn. Was it something we said?"

"Just me being a dumbass. Carry on." I turn in the direction Dahlia headed. It takes me a minute to find her outside, staring out at the lake with her good arm tucked against her sling.

"What was that back there?"

"A mistake." I've been stumbling my way across a tightrope of emotions, and one mention of Oliver had me tumbling straight into a pit of jealousy.

Her eyes remain focused on the view. "Do you like trying to make me feel small?"

My head rears back. "Of course not."

Dahlia turns. "If this is your plan to run me out of town, you better try harder than that. I didn't spend the last five years of my life dealing with internet trolls and a future monster-in-law to back down at the first sign of adversity. That much I can tell you."

"I'm not—" I try to center myself. "You've got this all wrong."

Although I want her to leave Lake Wisteria, I wouldn't embarrass her in front of my team to speed up the process, especially not when I see how much she struggles around people lately.

Her eyes narrow. "Then feel free to explain."

Thing is, I don't *want* to explain because then I would need to admit I'm still jealous of Oliver after spending years convincing myself I was over everything that went down between him, Dahlia, and myself.

So, instead of admitting the truth, I stick to my comfort zone.

I tuck my hands into my pockets. "I could have gotten rid of you weeks ago instead of going through the trouble of working together."

Her head tilts to the side. "Oh, really?"

"The mayor still has a reward listed for any information about who egged his Jaguar twelve years ago."

Dahlia's eyes go wide. "You wouldn't dare."

"Keep assuming the worst of me and I might."

Her nostrils flare. "If you don't want me to assume the worst, keep the blackmail to a minimum. It tends to send the wrong message."

I fight a laugh. "Fair enough."

CHAPTER TWENTY

Julian

Expanding my company beyond Lake Wisteria's borders was always part of the plan. I spent the last year researching neighboring lake towns, attending town hall meetings, and visiting countless open houses to make sure I picked the right second location for Lopez Luxury.

I should be ecstatic about purchasing my first house in Lake Aurora after how hard it was to get the town to warm up to my plan to drive up tourism and triple property values. Instead, I'm stuck with a hollow feeling while my signature dries on the dotted line.

My real estate agent tucks the contract into her file. "I'll reach out to your assistant once the owners of the manor on Juniper Lane agree to sell."

"You're confident they will?"

She slides the file into her briefcase before throwing the

strap over her shoulder. "Oh, yeah. It's only a matter of time. Plus, I already have two other families ready to sell a chunk of their land. It seems people are more willing to part with their properties after seeing what you did with the town."

"Great." My enthusiasm falls flat.

Her gray brows scrunch. "Is there anything else I can help you with?"

"No. Keep Sam posted about the other sales." I stand and walk her out of my private office.

Sam drops his sandwich and takes over walking the real estate agent out to the parking lot.

"The floors have to go," Dahlia's voice announces.

What the hell?

I scan the room and hallway for Dahlia, only to find them empty.

"We don't have the budget for that," Oliver's cheery voice follows.

An episode of Dahlia's show plays on Sam's computer monitor. I reach to pause the episode, only to stop before I hit the space bar.

Dahlia looks over at Oliver with a frown. "You told me yesterday we were under-budget and on track to finish early."

"That was before we found out about the issue in the attic." He tucks a screwdriver into his tool belt.

"What issue?" She looks genuinely confused by his statement.

"Two of the three support beams have termite damage, and the insulation needs to be redone," he enunciates with a fake smile.

"How much will that set us back?"

"Thirty thousand, give or take."

Dahlia's eyes shut for the briefest second before she recovers. "I can work with that."

Oliver wraps an arm around her shoulder, ignoring the way her body tenses as he pulls her into a hug. "Is now a bad time to tell you about the basement?"

The slight twitch in Dahlia's eye could be mistaken for a tic, but I know better.

I move the mouse around and check the episode details. It was prerecorded and released yesterday, which makes sense given Dahlia's longer hair and fuller frame.

Another thing I wouldn't mind punching Oliver over.

I find myself caught up in watching the train wreck of their relationship play out. Oliver seems to stare *through* Dahlia rather than at her while she talks to the camera, and his smile never quite reaches his eyes. Dahlia isn't much better at faking affection based on how she cringes when Oliver explains a few construction issues like a toddler in a hard hat.

Sam once referred to Dahlia and Oliver as the ultimate home improvement couple, but are we watching the same show?

Based on a quick internet search, a majority of viewers agree, describing the show as *uncomfortably bingeable* and the couple as *unfortunately doomed*.

"Oh, shoot. Sorry about that." Sam slams his thumb against the keyboard, pausing the video.

"That was..." I struggle to come up with the right word.

"Awkward to watch, right?"

I cross my arms. "You could say that."

"Dahlia is my queen and all, but Oliver sucks. I can't believe I once thought he was cool and laid-back."

Me too. At least he was before he made a move on the girl I liked, knowing full well how I felt about her.

I lean against the corner of Sam's desk. "What changed?"

"Every time Dahlia has an innovative idea, Oliver finds a way to ruin it with some recently discovered issue. It's a formula that was entertaining the first couple of times, but now I'm uncomfortable watching Dahlia pretend not to be annoyed at Oliver and him doing everything to push her buttons."

Are you any better than him?

"Is the show usually like this?" I ask, ignoring the usual self-doubt.

"No. But obviously their relationship issues bled into the show."

"I saw." *Painfully so.*

"According to some gossip accounts I follow, Oliver's family wanted to pull the plug on the show, and since they're the executive producers..."

"Dahlia was screwed."

"Production did Dahlia dirty with the way they cut scenes to paint her in a bad light." Sam takes a seat before chomping down on his sandwich.

"They can do that?"

He snorts. "Of course. Reality TV isn't exactly known for its honesty."

I shake my head. "What's the point, then?"

"Entertainment."

No wonder Dahlia is struggling. If there is one thing she values more than her career, it's her reputation, and Oliver couldn't even let her keep that.

I'm hit with a bloody desire to fly out to San Francisco and introduce Oliver to my fist. My lawyer might hate me for it, but the satisfaction of his nose crunching beneath my knuckles would be well worth the settlement money.

"How many more episodes until the season is over?"

"Eight? Maybe nine? I'd have to check."

For fuck's sake.

He takes a long sip from his paper straw. "But the production company hasn't canceled next season yet, probably because the ratings are higher than ever. Views nearly doubled last night after an article came out suggesting that Dahlia and Oliver broke up because of another woman—"

Dahlia's detached voice cuts Sam off midsentence. "You shouldn't believe everything you read on the internet."

"Dahlia! You're here!" Sam jumps up from his chair. While he gathers a few files from the cabinet behind his desk, I check Dahlia out.

Obvious anger aside, she looks better than when she first arrived in Lake Wisteria, having put on a bit of weight and taking the time to do her hair and makeup like she used to. The warm fall colors she chose for her eyes bring out the golden flecks of her irises, although her red lipstick steals my attention.

The color reminds me of the one she wore during a college Halloween party. Her red lips were a Trojan horse, and I was too enamored by her beauty to stop her from kissing me.

At first, I was surprised by her making the first move, but it only took me a few seconds to throw my inhibitions away and kiss her back after spending three long years resenting myself for dreaming about it.

Dahlia wasn't my first kiss, but it sure felt that way with how my mind and body reacted.

The memory wraps around my neck like an anchor, dragging me down until I'm left with only one thought.

Her.

Dahlia wipes the corner of her mouth. "What? Do I have lipstick on my face or something?"

No, but I wish I did.

A jackhammer to the heart might have been less shocking than the vision of Dahlia's red lips pressed against mine.

What the hell has gotten into you?

"Are you okay?" Her eyes shine brighter than Town Square during Christmas.

"Sam will help you get set up in the spare office room." I escape into my private suite before Dahlia has a chance to respond.

Have you learned anything since the last time? I begin pacing the perimeter of my office like a caged animal.

Obviously not, which is exactly why you need to keep contact to a minimum.

The idea of stepping away from the project fills me with dread, especially when I was looking forward to getting out of the office more and returning to my roots.

This is for the best.

If that's true, then why does it feel like someone turned my lungs into a pin cushion?

Because you're only punishing yourself by planning to avoid her.

Am I? Because I don't need a pro-con list to determine working with Dahlia is a disaster in the making. The best thing I can do for both of us is add distance, especially when my restraint is weakened by nothing more than red-painted lips.

I take a seat at my desk and fire off an email requesting a review of our schedules to ensure that.

Crisis averted.

CHAPTER TWENTY-ONE

Julian

Since I officially opened the Lopez Luxury office, I have always been the first person in and the last person out. Tonight's monthly board meeting for the Dwelling app took longer than usual, thanks to the latest bug discovered after Rafa's late-night tinkering.

By the time I shut down my computer and exit my office, my energy is sapped, and my stomach is protesting every few minutes for something better than coffee and a protein bar.

I'm surprised by the sound of off-key singing and country music streaming through the hallway. After spending the past few days avoiding Dahlia, it feels counterintuitive to seek her out now, so I don't bother checking in on her.

My escape route is blocked by a man standing behind the glass front door, holding a takeout bag from Holy Smokes BBQ.

My mouth waters as I unlock the deadbolt and open the door. "Yes?"

"I have a delivery for Dahlia Muñoz." The delivery man holds out the bag for me.

"Follow the music and terrible singing to the source."

The man's phone chimes. "Shit. I wouldn't ask this normally, but do you mind taking it to her? My next delivery is ready to be picked up, and the guy has been a real pill." He doesn't bother waiting for a reply as he places the bag on the sidewalk and takes off, running toward his parked moped.

"No problem," I grumble to myself as I lean down and pick it up off the ground.

Annoyance bites at my heels as I head toward the office Sam set Dahlia up in. It's on the opposite side of the building, far from my office and the conference rooms I frequently visit every day.

My loud knock goes unanswered, which only fuels my irritation as I turn the knob and open the door.

Dahlia jumps in place. "God. You scared me!" She reaches for her phone and hits pause.

I completely forget my reason for visiting her as I enter the office, which has been transformed in the short time she has been here. The chrome desk that originally took up half the space has been replaced by a reclaimed wood table covered with wallpaper samples, flooring chips, and ten different doorknobs.

Dahlia covered the plain gray carpet with an accent rug, added floor lamps to replace the bright overhead fluorescents, and installed a large bookshelf to organize the baskets full of supplies. She removed the previous paintings to make space for her design mood boards.

I head toward the six-foot pinboards covering the wall opposite the window. Fabric clippings, raw material samples, paint chip options, furniture printouts, and hand-sketched drawings are pinned to the surface, giving me a sneak peek into Dahlia's mind.

I knew she had an eye for modern rustic design—that much became obvious during my hours of researching her career—but seeing her in action takes my breath away.

I clear my tight throat. "Settling in okay?"

"Sam said I could do what I wanted with the room." A hint of defensiveness bleeds into her voice.

"I see that."

She peeks up at me through her dark lashes. "Do you hate it?"

"I don't think *hate* is the right word." I wince at how the sentence sounds.

Do you ever get anything right?

Reality is, I like her style more than I care to admit. Something about it is warm. Welcoming.

Homey.

"Perfect. Now if you don't mind, I'll be taking that..." Dahlia swipes the bag of takeout from my hand.

She searches for the best place to eat before deciding to sit crisscross on the rug and use a cardboard box for a table.

"Thanks for grabbing it for me. I must have missed the guy's call." She pops open the first takeout container. The aroma of freshly baked cornbread and pulled pork fills the room, drawing another disturbing grumble from my stomach.

Her gaze snaps toward the source of the noise. "Did you have dinner?"

"Not yet." I take a step toward the door.

She reaches inside the paper bag for another Styrofoam box and places it beside the first.

I pull out my phone to place an order at Holy Smokes, only to find out the restaurant closed fifteen minutes ago. "Damn."

"What?" She pops off the top of the barbecue sauce and drizzles some over the pulled pork.

Saliva fills my mouth at an embarrassing rate.

"Do you have a key to lock up?"

"No."

Great. "Did you expect to leave the front door open?"

She shrugs. "I thought I could sneak out of a window or something."

I tip my head toward her purple cast. "My liability insurance company is going to go bankrupt because of you."

Her soft laugh floods me with warmth. "Sam left me his key, so you're safe. *For now.*"

First thing tomorrow, I plan on having a chat with Sam about office keys and temporary guests.

"Fine. Be sure to lock up."

"Got it." She offers me a half-assed salute before popping open the box containing a whopping amount of brisket, mac and cheese, corn, and some coleslaw.

My stomach growls loud enough to have her looking up.

Her gaze flickers from her food to my stomach. "Do you want to stay and have some?"

I blink twice. "What?"

"I ordered way too much anyway."

"You're offering me food?"

"No need to make it a big deal and treat it like the Last Supper or anything. You're obviously hungry, and I'd hate for good food to go to waste." She holds out a plastic set of utensils and the container filled with brisket—my personal favorite.

"I'm surprised you're willing to share."

"You're the one who always had a problem with sharing. Plus, it's the least I can do after you drove me to the hospital and everything the other week."

I take off my suit jacket and throw it on the table before sitting on the floor opposite to her. "You're right." I stab into her pile of pulled pork and grab a forkful.

"Hey!" She smacks my fork away with her own.

"I thought you didn't have a problem with sharing," I tease before taking a bite. The burst of flavor nearly makes my eyes roll.

"You like it?"

"I didn't realize how hungry I was." I don't speak again until half the brisket is gone.

"Do you usually work this late?" She swallows a forkful of mac and cheese.

"Yup." I dig into the street corn since Dahlia would cut my hand off with a plastic knife before letting me have some of her mac and cheese.

"Why?"

"Not like I have much else to do."

She looks at me with a strange expression. "Oh, I don't know. Maybe you could enjoy life a little?"

"I do."

"Really? Because you're kind of a workaholic."

I frown. "So what?"

"It's not a bad thing, per se." She looks up at the ceiling.

"You sure make it sound like one."

"It's sad to think you made all this money at such a young age to make life easier, yet all you do is work anyway."

"I like my job."

"But do you love it?" She stays quiet as she takes a few more bites of her food.

Not anymore.

As if she can read my mind, she makes a confirmatory noise.

"What?" I ask.

"You don't seem happy."

Her acknowledgment shocks me.

She shakes her head. "I thought you were here living your best billionaire life, but honestly, everything about it is kind of pathetic."

"Gee. Thanks." I steal a scoopful of her mac and cheese in retribution, earning a little hiss from Dahlia.

She pulls the container farther out of my reach. "I'm not trying to be rude."

"Yet it seems to be your default setting around me."

My comment earns me a scowl.

"Your life is…" Her voice drifts off.

"What? Sad? Pathetic? Miserable? Take your pick."

"Not what I expected," she whispers.

My throat tightens. "What did you expect?"

"For you to be happy at least."

"Were you happy before you came here?" My tone comes off more accusatory than neutral.

Her shoulders stiffen. "For a time, yeah."

My napkin crumples in my tight fist.

Her brows furrow. "Julian…"

I rise in a rush and toss my crushed napkin and fork in the trash.

"Where are you going?" she asks.

"My house."

She doesn't need to stand to make me feel small as she asks, "Do you notice how you never call it your home?"

Fuck. Leave it to Dahlia to call me out on such a thing.

Truth is, I don't have a home, and I have no one to blame but myself. I spend way too much time living in my head, fearing I'll never be good enough without ever trying to prove to someone that I can be.

CHAPTER TWENTY-TWO

Julian

ey, boss. Do you have a minute?" Ryder's muffled voice
seeps through the cracks of my office door.

"Come in," I call out before locking my computer.

Ryder shuts the door to my office before leaning against it
with his arms crossed. "Your family friend has a special request
I wanted to run by you."

Lovely. Ever since last week's dinner disaster, I have done
my best to avoid Dahlia, which is probably why she enlisted
Ryder to do her dirty work.

I lean back in my chair. "What does Dahlia want?"

"She'd like to match the original moldings and woodwork
that came with the house, but I'm having trouble finding a
local carpenter with that kind of skill level who can work with
our short time frame."

"Can we find someone from Detroit to help?"

"She knew you would suggest that."

I shoot him a look. "Predictability is a sign of stability."

"And boredom." He brushes his hand over his buzz cut. "She wanted me to ask if you would be willing to do the work instead. She knows you're busy—"

"No."

He doesn't miss a beat. "But she said—"

"I don't care what she said. Either she works with whomever you hire or she can scrap her idea altogether." I type my password, only to screw it up twice from my agitation.

"Got it, boss." He nods before exiting my office, leaving me to take out my irritation on my keyboard.

The ache in my chest intensifies with each passing minute, and I'm quickly distracted from my work by the thoughts bouncing around my head.

Who does Dahlia think she is, making requests like that despite knowing I don't do carpentry anymore?

Are you annoyed at her asking for your help, or are you angry at yourself for being too afraid to follow through with her request?

I claimed to have processed my dad's death and moved on from my past mistakes regarding it, yet when given an opportunity to prove it, I shy away, allowing fear and grief to control my choices.

You're the one with all the power here.

And that's what scares me most.

As much as I wanted to avoid the building site and the woman who is working there, a few things needed to be addressed, including a formal introduction to the new team member Ryder hired.

It took him only one day to find me a carpenter fit for Dahlia's task and only one minute for me to hate him, breaking a new company record.

I glare at the blond, brown-eyed giant from across the lawn, although he is too busy talking to Dahlia to notice me.

Strike one.

"Hey, boss." Grass crunches beneath Ryder's work boots.

"Hey." I turn toward my project manager while keeping the carpenter on my radar. "Where did you find the new guy?"

"He comes highly recommended from someone I know out of Detroit."

"Hm."

Ryder shifts his weight. "According to my contact, he does the best woodwork on this side of the state."

Strike two.

That fact, along with the way he smiles at Dahlia, has me scowling.

Strike three. "Get rid of him."

Ryder freezes up beside me. "I'm sorry, sir. What?"

"I don't like him." God, it sounds as stupid to my own ears as it does aloud.

"Have you met him?"

"Seeing as he is too busy flirting with Dahlia to notice his employer, no."

Ryder's gaze swings from me to the carpenter. "I see."

"He seems too"—I pause in search of the right word—"unfocused."

"He's not on the clock yet."

"Perfect. Less paperwork for Sam."

He doesn't try to hide his amusement. "Boss, if you don't mind me making a suggestion…"

Working with Ryder for seven years comes with many advantages but also a few caveats, such as his ability to read me better than my own mother sometimes. I blame his military background and fascination with too many true crime shows.

"Go ahead." My deep sigh doesn't deter his knowing smile.

"If you don't want him around, then you'll have to find someone to replace him."

"Do you know any retired female carpenters?"

His laugh comes out like a low rumble. "I never thought I'd see the day someone got under your skin."

I peek over at him through the corner of my eye. "Dahlia doesn't have to try too hard."

"*Exactly.*"

"Don't you have a job to do or someone to manage?"

He holds up his clipboard. "Nope. I was actually about to go hand Dan some paperwork to sign before he starts working."

I snatch the paperwork from his hand. "Hold on."

His lips twitch. "Problem, sir?"

Dahlia shooting Dan a soft smile answers his question for me. Like a shot to the heart, the pain radiates through my chest.

Feeling jealousy toward Oliver was understandable given our history, but getting overwhelmingly frustrated at any man within her vicinity? That's a whole different issue I never thought I would have to face in this lifetime.

It was easy to ignore my feelings for her when she lived states away, but it wasn't until she returned to Lake Wisteria that I felt myself drowning in the what-ifs.

What if I hadn't made the choices I did after my dad died?

What if I had processed my grief differently and stepped up to be the person Dahlia deserved?

Would she have heard me out and given us a chance to fall in love? Or would we have gotten together only to realize we were better off apart?

My world spins around me as I consider the possibilities.

Attempting to avoid her clearly hasn't been working, so what are you going to do now?

"I have an idea." Ryder fidgets with the pencil tucked behind his ear.

"What?"

"If you don't want to hire Dan because he seems *unfocused*,"—Ryder shoots me a knowing look—"there is one guy I've heard who could easily replace him."

"Who?"

"You."

♚

"Really?" Excitement bleeds into Dahlia's voice.

The wood step creaks beneath my shoe as I pause halfway down the stairs. Dahlia doesn't notice my presence as she walks toward the back of my truck, disappearing from my view.

"Wow." Whoever is speaking to her on the other end must share something good based on the tiny squeal she lets out.

I'm not one to eavesdrop, but she is blocking my one way off the property.

"A show with them would be huge!"

My stomach sinks. "So much for sticking around until the house is done," I mutter under my breath.

"Would they want to film in San Francisco again?" She pauses. "Oh. That's good, then." She waits a few seconds to speak again. "January? That soon?"

I don't need to hear the entire conversation to jump to conclusions. Rather than feel relieved by her leaving town, I'm suffering from a serious case of heartburn.

You've done everything possible to make something like this happen, and now you're disappointed? Pick a lane and stay in it.

I ignore the pain in my chest and walk toward my truck, scaring Dahlia in the process. She steps out of the way, and I keep my eye contact to a minimum as I climb inside the cab and turn on the engine.

This is for the best, I lie to myself as I drive away from the Founder's house.

You wanted her to leave, I'm quick to remind myself as I park outside my office.

Dahlia dreamed of a life bigger than this small town, and you will never be able to give her that, so stop pining over her and pull yourself together. My mind goes blank as I get to work, drowning myself in paperwork rather than regrets.

CHAPTER TWENTY-THREE

Julian

When I got my mom's 911 text ten minutes ago during one of my last meetings of the day, I assumed a tent might be on fire or a cat stuck in a tree, but a quick walk through the park shows nothing amiss outside of the usual Thursday preparations for the weekend.

Come tomorrow, this place will be packed with volunteers since Fridays before the Harvest Festival are considered a town holiday, with everyone taking off from work to help prepare for a full Saturday and Sunday of events.

"You're here! Thank God." Mom makes a big show of throwing her arms around me and pulls me into a hug, turning my ears pink as the volunteers stare at us.

It takes an insane amount of strength to pry her off me. "So, what's the emergency?"

Her shoulders slump. "You're going to kill me."

"Only if you don't get to the point fast enough."

She pops her hands on her hips. "Luis Julian Lopez Junior. Don't you dare talk to your mother like that."

I swipe a frustrated hand down my face, erasing my scowl. "Sorry, Ma. I'm exhausted from the week." After a day full of meetings while avoiding Dahlia in my own office building, I'm spent.

"Make it up to me by saying you'll go to Detroit. *Tonight.*"

"Whatever you need."

She wipes her damp forehead. "I knew I could count on you."

"What's the issue?"

"I screwed up the dates for the festival with the rental company, so now I'm short on chairs and tables. The original one I chose for the event is booked solid, so I found another in Detroit that has enough."

"Why can't they come here?"

"They don't deliver this far."

There goes my date with a bottle of Merlot and a premade meal. "Do they know I'm coming?"

"Yes, but you'll need to borrow Fred's moving truck."

"Fred Davis?"

She grimaces. "Yeah."

"He hates me." The owner of the only moving company in town has loathed me since I accidentally plowed over his award-winning flower bed while learning how to drive with my dad.

"I know he does, which is exactly why you'll have Dahlia there to soften him up."

Where Fred's hatred for me has never wavered, his appreciation for Dahlia only blossomed after she single-handedly saved the flower bed I nearly destroyed.

"I don't need Dahlia's help," I say with a scowl.

"We both know you do, which is why I already sent her over to Fred's with a basket of Alana's baked goods and a fifty-dollar Holy Smokes BBQ voucher."

Dammit.

"Look at these roses." Dahlia flashes Fred a beautiful smile that makes the stunning flowers around her fade into the background. The usual tightness in my chest returns at the sight of her, making breathing a chore.

Will you ever get used to her being around?

Based on the uneven thump of my heart, the answer will remain a resounding no.

A twig snaps beneath my shoes, and her eyes flick over to me.

Fred turns on his heels, making his white-haired toupee flap from the sudden movement. "*You.*"

"Hey, Fred," I say with a half-assed wave.

"If you know what's good for ya, you'll get lost before I go searchin' for my granddaddy's rifle."

Dahlia muffles her laugh with the palm of her hand.

Glad one of us is amused.

I take a stab at being mature. "I want to be here as much as you want me here."

"Then feel free to see yourself off my property." He turns toward Dahlia.

"Mr. Davis," Dahlia says in that sweet-as-sin voice of hers. "The town could use your help." She uses those damn puppy eyes again—all big eyes and batted lashes—turning poor Mr. Davis into her latest victim. I've seen her use the same kind of tactic repeatedly throughout our lives. When we were teens, I hated it because there wasn't a situation Dahlia couldn't charm her way out of.

No one stands a chance against her when she does that thing with her bottom lip.

Fred lasts three whole seconds before breaking down. "Fine. But only if Dahlia stays with the truck the whole time."

"Of course!" She claps her hands together.

Fred disappears into the house.

Dahlia turns toward me with a wicked grin. "And that's how it's done."

"So how long will the trip take?" Dahlia asks as I turn onto the main road leading into town.

The brakes squeal as the twenty-six-foot truck jerks to a stop. "What?"

She checks her phone. "The highway is congested because of construction, so we probably won't get there until after the sun goes down."

"You're not coming with me."

"What do you mean?"

"I'm dropping you off at your house."

"Not if you plan on borrowing Fred's truck."

I angle my head in her direction. "Are you threatening me?"

"More like exploiting the situation for my benefit."

My fingers turn white from clenching the steering wheel. "What do you need to do in Detroit?"

"I wanted to pick up a few supplies since I left most of mine back in San Francisco."

"Like what?"

"Things that can't be found at the general market on Main. Tracing paper, drafting tape, alcohol markers, etcetera."

"Give me a list, and I'll grab them."

She peeks over at me through the corner of her eye. "The idea of being in a car with me for a few hours bothers you that much?"

While I'm tempted to agree, I don't want to give her the satisfaction of being right. So, instead, I say something incredibly stupid. "I was trying to be nice and save you the trip."

She laughs to herself. "Sure you were."

My hands clench around the steering wheel as I pass Town Square and head toward the one-way road out of town with the one woman I was trying to stay away from.

CHAPTER TWENTY-FOUR

Dahlia

I didn't mean to inject myself into Julian's mission to save the Harvest Festival, but with me having one arm out of commission, I can't exactly drive myself to the nearest city in search of interior design tools. Joining him is the best solution I've got.

Sure, I could order supplies online, but the estimated two-week delivery times have me quickly tossing out that idea. It's either join Julian on this trip or wait two weeks for supplies I needed yesterday.

The two-hour drive flies by, with Julian quickly vetoing my playlist for his own. I'm pleasantly surprised by new artists I hadn't heard of, and I find myself saving some of his songs to my own playlist.

Julian drives down a row of dark warehouses before stopping in front of the address his mom sent him.

"Is this it?" I look around the quiet street.

"According to my mom's pin, yeah."

I hop out of the truck despite Julian's protests.

"Do you have any survival instincts?" He slams his door shut.

I pat my purse. "Of course. I've got pepper spray and enough self-defense classes to hold my own."

"All it would take is one punch to your broken arm to have you begging for mercy."

I blink. "You clearly thought that one out."

He shoots me a look before heading toward the door. "Fuck."

My brows rise. "What?"

"They're closed."

"No." I check out the sign and confirm that fact while Julian calls his mother and explains our situation over speakerphone.

"What do you mean they're closed?" Josefina asks.

Julian shuts his eyes. "You got the hours of operation wrong."

Josefina gasps like one of her telenovela stars, which makes my brows rise. "Me? No. I would never."

And the award for the worst performance goes to…

"Ma." Julian shares a look with me.

She's up to something, I mouth. I should have known Josefina was planning something when she started drilling me with questions about the supplies I needed to pick up in Detroit. When I mentioned having them delivered instead, she insisted on me picking them up to prevent any more delays.

Julian shakes his head.

She laughs. "*Qué pena*. I guess you and Dahlia will have to stay there until tomorrow."

Julian's brows scrunch. "How did you know Dahlia was with me?"

"Fred promis—*told*—me that when he stopped by the volunteer tent."

"*Por supuesto*." He frowns hard enough to create permanent wrinkles.

"Gotta go, *mijo*! Someone left the petting zoo gate open. *Te quiero*. Give Dahlia a hug for me!"

The phone beeps twice before Julian's screen goes black.

He runs his hands through his hair. "I'm going to kill her."

"Feel free to do it *after* the festival; that way no one gets upset at you."

He pinches the bridge of his nose. "She gave me the wrong time on purpose."

"Honestly, it's a genius ploy to get us to spend time together."

"I'll call Sam and have him book us some rooms while we head to the store for clothes and your supplies."

I pull out my phone while Julian taps away at his.

"The mall closed an hour ago," I announce with a frown.

"We can shop at a big box store instead."

"*Perfecto*." On cue, my stomach growls loud enough for Julian's brows to rise. "Can we stop somewhere for food?"

Qué pena: How unfortunate.

Por supuesto: Of course.

"Together?"

My eyes roll. "I was going to suggest separate tables, but if you're that desperate for my company, I'm willing to make a sacrifice for you."

"Get your ass in the truck before I cancel our trip to the art store."

"Asshole."

"*Sweetheart*." His nickname penetrates my cold heart like a flaming arrow.

I instantly recognize the feeling. I'm tempted to carve out my heart and stomp all over it solely to remind me of what it felt like to be crushed by Julian all those years ago.

You're leaving in January to film your new show anyway, so no reason to get all flustered over a silly nickname.

Easier said than done.

🏆

Julian gets a call as soon as he parks outside the art store, so I take it as a sign of divine intervention. Spending time around him is one thing, but welcoming him into my sanctuary?

Absolutely not happening.

I reach for the handle, only to be stopped as he grabs my left hand. It's not meant to be an intimate gesture, yet my heart picks up speed anyway.

Wait, he mouths before releasing me from his grip.

He pulls a Centurion card from his wallet and holds it out for me. I blink at it a couple times and rub my eyes to be sure the name on the front of the card is correct.

How is he the same guy who lived off gift cards during his youth?

Why? I mouth.

Company expense, he replies.

I must not reach for the card fast enough for Julian's liking because his eyes roll as he tucks his Amex into the front left pocket of my jeans.

The heat from his fingers remains long after I rush out of the truck and head into the store.

With the art supply store closing in less than thirty minutes, I make quick work of my shopping list. Although it doesn't have everything I prefer to use while designing and planning, it has what I'll need to get me through the Founder's house project.

I throw a few extra things in my cart since this trip is being sponsored by Julian's bank account, including a few picture frames for my office, an artificial Christmas tree because 'tis the season to be spending, and enough yarn to crochet a scarf for every single person in town. I don't even crochet, but I had an insane urge to try after touching a hundred different balls of yarn.

With a swipe of Julian's company credit card and a quick signature for a fan across the back of a discarded receipt, I head back to the truck with the wheels of my cart squeaking from the sheer weight of my haul.

Julian leans against the truck with his phone still glued to his ear. My cart rattles, and he looks up.

"Gotta go, Rafa." Julian hangs up the phone with an arched brow. "A Christmas tree?"

"I thought we could liven up your office a bit." With all the time I'm spending there, I'd love something to stare at besides my own reflection in all the shiny glass and chrome fixtures.

"We haven't made it past Thanksgiving yet."

I tsk. "It's never too early to celebrate the birth of our Lord."

He plucks some bags from the cart. "Research suggests Jesus was actually born in the spring."

I rise on the tips of my toes and clamp a hand over his mouth. "Don't repeat that in front of my mother. *Ever.*" She's the type to put our family nativity scene out early, minus baby Jesus, because he doesn't make his official debut until midnight on Christmas Eve.

His eyes narrow.

I press harder. "You got it?"

He has the audacity to nip at the palm of my hand. I remove it with a gasp, only for him to clutch it within his punishing grip.

"My card?"

"I lost it."

The man scowls.

"Kidding!" I expect him to release me, but instead, Julian keeps me pinned against his chest as he searches my pockets for the card. The graze of his fingers is quick and clinical until they slide into my back pocket, gliding over my ass cheek as he takes his sweet time getting the slim credit card.

I battle between two feelings, neither of which is discomfort.

Surprise? Check.

Lust? Absolutely.

Although I'd rather gnaw on my own tongue than confess such a thing.

My enjoyment of his touchiness has me speaking first. "If you wanted to feel me up, all you had to do was ask."

The comment snaps him out of whatever daze he was in, and he pulls away. I mourn the loss of his touch as he tucks his card inside his wallet without looking me in the eyes.

"You can wait in the truck while I load your stuff in the back." He dismisses me without so much as a second glance, and I climb back into the cabin with a huff.

He was the one who felt me up.

Yeah, well, you were the one who liked *it.*

Julian and I hit a local big box store next. The clothing selection is grim, with me shuddering in my sneakers as I choose the most unattractive pair of flannel PJs, underwear with the days of the week plastered across the back, and a pair of paint-splattered jeans that would send the fashion police into full SWAT mode.

Julian gives me free rein over picking his clothes while he chats with Sam about a few things regarding next week's work schedule. I have a blast putting together the ugliest outfit for him, which he immediately rejects.

I pout. "I'm offended you don't trust me."

"No amount of trust in the world could convince me to wear those jeans." He frowns at the acid wash denim fit for an eighties music video.

"If you had your way, you'd wear plain ones and a black T-shirt."

He lifts his full basket of clothes in the air. "Exactly."

Ugh. "I'm going to put all this back." I head back toward the men's section with my cart, only to become distracted by the Christmas section near the checkout lanes.

Most of my holidays became opportunities for the Creswells and their agent to show off my design skills by having me make curated collections to be featured in magazines and social media pages. And while I love coming up with new ways to reinvent holiday classics, I can't help getting caught up in the nostalgic decorations lining the shelves.

Vibrant tinsel. Novelty ornaments. Multicolored C9 light bulbs. Everything about this holiday display reminds me of my childhood, and I want to take part in it without worrying about designing something perfect or aesthetically pleasing.

I want to have *fun.*

After struggling with intense sadness and chronic numbness for the last few months, I plan on clinging to my excitement and riding the high for as long as humanly possible.

Like a child with no self-control, I throw random objects into my cart. Tinsel shiny enough to blind someone. A nutcracker drinking a beer in a tropical shirt. Packages of themed ornaments that will no doubt clash with each other.

I go through each row, throwing whatever makes me laugh into the cart. At first, my haul was easy to navigate with one arm, but now I struggle to push it forward with all the added weight.

My neck prickles, and I turn to find Julian walking up to me.

"Is all this for that Christmas tree you bought for me?" He takes over manning the cart.

"On second thought, I think I'll keep the tree. We can't have you ruining your Ebenezer Scrooge image or anything."

"No."

My eyes widen. "You want the tree?"

"Yes."

"Why?"

Silence.

Jerk.

"What's all this about?" He pivots the cart toward the checkout lane.

"Some decorations for *your* tree."

His eyes drop to the nutcracker cracking open a Corona. "And the rest?"

"You'll have to wait and see."

"What are you planning?" His right eye twitches.

"Like I'd tell you."

"*Dahlia.*" That rough voice of his tugs at my lower half.

"It'll be great! I promise!"

I never thought going on a road trip with Julian could be a good time. Between fighting for control over the playlist and laughing over terrible restaurant reviews while searching for a spot that serves Detroit-style pizza, I find myself actually enjoying his company. It's a dangerous admission, and one I'm too afraid to acknowledge for more than a fleeting second, solely because I'm worried it won't last after we return to Lake Wisteria tomorrow.

I don't want to get my hopes up, so I'm careful not to set unrealistic expectations, although Julian makes it nearly impossible when he smiles at the jukebox.

The hostess drops our menus at the booth closest to it before going over to check on another couple.

Julian shuffles through the songs before swiping his card to pay and taking a seat as the beginning chords of one of my favorites, "Brown Eyed Girl", starts to play.

The memory of my dad spinning my mom around our living room to the same song flashes in front of my eyes. Mom would laugh often and worry less whenever my dad was around, especially when he danced with her.

Julian slides into the booth across from me, and the memory disappears.

"I love this song."

"I know." He grabs his menu while my heart thumps hard enough to almost jump out of my chest.

I drop my head into my hands with a sigh.

🏆

I'm exhausted by the time we make it to the fancy hotel Sam booked for us, with my eyes drooping and my posture slumping.

"Here you go." The concierge slides the key toward Julian.

"And the other one?"

The man's gaze flicks back to the computer screen. "You only booked one room."

Julian's shoulders tense. "That's impossible."

"I only have one reservation booked under Lopez."

"Try checking for a room under the name *Muñoz*," I say.

A few clicks of the mouse confirm I don't have a room. Julian walks away to call Sam, only to come back with the scariest scowl I've seen from him.

"He didn't answer."

I doubt I would answer my boss at midnight either, especially if I couldn't book a second room like he wanted.

"Can we reserve another room now?" Julian taps his fingers against the counter.

"I wish I could, but we're booked solid for the night. Most of the hotels in the area are, since we have three conventions, a hockey game, and an NFL player's wedding all happening this weekend. You could drive around and try your luck, but—"

"I want to speak to your manager."

Oh no. I better save Julian before he goes full entitled billionaire on this poor man.

"Thank you for trying anyway." I grab the key off the counter.

"We'll go searching for another hotel," Julian protests.

"I'm exhausted and want to get some rest." While my energy levels have improved significantly along with my mood, I'm still more tired than usual.

"But—"

"Come on." I lock elbows with Julian as I steer him away from the desk.

The anger pouring off of him keeps me quiet as we make our way up to our room. With the way he huffs and puffs, I'm a bit afraid for Sam's job security.

"At least the room is beautiful." I note the single positive before reality smacks me in the face.

Julian's hands clench and unclench as he glowers at the bed.

The *one* king-sized bed.

"Well, isn't this going to be fun?" I bite down on my tongue.

Although the lavish room has its own sitting area with the newest smart TV, it becomes clear that the leather couch and chaise lounge are more for looks than comfort.

"I'll be back." He shuffles past me.

I latch on to his arm and hold him back. "And you'll go do what? Threaten the guy? He already told us they don't have another room, so you're only wasting your time."

Julian's eyes shut. "What a nightmare."

"It could be worse."

"How?"

"Imagine if I snored."

He mutters something to himself before escaping into the bathroom with his plastic bag filled with clothes and toiletries. A pipe groans before the soft patter of water echoes through the room.

With Julian gone, I'm able to fully process the idea of sharing a bed with him. While our circumstances aren't ideal, I'm sure we can be mature adults about it and keep to our respective sides.

CHAPTER TWENTY-FIVE

Julian

Sharing a room with Dahlia proves to be a difficult challenge, especially after she takes a bath and climbs into bed beside me.

I reach over and yank on the cord of the lamp, plunging us into darkness.

"Good night," she says as she sinks into the mattress.

Regardless of the space between us, I'm acutely aware of every breath and move she makes.

"Night," I grumble up toward the ceiling with my arms crossed over my chest.

She shifts to the right before turning to the left, only to land on her back with a huff.

"You good?"

"Mm-hmm," she replies before moving back to her right side.

I try to fall asleep, but Dahlia's tossing and turning keeps me wide awake for the next five minutes. I'm not sure if she is typically a restless sleeper or if her cast makes finding a comfortable position difficult, but either way, she is driving me insane.

I turn my head to the side. "What's wrong with you?"

She fixes the comforter for the tenth time. "I can't fall asleep."

"Why?"

"Because…" She motions toward the two of us like it answers everything.

"What?"

"This is weird."

"Would you rather I sleep on the floor?"

Her smile can be seen in the dark. "Could you?"

"Hell no, but good to know you'd be up for me being exposed to more bodily fluids than a sperm bank."

My brain is sent into a tailspin by the soft, melodic sound of her laugh.

"Don't be dramatic. This has to be the nicest hotel in all of Detroit," she says.

"It could be the Ritz-Carlton, and I'd still refuse to sleep on the floor."

"There's always the couch."

"Thanks for the suggestion, but I like my spine alignment the way it is."

She giggles again, this time with a little wheeze at the end.

Both of us fall quiet, although this round of silence feels more comfortable compared to the others.

"Julian," she whispers a few minutes later.

I screw my eyes tight. "I'm sleeping."

"No, you're not." She nudges me with her cast.

I pop an eye open to confirm she closed the gap between us. She leans on her side, with her right arm tucked beneath her pillow and her dark hair billowing around her like a curtain.

"What?" I ask without hiding my annoyance.

"Something has been bothering me."

"About the mattress?"

"About *us*."

I remain quiet.

Dahlia sighs. "Sometimes it feels like…" Her sentence dies before she has a chance to finish it.

What? I want to ask.

Tell me, I wish to say.

But rather than give my curiosity away, I keep the questions locked away.

She returns to her original position on her back. "Forget it. I'm exhausted."

I let her get away with the lie because I'm not ready to face whatever she wants to say about us, mostly because there is no *us* to begin with.

Only because you are too afraid of what might happen if there was, the voice in the back of my head whispers.

Putting my history with Dahlia aside, there are plenty of issues standing in my way of pursuing anything serious, including her moving back to San Francisco next year and me not being good enough for her.

I don't even want a child, for fuck's sake. So, while I could acknowledge how I feel about her all I want, that doesn't mean we're a good match.

No matter how much I wish we were.

♔

I wake up to the sound of something thumping against the wall behind me. My eyes snap open, and my body goes rigid beneath Dahlia's. Her rhythmic breathing doesn't falter, so I doubt she notices anything, including the way she holds me like her favorite pillow.

Dahlia is always gorgeous to me—smile or scowl, made-up or barefaced, dressed like a runway model or wearing nothing but a sweatshirt and leggings—but right now, I find her absolutely stunning with her arm wrapped around me and her cheek pressed against my chest.

A smart man would slide out from underneath her and replace his body with an actual pillow, but obviously I lack the necessary IQ level required to move a single inch. Especially not when Dahlia burrows deeper into my chest and throws her leg over mine as if she senses my urge to flee.

Nothing has felt better than waking up with her in my arms.

The usual heavy feeling every morning I wake up alone is absent.

Just a few more minutes, I promise myself as the couple next door continue their sex marathon against our shared wall.

My eyes shut at some point, and I drift off to the sound of Dahlia's light snoring—a fact that she indeed lied about last night.

Yet I still fall back asleep with a smile regardless.

She doesn't plan on sticking around for long, I repeat for the umpteenth time during our trip to Detroit.

Then you might as well make the most of it and enjoy her company while you can.

🏆

At some point this morning, Dahlia slipped past my ironclad hold of her body against mine, leaving me to wake up all alone a few hours later to our door banging against the wall.

"*¡Buenos días, princesa!* I got you coffee and a ham and cheese croissant." Dahlia juggles two plastic cups of coffee in her arm while closing the door with her foot.

I blink up at the ceiling, rub my eyes, and let out a long yawn. She places my drink on the nightstand beside me before taking a seat near the bottom of the bed.

I don't need to check the label on the side to confirm it's the right order. Dahlia was the one who got me addicted to iced coffees with extra caramel, caramel drizzle, and a splash of cream, and I haven't found it in me to stop drinking them, though they always remind me of *her*.

After a single sip, I feel revived. I sit up against the headboard and brush a hand through my hair. "You sleep okay?"

"Mm-hmm." Her gaze shifts away from mine, although the flush crawling up her neck gives her away.

I nearly forgot about our neighbors until they restrart their

---

¡Buenos días, princesa!: Good morning, princess.

hourly ritual of fucking hard enough to make their headboard bang into our wall.

Dahlia's eyes widen. "Is that...?"

"Yup." My reply is followed by an obnoxious moan.

Her brows shoot up. "Wow."

"Only the tip," the lady coos.

Dahlia slams a hand against her mouth.

"Fuck, yeah, baby. You're so tight," the man growls.

Dahlia collapses face-first on the bed, right on top of my legs. The comforter does a good job of muffling her laughs, although I can feel them straight to my soul.

"Do you like it when I get rough?" A slap echoes through the walls before another moan.

"Oh, yeah." The woman moans. "Harder."

The man grunts, followed by the woman saying, "Just like that, baby."

"Just like that, baby," Dahlia repeats in a sultry voice as she peeks at me through her dark curtain of hair.

My dick should be the complete opposite of hard, but all it takes is her calling me *baby* while looking at me with bedroom eyes to have my blood rushing south.

"What are you doing?" I whisper.

"Having fun. Try it with me."

I don't know much about her life in San Francisco, but with the way she has been acting during this trip, one would think she was deprived of all the things she loved.

Dahlia crawls up toward the headboard and sighs loud enough to make our neighbors pause whatever the hell has them counting aloud like they're learning their numbers.

Holy shit. Tell me she isn't doing what I think she is doing.

She grabs the headboard with her right hand and shoves it with all her might. We could all hear a pin drop with the way everyone, including our neighbors, remains quiet.

"Did you hear that?" the woman asks.

"Fuck if I care. Let them listen," the guy admits.

"I won't lie. That's kind of hot," Dahlia says as her cheeks turn a deeper shade of pink.

I choke on my inhale. "What?"

A female moaning on the other side of the wall has my eyes widening.

"Put your finger up my ass like the last time," the guy grunts.

"Still find that hot?" I rasp.

"Only if he loves it." Dahlia's eyes glitter in a way I haven't seen since college, right before everything went to shit.

Fuck. Based on the way the guy is groaning, it's safe to say he enjoys whatever is being done.

Dahlia rattles the headboard again, making the couple quiet down.

Damn me straight to hell if I ruin her fun. I'm not sure she had much of it while dating that tool, and for once, I want to be the reason behind her smile.

Screw it.

I rock back and forth hard enough to make the headboard bang into the wall. Instead of our neighbors worrying, they seem to be encouraged by our eavesdropping.

"Where do you want me?" Dahlia's husky voice has my dick standing to attention.

"Sitting on my face sounds like a good start."

"What?"

"You heard me." I tap my lips. "Spread your legs and show me what's mine."

Her face goes from pink to red. "I— We—"

"If you're going to run your mouth, might as well do it with your lips wrapped around my dick."

She grabs the nearest pillow and launches it at my head, only for me to deflect it.

I trace a line from her neck to her tomato-red cheek with the tip of my index finger. "Someone's shy." After all the years of dealing with her constant teasing, it feels good to be on the other end of it.

Her nostrils flare. "Cut it out."

"Why? Afraid you might like it?"

"Like I could want your cock anywhere near my mouth."

"Does that mean the other two holes are available?"

"Only if yours is too, *mi amor.*" She swipes her thumb across my bottom lip.

Fuck. Me, along with our neighbors, both shut up. Her comment shouldn't be hot, but damn, my dick feels hard enough to snap in half.

Dahlia is breathing so heavily that I question if she might shoot fire from her nostrils.

You took things too far. Way *too far.*

"Dah—"

She straddles my lap and slams her right hand over my mouth. "Shh. No names," she whispers.

"*Sorry.*" My reply is muffled.

She moves to slide off my lap, but I hold her in place by clamping my hands around her hips.

We both stare into each other's eyes.

What are you doing?

Her gaze drops toward my lips, which tingle from a single glance.

Something I will probably regret.

Wouldn't be the first time.

She seems to come to her senses first as she attempts to wiggle out of my grasp, only for her eyes to bulge.

"Are you…" She swallows hard enough for me to see before shifting her hips again, making me hiss as she grinds against my erection. "Oh my God."

"*Stop.*"

"You're hard," she announces, her cheeks flushed. "Is it because—"

Something loudly crashes against the wall, followed by another moan.

"Take a guess," I snap.

She swivels her hips, and my head drops back with a groan. The giggle she unleashes has me battling two different emotions—neither of which are good.

She trails a finger down my chest. "I'm flattered."

"Shut up."

"No. To know I affect you like this…" She presses her fingers to her lips and makes a kissing sound. "Justice is served."

"I'll show you justice." I grip the back of her neck and pull, dragging her toward me. Her eyes shut as she leans forward, only for them to snap open at the ear-splitting sound of our neighbors finding their release.

Dahlia shoots off the bed and dashes toward the other side of the room while I drop my head back against a pillow and groan.

I don't need a pro-con list to remind me of all the reasons kissing Dahlia is a bad idea. It would only complicate things more, and with everything going on in our lives, it's best not to rock the boat when it's more structurally compromised than a sinking *Titanic*.

I climb out of bed, grab my phone, and head toward the bathroom while shielding Dahlia from my raging hard-on. My voicemail is clogged with messages from my mom, Sam, and Rafa, all of which I ignore for a hot shower.

Jacking off is the smartest choice, although thinking about Dahlia while doing it is most definitely not. At first, I try to resist, but my task seems impossible as I'm flooded with images of her.

I work myself to the array of ideas floating in my head from our theatrical performance.

Her sitting on my face.

My tongue and mouth fucking her until she threatens to cut off my oxygen supply.

Her lips wrapped around my cock—licking, kissing, sucking—as she wrecks my world with a single orgasm.

My spine tingles with each frustrated tug, and my breathing quickens until I'm gasping at the fantasy of Dahlia choking on my cock while swallowing my release.

Fuck. Fuck. Fuck!

The final image has me exploding. I ride out my orgasm while fisting my dick, pumping hard enough to make me hiss.

It's not until I come down from the high and am thrust back into reality that I realize what I did. Thinking about fucking Dahlia is one thing, but coming to the vision of her? That's a whole other level of fucked up.

I wait for the shame to sink in, but it never comes. Instead, my mind spirals with the possibility of what might happen if I stopped ignoring the obvious.

Fighting my attraction toward Dahlia is a losing battle, and if there is one thing I hate most, it's being defeated by her.

CHAPTER TWENTY-SIX

Dahlia

should have known today would be a disaster from the moment I woke up in Julian's arms as he grumbled my name in his sleep. It wasn't the idea of him dreaming of me that scared me, but rather the way it made me *feel*.

Our day quickly took a drastic turn into uncharted territory, and I feel like a lost ship trying to navigate a brewing sea of mixed emotions.

I press my ear against the bathroom door after hearing a strange noise coming from inside. Goose bumps spread across my skin when Julian groans my name, followed by a curse. My skin burns at the sounds, and I'm overwhelmed by a new sensation tugging at my lower half.

You could suggest a friends-with-benefits kind of thing.

Except Julian and I aren't friends.

Just benefits, then?

A tempting offer, but I've never been the casual-sex type. I'm the *fall first, have sex second* kind of girl, so suggesting anything else could be a recipe for disaster.

Or it could be exactly what you need.

When a pipe creaks and the water shuts off, I dash to the corner of the bed, take a seat, and pull out my phone.

A few minutes later, a cloud of steam follows behind Julian as he steps out, clad in a pair of blue jeans and a T-shirt.

"Hey." He rubs the back of his head with a towel.

"Have a good shower?"

"Mm-hmm." He can't hold my eye contact for long.

Let it go.

Nope. An opportunity to tease Julian is too hard to pass up.

No pun intended.

"Did you get the job done?" I ask while fighting a smile.

A wrinkle cuts across his forehead. "I guess?"

"Was it *hard*?"

"Was it…" His voice trails off, only for his cheeks to explode with color a few seconds later. "You heard me."

"Out of curiosity, was today a special occasion, or do you typically moan my name while making yourself come?"

"Only when I'm thinking about you sitting on my face." He tosses his towel on the back of a chair.

I'm afraid my jaw may need to be popped back into place after the way it fell open. I expected Julian to stay quiet and break eye contact, but it looks like he found some post-orgasm confidence.

"Dream about it often?" I ask.

"Enough to question my sanity."

I blink hard.

"Do you like that?" His question has my thighs pressing together.

"More than I probably should."

My body temp spikes from his attention.

I hate myself for breaking eye contact first. "We almost kissed."

He says nothing.

"What do you want, Julian?"

He leans against the opposite wall, looking cool, calm, and collected as he crosses his arms against his wide chest. "You tell me."

Is he unfazed by all of this?

God. How embarrassing would that be?

I shake my head. "This is a mistake."

"Only if you want it to be."

"What are you saying?"

He lifts a shoulder.

I grimace. "You're a thirty-year-old man. Communicate like one."

His eyes narrow. "Isn't it obvious?"

"Would I be asking if it was?"

His eyes narrow.

Mine glare.

His lips curl. "You. I want *you*."

My throat feels like I swallowed a bag of sand. "I recently got out of a serious relationship."

"No one is saying you have to jump into another one."

Not exactly the answer I was hoping for, but a decent one nonetheless.

I gather some courage and ask, "So then, what exactly are you suggesting?"

He pauses for a beat too long. "Whatever you want."

"What do *you* want?"

His gaze flickers over my face. "Anything you're willing to give me."

"That's it?"

He nods.

"So if I suggested something casual?" The question leaves a bad taste in my mouth.

"That's fine."

My heart sinks. *He isn't looking for anything serious.*

Things are better this way. Fewer expectations. Less disappointment.

"Okay," I reply.

Are you going to enter a no-strings-attached relationship with Julian?

My eyes blaze a trail down his body, taking him in without feeling self-conscious about it. Muscles for days. Abs worth drooling over. A mouth that promises the dirtiest things I'd love to experience firsthand.

Hell yeah, I am.

Why bother ignoring what we are both already painfully aware of? He is attracted to me. I'm attracted to him. The whole situation isn't exactly rocket science, although our history might as well be.

"Dahlia."

Our gazes collide.

"Do *you* want something casual?" he asks in a soft voice I never knew he possessed.

I chew on the inside of my cheek until I taste blood. "Fun and simple sounds nice after everything."

His index finger taps against his thigh. "Fine."

"*Fine?*"

"Did you expect me to object?"

"Kind of?" Or at least take more than a single second to think it over.

"You want fun and simple, then I'll give you that." He is saying all the right words, yet my lungs painfully constrict.

"For how long?"

"You tell me."

"I don't know. It's not like I've done this before."

His nostrils widen. "That's fine."

"But you have." The thought makes my stomach roll.

"Does that matter to you?"

Far more than it should. "Nope."

He stares at me for a moment before taking a step in my direction. "We keep going until one of us stops having fun."

"No." I need something more concrete than that. A clear boundary that will hold me accountable and stop me from doing anything stupid. "Until the New Year." That should give me enough time to get him out of my system.

"Because you'll be moving back to San Francisco?"

I nod. "The house will be pretty much finished, and I have a pending contract for a show."

The muscles in his neck strain. "I can work with that."

My stomach becomes a chaotic mess of buzzing butterflies as he walks over to me, pushes my thighs apart, and steps between them.

A shiver rolls through me as he curls his hand around the back of my neck and exposes my biggest secret with a single brush of his thumb over my pulse.

"You're nervous."

"A little bit," I confess.

"What else?" He leans in and kisses my neck, drawing another shudder from me.

"Excited." I *want* Julian, and I'm done avoiding my feelings in hopes of my attraction fading. I've tried that strategy for years to no avail, so I might as well give in and enjoy myself.

I can feel him smiling against my skin. "I've waited a long time for this."

"Exactly how long are we talking here? Because maybe I didn't make you work hard enough for it—"

He presses his mouth against mine for the first time in almost a decade, effectively shutting me up. All my brain cells go on strike as Julian kisses me like it might be his last chance to do so.

I've had a lot of kisses in my lifetime, but none compares to this. The longing. The passion. The spine-tingling, mind-melting, decade-in-the-making kind of kiss that sends my body into a spiral of sensations.

Julian takes his sweet time, teasing me with every brush of his lips and every swipe of his tongue.

His movements are intentional, meant to drive me mad as I wrap my legs around his waist and drag him closer. His fingers slide through my hair and cradle my head as he grinds against me. We both groan, and I take advantage, swiping my tongue against his.

Our kiss grows more desperate. At one point, I rip myself away from him and tug at his hair. Julian's muscles tremble as I kiss a path down the slope of his neck, his skin flushing.

His hips swivel as he teases me with the press of his cock, and my head falls to the side as he snatches back control and turns me into a breathless, throbbing mess. He claims my mouth. Neck. *Chest*. He blazes a trail, burning away the memories of any men who came before him.

I'm not sure how long we battle for dominance, but neither one of us stops until I'm lying flat on my back with my legs hanging over the side of the bed and Julian hovering above me.

Before I have a chance to protest, he drops to his knees and makes quick work of my shoes and jeans.

He kisses his way up my thigh before stopping in front of my underwear. "Cute, although today is Friday."

"I thought these were cuter."

He smirks at the *Wine Wednesday*-themed underwear. "I agree."

"Great. Now, less talking, more kissing." I push his head down with my good arm, only for him to turn away and bite down on the inside of my thigh.

I jolt. "What the—"

"Stop rushing me."

"By all means, take your time."

His eyes blaze with silent challenge. He tugs on the band of my underwear, pulling them down while kissing every available inch of skin within reach. While I love his soft kisses, I quickly lose patience.

"To clarify, when I said take your time before, I meant with your tongue inside my pussy."

"Did you?" he asks in that annoyingly dry voice of his.

"I get you've been waiting thirty long, painful years to lose your virginity and all—"

My mind goes blank as he yanks my thighs apart. Whatever control he had before snaps after only one pass of his tongue over my dripping center.

He devours me with a ravenous hunger I've never experienced from a partner before, and I'm afraid he may truly stop breathing from the way he sucks, licks, and teases me without ever coming up for air.

I lose all concept of time as he pleasures me. He studies my reactions like I'm his favorite subject, perfecting his technique of stroking, licking, and sucking until I'm begging for release.

Pressure builds in my lower half, the ache strengthening with every pass of his tongue and each suck on my clit.

My thighs tremble beside his head as I fight my orgasm, battling between wanting to come and wishing for this to last.

His eyes flutter shut. "So beautiful."

I jolt as he flicks his tongue over my clit while sinking a finger inside me. My limbs shake as he adds another not long after, sending my nerves into meltdown mode.

"So responsive." He pulls his fingers out to show me exactly that. My entire face flushes, drawing a devilish smile from him.

"So perfect for me." He curls his fingers and strokes my

clit from deep inside, instantly making me see stars. The way Julian knows how to manipulate my body from all angles makes me regret doubting his skills in the bedroom. I've had good sex before…but this?

Julian could teach a class on female orgasm.

I don't have a single thought left in my head as I come with a cry. Warmth floods my body like a tidal wave, consuming everything in its path. Julian doesn't stop his teasing as he continues to pump his fingers, riding out my orgasm with me.

I'm not sure how long it takes me to come down from the high. All I know is that at some point, Julian crawled back over my limp body and caged me between his arms.

I cup his cheek. "You're telling me we've been fighting this whole time when we could have been doing *that*?"

He leans into my touch with a smile. My heart doesn't stand a chance at slowing down if he keeps doing sweet things like that, so I pull away.

His head tilts. "Having second thoughts?"

"No." Although I probably should, especially when he makes me feel like *this*.

"Good." He kisses me one last time before crawling off the bed.

"Where are you going?" I motion toward his thick and equally impressive bulge.

He checks his watch. "Next time."

My cheeks burn as Julian helps me get dressed.

"What now?" I keep my head down as I begin packing up my recently purchased belongings.

"We keep things fun and simple."

My stomach takes a dive off a long, steep cliff.

"Shouldn't we set some rules, though?" I might not have the most experience when it comes to relationships, but I have enough to know it's best to set expectations. That way if I get hurt again, I'll have no one to blame but myself.

He lifts a shoulder. "If you want to."

"I think it's probably best, so we don't set ourselves up for hurt feelings."

"Feelings? What are those?"

With my good arm, I toss a pillow at his head, only for him to catch it with ninja-like reflexes.

"I'm willing to go along with whatever you want, but I need you to be up-front and honest with me."

Right. Easier said than done after the last time I was vulnerable with him.

People will never learn from their mistakes if you don't give them a chance to.

I take a deep, empowering breath. "We should keep this private."

A dark look passes over his face. "Got it."

"It's not that I'm embarrassed or anything."

"Sure."

"I don't want people to think…"

"That we're together," he finishes for me.

My eyes drop to my lap. "Our mothers would get their hopes up."

"More than they already have?"

I grimace.

"What else?"

"We should be mutually exclusive." The thought of him being with anyone else makes my stomach churn.

"We already established that I don't like sharing."

"Obviously, based on the way you acted like a jealous caveman around Evan, Dan, and anyone else who stared at me for longer than a few seconds." My eye roll gets interrupted by a pillow smacking into the side of my face.

Julian laughs, only to profusely apologize after I pretend he hurt my eye.

"Ow." I stick out my bottom lip and sniffle.

"I'm sorry." He kisses my temple, right above my "injury," only for me to break out into a fit of laughter.

His hand moves from cupping my cheek to wrapping itself around my neck. "You played me."

"You have no proof."

His fingers press into the side of my neck.

"Fine." I crack. "I did! But it's not my fault you're so gullible."

He gives my neck one last squeeze before he gives my shoulder a shove. I fall back onto the mattress with a wince.

Panic flashes across his face as he reaches to help me sit up. "Shit. I'm so sorry. Are you okay? I should have been more carefu—"

I fix my sling. "Relax. It was an accident."

His face pales. "On second thought, we should wait until you're cleared by a doctor before doing anything else." He takes a large step back.

"That's not for another two weeks!"

"I'm not going to risk you getting hurt again."

My heart does a betraying dive straight into enemy territory, exposing my weakness.

Him.

I'm not sure how long this thing will last between Julian and me, but I plan on making the most of it—and him—until the time comes for me to leave.

CHAPTER TWENTY-SEVEN

Dahlia

It's easy to spend the rest of the morning in our own little bubble while picking up the party supplies and driving back to Lake Wisteria. With Julian playing our favorite songs from high school while I belt out the lyrics at the top of my lungs, time flies as we drive back to town.

I'm hit with a weird feeling when Julian removes his hand from my thigh, and I mourn the loss as we drive toward the park where the Harvest Festival is being set up.

We both stick to opposite ends of the park while we help his mom with anything she needs for tomorrow's event. Julian holds true to his promise of not touching me in public, although I do catch him staring at me a few times with a strange expression on his face.

I wake up Saturday pleasantly surprised by the way I'm buzzing with excitement rather than feeling heavy with dread.

It's a positive sign I plan on sharing with my therapist during our next session, and one I plan on taking full advantage of today as I head to the Harvest Festival for my morning shift.

Not many people are interested in *buñuelos* at this time of day, so I entertain myself by watching Julian struggle his way through running the *champurrado* booth.

"All good?" I ask when he curses at himself in Spanish.

He wipes his face with the back of his hand. "Perfect."

"Hey, mister. Hurry up! I'm losing my patience here," a ten-year-old hollers from the back of the line.

I laugh as a few others start a chant.

"Thank God I'm never having children," he mutters under his breath.

"No?" I'm surprised I can manage the word with how tight my throat feels.

"Don't tell me you want them after listening to these guys all morning."

I take a huge bite out of a *buñuelo* despite my stomach rolling while Julian makes his way through the line of children at a snail's pace. A few of the kids find their way over to my booth after they pay him, and I set them each up with a mini *buñuelo* and a suggestion to dip it into the drink Julian made.

"That's disgusting." Julian's nose twitches.

"You haven't tried it."

A kid follows my advice, and his eyes light up. "This is *awesome*!" He holds up his hand.

I high-five him before turning to Julian. "Told you so."

"No one likes a know-it-all."

"I wanna try!" The blonde girl I saw with Alana pops out

from behind a group of kids and passes me a hundred-dollar bill.

"Umm…one second." I open the cash register and attempt to gather enough bills together to give her change.

"Don't worry about that." A deep male voice has me turning to find the blond guy I'd seen with her before.

What was his name again? Al?

I hold the crisp bill in the air for him to see. "She gave me a hundred-dollar bill."

"Save it for college." The little girl winks.

While I'm flattered she thinks I look young enough to attend college, I'm mildly concerned that she hands out hundreds like singles.

"Are you Alana's kid?" I throw some batter into the fryer.

"Yup! I'm Cami."

"You know my fiancée?" the man—possibly Al—asks.

"Yup. The three of us went to high school together." I point my thumb back at Julian, who scowls at the man across from me.

"You didn't tell me that, Julian," Al says.

"You didn't ask," Julian replies with a bored tone.

Hm. "You two know each other?"

"I remodeled his house last year," Julian states.

"Of course you did."

Alana's fiancé offers me his hand. "Callahan Kane."

Callahan freaking Kane?

I've been in the presence of American royalty and I had no idea. While Declan Kane, the eldest grandson of the Kane Company's founder, is instantly recognizable given the number of articles published about him becoming CEO, Callahan Kane has been under the radar and out of the press spotlight for years.

If I were an heir to the biggest media conglomerate and Dreamland theme park empire, I would want to stay out of the public eye too. Those reporters are vicious, and I can't think of a better target than three handsome billionaires.

"I had no idea you went to high school with my fiancée," Callahan says.

I regain control of myself. "Julian and I weren't exactly part of the cool crowd."

"No?"

"We were a bit busy making honor roll and whatnot."

"Ahh. Got it." His head tilts and his eyes squint in a way I know all too well. "Wait. Are you that interior designer who has a show on TV?"

My cheeks heat. "Yup."

"I knew it! My sister-in-law is a huge fan of your show."

"Really?" I manage to squeak out.

"Oh, yeah. She binged all your episodes before renovating her house."

"That's nice." My nerves take over because a freaking *Kane* watches my show.

His smile is nothing but warm. "I didn't realize you were from around here."

"Born and raised." I throw a thumbs-up like a complete loser.

"Do you plan on sticking around town for a while between filming seasons?"

"Um…sure."

Julian tenses.

Callahan claps his hands together. "That's great news because my brother and his wife want to buy a property around here, so I'm sure they'll need a local interior designer. I know Iris will flip out if you're free."

Me? Designing a house belonging to the Kane family? I'm afraid I might pass out at the mere idea.

Julian's glare could increase the world's temperature by a few degrees. "She's not available."

"*She* can speak for herself." I turn toward Alana's fiancé with a small smile. "I might be filming by the time that happens, but even if I am, I'd still love to help your family."

"Dahlia!" Alana rushes over. "I should have guessed you would be working the *buñuelos* booth this year." She pulls me into a hug before grabbing Cami's hand and tugging her away from the booth. "I told you no more sweets until after lunch."

"But Cal said it was okay."

Alana shoots him a look. "Did he now?"

He lifts his hands in the air. "You try saying no to her when she does that thing."

As if on command, the girl pops out her bottom lip and wobbles it, making me laugh.

Alana spares me a halfhearted glare. "Don't encourage her."

"He's right. I wouldn't stand a chance at saying no to that kid."

"When you have a kid, you'll understand."

My smile slips as a cold feeling of dread takes over. "I'm sure I will," I manage to say despite the invisible rope wrapped around my throat.

Alana's expression quickly morphs into one I recognize all too well. "Is everything okay?"

Julian's head snaps in my direction.

I plaster on the same fake smile I wore while filming the entire last season of my show. "Yup. All good."

My phone vibrates in my back pocket. I pull it out and read the name before facing Julian. "Hey. Do you mind watching the booth for a second?"

Julian's brows scrunch together. "Everything fine?"

That's the third time he's asked me the same question in the last hour, and while my answer hasn't changed, his concern has.

"Hope so. Be right back." I throw him one last wave over my shoulder before taking off down a row of booths.

I don't answer Jamie's call until I'm out of sight and earshot of any festival attendees or volunteers.

"Hey!" Though Jamie and I haven't worked together long, whenever she hits that high pitch, I know something is up.

"Hi."

"So…" she says. "I swear I wouldn't have called you unless I thought this was important."

"Oh? Is everything all right?"

She pauses for the longest three seconds of my life. "No."

"What's wrong?"

"Oliver was caught outside of a club in Vegas by paparazzi last night."

"Okay." Acid climbs up my throat.

"I think the whole thing was staged."

"What was?"

"I don't know how to say this."

I feel like I swallowed a rock. "What's going on?"

"He eloped."

"I'm sorry. *Who* eloped?"

"Oliver."

I squeeze my eyes shut as I'm hit with a dizzy spell.

"I'm sorry, Dahlia. I wish I didn't have to be the one to break the news to you, but I thought you deserved to hear it from someone in your corner."

My breaths come out in short bursts. The tingling in my left arm has me debating whether I'm going into cardiac arrest or suffering from another panic attack.

Jamie shuffles some papers on the other side of the phone. "According to the article in the *Golden Gate Gazette*, he was reunited with his high school sweetheart during a family trip to the Swiss Alps a couple of weeks ago."

"Olivia Carmichael?" I'm surprised I can manage a single word.

"Yes, but—"

I stop hearing her. It's an impossible task anyway with the way my ears ring.

Oliver's mother wouldn't shut up about how Olivia was the one who got away. With the way the Creswells spoke of the Carmichaels' daughter's perfect pedigree, one would assume the family was breeding horses rather than people.

I bet *she* can give him the perfect kids he and his mother want.

Rage quickly replaces the shock. My emotions rise to the surface, more chaotic and dangerous than a riptide.

Surprisingly, I'm not upset with Oliver.

I'm angry at *myself*.

"Thanks for the update, Jamie," I say despite the tightness in my throat.

"I've already got my people on the phone managing PR. There are many fans rallying behind you on social media."

"That's good."

Her long pause reminds me of a death knell. "But because of everything going on in the media..."

The pounding in my ears can't drown out her next sentence.

"The network is pulling out. They don't want to get involved in all this drama."

"But..." My voice cracks.

"I'm so sorry. I tried my hardest to save the deal, but they thought it was best for you to pursue other options."

"Of course. I totally understand." I try to keep my tone light.

"Give me time to find the perfect home for your show."

"*Right*."

"I mean it, Dahlia. You're talented, and once the dust settles, people will be begging to work with you."

I appreciate her vote of confidence, but the catastrophizer in me is questioning if anyone in the industry will touch me with a ten-foot mic pole after all this drama.

This is your anxiety talking. I try to reason with myself.

Is it, or am I being realistic after losing the deal because of Oliver?

"I've got to go." I hang up the call and walk away from the

festival. Almost all the businesses in town are closed except for one.

Last Call.

Making a choice between crying my eyes out or heading to the bar is a no-brainer, although I'm sure I'll regret my decision later.

You're not supposed to numb your depression with alcohol.

Tomorrow, I plan on confronting my feelings, but today, I need a break. Plus, a few drinks won't send me into a downward spiral.

Or so I hope.

The smell of stale beer makes my nose twitch, but I ignore it as I drop onto a stool across from the bar owner. "Hey, Henry."

"Dahlia? What are you doing here?"

"Getting a drink."

His brows scrunch together. "Are you okay?"

"I will be once you pour me a shot of tequila." I reach for my purse, only to remember I left it back at the booth. "Shit. I forgot my purse."

"I got you." A guy from across the bar lifts his glass of brown liquor in my direction.

I frown. "And who are you?"

"Depends on who is asking."

I look around the empty dive bar.

His lips twitch. "Lorenzo. You?"

"Someone who isn't interested in talking."

Henry snorts as he grabs an empty shot glass and fills it up to the top with tequila. "It's on the house."

"I'll come back and pay you tomorrow."

"I know you're good for it."

I reach for the glass and knock it back. The alcohol blazes a burning trail down my throat, helping with the anger.

My phone vibrates throughout the next hour from incoming texts from Julian.

SECOND BEST

Where did you go?

SECOND BEST

Is everything okay?

SECOND BEST

Stop screwing around and answer me.

His last text makes my entire chest ache.

SECOND BEST

Tell me what's wrong and I'll fix it.

I'm afraid not even Julian, the ultimate fixer, can repair the damage that's been done to my career, self-esteem, and confidence.

But look at all the progress you've made.

Sure, I've improved somewhat thanks to therapy, meds, and taking on a new project with Julian, but the darkness is creeping back in, threatening to destroy all my hard work.

Having one bad day doesn't discount ten good ones.

Then why do I feel like a failure for running away from my fears and drowning my sadness with alcohol?

Maybe because you are *a failure*, the toxic thought strikes out like a venomous cobra.

I hold my glass out for Henry. "Another one, please."

CHAPTER TWENTY-EIGHT

Julian

I pull my mom aside. "Have you seen Dahlia?"

She shakes her head. "Check with Rosa."

"I already did."

It's been two hours since Dahlia took off to answer a phone call. I have tried my best to ignore the churning sensation in my gut, yet it has only grown stronger with time.

I message the family group chat again.

ME

Has anyone seen Dahlia?

LILY

Since the last time you asked five minutes ago? No.

LILY

Try Cisco's tent?

I already did twice, along with all her other favorite local food stands. I'm about to reply, but then my phone buzzes from an unknown number.

"Dahlia?" I ask before the other person has a chance to speak.

"Nope."

It takes me a moment to place the voice. "Vittori."

"Please, call me Lorenzo. Vittori reminds me of my uncle, and he's a real dick." Lorenzo's mocking tone only irritates me more.

"How did you get my number?"

"You're not the only one with connections."

Something that sounds distinctly like Dahlia's laugh has me nearly crushing my phone within my grip. "Is that Dahlia?"

"Yup."

"Put her on the phone."

His deep chuckle lacks any warmth. "I don't think so."

"I'm not asking you."

"Unlike the majority of this town, I'm not on your payroll, so treat me accordingly."

I take a deep breath to stop myself from cursing him out. "Fine. Please put her on the phone."

Something muffles his question, although I can distinctly hear Dahlia rejecting his request.

"She's not available right now."

"Where are you?"

He releases a big, dramatic sigh. "I'll tell you once you promise to end your personal vendetta against me."

My teeth grind together. "Extortion won't make you any friends."

"Maybe, but it will get me a house."

The soft rattling of ice in the background has my ears perking up.

"Speaking of houses, I'm curious why you need one to begin with…" I let the thought drift like chum in the water.

He scoffs. "Wouldn't you like to know."

I pause to listen for any other clues about his location. "I'm trying to figure out if you're competition or not."

"If I wanted to compete with you, you'd know it."

"So that only leaves one other reason."

"Sounds like you have it all figured out." Ice rattles again at his end of the call.

"You can't run for mayor without actually being a tax-paying citizen, can you?"

Blissful silence greets me.

Who knew Lorenzo was capable of such a thing?

"One more. Please." Dahlia's plea is followed by a rough voice I'd recognize anywhere.

"I'm cutting you off," Henry replies in that serious tone of his.

I hang up the call and head toward the one place I'm kicking myself for not checking.

"Dammit." Dahlia's plastic cup clatters to the floor while Lorenzo lands his perfectly on the first flip. The speakers blare a female singer's voice, making my ears ache.

"What the hell is going on here?" The door slams shut behind me.

"Julian?" Dahlia turns on her heels so fast that she loses her balance.

Lorenzo reaches out to stabilize her.

"Get your fucking hands off her." I practically snarl the words.

He lets her go. "Would you have preferred for me to let her fall?"

"I would have preferred for you not to take advantage of a woman. Period."

Henry knocks his hand against the counter. "Hey. I was here the whole time watching them. Lorenzo did nothing but keep Dahlia company."

Lorenzo places a hand over his heart. "Henry? Are you defending me right now?"

He looks away with an eyeroll.

"I'm touched. Truly." Lorenzo taps his fist against his chest.

My patience snaps. "Someone tell me what's going on."

"Nope." Dahlia returns to flipping her cup and failing miserably.

Lorenzo must possess at least a quarter of a brain because he doesn't return to his part of the game.

"What's wrong? Keep going." She points at his cup.

"I think it's time you go home."

"You suck."

"Hey."

She pouts. "I thought we were friends."

"You're not," I answer for him.

Lorenzo scowls at me. "That's not for you to determine."

"Yeah." Dahlia crosses her arms against her chest.

"You're drunk," I add.

"I'm barely tipsy." She taps her nose and spins in a circle like that means anything.

"Either way, it's a bit early to be drinking, don't you think?"

She crosses her arms. "You sound like Lorenzo."

"Over my dead body."

Lorenzo covers his smile with a fist.

Cabrón.

I situate myself between him and Dahlia as I pass their cups to Henry. "Get rid of these. And him while you're at it."

Lorenzo's gaze flickers from Dahlia to me. "I'm the one who called you, asshole."

"What? Why?" Dahlia whines.

Nice to know she feels so strongly against being around me at the moment.

She's obviously struggling, so don't take it personally.

Lorenzo frowns. "Henry recommended it."

Henry holds his hands in the air at the sight of Dahlia's glare.

"Henry?" She frowns. "How could you? You know he's the enemy."

Back to square one. Fantastic.

"Why's that?" Lorenzo leans against the bar.

"Because if he hadn't pushed me away all those years ago, I would have never fallen for Oliver's shit."

Coño.

Henry and Lorenzo's eyes bulge as they swing from her to me.

I clear my throat. "We need a minute. *Alone.*"

"Take all the time you need, kid." Henry hauls Lorenzo out of the bar after flipping the sign from *Open* to *Closed.*

"Hey." I turn her around, but Dahlia doesn't look up from her feet.

I tuck my hand under her chin and lift. Someone could drown in her watery eyes, and I already know that someone will be me. "What's wrong?"

A single tear slips down her cheek. "Everything."

I'm quick to wipe it away, only to watch another follow a similar path.

"Dahlia." My voice cracks, along with something in my chest.

"I don't want to cry in front of you." She wipes at her cheeks with a frustrated growl.

"It's okay."

"No, it's not." She shoves me away when I reach for her. "Anyone but you."

I keep my face blank despite the slice of pain tearing through my body. "I want to help you, *cariño.*"

She unleashes the most heart-wrenching sob. I act on instinct and impaired judgment as I tug her against me and wrap my arms around her, right before her legs give out.

Having a front-row seat to Dahlia's breakdown nearly

Cariño: Sweetheart.

drives me insane with an urge to pummel something, although no one would be able to tell with the soothing way I caress her back.

Neither of us says anything, but I don't need her to.

Whatever it is, I'll fix it.

Whoever hurt her, I'll ruin them.

And whenever she needs someone to lean on, I will be there.

The final thought rocks me to my foundation. Somehow, I went from fearing how Dahlia could hurt *me* to wanting to stop anything and anyone from hurting *her.*

I've always cared about her well-being, that much became painfully obvious after how I reacted when she broke her arm, but there is an undercurrent of something *more.*

I know I will never be good enough for her, but if I can help her heal and protect her from any more assholes, then I've served my purpose.

It takes her ten minutes to calm down and for her tears to relent.

She snuggles deeper into me. "Can you play some music?"

I pull out my phone and search for a playlist before placing it on the bar. The soft strumming of a guitar paired with the melodic voice of her favorite artist fills the air.

At one point, we both begin swaying to the music, our bodies in perfect harmony except for a mishap when I step on her foot. She looks up at me with a small smile that acts like a release valve for the pressure building in my chest.

I cup her face. "I hate to see you cry."

Her eyes focus on something over my shoulder, but I draw them back with a caress of my thumb across her cheek.

"Tell me what happened."

Her chest rises and falls from her shallow breathing. "Oliver got married."

"Come again?" Of all the things I expected her to say, that didn't even make it into the top thousand.

"He had an impromptu ceremony in Vegas."

"Who's the unlucky bride?"

She half laughs, half sobs. "His high school girlfriend, Olivia."

"Should I send a sympathy card on our behalf?"

"Do they make one that says, 'I'm sorry you married him for an inheritance he will always value more than you'?"

My mouth falls open.

Her gaze drops to the floor. "There was a reason he broke up with me."

"I thought we already established that he is an idiot."

"Yes, but that's not the reason he broke things off. At least, not the only one."

"Then why?"

"Because his inheritance is contingent on getting married."

"And?" I press.

"When I found out I couldn't have kids with him, he didn't want to get married anymore."

"Why not?"

Her eyes may be dry, but the look in them haunts me. "We're not compatible."

"What the hell does that mean?"

"The prenup required me to take a genetic screening test with him. I thought it was a normal request—"

"That should be a choice, not a contingency for marriage." I seethe.

"I realize that now." She lets out a heavy sigh.

"Why?"

"Because I wish I hadn't found out what I did. I know it makes me sound so damn selfish and awful—"

"You're not." My hold on her tightens.

"You don't know enough to make that call."

"I know *you*, which is all that matters."

Her eyes swim with unshed tears.

"What did you find out?" I push.

"I shouldn't have a child with Oliver—or anyone else, for that matter."

"Because of some genetic test?"

Her face twists in agony as she nods. "I'm not...compatible...with anybody. I carry recessive genes that shouldn't be passed down unless I want my child to suffer."

Fuck.

CHAPTER TWENTY-NINE

Dahlia

I'm not sure how long Julian holds me while I process everything, but I'm grateful for his company.

Slowly, the grief I felt before fades until I'm left with something I didn't expect.

Relief.

It feels good to talk to someone about everything, even if that someone is Julian. And maybe—just maybe—it was meant to be that way.

He isn't overly emotional and anxious like my mother, who would probably break down crying with me, and he isn't like Lily, who would go into graphic detail about the ways she plans on murdering Oliver. Neither one of them would truly understand me and what I need.

I don't want crying or revenge. I want *this*.

At some point, Julian carries me to one of the booths

in the back of the bar. After spending the last twenty minutes using his shirt as a tissue and his chest as my personal punching bag over the subject, I'm emotionally and physically spent.

Julian brushes my hair out of my face. "Aren't those tests a bunch of probabilities? There's no way they can be one hundred percent accurate."

"Yes, but the risk…I can't consciously bring a child into this world who might spend most of their short life in agony." My voice sounds so small and uncertain.

"I understand."

We stay quiet for a few minutes until Julian breaks the silence.

"Oliver and his family are obviously still stuck in the 1700s, but you know there are plenty of ways to have a child."

My shoulders slump. "I know."

Oliver said the same thing countless times, but his story eventually changed once the terms of his inheritance became clear. He stopped making an effort while gaslighting me into believing I was the problem.

Everything about our relationship imploded, along with my mental health.

"Then, what's the matter?" Julian asks.

I twist one of my rings. "He made me feel…"

He crushes my body against his. "What?"

"Defective." I choke up.

"Did he say that specifically?" The way Julian's voice quickly shifts into something dark and menacing has the hair on my arms rising.

I don't answer—not out of fear for Oliver's safety but because I don't want Julian's pity.

"I'm going to kill him." Julian's expression sends a shiver down my back.

"When did we go from wanting to murder each other to wanting to murder *for* one another?" I tease in a desperate attempt to change the subject.

"Since I found out how much he hurt you."

I bat my tear-soaked lashes. "That might be the sweetest thing you've said to me."

"Don't get used to it."

"I wouldn't dare."

"He never deserved you."

My next confession rushes out of me. "I'm not torn up about him or his marriage."

"No?"

"No. It might not seem like it, but I'm *relieved*. I know all of this is for the best, although I wish my breakup and life weren't so publicized."

"Then, why are you crying?"

"For myself, mainly. And for the show I was promised."

"What happened?"

"The network pulled out of the contract this afternoon after the news broke."

His jaw ticks. "If a network doesn't stand by you for something like this, you're better off without them."

I sniffle. "What if another opportunity doesn't come around?"

"It will."

"You sound awfully confident about that."

His eyes narrow. "I'm surprised you're not."

My gaze drops.

He lifts my chin. "You can tell me anything. I won't hold it against you or think any less of you."

My shoulders slump. "I let Oliver redefine my self-worth. I doubted everything that made me feel like *me* because I thought that was part of growing up. That love was about compromise."

"If you have to change yourself to fit someone's ideal version of you, then that's not love."

I stare down at my clasped hands. "I realize that now."

"What took you so long?"

"Honestly? I forgot who I was before. But then coming back here by myself…it's given me time to think."

We share a knowing look before Julian motions for me to exit the booth.

"What?" I stand on shaky legs.

"How do you feel about getting out of here?"

"And going where?"

"To do something fun."

🏆

I don't realize where Julian is taking us until I see the lit-up Ferris wheel slowing to a stop as Harvest Festival attendees hop on and off.

"No way." I dig my boots into the ground.

"Why not?"

"I'm embarrassed."

His head tilts. "About what?"

"All the stories being posted about me."

"People around here barely read the news, let alone gossip columns."

"But I look like a hot mess." I point at my swollen face.

He closes the gap between us and gently brushes his thumb beneath my right eye, wiping away a spot of mascara I must have missed during my visit to the bar's bathroom. "You look beautiful."

My head spins faster than the teacups in the distance. "You're only saying that so I go along with your plan."

"If I wanted you to go along with my plan, I would have told you about the competition I have planned."

My ears perk up. "Did you say competition?"

His laugh acts like a shock to the system. "Told you."

"What do you have in mind?"

"I'd rather show you." Julian places his hand on the small of my back and pushes me in the direction of the entrance to the festival. I try to shake him off a few times and remind him of our established rules, but he chooses to ignore me while leading me toward the food area.

"Please tell me you're not suggesting a food-eating competition."

"No, but we should get you fed and hydrated."

"I only had two shots of tequila before Henry cut me off."

He shoots me a look.

"Okay. Three. But that's it. I swear. See." I walk backward in a straight line while reciting the Pledge of Allegiance.

Julian rolls his eyes as he steers me toward the barbecue

tent. He stacks our plates to the top with enough food to feed a small family. I can barely eat half of it, although I do guzzle three cups of water to appease him.

My experience with casual relationships might be scarce, but I'm smart enough to know him comforting me like this isn't standard protocol. Neither is me accepting it without putting up my walls.

I didn't realize how much I needed to be taken care of until Julian showed me what I was missing, and I'm not sure how to process that information.

Luckily, Julian doesn't let me get lost in my thoughts as he pulls me away from the food tent. With my stomach full and my head no longer feeling fuzzy from crying and tequila, he leads us toward the opposite side of the festival.

A ringing bell in the distance catches my attention. "Carnival games?"

He stops near a tent and turns to me. "I can't think of a better way to have a friendly competition."

"Is there such a thing as far as we are concerned?"

"I suppose not."

"What are you thinking?" I ask.

"Whoever wins the most games is crowned the victor."

"And what do we get if we win?"

He scratches his cheek. "I don't plan on letting you win, so I doubt it'll be much of an issue for you."

I scoff. "Game on."

Julian and I pick the tent closest to us, which happens to be one of my old favorites, the ring toss. He swaps a few singles for two sets of rings.

"Good luck." He passes me the rings.

I roll my eyes and toss my first ring. It hits the side of the glass bottle before falling to the ground.

He goes next and tosses his ring in a way that comes off well-practiced with how it slides down the neck of the bottle perfectly.

My mouth drops open. "How did you get that on the first try?"

"Nico loves this game."

My eyes narrow. "How many of these games have you played?"

"All of them."

"You're a cheat." I shove his shoulder.

"Don't be a sore loser."

"I haven't lost *yet*."

"Emphasis on *yet*."

I throw my next ring with a little more force this time. Unlike the last one, it hits the rim of the glass, although it never makes it around the bottle.

Closer.

Julian tosses his next two back-to-back, landing both of them like a show-off.

I turn to face him with a frown. "What do you want if you win?"

"*When* I win, I'll let you know."

Asshole.

Julian and I bounce between tents. Thankfully, he picks games that only require one good arm, although my relief is short-lived as he kicks my butt at the ring toss, the dunk tank, a milk-bottle knockdown game, and a shooting hoops game.

Much to his surprise, I win a game of Skee-Ball, balloon darts, shooting targets, and a match of cornhole.

After drinking some apple cider and snacking on a couple of Coney dogs, we arrive at the final competition with an even score.

"Feeling nervous?" I ask.

"Nope."

"You're mighty confident."

"Because I already know I won." He guides me toward the last game.

Someone slams the mallet against the plate, and the bell at the top of the high striker game rings like a death knell. This game was Julian's favorite, so I usually passed on playing it solely because I knew I could never hit the bell like he did.

"I'm down one arm."

"Is your good one acting up? It wasn't an issue for the other eight games."

My eye twitches.

"Do you want to go first?" He offers me the mallet.

"Take it away." I motion toward the base. Despite knowing I lost, I plan on being a good sport about it and at least trying my hand.

He modifies his grip before slamming the mallet down against the metal base. To no one's shock, the metal piece shoots up toward the top and smashes into the bell.

"Winner." The game attendee offers Julian a choice from the wall of plastic toys and stuffed animals.

"*Qué lástima*," I say. "It seems like they're out of blow-up dolls for you."

He flips me off, making a parent gasp as they walk by.

"Sorry, ma'am." He looks away with pink-tipped ears.

"*Ma'am*," I mimic in that rough, hushed voice of his.

"Shut up and lose already." He passes me the mallet.

I step up toward the base while adjusting my grip to match Julian's hold on the mallet. With a deep breath, I swing my arm up before slamming the mallet against the base. The metal piece climbs to the center of the strip, never reaching the bell like Julian did.

"If only I could use both arms." I glare at the bell.

"That doesn't matter."

My eyes roll. "Yeah, right."

"It's more about science than strength."

"*Sure.*"

"Nico can do it, and he doesn't have half your power—even with a broken arm." He passes the carnival worker a ten-dollar bill. "Let me show you."

"Here." I pass him the mallet, only for him to shake his head.

"It's easier if I demonstrate with you." He steps behind me and places his hands over mine.

"You want an excuse to touch me." I speak low enough for only him to hear.

His lips press against my ear as he whispers, "Only because

Qué lástima: What a pity.

you won't let me otherwise." He fixes our hands while ignoring the slight tremble in mine.

"If we smash the plate with all our might"—he swings back with me and whacks the mallet against the base, making the metal piece slide a little higher than mine—"we still won't hit it."

"Why?"

"Because you have to hit it just right."

"All right, Goldilocks. Prove it."

He repeats the same motion, although this time the mallet hits the center. The metal piece skyrockets to the top and slams into the bell, making it ring.

"See?"

I stick out my tongue. "Show-off."

He lets go of my hands with a laugh. "Try again and aim for the center."

I repeat the motion like he taught me. The metal piece climbs higher than before, but it doesn't hit the bell.

He passes the worker another ten-dollar bill. "Keep going."

My eyes slide toward the line building behind us. "There are other people who want to try."

"They can wait."

I try once more, aiming for the same spot Julian showed me. Although I don't hit the bell, I'm getting closer.

"Again." He taps the center of the base. "Right here. Focus more on hitting the target than how hard you hit it."

"All right." I follow Julian's exact instructions to a T, hitting the spot he showed me at the perfect angle with the right amount of strength.

The ring of the bell has me throwing myself into his arms with a huge smile. "I did it!"

He wraps his arms around me, giving me a squeeze, and lifts me up. "You did."

"I don't care that I lost the competition."

"No?"

"Nope! Because that was awesome. I've never been able to win that one before."

"I know." His eyes shine brighter than the flashing light above us.

A few people around us laugh and clap, reminding me of our audience.

"You can let me down now."

He follows my request, turning it into a whole ordeal as my body slides down his.

My cheeks burn by the time I land on my feet.

"You put up a good fight." He hands me the stuffed unicorn he picked out.

"Save me from the fake display of sportsmanship and get on with your gloating."

"Fine. It felt good kicking your ass again."

"There's the cocky Julian I know and despise." I grin.

Before I have a chance to stop him, he steals a quick kiss. It's nothing more than a soft brush of his lips over mine, but it makes my head spin and my heart race like I ran a marathon.

"Sorry." He pulls away and scans the group of random festival attendees waiting for their turn at the game.

"Just…You…We have rules for a reason."

His gaze drops to my lips. "I know. It won't happen again."

Except the strange look on his face doesn't fill me with confidence.

Julian places his hand on the small of my back and steers me toward the other side of the fairgrounds, keeping his touch to a minimum as we navigate the large swarms of people.

"So now that you've officially won, what do you want?" I ask as we near the entrance.

"You'll find out when the time is right."

"Julian!" I grab at his arm, but he steps out of reach before I have a chance to latch on. "Where are you going?"

"Far away before I give in to temptation and kiss you again."

I'm beginning to hate my rule about no touching in public, especially when I'm hit with a sudden feeling of emptiness as he disappears into the crowd.

I was so distracted by his words that I forgot to get an answer from him.

Damn.

CHAPTER THIRTY

Dahlia

While Julian's carnival competition kept my mind occupied last night, I wake up on Sunday at four a.m. with a heavy weight pressing against my chest. I battle between wanting to get out of bed and wishing I could disappear into the dark pit of despair threatening to swallow me whole.

That's the depression talking, I remind myself.

I'll be damned if I let myself sink into deep sadness today, no matter how tempted I am. So instead, I reluctantly slide out of bed, throw on some workout clothes, and head out for a run like my therapist suggested once.

Good for you for getting out of bed, I chant to myself as my sneakers smack against the pavement.

No one but you defines your life's purpose. I wipe my sweaty forehead.

There are plenty of ways to have a child. Julian's words from yesterday ring true, erasing the last bit of self-doubt.

By the time I return home an hour later, I'm feeling loads lighter after challenging every single one of my negative thoughts.

And now that my mind feels clearer, I'm able to take on the second day of the Harvest Festival.

But first…

I pull out my phone and get to work, planning something much more worthy of my time and energy.

After Julian tricked me into losing yesterday's carnival games, I have one goal in mind. Thankfully, Lily, Josefina, and my mom are all on board for my prank since I'm down one arm and need all the help I can get.

"He's never going to forgive me." Josefina unlocks the front door to his office building.

Mom's face pales. "Will he be mad?"

"Mom. Relax." Lily grabs her shoulders and gives them a squeeze. "You're so tense all the time."

She does a quick prayer under her breath before passing over the threshold with bags filled with Christmas decorations.

My prank is silly and unexpected, which will only make the whole thing that much better when Julian enters his office tomorrow morning.

"Do I need to ask?" Lily pulls out a nutcracker smoking a joint.

Josefina and I break out into a fit of laughter while my mom covers her eyes.

"*Ay, Dios. ¿Dónde está la natividad?*" My mom searches through the plastic bags of stuff I bought.

I cringe. "I forgot to grab one."

"No, no, no. That's unacceptable. I think I have a spare one from the flower shop." Mom rushes out the front door and toward the store.

Josefina steps outside and returns with the fake Christmas tree. "Where do you want to put this?"

"I'm thinking Julian's office."

She steers me in that direction. "He'd absolutely love that."

"Wait until you see the ornaments I bought. They're truly one of a kind."

Her cackle bounces off the tall ceilings, making Lily and me burst into laughter too. Mom shows up with a nativity scene and sets it up on a coffee table in the waiting room while Lily gift-wraps Sam's desk.

Josefina and I enter Julian's office and get to work assembling the Christmas tree in the corner opposite his desk.

"What gave you this idea?" She plugs in the cord in a socket, and the bulbs covering the tree flicker to life. The twinkling lights reflect off every shiny surface, nearly blinding us with their sheer intensity.

"Well, it all started with finding the Christmas tree at the art store in Detroit, and the plan kind of spiraled from there."

"Does Julian know?"

"Vaguely."

She laughs while shaking her head. "You two and your pranks."

"Do you think he'll hate it?"

Ay, Dios. ¿Dónde está la natividad?: Oh, God. Where is the nativity?

"Maybe for a moment. He hasn't decorated his house for Christmas, let alone his office."

I gasp. "Like ever?"

She nods.

"That's blasphemous."

"I know. I bought him a fake tree because of his allergies, but it's still in the garage gathering dust."

"Why?"

"I haven't wanted to ask. But I know this"—she motions at the pile of ornaments waiting to be hung—"will be good for him."

"How so?"

"Because this is what life is all about."

My brows tug together. "Decorating?"

"*Living* rather than going through the motions."

Her comment hits far too close to home, so I thrust myself into the task of hanging the first ornament.

Ho for the Holidays.

Josefina breaks out into laughter at the cartoon image of Santa wrapped around a candy cane stripper pole.

"I love it."

"My mom would have a heart attack."

"Should we bring her in to watch her gasp and clutch at her cross?"

I laugh. "Tempting, but we're on a time crunch."

Josefina grabs one of an elf smoking out of a candy cane bong. "Classy."

"Wait until you see the other ones I got."

The twinkle in her eyes has little to do with the lights of

the Christmas tree reflecting off them. "I'm so happy you're back."

Her sentence has two meanings, one of which has my throat getting all scratchy. If anyone understands the ups and downs that come with depression, it's her.

"I'm happy I'm back too."

She wraps her arms around me. "I've missed you."

My sniffle could be misconstrued as an allergy to the Christmas-scented candle I lit, but I know the truth. I lost myself over the years and became a fraction of who I was meant to be, all because I thought that was a part of growing up.

I don't plan on making that mistake again.

♛

According to a late-night Sunday text from Sam, Julian wakes up at five a.m. and works out at his home gym before stopping by the Angry Rooster Café for a cup of iced coffee. Sam, who was sworn to secrecy about the surprise, promised me that the best place to intercept Julian would be at the coffee shop.

So I begrudgingly wake up at the crack of dawn, get dressed, and head over to the coffee shop before he gets there.

"Hey." I wave from my spot at the back of the empty café.

"Dahlia?" Julian stares at me with a pinched expression.

"Morning."

"What are you doing up this early?"

I take a long sip of my iced coffee. "I've decided to take a stab at being a morning person."

"And how's that going for you?"

"Ask me again after my next cup of coffee in ten minutes."

"How many have you had?"

"Not enough to make me want to talk to you at six a.m."

He heads over to the register and places an order for two iced coffees the way I taught him while I drain the rest of mine and dump the empty cup in the nearby trash bin.

He returns with our two drinks. "Here. Can't risk you starting off the morning with only one cup."

I could blame my escalating heart rate on the steady stream of espresso pumping through my veins, but then I'd be lying.

"Thanks," I manage despite the tightness in my throat.

The gesture is as sweet as the drink I take a sip of. While I chalked up his taking care of me the other night to being nice, this feels like so much more.

Go with the flow, Dahlia.

Easier said than done. I've never been that kind of person, thanks to my anxiety and chronic overthinking, so I'm not exactly one to roll with the punches and throw caution to the wind.

If I'm going to crash and burn, Julian isn't my first choice for an eyewitness, but at least he knows me well enough to expect the worst.

Nice job finding the silver lining.

I have an extra bounce in my step as I follow Julian out of the coffee shop. Main Street is dead, with a majority of the shops remaining closed for the post-Harvest Festival blues, also known as cleanup day.

By the time we make it halfway to Julian's office, I'm trembling from the slight chill in the air and the iced coffee in my hand.

"You good?" He peeks over at me.

"Yup. Just cold." I struggle with a button on the front of my pink tweed jacket.

His suggestive gaze explores my body. "Where's your coat?"

"It clashed with my outfit."

Julian catches me off guard as he places his iced coffee on a nearby bench and sheds his coat. He grabs my cup and does the same before helping my right arm into the sleeve of his jacket.

Two sweet gestures in a span of ten minutes? If this is the kind of treatment I get after a make-out session, I can't imagine what will happen once I finally suck his cock.

"Do you plan on sticking around for winter now that the TV deal fell through?" Julian's loaded question seems to kill two birds with one stone as he fixes the jacket to cover my broken arm.

I nudge him with my hip. "Why? Are you trying to get rid of me already?"

"I haven't gotten started with you yet." His tongue darts out to trace his bottom lip.

My body floods with warmth, banishing the chill.

Who needs a winter coat when a few sentences from Julian have my temperature spiking like I'm running a fever?

When we stop outside his office building, he doesn't make a comment about the blinds being closed as he pulls out a set of keys from his pocket and incorrectly interprets the reason for my trembling fingers, swapping my iced coffee for his key.

"Open the door."

Despite my shakiness, I unlock the door on the second

try. I step inside and flip the switch as Julian crosses over the entryway.

The Christmas lights reflect off his dark eyes and face, basking him in a warm glow as he takes in the lobby. "Holy shit."

Out of all the pranks we have pulled on each other over the years, this might be my absolute favorite, and that's saying something since I managed to temporarily dye his skin blue during high school.

"When did you do all this?" He walks up to Sam's gift-wrapped desk.

"Lily and our moms helped yesterday morning before the festival."

"My mom was in on this?"

"How else would we have gotten a key after you banned Sam from lending me his?"

He tries so hard to frown, but it's a losing battle against the smile slowly stretching across his face as he takes in the array of decorations mounting the walls, furniture, and fireplace behind Sam's desk.

"Do you hate it?" I ask.

"With every fiber of my being."

"Will you tear it down?"

"Come January first."

I laugh. "Wait until you see your office."

He ditches both our coffee cups on Sam's desk before taking off down the hall toward his private office suite. I have to run to keep up with his long strides, but luckily, I make it in time to see his face as the door swings open.

His eyes widen. "Damn."

Julian's office looks like the bargain bin section of a holiday store, with the obscene nutcrackers lining the shelves behind his desk and the eight-foot inflatable lawn decoration of Santa riding a dinosaur.

A nice touch, if I do say so myself.

He quickly turns his attention toward the tree standing in the corner beside the window facing the road.

He shakes his head hard enough to ruffle his perfectly styled hair. "This is the tackiest setup I've ever seen."

"I know."

"It could be your best prank yet, but I have to check my list."

His admission makes my cheeks warm. "You think so?"

He smiles at me, and I lose all train of thought.

"Not better than the time I snuck your car onto that floating dock and anchored it to the middle of the lake, but close enough."

I laugh at the memory. "You haven't seen the ornaments I picked out yet."

Julian motions me toward the tree, and I spend the next five minutes showing off all the ornaments I chose, earning a couple of deep chuckles from the formidable man beside me.

He carefully places them back on the branch. "I can't believe my mother was in on this."

My laugh steals his attention from the tree. "In on it? She was practically running the whole operation once I told her about my idea."

"Did you have fun?"

I laugh. "Tons."

"Good." He steps toward me.

"What are you doing?" I take a step back.

"You had your fun, so now it's my turn."

"Julian…"

He wraps his hand around the back of my neck and slams his lips against mine, killing my protest with a single kiss.

CHAPTER THIRTY-ONE

Julian

I wanted to kiss Dahlia since I saw her sitting by herself, sipping on a cup of coffee while scrolling through her phone, doing God knows what at six a.m.

Dahlia isn't a morning person, which should have been my first clue that something was wrong.

Her prank was great—master level even—but I can barely appreciate it when all I can think about is kissing her stupid.

So I do just that.

At first, she is surprised, but it only takes her a few seconds to match my tempo. Her nails dig into my skin from her tight grip around my neck, and I pay back the bite of pain by sliding my hands through her hair and tugging at the roots until she gasps.

Kissing Dahlia feels like a battle of teeth and tongues as I fight the temptation to hike up her skirt and fuck her against my newly decorated desk.

You need to take things slow, I tell myself while dragging my tongue across hers.

You're supposed to wait until her arm is cleared. I groan as she slides a hand over the material covering my cock.

Stop before you can't anymore. I rip my mouth away from hers, earning the sweetest frustrated sigh.

Only a few more seconds, I promise as I tug on her hair and expose her neck.

She teases my cock, brushing the tips of her fingers across it while I kiss, nip, and suck on the column of her throat.

She latches on to my hair and yanks hard enough to have my head snap.

"Hey." I rub at the sore spot.

"My mom would freak out if she saw a hickey."

"Perfect time of year for a scarf." I lean in, only for her to hold me back with a single finger to the middle of my forehead.

"Who knew you were so desperate to mark me?"

"Your neck might be off the table, but your ass is still fair game."

Her eyes widen.

I brush my index finger across the red blotchy skin of her neck. "Would you like that?"

"Not sure, but I'm up for finding out."

"I'll hold you to that *after* you get your cast off."

"Fine." Her deep sigh of resignation can probably be heard a mile away. "I better get to work anyway. I'm on a tight deadline for my décor launch, and I don't want to miss it."

"See you at the Founder's house later?" I ask before she disappears out the door.

"Why?"

"I want to check on a few things and make sure we're still on schedule."

"Still itching to get me out of here?" Her eyes glimmer.

"You knew about that?"

"There was only one reasonable explanation for why you wanted to get the project finished in half the time."

"Perhaps I should slow things down, then." Now that I admittedly want to spend time with Dahlia, there is no reason to rush things.

What happened to keeping things casual? The small, paranoid voice in my head asks.

"Why—" Her question is cut off by the rattling of keys. "I need to see Sam's reaction! Bye!" She darts around the corner, leaving me alone with the silliest smile on my face.

🏆

I'm not sure if Ryder hired another male carpenter to spite me, but he's lucky I need him, or else I'd fire him.

Hell, I'm tempted to do so to prove a point.

The attractive carpenter leans into Dahlia's side under the guise of getting a better peek at her drawing.

My blood pressure spikes. "You there. With the goatee." I keep my voice neutral, although my stiff posture seems to draw Dahlia's attention.

The carpenter beside her looks up. "Me?"

"Well, I'm certainly not talking about Ms. Muñoz."

"Of course not, Mr. Lopez."

"What's your name?"

"Patrick."

"Congratulations, Patrick. You've been promoted."

His brows jump. "What?"

"Go find Ryder outside and tell him I want you working on the Lake Aurora project."

"Really?"

"Yup." I wave him away.

Patrick takes off running for the door, leaving Dahlia and me behind.

Dahlia's brows furrow. "Is everything okay?"

"It is now."

Her eyes light up. "What did Patrick do to earn a promotion after only a day of working here?"

"I needed his skills elsewhere."

"And what about the house?"

"I'm going to take over Patrick's job."

Dahlia blinks a few times. "You can't be serious."

Deadly so.

Jealousy might be one hell of a motivator, but it doesn't change the facts. I'm tired of avoiding what I love because of the pain associated with it. Just like I'm tired of pretending I would rather be in meetings when I would prefer to be out here, getting my hands dirty with every project Dahlia throws my way.

My plan to work on the Founder's house goes beyond jealousy or my need to impress Dahlia.

It has everything to do with *me*.

CHAPTER THIRTY-TWO

Julian

knew it was only a matter of time before Dahlia and you began pulling pranks again." Rafa checks out the tree beside my office door.

"What do you think?"

He glances around the suite. "The whole place is an eyesore."

"Most definitely."

"Do you plan on taking it all down anytime soon?"

"Probably after New Year's." My lips curl.

His brows rise. "You want to keep the decorations up for another six weeks? Why?"

"They've grown on me."

"Oh no," he mutters up to the ceiling.

"What?"

"You're falling for her. *Again*."

"So what if I am?"

"The fact that you're not denying it is proof enough."

I sigh.

He follows with one of his own. "Should I go ahead and warn the rest of town?"

"We won't involve civilians this time."

He glares.

"Or animals," I add.

His lips press into a thin line.

"And I made sure no one will get hurt." *Especially Dahlia.* God forbid she has some crazy reaction and breaks her other arm in the process.

Rafa cocks his head. "What do you have planned?"

"Depends on whether you're willing to help me or not."

He shakes his head. "Hell no. You can both keep me out of whatever is going on."

"You haven't heard me out."

"Anything that makes you smile like *that* is a bad idea."

I wipe the stupid grin off my face. "But I'm going to need your help if I plan on pulling this one off."

"Helping you start another prank war is a recipe for jail time." His arms cross against his chest.

"That only happened one time."

"Do you know that I'm still not allowed to park within a hundred feet of a fire hydrant?"

I laugh. "Must make parking in town a total pain in the ass."

"Which is exactly why I am steering clear of you two."

I clasp his shoulder and give it a squeeze. "Come on. It'll be like old times."

He grunts something unintelligible. Pranking Dahlia again wouldn't only be good for her but also for Rafa, who could use a little fun in his life.

"I can't do this one without you, man."

He glimpses at the ceiling decorated with flickering icicle lights. "Don't you pay Sam to help you?"

"His loyalties are split."

Rafa rubs at his stubble. "Fair enough."

"Does that mean you'll help me?"

"I don't remember you being this pathetic when we were younger."

"Only because you were willing to *prank first, ask questions later.*"

His eyes narrow. "What do you have in mind?"

"Something that will have her sleeping with a light on for the next four to six months."

"I do enjoy scaring people."

"Doubt you have to try too hard lately with your attitude problem."

"Fuck off." He shoves me aside before taking the empty seat across from my desk.

I drop into the rolling chair on the other side. "I never thought I'd see the day you came to your senses."

"Only because you've never been able to pull one of these off without me."

I better enjoy Rafa's playfulness while it lasts and make this prank worthy of his efforts.

With a quick pass over my keyboard, I unlock my computer screen and turn it toward him. "So, here's the plan…"

After spending the last few days rescheduling my meetings and finalizing my new schedule with Sam, I can finally start working part-time at the Founder's house.

The makeshift tent in the backyard is set up with all the tools I need for a project of this magnitude, which makes the process of returning to carpentry easier. I'm not sure I would have been able to follow through with the task if I had to work in my father's old woodshop.

One step at a time.

I fight the ache in my bones as I cover my eyes, nose, and mouth with protective gear. The smell of fresh wood chips and the sound of my tool scraping across the wooden post fill the air as I start working on the first baluster.

It takes me longer than it should, with me being out of practice, but the skills I acquired over the years come back to me.

Remember why you're doing this in the first place, I chide myself when I get frustrated at making a mistake. I toss the wooden post into a pile and grab a fresh one.

This is for you, I tell myself as I start all over again.

It takes me two more tries to perfect the design. "One down, a few hundred more to go." I blow on the post and twirl it in a circle, cataloging every single detail.

My good mood is quickly destroyed when my phone buzzes with new text messages from Sam.

SAM

> Issues with Lake Aurora
> project. Call Mario ASAP.

SAM

> Also, design team wants to meet about
> the townhouses tomorrow. Something
> came up that they need to run by you.

SAM

> Flooring for the cul-de-sac is delayed.
> Should get here in a few weeks.

Balancing my office schedule with the carpentry tasks Dahlia planned is going to be difficult. I haven't been at the Founder's house for more than an hour and Sam is already blowing up my phone.

I rip my protective mask off, place my phone on the worktable, and grab a hammer.

So freaking tempting.

"Whoa. Put down the weapon and step away from the phone." The tent flaps slap shut behind Dahlia.

I drop the hammer on the table. "It's not what it looks like."

"So you weren't about to destroy your phone?"

I glance at her left arm. "You finally got your cast removed."

"Smooth change of subject."

I stay quiet.

She reaches for one of the wooden posts and assesses it from every angle. "This is…beautiful."

"You think so?" I stumble over the words, sounding pathetic to my own ears.

"Your dad would be so incredibly proud of you."

I choke on the ball of emotion building in my throat. "It's nowhere near perfect."

"You're right. It's far above."

A surge of pride floods my system as she places the post back on the table.

My phone buzzes again, and my head drops back with a sigh.

"So, what's going on?" She drags a stool out from underneath the worktable and takes a seat.

My eye twitches. "Having a few issues with scheduling."

"Anything I can help you with?"

"Not really."

Her gaze narrows. "Are you saying that because you don't want to ask for help?"

"I'm saying that because no one can do what I do."

"And what's that?"

"Meet with teams, realtors, and committees each week. Discuss plans and permits and all that boring stuff."

"No offense, but that's not exactly rocket science or anything."

I tuck my hands into the front pockets of my jeans. "No, but it *is* time-consuming."

"Have you considered hiring someone to split your responsibilities?"

So many times I've lost count. "Yes."

"And?"

"I haven't found the right person for the job."

"Have you searched hard enough?"

I go completely still.

She glances up from the wood piece she was focused on. "You have a good team. I'm sure one of them would be more than happy to help take the load off."

"I know." I'm lucky to have people I can trust working for me, and I pay them accordingly, but that doesn't mean any of them are ready for the responsibilities my job entails.

I place the baluster on top of the table and grab another unfinished piece of wood.

Dahlia leans against the worktable. "You know, if you needed a little break, I'd be happy to help you with some of the meetings."

"You would?"

Her shoulders hike. "Sure. I've worked with plenty of design teams and general contractors throughout the years."

"I don't know…"

"Think about it. While the Founder's house has been a welcome creative challenge, I'm used to juggling eight different houses and a hectic filming schedule."

"Don't tell me you're bored."

"Well, that and underutilized." She grabs a two-by-two from my pile and fidgets with it. "Your design style isn't my favorite, but I can put my personal views aside if it means having your full and undivided attention with the Founder's house."

"I'd much rather have your full and undivided attention on other pressing matters." My devious smile makes her scowl.

"I'm being serious, but if you don't want my help, then that's fine."

Her comment sobers me. "You want to help me? Really?"

"Sure. At least until the New Year."

The knot in my stomach tightens. "You still plan on leaving so soon?"

"Without a busy filming schedule, I can finally tackle Design by Dahlia's mile-long waitlist. Some of those clients have been waiting over two years for my services."

"You can't design their houses from here?" The question slips out.

"Uhh…I don't know. I haven't given it much thought."

That's not a *no*, so I'll take it. Dahlia needs a special kind of challenge, and it's up to me to figure out what.

CHAPTER THIRTY-THREE

Dahlia

After spending the last five minutes questioning my sanity, I grab Julian and bring him into the house.

"What are we—"

"Shh!" I whisper.

Julian wipes his forehead with the bottom of his T-shirt, giving me a glimpse of his abs.

A low rumble akin to furniture being dragged across the floor has the hairs on my arms rising. "That! Did you hear it?"

"It's probably Ryder upstairs drilling something."

My eyes widen. "That's not possible. Ryder and the rest of the team left an hour ago."

Usually, I would also have headed out, but I didn't want to ditch Julian, so I stuck around and took advantage of my newly healed left arm. Without the cast, I'm able to work throughout the house on little projects, like paint swatches, testing wallpaper samples, and obsessing over whether or not I should picture-frame mold half the house.

Another scraping noise has me stepping closer to Julian. "I know you heard that one."

"Are you sure Ryder left?" he asks.

I nod. "Positive."

Julian shrugs. "It could be materials rubbing—"

"Together as the house cools down. Yeah, no. I'm not buying it, Mr. I Don't Believe In…" I let the statement hang.

"Ghosts?"

I press my index finger against my lips. "Shh! Don't say the word!"

His eyes roll as the chandelier above our heads flickers.

"Ah!" I shriek and clasp Julian's hand in a death grip.

He attempts to pry my fingers off, but to no avail. "Can you relax?"

I scowl. "You know what happens when you tell an anxious person to relax?"

"What?"

I squeeze his hand harder. "The complete freaking opposite!"

His heavy sigh comes off as condescending. "The electrical crew was here today working on that same chandelier."

A sudden cold draft blasts through the air vents, sending the hairs on my arms rising. "Want to explain that?"

"Explain what?"

"Forget it." My voice drops low enough for only Julian to hear. "I think he's here."

"Who is here?"

"G.B.," I squeak.

"G.B.?" He pauses for a few seconds. "Oh. Gerald Baker?"

"Are you for real right now?" I pinch him between the ribs.

He rubs the sore spot. "Ow. What was that for?"

"Don't say his name aloud."

"Now you're being ridiculous."

I frown. "I swear, it's like you have never seen a scary movie before."

"Why?"

"Because you wouldn't be saying that if you had."

"What happens to the person who says that?" he asks with a neutral tone, although his eyes glimmer with hidden amusement.

"They end up like G.B." I drag my middle finger across my throat and make a slashing noise.

"You're so—" His voice cuts out, along with the electricity.

"Julian!" I wrap my arms around his waist.

He pulls out his cell phone and turns on the flashlight, nearly blinding me. I'm too afraid to extract myself, so I hold on like a baby monkey as he walks toward the stairs.

I dig my feet into the floor in a wasted attempt to stop him. "Where are you going?"

"To go find the breaker panel." He attempts to break my hold.

"No!"

A chilling sound echoes through the house.

Julian's eyes widen.

My voice drops. "What the hell was that?"

His Adam's apple bobs. "I don't know."

"Did that sound like Ryder to you?"

"Maybe a wounded animal got into the attic?"

"Yeah, and what? Bit the electrical cables and caused a power outage?"

He makes a face. "Plausible. It happened once with a lizard that fell into a power box at one of our sites."

I rub my throbbing temple. "Will you stop being so damn logical for once?"

"Would you prefer for me to break out into hysterics like you?"

"I am *not* breaking out into hysterics."

Another hair-raising sound echoes through the corridor above, followed by the ominous sound of a hacking cough.

Julian only makes it up one step before my fingernails are embedded into his arm.

"You can't go up there."

He pats my hand like one would a scared child. "Don't worry. I'll be back."

"No! You can't say shit like that!"

"You're something else." He shakes his head and laughs before darting up the stairs with his phone in hand.

I turn my phone's flashlight on and stay frozen in place as he disappears up the stairs and around the corner in the direction of the east wing.

"Julian!" I whisper-shout a minute later, only to have my call go unanswered.

"Seriously. Quit fooling around and come back here. We can fix the power tomorrow, once it's daytime." I speak louder this time.

Something crashes above, sending my heart into overdrive. "Julian?"

I last four whole minutes without power or proof of life before I walk up the steps myself.

"If he's not dead by the time I get up there, then I'm going to kill him myself." My own voice can barely be heard over the hard pounding of my heart.

"Julian? Where are you?" I call out as I reach the landing.

I call his phone again, but it goes directly to voicemail.

Shit.

A noise similar to heavy furniture being moved around sounds from above.

"Not the attic," I moan to myself.

My neck tingles, and a sensation of being watched makes the hairs on my arms rise.

I don't turn around despite wanting to check if someone or something is behind me. "Hey, Gerald. We come in peace. Please don't kill me or my naïve friend who doubted your existence. I swear he didn't mean it when he said ghosts aren't real."

The feeling of being observed never goes away as I walk toward the stairs leading up to the attic.

I pause at the bottom step. "Julian? Are you up there?"

The door to the attic is shut, and a soft light that matches Julian's flashlight pours through the bottom crack.

I press a hand against my chest, right over my racing heart.

You're Dahlia Muñoz. You're not afraid of anything.

Says the woman diagnosed with anxiety when she was a teen.

Despite my stomach churning, I climb the stairs before

stopping in front of the attic door. After a second of hesitation, I roll my shoulders back and turn the knob.

The door opens with a creak, and I take a cautious step inside. Another blast of cold air hits me from behind, and the door slams shut, causing me to jump in place.

"Hello?" I'm afraid I might burst into tears if anything else happens.

Soft scampering has me turning my flashlight in the direction of the noise.

"Oh, fuck!" My phone drops as I let out a bloodcurdling scream.

A massive, fuzzy spider with beaming red eyes, incisors the size of my fist, and legs the width of my thighs stares back at me.

It moves, and I lose my shit.

"Julian!" I scream.

Light floods the attic, and it takes me a few seconds to process the laughs of the two walking dead men hiding behind the support beams.

"I'm going to kill you!"

Their laughs cut out as they show themselves. I completely ignore Rafa as I launch myself at Julian. He catches me, locking my arms behind my back before I have a chance to wrap them around his throat.

"Gotcha."

"I hate you!" I lift my foot, only to smash it against the wood floor as Julian avoids my stomp.

He tugs me closer to his chest. "That's not nice."

"Neither was setting me up to believe you died!"

Rafa chuckles at his phone screen before the sound of me crying out Julian's name fills the room.

"I can't believe you helped him with this." I jab a finger at him.

Rafa shrugs. "Julian was right. This *was* fun."

"Fun? I'm *traumatized*, you jerk."

The sound of my screams echoes off the walls as Rafa replays my video again while he walks toward the stairs. "Can't wait to send this to the family group chat."

"Rafa! Get back here!" I fight Julian's hold. My phone pings on the floor. "You sent it already?"

Rafa tips his chin in Julian's direction. "Thanks for the invite."

"I'll be sure to extend one for Julian's funeral," I call out.

He turns away and heads down the stairs. "See you on Sunday, Dahlia," he says from a safe distance.

I lash out against Julian's hold, only to pause as I rub against something that shouldn't be hard.

"You're turned on?"

"With the way you've been squirming against me for the last minute, it's impossible not to be."

I fight harder, earning a hiss from him.

Good. Serves him right.

"Cut it out, and I'll let you go," he says while tightening his grip.

I still in his arms. "I can't believe you did this."

"Consider it payback for my office." He pulls away.

I throw my hands in the air. "What I did was cute! This is…disturbing!"

"Were you scared?"

"Terrified."

His head tilts. "Yet you still came to my rescue despite being afraid."

"A temporary lapse in judgment."

"Were you afraid I got hurt?"

I frown. "More like I was scared you got possessed by a demon, but then I should have remembered that's been the case since you were born."

His smile expands, easing some of my annoyance. "You called my name when you were afraid."

"I shouldn't be held responsible for what I said when my life flashed before my eyes."

He traces my bottom lip with his thumb. "What did you see?"

I slowly brush my hands across his chest, earning the sweetest inhale from him. "You."

He cups my cheek. "How?"

"You held me like this." I drag his hands toward my hips.

"And?" His fingers press into my skin.

"And I choked you like this." I latch my hands around his neck and squeeze hard enough to make his eyes widen for a second.

He places his hands over mine, pressing them deeper into his neck. "If you wanted to act out one of your fantasies, all you had to do was ask."

I trace a finger down the center of his chest. "It's not like you would have followed through until my arm was cleared."

"Speaking of…" He brushes his hand across my left arm.

I shiver as he pushes his hips forward.

"It was a sacrifice I plan on making up for tonight."

"Why wait until later?" My fingers tremble with anticipation as I reach for his belt and work on undoing it.

"What are you doing?" He attempts to step back, but I hold him in place by the buckle.

"Use context clues." I pull the undone belt through the loops before tossing it aside.

"I had other plans for you." His deep voice makes my stomach flutter.

"Save them for later."

"Dahlia…"

The slide of his zipper sends a shiver skating down my spine. His abs clench as I kneel and pull his pants down far enough to reveal his straining erection pressing against his briefs.

"Did scaring me turn you on?" I swipe my finger across the damp material covering his tip.

"More than it should have."

"That's sick." I tease his length with a featherlight touch.

"I'm aware."

I kneel before gripping the band of his boxers and sliding them down his thighs to free his dick.

He grips my chin hard. "Maybe I should scare you some more if this is the reward I get."

I tilt my head back so I can glare properly. "I prefer you when you're quiet."

"What—"

I run my tongue up the length of his cock before tracing the tip. His groan has my toes curling within my sneakers, and I repeat the same motion on the other side.

His fingers slide through my hair and hold me in place. "Let me take you out to dinner first."

"We never agreed to a date." I flick my tongue across his tip, collecting a drop of his arousal in the process.

My comment earns me the hottest scowl.

"Open." He practically snarls the word.

My lips part out of surprise rather than submission. Julian doesn't seem to notice or care about the difference as he slams inside. I gag, digging my fingers into his thighs.

It takes me a moment to adjust to his size, and he patiently waits until my eyes are no longer cloudy from my tears.

"Turns out I like you better when you're quiet too." He flashes me the most unhinged grin as he repeats the same move, although I'm better prepared to take him this time.

My attempt at controlling the situation slips away as Julian finds his tempo, fucking my mouth in the most deliciously depraved way. I should hate the lack of control—should despise everything about Julian using me like this—but I'm too turned on by it all to care.

I press my thighs together as his gaze burns a hole straight through my heart.

He chants my name in a hoarse voice that makes my stomach muscles tighten. I alternate between flattening my tongue and sucking hard enough to make him hiss.

He curses as he nearly rips my hair out by the roots gripping the back of my head, and I return the bite of pain by digging my nails into the back of his ass hard enough to leave half-moon indentations.

"Do that again and I'll find a better way to keep your hands occupied."

Fuck him. I'll show him.

I lift the hem of my skirt, exposing my soaked underwear.

His gaze follows my every move as I push my underwear to the side and trace my slit. I'm careful to avoid my clit, wanting to drag this process out.

His muscles bulge as he pauses mid-thrust. "Let me see."

I lift my glistening middle finger into the air.

"Fuck."

My body lights up like the sky on the Fourth of July.

"Show me how you like to be touched."

His demand feels like a test in a way, and I'd like nothing more than to pass with flying colors. He pulls back, giving me a moment to collect myself before restarting his ownership of my mouth.

God. This is so wrong.

I spread my thighs wider and match his thrusts with my own. Every pump of my fingers sends a fresh wave of sparks down my spine, and after a minute, my muscles are trembling.

I play with my clit and shudder at the building pressure in my lower belly.

"That's it, sweetheart." His maddening pace quickens.

The butterflies in my stomach rage and riot at his nickname, threatening to burst free. My eyes roll into the back of my head as I tease myself to the sounds of his groans.

"Dahlia," he chants as I wrap my lips around his cock and suck hard enough to make him shake.

"Fuck, sweetheart. You are too fucking good at that."

Julian cursing twice in one breath? A girl could get used to that.

"Screw this." He pulls out of my mouth, yanks me to my feet, and drags me by the hand toward the wall with the window facing the lake.

"What are you—" My question gets cut off as he drops to his knees, throws my leg over his shoulder, and yanks my underwear to the side.

He gazes at my pussy like one does a work of art—with utter fascination and devotion. My legs tremble, which seems to snap him out of his trance.

He glides his tongue over my slit, sending sparks down my spine.

"Oh, fuck." My head knocks back against the wall.

Whatever self-control Julian had snaps as he alternates between long strokes and deep thrusts of his tongue. He studies my reactions like I'm his favorite subject, his attention never straying from my face, and I have to break eye contact multiple times because what reflects in his eyes excites me way more than it should.

I detonate with a single thrust of his finger and a rough tug of my clit with his mouth. My leg locks around his neck as I trap him against my pussy, forcing him to keep going while I ride out my orgasm.

I'm so lost in my lust that I don't notice Julian's jerky movements until he is groaning against me. I glance down at the mess he made of the floor.

Holy shit.

Julian came to the sound and taste of *me*. I've never felt

more powerful in my life than with him on his knees, still trembling from the aftershocks of his orgasm while he stares up at me with an expression I'm too afraid to dissect.

He got my hopes up once before, and I refuse to fall for it again.

CHAPTER THIRTY-FOUR

Julian

After cleaning the floor and fixing our clothes, I take advantage of Dahlia's post-orgasm bliss before she has a chance to come to her senses.

"Have dinner with me?" The words rush out of my mouth as I grab her hand and tug her away from the attic door.

Her eyes widen. "You were serious about that?"

"Yes."

"Where?"

"My place."

She glares. "I should say no after the prank you pulled."

"But you won't." I kiss her knuckles.

Her brow rises in a silent taunt. "You sure about that?"

"Don't make me beg."

"I'd love nothing more." She pushes on my shoulder with a single finger. "Ask me again. On your knees."

Dahlia is the only woman I would enthusiastically get down on my knees for, and I prove it to her as I follow her order.

I tease her hip with the pad of my thumb. "Put me out of my misery and say yes."

"That's possible?" Her eyes gleam.

"Hilarious."

"Fine. I'll join you, but only because you're doing that sad puppy dog look again."

I had no idea I had one, but I'm glad to have the weapon in my arsenal as far as she is concerned.

"Let's go before I change my mind." Dahlia interlocks our fingers and pulls me through the house and out the front door. We stop in front of her car, right beside the driver's side.

"What are you thinking about having for dinner?" she asks as she digs through her purse for her keys.

I cage her against the door and steal one last kiss. "Takeout."

"So much for being a good dirty talker."

"You asked me what I wanted for *dinner*. Not dessert."

Her skin turns the prettiest shade of pink. "*Oh.*"

I trace the curve of her cheek with my thumb. "Is there anything you're in the mood for in particular?"

"Some sushi from Aomi sounds amazing."

It takes me a moment to process her request. "That fancy place in New York?"

"Yeah." She laughs. "But anyway, joke aside, I'm up for whatever. Surprise me."

"That I can do." I kiss her forehead before grabbing my key ring and detaching the one to the house. "Here."

She gapes at the key. "Moving a little fast, aren't you?"

"Shut up and take it before I revoke your chance to snoop around without me being there."

Her face lights up. "¿*Neta?*" The slight raised pitch in her tone makes the possible blackmail worth it.

I'm positive Dahlia's love for investigating began when she borrowed her first Nancy Drew book from the library, and it's never stopped.

I dangle the key in front of her, keeping my grip tight to stop her from noticing my twitching muscles. "Stay downstairs."

She cocks a brow. "What are you hiding up there?"

My heart thumps wildly in my chest. "You'll have to wait and see."

♆

Dahlia takes off toward my house while I drive to town. While I can't get her sushi from Aomi at the last minute, I place an order with Lake Wisteria's best—and only—sushi spot before they close their doors for the night.

Although I planned on taking the long way back home to give her time to conduct a thorough investigation of my place, I decide differently. I'm afraid she might end up going upstairs and checking out my bedroom solely to satiate her curiosity.

Unlike the usual oppressive loneliness that hits me

Neta: Really?

whenever I turn into my driveway, my body buzzes with antic-ipation as I park my car in the garage and walk inside the brightly lit house.

I'm welcomed by the sound of Dahlia messing around on the piano in the distance. Unlike Nico, she lacks the proper skill and training to do anything but massacre her way through "Twinkle, Twinkle, Little Star."

My spine tingles as I walk through the long hall leading to the formal sitting room. Never have I felt this excited at the end of a workday, and I pause to process why.

No painful silence. No dreadful loneliness. Nothing but a strong sense of contentedness as I think of the person waiting for me.

You're getting attached, the cautionary voice speaks up.

I'm pretty sure it's far more serious than that.

It's *love*.

Something is shifting inside me—that much was made clear when I returned to carpentry after almost a decade avoid-ing it—and it has everything to do with Dahlia.

When she hits the last note, I enter the room.

"Dinner's here."

She startles, banging her fingers against the keys. "You scared me."

"Did you have fun looking around?"

"Tons. Check out what I found next to your prized *The Little Prince* collection." She stands and reveals the *Second Best* trophy she gave me.

Damn. I was so focused on keeping Dahlia away from my bedroom that I forgot about the incriminating trophy.

"I'm flattered you kept it after all this time." She rubs at an invisible stain.

"It's a reminder of what failure feels like." The words come out at lightning speed.

"So you keep it beside your most prized possessions? Interesting location choice given how big your house is."

I blink slowly.

She smirks. "I know you bombed our physics final on purpose."

"You have no proof."

"Physics was your strongest subject and my weakest. There was no way I could have beat you any other way."

I exercise my right to remain silent.

"Why did you do it?" she asks.

The hum of the heater starting up echoes around the house.

Her brows scrunch. "Did you do it because you felt bad for me?"

"No," I blurt out.

"Then, why?"

"Because I *liked* you."

Her eyes widen. "Since when?"

"I'm not sure when it started," I lie.

"Why didn't you say anything?"

"Risk-averse, remember?"

She gives her head a good shake, although it doesn't wipe the disbelief from her face. "If I hadn't kissed you during that Stanford Halloween party, would you have made a move?"

"I had no idea what I wanted back then."

Her brows crinkle with confusion. "But you liked me."

"Yes."

"Then why did you push me away when your dad died?"

"A few misguided reasons, but mainly because I was too proud to deal with my grief in the way I should have."

Her mouth drops open.

"I took on way too much all at once, thinking if I fixed the struggling business or helped my mom through her depression, my own pain would go away."

Her bottom lip trembles. "And you couldn't do that if I was distracting you."

"I should have never called you that."

She reaches for my hand and gives it a squeeze. "I'm sorry for not seeing your actions for what they were."

I rapidly blink. "What?"

I'm the one who hurt her.

I'm the one who drove her into the arms of another man, who ended up breaking her heart.

And *I'm* the one who took ten years to apologize, solely because I was a coward who didn't want to face my fears, instead choosing to let my insecurities about my worth dictate my actions.

"Despite being hurt by all the things you said, I should have put my feelings aside and stepped up to be the bigger person. Because even though you pushed me away, I was the one who made a conscious choice to let it stay that way."

My lungs ache. "None of this was your fault."

"The same can be said about you."

"Let's agree to put the past behind us?"

"Deal."

I wrap my arm around her before steering us toward the kitchen. She sits in my usual corner seat on the island while I fill two glasses with water.

"What did you get?" She reaches for the nondescript paper bag.

"Sushi."

"Yes!" She grabs the top container, only for me to swap it for the other one.

"What?"

"That one is mine."

Her brows furrow.

"It has cream cheese."

The cute way her nose scrunches has me smiling to myself. She rips the lid off the container. "Shrimp tempura?"

"Here." I pass her a large container filled with spicy mayo.

"You're annoyingly perfect at predicting my every move."

I toss her a pair of chopsticks, and she rips them apart before plucking her first sushi roll off the tray.

I don't dig into my food right away, which earns me another speculative glance.

"Are you going to eat?" She points at my tray.

"Yeah."

"Well, get to it." She clicks her chopsticks together a few times.

"What's the rush?"

"Someone promised me dessert."

My heart pauses for a second before returning to its normal pace.

"I'm enjoying the moment," I confess.

Dahlia processes my words with a slow blink. "It's only dinner."

I pop the lid off my takeout container to give myself something to do. "I know."

"We can do this again tomorrow if you want." A faint pink blush creeps up the collar of her shirt.

"Would *you* want that?"

"Depends on how tonight goes." She winks.

I know her words are meant as a tease, but they seem to widen the gap in my chest until the ache becomes unbearable.

Her forehead creases from her frown. "What's that look for?"

"Huh?"

Whatever expression she copies makes me feel ten times more pathetic.

"Nothing." I pop a sushi roll into my mouth to stop myself from revealing anything else.

"You seem sad."

"I'm…"

"Lonely?" she offers.

I nearly break one of the wooden chopsticks because of how hard my fist clenches.

The worst kind of expression flashes across her face.

Pity.

"For how long?" she asks.

Too long.

"Not going to lie, I expected you to be married with a kid by now."

"Married, yes. A kid? Not so much."

"You don't want children? For real?" Her throat visibly tightens from how hard she swallows.

"Not really."

She only frowns harder. "Since when?"

"Since my mom returned from the hospital without my baby sister."

She wraps her hand around my bicep and gives it a comforting squeeze. "I'm sorry."

I halfheartedly shrug. "It's in the past."

She spares me a look. "We're quite the pair, you and I."

"Tell me about it."

Her hand drops. "You know, a wise man once told me there are plenty of ways to have a child."

"Is that right?"

"Yup."

"I think I'll start with finding a wife first and see where life takes me."

"Right." Her grip on the chopsticks tightens.

Cute.

Warmth spreads through my body. "Maybe when you head back to San Francisco, I'll reconsider my mom's matchmaking services."

"I sucked your dick less than an hour ago, and you're already talking about going on dates with other women?"

"Does that bother you?"

Her nose scrunches. "*Ugh.* You're such an asshole."

"And you're *jealous.*"

"No, I'm not."

"It's nice to be on the receiving end of it for a change." I uncurl her fingers, releasing the chopsticks from her punishing hold.

Her gaze narrows. "You said all that on purpose."

"I did."

"Next time you go down on me, I plan on suffocating you to death."

I drag her hand to my lips and kiss it. "I can't think of a better way to go."

CHAPTER THIRTY-FIVE

Dahlia

So, do I get to see your bedroom now?" I toss our empty containers in the hidden trash can beside the sink.

"I have a better idea." Julian grabs me by the hips and lifts me onto the counter. My dress does little to protect me from the cold marble below, especially when Julian pushes it up until I'm completely exposed.

"Here?" I peek at all the curtainless windows.

He drops to his knees.

"Someone could see us from a boat or their dock," I protest.

"Relax." He slides my underwear down my legs before pocketing them.

"But—" My protest dies in my throat as Julian rips my thighs apart and peppers them with soft kisses.

His stubbled cheek scrapes against my skin on his mission toward the spot aching for his attention. He teases me with a flick of his tongue, making me jump in place before he pulls back.

"Should I stop?"

"Don't you dare." My head drops back as he rewards me with another lick.

"Are you sure? I'd hate for someone to see you like this." He drags his tongue toward my clit and presses against it with the flat of his tongue.

"Shut up," I hiss as my fingers sink into his hair.

"You're so demanding." He tsks before sliding his tongue over my clit again.

I'll show him demanding. I throw my legs over his shoulders and line him up with my entrance. "Lick."

We hold eye contact as he collects my arousal with the tip of his tongue. Goose bumps spread across my skin, and he runs his hands across my pebbled flesh as he sinks deeper inside me.

"Fuck." I allow him a few more seconds of teasing before I take control again. Despite how good everything feels, I drag him away by his hair, straight toward my clit. "Suck."

Something flashes behind his eyes as he wraps his lips around it and sucks hard enough for my hips to jolt off the counter.

The scrape of his teeth is something new, and my body lights up at the sensation.

He grins against me before repeating the move again.

Damn him straight to hell.

"Oh God," I groan as he does something with his tongue no one has ever done before, and then shiver when I press my thighs against the sides of his head.

He pulls away. "Your needy cunt is making a mess of my counter."

"This mess?" I spread my legs wider and gather some of my arousal on the pad of my thumb, earning a delicious groan from the man kneeling in front of me.

"I should make you lick everything clean."

"Or you should, since you love the taste of me."

His sharp breath makes me smile.

"I bet you'd like that." I hold my soaked thumb out.

His mouth wraps around it, sending a pleasant rush of heat through me as he licks my skin clean before he bites the tip. "Keep talking and I'll gag you."

"With your cock?"

"Don't tempt me." Julian sinks one finger into me, and my eyes roll as I'm overwhelmed by the sensation. He rewards my moan by pressing his thumb against my clit while adding a second finger.

My head drops back. "If you don't fuck me in the next minute, I'll find a way to do it myself."

"Threaten me again while my fingers are inside you, and I'll stop."

Oh shit.

"You got it?" He curls his finger to reach my most sensitive spot.

"Yes," I moan.

He makes a confirmatory noise before removing his hand. "Be back in a minute."

Julian runs away before returning a minute later, breathing heavily with a shiny condom wrapper in his hand. Somewhere along the way, he ditched his pants, giving me the best sight of his straining erection concealed by his boxer briefs.

"Just one?" I brush my index finger over his bulge.

"I have more upstairs." He tugs my dress over my head, making a mess of my hair in the process.

I'm breathless as his gaze roams over my body, taking in every detail before he pulls me into a searing kiss.

He breaks away first. "I don't know what I did to deserve this, but I feel like the luckiest bastard in the world right now."

The butterflies in my stomach break free in a desperate swarm, making me light-headed.

"The things I want to do to you…" With his index finger, he traces a path from the base of my throat to my pussy.

Attraction we have both spent years ignoring rises to the surface, making my heart pound as he presses the pad of his thumb against my clit.

I want Julian. I want him so damn badly, and I've spent far too long acting like I didn't.

That ends tonight.

"Feel free to skip past the sexy talk and get started because I'm beyond ready."

He dips his thumb inside. "I'm enjoying the moment."

"You tend to do that a lot lately."

"All because of you."

I'm afraid I may not survive the night if he keeps talking to me like that.

I fight the emotions swirling in my chest as I reach for the foil wrapper. I'm a seductive showman, making Julian's muscles ripple and tense as I rip open the wrapper and carefully pluck the condom out of the package.

He sucks in a breath as I grab him by the cock and tug, pulling him closer so I can roll the condom on.

"You could have asked nicely."

"And miss out on that sweet little gasp you made? I think not." I drag a finger across the rubber, relishing the way his thighs strain.

His head drops back with a sigh.

Maybe Julian is onto something when he says he wants to take things slow. I want to catalog every single second of tonight and lock it away in my memory bank because, while I can't have him forever, I can have the memory of us.

With shaky hands, he wraps my legs around his waist. My thighs tremble, and a shiver rolls through me as the tip of his cock slides over my clit before stopping.

He cups my cheek with one hand while fisting his cock with the other. "Are you sure about this?"

Am I sure I want to have sex with Julian? Absolutely. I fear I may combust if we don't, and my pussy throbs in agreement. Am I certain about what will happen after we blur that final line between us? Nope, but I'll be damned if I let my fear of uncertainty ruin tonight.

I place my hand over his, line his cock up, and push until his tip disappears inside me. "Does that answer your question?"

His eyes screw shut. "*Dahlia.*"

I've never heard him say my name like that before, and holy shit, I need him to do it again.

My legs tighten around his waist as I pull him in, driving him deeper. "Repeat that."

His hands shoot out to clutch my hips. "*Dahlia.*"

Sparks fly down the base of my spine, but I'm not able to soak up the feeling before Julian slams into me hard enough to make me gasp.

He fights a tremor. "Shit."

My chest rises and falls with each rapid breath as I take in the pure look of adoration on his face.

Stop overthinking everything.

The trance Julian has over me is broken as he pulls out.

Both of us tremble as he drives into me again. It doesn't take him long to find the most perfect, tantalizing pace, and I'm desperate to make it last for as long as possible.

His fingers grip my hips as he fucks me like a man on the brink of madness, and I'm the only thing keeping him tethered to reality.

I cling to him with desperation. My heels dig into his ass as he switches his rhythm, pounding into me hard enough that I slide across the counter.

He finds the sensitive spot between my shoulder and my neck before he sucks on the skin.

"Hey." I smack him away.

He shuts me up with another eye roll-inducing grind of his hips. His blunt nails scrape against my ass as he holds me in place, fucking me within an inch of my life.

Julian, with his dark, dilated eyes, acts like a man possessed by my pussy as he collects my wetness and teases my clit with it. "You like my cock?"

I fake gasp. "Did my dripping pussy give me away?"

"That mouth will get you in trouble one day." He swipes my bottom lip.

"I hope so." My tongue darts out to tease his finger.

His deep chuckle is the only warning I get before he pulls all the way back until only the tip remains. I get ready to protest, but I'm cut off when he pushes back into me with every ounce of strength he possesses.

I gasp for air.

It's too much. From the sting of his cock stretching me to the pace he sets, I'm a goner.

I shatter around his cock with a loud cry. My vision turns dark as I lose touch with reality and free-fall headfirst into my orgasm.

"*Hermosa*," he says as he tips my head back.

My stomach takes a dive into deep, dangerous waters. Julian swallows my moan with a kiss, pressing hard enough to bruise my lips.

He fucks me through my orgasm while whispering sweet praises into my ear.

"That's my girl," he says without breaking his rhythm. "Look at me." He tugs on my hair until my eyes snap open.

"*Mi preciosa*," he whispers against my ear before nipping at the curve.

Hermosa: Gorgeous.

Mi preciosa: Beautiful.

My fuzzy brain fails to fully process the words fast enough as he comes with a groan.

His swift movements turn jerky before they halt altogether. I brush my fingers through his hair, fixing the strands while he comes down from his high.

"Shit." His forehead presses against mine.

"You liked it?" I'm not usually so demanding in circumstances like these, but Julian challenges me at everything, so I find myself desperate to gain some kind of control over him.

The thought makes me laugh at myself.

No one can control Julian—least of all me. If anything, I unleashed a devious part of him that he has kept locked away, and I can't wait to do it again.

You're playing a game you won't win, the cautionary voice in my head calls out.

Then you better make sure Julian can't win either.

He kisses the top of my head as he pulls out with a groan. "I'm afraid you might have ruined sex with any other woman for me."

Best news ever.

CHAPTER THIRTY-SIX

Dahlia

S o, about my room…" Julian hesitates outside his bedroom door.

"What about it could possibly make you this nervous?" I reach for the knob, only to be blocked by his wide body as he steps in front of it.

He rubs the back of his neck. "Well…"

"Is it your bobblehead collection?"

His head shakes. "No. I got rid of that years ago."

"Thank God, because they creeped me out."

He shoots me a look.

"Do you have porn magazines or posters or something?" I ask.

"Seeing as I'm not a teenager who was born before the internet existed, no."

"Maybe a pocket pussy in your nightstand drawer?"

His entire face turns red. "A pocket—you know what? Screw this." He throws the door open and steps out of the way. "Go ahead."

My feet remain firmly planted against the floor as I take in his bedroom from the doorway. I blink a few times to be sure.

"You... This..."

Julian's eyes shut. "I can explain. It's..." His voice drifts off, along with his confidence.

Everything.

I take a few steps inside and stop in front of the hand-knotted wool rug I designed with Curated Living. It took me a whole month to nail my vision, and I went through hundreds of sketches and samples before everything clicked.

The same can be said for most of the furniture and custom décor scattered around Julian's bedroom. Each piece holds a memory of my career, and I find myself getting choked up as I catalog at least one item from each of my collection drops.

He didn't buy everything, because that would have been excessive, but he purchased enough to prove that he followed each launch and chose a favorite.

A burst of warmth barrels through my chest, stronger than any solar flare.

He supported your dreams without you knowing it.

I blink away the mistiness in my eyes before turning to him.

"I thought you weren't a fan." My voice cracks.

"Of the show? Fuck no." He scowls.

"Of *me*."

His eyes drop to the hardwood floor.

I walk up to his dresser and run my finger across the edge of the ceramic bowl I designed. "Why were you afraid of how I would react to your shrine?"

"That's not what this is." He stumbles over the words.

I laugh. "Then what would you call it?"

"An appreciation of someone who deserves it."

If he keeps talking that way, I might do something incredibly stupid and fall in love with him.

You have rules for a reason. Stick to them.

The tightness in my throat only worsens as I take a tour of his room, freaking out internally over the pieces he chose.

I readjust an already balanced lampshade before turning it on. "You have stuff here from my very first launch."

"I know."

"How long have you been following my career?"

"Since you first learned your ABCs and 123s?"

I shake my head with a laugh. "I'm being serious."

"So am I. I was always invested in your success."

"Even when you were hell-bent on beating me at everything?"

"Even then."

"All this time, I thought you hated me…"

He walks up to me and wraps his arms around me. "I never hated you, Dahlia. Not for a single second of a single day."

"Then why did you avoid me for so long?"

"Because I knew what would happen if I got close to you again."

"What?"

He ignores my question as he leans in and kisses me. This

one is different—*he* is different—and I can't help but obsess over every single detail.

The way his hands cradle my face like I'm the most precious thing in this world.

His thumb softly caressing my cheek, stroking back and forth in a way that has me shivering against him.

The tug on my heart as he answers my question without uttering a single word.

I'm terrified of acknowledging the serious feelings growing between us. He already got close to me once and pushed me away, so who's to say he won't do the same thing again?

Be present-minded and enjoy the moment. My therapist's words of wisdom pop up in my head.

With the way he kisses me like I'm already his, I'm having a hard time ignoring the obvious.

You'll have to admit these feelings eventually, the rational part of my brain adds.

I plan on it…just not tonight.

♟

I half crawl, half hobble out of bed to use the restroom and clean myself up after a second round of sex. When I return and start searching for my clothes, Julian grabs me and throws me back into the center of the mattress.

"Put something on." He hands me the TV remote after climbing into bed.

"How domestic of us." I lay the sarcasm on thick, hoping it will shield the trembling in my voice.

"You haven't seen anything yet." He grabs a book from his nightstand and a pair of reading glasses from a drawer.

I never realized how much I needed to see a shirtless Julian reading a book with glasses on, but I believe the image may have permanently altered my brain chemistry.

I end up cuddling against his chest and watching a *Silver Vixens* rerun while he reads from a leatherbound book I don't recognize.

"What are you reading?" I pause the episode halfway through.

"An unofficial Lake Wisteria history book."

"What?" I sit upright and knock the book from his hands in the process. Thankfully, he catches it by the worn spine before it falls to the floor.

"Sorry."

He places the book back on the table. "Trust me. It isn't as exciting as it sounds. The agricultural talk and detailed accounts of the first few brutal strawberry seasons put me to sleep two nights in a row."

I chuckle.

"Did you know the Strawberry Festival was first started over a hundred years ago as a way to entice farmers into moving here?"

"That's great and all, but I want to know if there is anything in there about Gerald and Francesca!"

He makes a face. "After reading Gerald's backstory and his brothers' reason for moving to Lake Wisteria, I almost feel bad about tearing down all his houses."

"See! I told you understanding history is important."

"I said *almost*."

I huff. "What did you find out?"

"His family moved here because his sister was shunned by their old town after she was caught, and I quote, 'rolling in the hay' with another man before marriage. So instead of staying within the Upper Peninsula, they moved here after hearing about the beaches."

"No way."

He nods. "There were four Baker brothers and their sister, Wisteria, who refused to be called anything but Ria. She's the scribe who kept a detailed account of everything."

"They named the town after her?" I squeal. "How come no one talks about this?"

He shrugs. "Probably because she didn't want people to know her real name. She said the name 'Wisteria' was a dainty mouthful that didn't fit her personality."

I clutch his arm. "What else did she say?"

"She had a lot of great things to say about her oldest brother, including how much heart and love he poured into every house."

"Sounds like one of us."

Julian brushes his fingers over a spot that has me bucking and laughing against him.

Once I calm down, I trace invisible patterns across his chest. "Anything about Francesca?"

"She was from their old town."

"Oh no."

"It gets worse. Turns out she was the mayor's daughter."

My bottom lip wobbles. "*No.*"

"It explains why Gerald never got married to her or anyone else."

"That's so unfair. Gerald and his family sounded like good people." My voice shakes with outrage.

"They were, but what can you do? Not everyone was as progressive during that time."

"It's a shame you're tearing down his legacy, one house at a time, especially after learning why he started this town to begin with."

His scowl makes me shiver. "What else do you expect me to do?"

"Find whatever town shunned his sister and take a wrecking ball to those houses instead." I smile.

His eyes sweep over me. "You'd like that, wouldn't you?"

"Of course. Lake Wisteria needs to be protected at all costs from people like you."

"And who will protect *you* from people like me?" Julian climbs over me, locking my hands above my head as he traps me beneath him.

I lock my legs around his waist and pull him closer. "You're the one who will need to be protected from someone like *me*. Mark my words."

Julian shuts me up by kissing me until I can no longer remember anything about Gerald, the towns, or my own name.

CHAPTER THIRTY-SEVEN
Dahlia

A doorbell chimes in the distance after another round of unbelievable sex. Julian has more stamina than ten triathlon winners, and although I want to keep up with him, my pussy officially tapped out for the night, and no amount of lube or oral sex will change my mind.

"Expecting someone?" I roll off him so he can get up.

"No." He reaches for his phone and curses.

"What?"

"It's my mom."

I jolt upright. "What is she doing here this late?"

Loud banging against the front door has both of us staring at each other with wide eyes.

"My car is outside."

He nods.

"Do you think she will suspect something?"

"I'm pretty sure she jumped to conclusions the moment she saw that you were here."

I throw the comforter over my head. "Don't mind me. I'm going to stay here forever."

He chuckles as he pulls the comforter down. "I'll tell her not to make a big deal of it."

"This is your mother we're talking about. I'm pretty sure she is already calling the *Wisteria Weekly* to announce the news."

"I'll swear her to secrecy."

"It's cold out here!" The doorbell app echoes her shouting from downstairs.

He presses a button on his phone. "I'm coming now."

"And Dahlia?"

Good luck getting out of seeing her.

"I heard that," his mother responds, startling me.

I said that out loud?

Julian muffles his laugh with his fist while I glare at his phone screen.

"Be right there." My attempt at a cheery voice falls flat.

Julian collects our clothes and helps me get dressed in record time before leading me downstairs. I smooth out a wrinkle running down the center of my dress while he opens the front door.

"Ma. What are you doing here?"

"Dahlia!" Josefina brushes past her son and throws her arms around me. "What a nice surprise."

I give Julian a look.

She holds me at arm's length. "Are you okay?"

"Sure? Is there a reason I shouldn't be?"

She shoots her son a terrifying glare. "I saw Rafa's video." She turns back to me. "I came here to give Julian a piece of my mind, but I see it's not necessary." The grin on her face should come with a warning label.

"Oh, I won't stop you from giving him hell." I gesture toward the man standing off to the side with his arms crossed.

"Don't tempt me." She plants her hands on her hips. "Luis Julian Lopez Junior, what were you thinking, scaring her like that?"

He doesn't speak.

I place my hand on her shoulder. "It's fine, Josefina. Julian and I talked it out."

She turns toward me with hearts in her eyes. "Did you?"

"Yup."

"I was wondering why your dress is on inside out…"

"What?" I turn my neck to check for a tag.

"Kidding!"

"*Ma*," Julian groans.

She shrugs. "What? I wanted to confirm something."

"The fact that you're crazy?"

She cackles.

Julian shoots me a look over her shoulder.

"Josefina," I say.

That seems to sober her. "Yes?"

"Do you mind keeping this between us?"

She winces.

"Who did you tell?" Julian grumbles.

"Rosa."

I want to get annoyed, but Josefina truly can't help herself.

The woman was born with a big heart and an even bigger mouth.

Julian glares at his mother.

Her arms shoot up to her sides in submission. "That's it. I swear."

Julian reaches for the door. "Call Rosa on your way home and tell her not to tell anyone else."

Her left brow curves into a perfect arch. "Don't tell anyone *what*?"

"What you saw." He kisses the top of her head before yanking the door open.

Josefina walks outside. "And what exactly did I see?" She bats her lashes at her son.

"Too damn much."

"Don't—"

"*Te quiero. Cuídate.*" He swings the door shut, closing us off yet again from the outside world.

Just how I like it.

Julian tried his hardest to have me stay over, and I nearly caved to his request, but then I remembered our agreement. If I want to protect myself from getting hurt by him again, I should steer clear of cuddling, late-night pillow talk, and sleepovers.

Te quiero. Cuídate: Take Care.

When I wake up the next morning, I find my mom waiting for me in the kitchen.

"*Mami*?" I rub the sleep from my eyes. "Shouldn't you be at work?"

"I wanted to be here when you woke up."

Ah, shit. I knew this conversation was coming once Josefina found me at Julian's house last night, but I didn't expect it to happen so soon.

I place a coffee pod in my mom's Nespresso machine before turning around. "I'm sorry you had to find out about everything the way you did."

"You think I'm upset?"

"Yes?"

"No, *mija*. I'm worried."

Unlike my mom's usual bouts of anxiety, this feels different.

"You came back…so sad. I don't want to see you like that again."

I drop a teaspoon of sugar in my cup. "I'm doing better."

"I know, which is why I worry."

"This is different."

"How so?"

"Um…" *Yeah, it's a hard pass on talking about my sex life.*

"It's not too serious yet," I say.

She makes a noise in the back of her throat.

"We're seeing how things go," I add.

She nods. "You're old enough to make your own decisions."

I'm stunned into silence. I expected my mom to be rattling off about sex before marriage and rushing to have a church wedding to save my soul, not this.

"That's it?" I ask.

She rises from her stool and drops a kiss on the top of my head. "That's it."

"You're not going to warn me about getting hurt or being stupid or something?"

"Julian won't hurt you."

I rear back. "How do you know?"

"The answer is obvious every time I catch him staring at you."

My heart misses a beat. "What do you mean?"

"That man would rather hurt himself before putting you in true harm's way."

I lock my knees together to stop myself from toppling over. "*Mami.*"

"It's been that way since you were kids."

"Do you…" My voice trails off.

"Do I *what?*"

Think he could be the one?

Are you serious, Dahlia? You got out of a serious relationship less than five months ago.

I shake my head. "Nothing."

♕

Lily replays the video of me screaming for the fifth time this afternoon. She has spent our entire lunch together showing everyone who will spare a minute of their day.

At this rate, by five p.m., everyone in town will have seen me losing my shit over a ghost that doesn't exist and a Halloween lawn decoration Rafa found in Josefina's garage.

I rise from my seat to the sounds of the waitress and Lily laughing together.

"Hey! Wait up!" Lily calls after me.

"No." I walk out of the diner.

Lily chases after me. "Stop!" My sister huffs and puffs as she grabs my arm and yanks me away from my car. "What was that about?"

I throw my hands in the air. "I'm sick of seeing that video."

"Come on. You have to admit it's kind of funny."

"It's *embarrassing*."

"I beg to differ. It's so cute how you cry out for Julian." She repeats the part where I almost break into tears.

I bite down on my tongue until I taste blood. "I'm going to kill Rafa for sharing that video in the group chat."

"It would have been a hate crime to keep this gem hidden from us." Lily shows me the screenshot she saved as her phone's lock screen.

"I won't sleep well until I get my revenge."

She rubs her hands together. "What are we thinking?"

"We?"

"You're not seriously thinking of doing something fun without me."

"The fewer the witnesses, the better."

She winks. "Just how I like it."

"You want to help?"

"Of course. You and I are partners in crime."

"Speaking of crime, your friend's brother is a deputy, right?"

Her smile alone could land her on the FBI's Most Wanted list. "Yes."

"Do you think he is the type to willingly arrest someone who isn't actually guilty of a crime?"

"I'm sure he can be enticed into the idea with a gift card to the town's bookstore or something like that. Why? What's the plan?"

"You can't tell anyone."

She holds out her pinkie like we did as kids. "Pinkie promise."

I lock mine with hers. "I'm thinking of waiting until after Thanksgiving so he doesn't suspect a thing..."

CHAPTER THIRTY-EIGHT

Dahlia

Julian and I have fallen into a comfortable pattern over the last few weeks. Somehow, he finds the energy to balance his busy work schedule and me, making time every evening for us to hang out together.

I'm not sure what the standard is regarding casual relationships, but I have a strange suspicion that Julian's insistence on having dinner together and cuddling for an hour after sex isn't it.

Neither are your growing feelings toward him.

The timer rings, banishing my thoughts. I open the oven and check on the turkey.

"Hey." The door to the kitchen swings shut behind Julian.

I wipe my sweaty forehead with the back of my hand. "I thought you weren't coming until later."

"Based on the last photo Lily sent in the family chat, you seemed like you could use some help."

"Remind me to never volunteer to prepare Thanksgiving dinner again."

"It was a thoughtful gesture."

After spending the last ten Thanksgivings with Oliver and his family, I *thought* it would be nice to prepare the meal for once.

I wipe my hands down the front of my apron. "I'm severely underqualified."

"What do you need me to do?" He starts rolling up his sleeves before I even answer his question.

"For the record, you're going to regret asking me that."

"Noted. Now put me to work before I rescind my offer."

I rattle off instructions. Julian follows my mom's recipes down to the last letter, all while making the process ten times more enjoyable for me.

And ten times harder to stay away from him.

Julian goes out of his way to turn cooking together into some kind of romantic date. Him spoon-feeding me under the guise of wanting my approval. The way he pulls me into a quick dance whenever my favorite song pops up on the playlist. How he steals kisses between random visits from Lily, who spends more time taste-testing food than actually helping.

After all the food has been prepped, he traps me against the counter and steals another heated kiss. It's incredible how quickly I've become addicted to Julian in such a short amount of time. He makes it impossible not to crave him, making my head reel with a single kiss and my body buzz with the need for *more*.

He readjusts my headband so my hair is no longer a puffy

mess from his fingers. "Did I tell you that you look beautiful today?"

The fluttering sensation in my chest intensifies. "Only once or twice."

He fights a smile and fails. "Keeping count?"

"Words of affirmation are my love language."

He wraps his hand around the back of my neck. "Explains why you love being called a good girl while riding my cock."

Someone chokes on a cough behind me. I turn to find my sister slamming her fist against her chest.

"Lily." My eyes stretch to their maximum width.

Julian trips over his own feet in his rush to get away, which only makes Lily burst out into laughter.

"I knew something weird was going on when Mom said Julian was coming over to help. I've been trying to catch you in the act all afternoon."

"Now I understand your hourly need to taste-test everything."

She grins while Julian remains silent and brooding.

She gestures to us. "How long have you two been together?"

"We're not," I rush to answer.

The veins in Julian's arms strain from how hard he crosses them.

Lily raises a brow.

"At least not like that," I finish.

"Hm." She glances over at Julian. "Interesting."

"I'll let you two talk this one out…" He speaks to my sister rather than me.

"Take me with you?" I reach out for him, but he sidesteps me.

Julian disappears behind the swinging door leading into our living room.

"Tell me everything," Lily says before I have a chance to consider the weird look on his face.

"Not here." I grab her hand, tug her outside, and shut the door behind us. Fresh snow covers every inch of the porch like a white blanket.

"It's freezing out here!" she whines as she rubs her arms.

"Then we better make this fast."

"Why are we talking out here anyway?"

"I don't want Mom to walk in on us or something."

"Does she know?"

"Vaguely."

My sister frowns. "I'm insulted you didn't come to me first."

"We didn't want anyone to know about our arrangement."

"A little too late for that, so spill."

"There isn't much to share. We agreed to keep things casual."

"Did that seem casual to you? Because it sure didn't look like it to me."

It sure didn't *feel* like it either, but I can barely admit it to myself, let alone Lily.

I swallow the lump in my throat. "We were talking."

"How long do you plan on lying to yourself? Days? Weeks? *Months?*"

"*Lily.*"

Her deep sigh produces a cloud of air. "I'm kidding. I worry about you."

"Why?"

"Because you don't *do* casual."

"No, but it's not like I've had much of an opportunity to try."

And see where that got you.

A strange look passes over her. "It's not as fun and easygoing as it sounds. Take it from me."

My stomach churns. "Is everything okay? With you, I mean?"

Lily recovers with a smile. "Of course. Why wouldn't it be?"

"You sure about that?"

"Yes. I'm more worried about you and whether you'll end up with hurt feelings."

I scoff hard enough to create a puff of air in front of me. "That won't be an issue."

Her eyes roll. "That's what everyone says."

"Yeah, well, this is different. Neither of us is interested in anything serious."

"Are you sure about that?"

I wiggle my empty ring finger. "Positive."

"Make sure to tell him that, then."

My stomach drops. "What do you mean?"

"Julian doesn't do casual relationships. Sure, he agrees to go on dates to appease his mother, but he's not interested in something temporary. That much I know."

My gaze drops. "We would never work long-term."

"I've yet to hear why."

"For starters, we both have businesses to run in separate states." Designs by Dahlia is all I have left after losing my show and my relationship, and I'm not about to walk away from it because of a man.

She shakes her head. "Long distance is an obstacle to over-come, not a reason to stay apart."

A condensation cloud forms around me as I let out a heavy sigh. "I don't trust him not to hurt me again."

"I think your biggest issue is that you don't trust *yourself*."

I let out a low whistle. "Damn."

She locks elbows with me and steers us back toward the house. "You know I'm giving you a hard time because I care about you both and don't want to see either of you get hurt."

I lean my head against her shoulder. "That's why I love you."

"Even if I steal your clothes?"

I check out the pastel jacket she stole from my closet. "Even then."

"Or if I borrowed your expensive face cream this morning and accidentally dropped all of it?"

My body tenses. "Tell me you didn't."

She dashes away before I get a chance to wrap my hands around her throat.

"Lily!" I chase after her.

"I'm sorry!" She shouts before entering the house, leaving an incriminating trail of footprints in the shape of my red-bottom boots.

"Nico and I got the dishes." Rafa stands while Nico groans.

"Don't worry about it. I like doing them anyway." Julian rises from his seat and begins collecting the dirty plates and utensils.

Lily kicks my chair leg hard enough to make it shake.

"I'll help you." My chair scrapes against the wood floor as I rise.

My mom has the most approving look on her face while Josefina winks at me. Rafa's gaze swings between the two of us before landing on his cousin with a pinched expression.

Rather than feel embarrassed by everyone knowing about us, I'm nervous about what they think. I don't want to get anyone's hopes up, least of all Josefina's, whose evergreen smile only brightens whenever we lock eyes.

I ignore their gawking as I gather everyone's glasses and follow Julian into the messy kitchen. Dishes on a normal day are tolerable, but post-holiday cleanup duty after cooking the whole meal?

I'd rather stab my eye out with my new acrylic nail set.

Julian places the dishes in the sink and turns on the tap before grabbing the dirty ones from my hands.

"Was there a reason you volunteered for this job?" I ask.

"I wanted some alone time with you before we got roped into a three-hour Pictionary game." He grabs my hips and crushes me against his body.

"We already spent the whole afternoon together."

He replies by pressing his mouth against mine. The kiss ends as quickly as it began, leaving me wanting more.

"You don't have to help." Julian places the dishes in the sink and turns on the tap.

"Perfect, because I'm only here to watch you work." I snatch the pink gloves from the dish rack and drop them into his open hand.

He shakes his head with a smile.

"I'll go grab the last few plates while you get started."

"Thank you." He reaches for the first wineglass and dumps it underneath the water.

I stack the last few dishes on top of one another while our families gather in the living room, setting up the easel and large pad of paper.

"You and Julian are going to be paired up together," Lily says.

I frown. "Only because none of you want him on your team."

Rafa shrugs. "He's deadweight."

"I heard that!" Julian shouts from the kitchen.

Josefina holds her hands up. "No way was I having him on my team after the last time."

"Remember his version of a cat?" My mom laughs.

"Or when he tried to convince us that whatever he drew was a spaceship."

"It truly was out of this world." Lily's brows waggle.

I laugh as I turn toward the hall, only to be stopped by Nico jumping in front of me.

Dishes rattle as I pull to a stop. "Hey."

He rocks back on his sneakers, making the heels light up. "You don't have to play with us if it makes you sad."

"Why would…" Realization dawns on me, and my knees wobble. "Playing with you won't make me sad."

His brows rise behind his glasses. "It won't?"

I kneel down so we can be at eye level. "No. Before, I was so sad that it made me feel sick, but now, I'm feeling much better."

"Can you teach my dad how to feel better too?"

My stomach sinks.

The light in his eyes dies as I shake my head. "I wish I could, but I can't help with that kind of sadness."

He stares at his sneakers. "Oh, okay."

I put the dishes down and pull him into a hug. "But he is going to get better all on his own because he's one of the strongest people I know."

"Like a superhero?"

"Even better. He's a dad."

Nico's arms tighten around me before letting go.

I stand with shaky legs and fix his lopsided glasses. "I better get these dishes to your uncle."

"Okay. Love you!" Nico takes off, running back to the living room.

I take a moment to center myself before heading to the kitchen with the remaining dishes.

"Shit." Julian shakes his hand with a sneer.

"What happened?" I dump the plates on the counter and rush over to him.

"Burned myself with the stove while grabbing a pot."

"Sorry! I must have forgotten to turn it off." I reach for the knob and turn it all the way to the left before grabbing his hand. "How bad is it?"

"It's not a big deal." He tries to tug his hand free.

I tighten my grip. "Stop moving."

"I'm fine."

Based on the way he hisses when I brush my hand over his palm, I would say the opposite. "We have some of that silver burn cream stuff after Lily had an incident with a curling iron." I pull him toward the fridge.

"Completely unnecessary for a little mark." He wiggles his fingers.

"Stop fussing and let me help you."

His deep sigh of resignation shouldn't be endearing, but Julian has a way of making the most mundane sounds interesting.

I find the cream and open the jar.

He reaches for it. "I got it."

I pull away. "Seriously, what's your problem? I'm trying to help you."

"No need to burden yourself," he whispers to himself.

I didn't expect my comment to elicit that kind of response, which makes me momentarily feel bad. "It's okay to ask for help. In fact, I encourage you to be the biggest burden since it does wonders for my ego."

"My dad didn't need anyone else's help."

"Your dad was also *un cabeza dura*, no offense."

He laughs. "None taken."

"You can admire your father without trying to emulate everything about him, you know?"

He nods. "Yeah, I'm aware. It's a bad habit I picked up as a kid, and now it's more of a pride issue than anything else."

"What happened when you were a kid?"

He gives the door a forlorn glance.

"You can tell me." I press my hand against his stubbled

Un cabeza dura: A hard-headed person

cheek. My touch only lasts a second, but it does the trick of getting Julian to open up to me.

"It's no secret my mom suffered from depression. It started as postpartum after giving birth to me, but then it became more permanent after the miscarriages, a stillbirth, and the financial struggles my parents had."

My nose stings. I always admired Josefina and her battle against depression, but now that I've gone through my own experience, I have a whole new level of respect for her. Little by little, I hope to be as carefree and fearless as Julian's mom.

Julian leans into my hand cupping his cheek. "At first, I didn't want to add to my dad's worries because he was already struggling with my mom's episodes. But then Rafa moved in with my family, and I felt self-conscious about complaining because his problems were so much bigger than mine. Asking for help seemed selfish when he and my mom needed it so much more."

I can't keep my eyes from watering.

His gaze hardens. "It's nothing to feel sad about."

"I'm not sad. I'm…" *Dammit, you* are *sad.* "Emotional."

Julian's face reveals nothing. "Why?"

"Because you've put other people first, even when it meant struggling on your own."

He shrugs. "At least I'm living up to my title of Second Best."

My heart might implode. "Our competitions only made your insecurities worse, didn't they?"

"No. They pushed me to be better."

"You were always the best, Julian, with or without the trophies or accolades."

He blushes.

"Expressing our feelings has never been our strong suit, but I mean it. You're the best son, brother, godfather, and businessman I know."

"I'm the best god*parent*, but we can agree to disagree."

I laugh, and his dark gaze traces the curve of my face.

"Asking for help doesn't make you a burden or less than." I swipe some of the burn cream over his red skin. "So stop telling yourself that."

His body ripples with tension until I finish treating his burn.

"There." I give his wrist a squeeze before taking a step back.

He latches on to mine and holds me in place. "Thank you."

"Thank me by channeling your inner Picasso during Pictionary."

He laughs. "Deal."

Turns out losing *with* Julian is far better than winning against him.

And I can't wait to do it again next week.

CHAPTER THIRTY-NINE

Dahlia

want to take you somewhere." Julian tugs on my hand.

"Now?" I check the empty living room. Josefina, Rafa, and Nico headed out ten minutes ago to see a movie together, while Lily and my mom are busy finding a way to fit all the Thanksgiving leftovers in the fridge.

"Yes."

I must not answer fast enough because he rushes to say, "I have a surprise."

"What kind of surprise?"

"Telling you would defeat calling it one." He leads me toward the front door, but before he opens it, he grabs my winter coat off the rack and helps me into it.

It's the smallest gestures that send my heart into overdrive, like the way he wraps a scarf around my neck and fixes my hair without me asking.

He's perfect.

Which makes him that much more dangerous. The more he takes care of me, the less confident I feel about our arrangement.

I peek into the empty living room. "But my mom—"

"Has plans to spend the rest of the night catching up on a telenovela with your sister."

"If you're trying to convince me to leave, you're doing a terrible job."

"It'll be worth the sacrifice. I swear."

"That's a big promise."

His smile says he plans on delivering.

"Tonight was…nice," I say after the first song finishes playing.

Julian turns down the volume. "I thought so, although your turkey was a little dry."

I slap his shoulder. "Jerk! You're the one who told me to keep it in the oven longer."

"I only said that so you had to keep bending over to check on it."

I laugh until my lungs hurt.

"I like it when you laugh like that," he says in that quiet, shy voice of his.

A rush of warmth flows through my body, spreading all the way to my toes.

"But I like it even more knowing I'm the reason behind it."

Forget a rush of warmth. Julian's words are like an inferno, obliterating whatever ice I had left to protect my heart.

I become fascinated by the window. "When you say things like that…"

"What?" he asks after a few moments of silence.

"It makes me feel *things* I shouldn't."

"According to whom?" His question comes out sharper than a blade directed at my chest.

"Me."

"Because you're afraid?"

"Because I'm a *mess.*"

He focuses on the road, giving me a side view of his jaw clenching. "You're many things, but a mess isn't one of them."

My eyes drop to my lap. "I've only just started feeling like myself again." After fighting my way out of a mental fog, I don't want to sink back into that black hole.

Julian stays quiet, which emboldens me.

"I've been taking the right steps to get better. Therapy. Antidepressants. Exploring who I am post-breakup while forgiving the person I was before it."

His grip on the steering wheel tightens. "And how is that going?"

"I'm finally happy." I take a deep breath. "So freaking happy but also terrified that the feeling might disappear again, and then I'll be sucked back into that dark place."

"It could happen. You could slip back into another depression, and that isn't something you can control."

"I know." I fidget with my hands.

He reaches over and interlocks our fingers. "But that

doesn't mean you have to go through that kind of feeling by yourself anymore." His hand squeezes mine.

"I'm afraid to depend on people."

"Your issue isn't depending on people but rather finding the *right* people to depend on."

It takes me a good minute to wrap my head around that one. "Did everyone see what I was clearly missing?"

"No, although I wish I had." His hold on my hand loosens, so I tighten my grip to stop him from slipping away.

"You wouldn't have known regardless." Keeping up false pretenses was a craft I honed over the years, making sure no one could see through the mask I held in place to shield my anxiety, insecurities, and relationship issues.

"Maybe, maybe not. But I regret not owning up to my actions and trying to reconnect with you."

No amount of deep breathing will save me from the ache in my chest. "We both need to let go of our regrets if we plan on moving forward."

It takes him a full minute to say anything. "I can do that."

"Do you think…" I bite down on my cheek.

He peeks at me out of the corner of his eye. "Do I think *what*?"

"That we could remain friends, even if I move back to San Francisco?"

"If?" His fingers stop tapping against the steering wheel.

"*When*." I power through the next sentence before I second-guess myself. "Our families are so happy that we're all together, and I'd hate for things to be strained again if we have a falling out or things get weird between us."

"*If* or *when* you move back, I don't plan on letting things go back to the way they were before."

My brain takes his statement and runs a marathon with it until Julian interrupts my overthinking power hour by stopping his truck at the intersection leading out of town. "Put this on."

I check out the silk eye mask. "Is this surprise a kinky one?"

"Don't take it off." His burning gaze is the last thing I see before he pushes the mask down, blocking my view.

My body trembles, a fact Julian notices based on his low chuckle.

The engine roars as he takes off again, driving for another twenty minutes before the car finally rolls to a stop.

"Wait here," he announces before climbing out of the car.

I have no idea what surprise Julian has planned, but I can't wait to find out.

He opens my door and helps me out.

"Can I take off the blindfold now?"

"Give me a minute." He grips my elbow and leads me into the unknown. Funny how two months ago, I didn't trust him near me with both eyes open, yet now I'm willingly taking a blind leap of faith with him.

Gravel crunches beneath my boots as we walk uphill.

I strain my ears while searching for clues about our location. "Where are we?"

"Lake Aurora."

"Why?"

"You'll see in a second."

I'm not sure why Julian brought me out here, but anticipation bites at my heels. Lake Aurora was founded ten years after

Lake Wisteria and was heavily influenced by London architecture. With houses of every color and rows of unique townhomes that stretch for miles, the town is a designer's dream.

After ten more steps, Julian holds true to his promise as he rips the eye mask off. I blink a few times, allowing my eyes to adjust before I take in the massive mansion in front of us. The Queen Anne-style matches the Founder's house style, although this one was kept in slightly better condition.

"What's going on?"

He holds up a pair of keys. "You said you were bored."

"So you bought me a house?"

"I thought we could fix it."

"*Together?*"

The slight tightening of his throat gives his nerves away.

"What happened to destroying houses to build neighborhoods?" I ask.

"I still plan on doing so."

"Oh."

"But unlike our town, Lake Aurora has plenty of land to spare without me needing to tear down historic homes in the expansion process."

"I like this plan more and more."

The moon highlights the faint blush creeping up his cheeks. "Do you want to check it out?"

Shy Julian might be my favorite Julian, especially when it comes with surprises like this.

I slip my hand into his and lock our fingers together. "Let's go inside."

The fresh scent of cleaning solution fills my nose as we

walk into the house. The tightness in my chest becomes impossible to ignore as I consider Julian hiring someone to get the house ready for me to see it.

I catch him devouring my reactions like a ten-course meal as we walk through the perfect mansion.

A room full of empty shelves begging to be lined with books and accessories. A sunroom facing the lake and the surrounding tree line. Windows lining the whole back wall, allowing plenty of moonlight to stream inside.

With each room, I fall more in love with the property. Sure, it could use an interior designer's touch, but the bones are stunning, and the view of the lake is a huge selling point.

"I thought you didn't like restoring houses." I turn and find his eyes already focused on me.

"The Founder's house and Gerald's story may have changed my mind."

"Oh, really?"

His Adam's apple bobs from how hard he swallows. "And you."

"I did?"

"Yes."

"Who knew I was such a good influence?"

He wraps an arm around me and pulls me into his warm embrace. "Do you like it?"

"I *love* it."

"Good, because you're in charge of it."

"Me?"

His right brow rises. "I thought you wanted a challenge."

"This is…" *Everything I could have dreamed up and more.*

I blink hard and fast. "What's your timeline?"

"I was thinking the team could get started on demo next week."

My brows jump. "So soon?"

He breaks eye contact. "I don't want you to be bored here."

"Why?"

He takes so long to answer, I almost give up waiting for one.

"Because I want to give you a hundred different reasons to stay."

Wait. What?

"Julian," I plead.

He holds my chin in a firm grip, cutting me off. "I need to get this out." Instead of five deep breaths, he takes one long inhale.

Progress.

"Tonight, when you told Lily we weren't together, I wasn't angry…"

My lungs stop working.

His arresting stare holds me hostage. "I was disappointed because of how much I wanted us to be."

"I never meant to hurt your feelings," I rush to get out.

He presses his forehead against mine. "I know that. We had our rules, and I went ahead and broke them."

"What do you mean?" My voice cracks toward the end of the question as I pull back.

"I'm falling in love with you, Dahlia. I don't expect you to say it back after everything you've been through this year, but I didn't want to go another night without you knowing how I feel. Just like I can't go another day with you thinking I'm okay with us keeping things casual."

Por Dios.

His eyes shimmer from the moon peeking through the clouds. "I missed out on a chance to make you mine before, but I don't plan on making the same mistake again. We're the real deal, sweetheart, and I'm done letting you believe anything else."

My heart soars like a bird released from a ten-year cage of wishful thinking and haunted what-ifs.

Julian doesn't wait for a reply before he bends down and captures my mouth with his. I bask in the afterglow of his admission as he kisses me, making me *feel* the truth behind his words.

Every kiss feels like a promise. Every touch an oath. A vow that Julian will love me, cherish me, and protect me—no matter if I choose to believe it or not.

There is a fundamental shift happening inside of me, and I'm overwhelmed that it all has to do with Julian.

You're falling in love with him too.

The thought is scary, but then again, the truth typically is.

As if he senses my wandering thoughts, Julian tugs me back into the moment by biting down on my bottom lip. He draws blood before licking the evidence away with the tip of his tongue.

I return the favor, earning a sharp hiss I feel straight to my clit. He grabs my ass and lifts me, and I wrap my legs around him before he presses my back against the wall, trapping me as he ravages my mouth.

I swivel my hips, and Julian moans. His nails stab into my flesh as I rub against his cock.

I'm not sure how long we tease one another, but he only breaks away from kissing me to focus his attention on my neck.

"I can't get enough of you." The adoration in his voice has something in my chest twisting. He sucks on my neck hard enough to bruise, no doubt marking the skin.

"We weren't supposed to fall in love." I pull him away by the roots of his hair.

Shit!

Before I have a chance to panic about what I said, Julian distracts me by kissing the spot beneath my ear that makes me tremble.

"What are you going to do about it?"

"I'm not sure yet. Ask me again after you make me come."

He smiles against my skin. "Sounds like a plan."

CHAPTER FORTY

Julian

Telling Dahlia that I'm falling in love with her wasn't part of tonight's plan, but neither was reacting the way I did to her conversation with Lily. When she said we weren't together, it felt like taking a missile to the chest, and nothing could ease the ache but admitting how I feel.

I don't want casual, and I'm done pretending otherwise.

While I'm afraid Dahlia might not reciprocate, I'm more afraid of the regret I'm guaranteed to feel if I allow my fear of losing her to rule over my actions.

There is no place for pride or denial when it comes to falling in love with Dahlia. I got my second shot at winning her over, and I refuse to squander it because of my ego or stubbornness.

I carry her over to the living room, only breaking our kiss to place her back on her feet. She sways a little before reaching out for the back of the couch.

Now that's an idea.

I spin her around. "Bend over." My hand pushes on the small of her back, and she curls over the cushion.

I lift the hem of her dress, exposing her ass.

She squirms with every pass of my palm over the smooth flesh. "Did you plan for all this to happen?"

"I hoped." I push her feet apart with the toe of my shoe. "Get yourself ready."

Her hand trembles as she slips it inside the elastic band of her underwear to reach her pussy. To stop myself from touching her, I focus on grabbing the condom from my wallet and undoing my belt.

The jangle of the buckle stops her.

I slap her ass hard enough to leave a mark. "Stop touching yourself again, and I'll take you here instead." I drag a finger along the crease, and she responds with the sweetest shiver.

She pushes her underwear all the way down. The lace stretches around her ankles, trapping her in place like a pair of leg restraints.

She pushes her underwear all the way down. The lace stretches around her ankles, trapping her in place like a pair of leg restraints.

I don't take my eyes off her as I undo the button of my jeans and slide them down my legs, freeing my aching cock in the process. The tip glistens from precum, and a single pump draws more out.

Fuck.

Dahlia's hand pauses, only to resume her efforts when I catch her staring.

"Like what you see?" I slide my hand up and down.

Her eyes land on my lower half. "Come a little closer so I can get a better look."

"I think I'll stay here and enjoy the view for a little longer."

She leans forward a bit so I can get an unobstructed show of her finger sliding over her slit.

I tug on my cock again, and Dahlia matches by pumping a single finger inside herself.

"Just like that." I grind out the words.

She follows my pace, slow and steady.

"Another one," I command.

She bites on the inside of her cheek as she adds a second finger. My languid pace frustrates her, and I find myself smiling more than once at the small huffs of irritation she makes every time my tempo slows back down.

"Julian. *Please.*"

I pause mid-stroke. "Stop."

Her brows furrow.

"Show me your hand."

She lifts it.

"Another pretty little mess." I lick my bottom lip.

"Clean it," she orders.

I bend down to suck her fingers. Her sweet gasp sends a wave of pleasure straight to my dick, already hard as steel.

I break away to roll the condom on before stepping between her legs. She shudders when I drag the tip past her entrance, coating my length with her arousal. The torturous back-and-forth slide seems to drive her mad based on the noises she makes.

Her patience runs out, and she digs her fingers into the couch before pushing back until my tip slips inside her.

"If you wanted me to fuck you, all you had to do was ask nicely." I grip her hips hard enough to bruise.

"I'm done playing nice." She pushes back some more, and I sink deeper.

"Fuck this." I thrust with enough power to make Dahlia and the couch shake. She claws at the cushions as I slam all the way inside her, pinning her in place with my cock.

Right where she belongs.

She just hasn't accepted it yet, but she will soon enough. Deep down, I know she feels the same way, but my girl is as stubborn as they come. Her fighting against the idea of us is to be expected with our history…but so is my victory.

She whines as I withdraw fully. Sparks shoot down my spine as I slide my cock back and forth over her entrance, using her arousal as a lubricant while I tease it. Every time she wiggles her hips, I nearly give in to her request to fuck her.

I'm a bastard for edging her this way, but the outcome will be worth it. That much I know.

"Please fuck me." Her voice cracks.

"My three new favorite words." I slam back inside her.

Her request might not have been the three-word phrase I would have preferred to hear, but it will do for now.

Both of us groan at the pressure, although I recover quicker than Dahlia and find my tempo. The push and pull between us intensifies as I draw out her orgasm by constantly switching my rhythm. She begs, cries, and pleads for me to let her come, but I only plan on helping her find her release once I'm ready to follow her.

I slide my arm underneath her, and with a few more strokes of her clit, she comes around my cock. It only takes a few jerky thrusts for me to come with a curse. My whole world threatens to go black from the overwhelming pleasure, but Dahlia's lazy grin keeps me grounded.

Her smile rivals the brightest gem, and I'll be damned if anyone threatens her happiness again. She is more valuable to me than anything else, and it's only a matter of time before she realizes that.

And it's my job to help get her there.

🏆

After cleaning up, I drag Dahlia to the couch situated in front of the window facing Lake Aurora. At some point, I will have to drive her home, but I won't be the first one to suggest it now that I have my arms wrapped around her.

"I can't believe you bought a lakefront mansion because I was bored." Dahlia leans her head against my shoulder.

"I'm doing everyone a favor. People get hurt or arrested whenever that happens."

"Rafa got arrested because *you* convinced him to break a fire hydrant."

"He never would have done it in the first place had you not pulled that prank on us with the skunk."

She flips her hair over her shoulder. "One of my finest moments, if I do say so myself."

"I'm afraid of whatever you've planned next."

Her smile borders on certifiable. "Don't be."

"Is it too late to call a cease-fire?" I pull her white lacy underwear from my pocket and wave it.

She laughs as she snatches it back. "Nothing will save you after the stunt you pulled in the attic."

I drop my head back with a sigh. "It was worth asking."

She shrugs. "You'll forgive me eventually."

"You're that confident, huh?"

"Oh yeah. Because you're falling in love with me."

"I'm going to regret admitting that, aren't I?"

"Never. Your precious little heart is safe with me." She taps the spot over my chest.

Rather than focus on the cold thread of fear slithering through my chest, I choose to believe her.

CHAPTER FORTY-ONE

Dahlia

Julian goes on his annual Thanksgiving weekend trip with Rafa and Nico to his Lake Aurora cabin, leaving me alone to process how it feels to be without him. After seeing Julian almost every day, I feel his absence already during the first day—a shocking development to say the least.

My mom, Lily, and I binge the latest season of our favorite telenovela together, which keeps my mind occupied for a day or two, but it never fixes the empty feeling plaguing me since Julian left for the cabin.

Because he fills a void that nothing else can.

A terrifying realization after everything I've been through over the last year.

You knew something like this could happen.

Yeah, well, knowing and experiencing are two very different things.

Despite my fear of getting hurt, my feelings are becoming difficult to ignore, especially now that I know how he feels.

I'm falling in love with you.

I've replayed the memory a hundred different times this weekend, expecting the buzz to go away, yet it remains throughout the weekend and well into Monday.

My heart slams against my rib cage when Julian walks into the Founder's house kitchen with a paper bag I instantly recognize.

I ditch the tile samples and run up to him to confirm the name stamped on the side of the bag.

"No freaking way!" I squeal as he passes me a takeout bag from Aomi. "I thought they didn't offer takeout?"

"They don't."

"Then, how?"

"They make exceptions."

"For a price?"

He nods, and I laugh at the insanity of it all.

I place the bag on the counter and rip it open.

"I ordered a few different rolls since I didn't know which one you liked most."

"Are you kidding? I'd eat anything from there." I reach inside and pull out the first container with a sigh. "How is this possible? They're in New York."

Aomi is the most luxurious and expensive sushi restaurant in the U.S., with most meals costing over a thousand dollars per head since they import fresh seafood directly from Japan. I only went once at my television network's expense and never returned because I couldn't justify the price or trip.

He avoids my gaze. "I hired a guy to pick it up."

"With what? A private jet?" I laugh off the idea.

His lips form a thin, white line.

My eyes widen. "Oh my God. Tell me you didn't."

His silence says enough.

"That's terrible for the environment."

"Are you going to make me promise to never do it again?"

"Hell no. Next time, we'll have to go together to make it worth the carbon footprint."

He shakes his head. "You never cease to surprise me."

"That's why you like me. Challenge, remember?"

He kisses my forehead before stepping away. "Enjoy your lunch."

The excitement I felt about eating seven-hundred-dollar sushi rolls disappears as Julian walks toward the door.

"I haven't seen you all weekend," I say to his back.

He turns. "Did you miss me?"

I bite down on my tongue.

"You did." He smirks.

"Shut up," I snap.

"When you're ready to admit you couldn't stand being away from me for four days, come find me." His eyes glitter as he moves toward the archway.

"Wait!"

He pauses. "Yes?"

"Fine. I missed you. *A lot.*"

"Me too. I considered ditching Nico and Rafa on the second day."

"And that right there is why I'm the favorite godparent." I stick out my tongue.

He spares me an icy glare. "It was for their safety more than anything. I nearly poked Nico's eye out while making s'mores because I was busy daydreaming about the other night with you."

My cheeks flush.

He nods toward my container. "Hope the food is as good as you remember. I'll stop by later and check on you once I'm done with the molding in the dining room."

"Will you join me?" After spending a whole weekend without him, I want a little more than three minutes of his time.

"I was hoping you'd ask." He *winks*. My whole world stops spinning for a second before I gather my bearings again.

"The house is coming along." He stands on the opposite side of the island.

I glance around the half-finished kitchen, taking in the grand, warm oak cabinets Ryder and his team hung last week.

"I like the color of the island." Julian glances over at the deep blue wood paint. "And the waterfall counter adds a nice touch."

"What about the pendant lights?" I tilt my head toward the lampshades hanging above the off-white quartz counters.

"Fits the blend of modern and Victorian you're going for, although I like the vintage light above the sink most."

"Me too. I found it at Another Man's Treasure and knew we needed it."

He steps away from the counter and checks out a few paint swatches. "I like this one." He points at my least favorite one.

I must make a face because he asks, "No?"

"Too dark, especially if we're trying to balance out the island."

"Good point."

Julian and I spend the rest of our lunch break discussing other parts of the house while stealing pieces of sushi from each other's containers. Compared to Oliver's go-to *you got this, babe* reply and general apathy toward my design process, Julian not only seems interested but also gives opinions. We have become a *team*.

At one point, he smacks my chopsticks away with his own before lifting the piece to my mouth himself. Goose bumps spread across my skin as he feeds me, turning a casual lunch into our own version of foreplay.

I love the little ways he shows he cares, like giving me the last piece from his favorite sushi roll or only stealing a single bite of dessert before handing it over, although I know we both suffer from the same unfortunate sweet tooth.

As a thank-you for today's meal, I lift the spoon and feed him the last bit of dessert. His eyes darken as he steals a kiss, flooding my mouth with the taste of peaches.

I tug him closer, not wanting to let him go.

"People are working upstairs." He pulls me to him.

I reach for his shirt. "We can be quiet."

"You just don't want me to go."

Not at all. The more time I spend around Julian, the less time I want to spend apart, and that kind of reliance on someone else is what scares me most.

♛

After Julian went out of his way to bring me sushi from Aomi earlier, I *almost* feel bad about the prank Lily and I have planned.

It only took me finding one of the crew members laughing at my video for me to remember today's mission. Lily assured me the plan is still on, so I need to get Julian into position and let the rest fall into place.

The flaps of the tent slap together after I walk inside. "Oh, good. You're still here."

Julian looks up from the half-carved wooden post. "Yeah. Why?"

I walk around the makeshift woodshop. Based on the number of balusters stacked in neat columns beside him, I doubt Julian has taken much of a break since he arrived at noon.

"I was wondering if you had plans tonight."

"We both know I don't." He wipes his damp brow, spreading sawdust across his forehead.

I walk up to him and wipe it away. "Do you want to get out of here? I'm hungry."

He leans into my touch. "Sure."

"I was thinking we could grab something to eat on the way back to your place."

His brows jump. "Where are you thinking?"

"Nothing *too* fancy."

"That's a relief, seeing as the upscale restaurant options in town are probably closed for the night."

"Maybe another time." I wink.

"What about Early Bird?"

"That's perfect."

Julian holds the tent flap back for me, turning my stomach into a ball of knots.

It's not too late to cancel everything.

I give my head a hard shake. There is no way in hell I'm skipping out on the opportunity to pull the ultimate prank, especially after what he did to me in the attic.

"Should we go in two cars or one?" I bat my lashes.

His thick swallow nearly makes me drop my cover. "You could drop yours off at your house, and I'll drive us to the diner."

"Sounds good to me."

I pull out my phone and shoot Lily a text.

ME

Plan is a go.

🏆

My phone vibrates from an incoming call from my agent before we make it out the front door.

"Give me a second," I tell Julian before answering. "Hey, Jamie."

"Dahlia! How are you?"

"Good. And you?"

"Doing well. I know it's late, but I couldn't wait until tomorrow to call you."

My heart rate increases with each beat. "What's up?"

"We got a new offer."

"Really?"

Julian's face strains as he tries to listen, so I put Jamie on speakerphone to save him the trouble. "An offer from who?"

"Archer Media."

"No way." The Creswells always complained about their growing web of networks and record-breaking viewer numbers.

Julian pulls out his phone and taps away while I process Jamie's news. Until I have a contract in my hand, I probably won't believe Archer Media wants to work with me, especially after being burned once before.

She laughs. "They're in the market for a show like yours for their fixer-upper network."

"Wow."

"And the best part? They're willing to pay you double what you made with your last contract."

My lips part.

"I can get started on discussing logistics with filming in San Francisco. They seem eager to get started as soon as possible."

Julian gives me his back, either out of privacy or to shield his disappointment. My excitement dies with every rise and fall of his shoulders.

"If you're interested, we can schedule a meeting with them to discuss everything."

I shake my head to clear my thoughts. "Yes. Of course I'm interested."

Then why do you sound less than enthusiastic about the offer?

Probably because while renovating the Founder's house, I fell in love with the man who bought it.

Are you considering giving up a television opportunity like this for Julian?

Yes? No? Probably, although I hate admitting it. As much

as I love connecting with families and helping make their dream homes come true one television episode at a time, I also love working with Julian and his team. Just like I love being back at Lake Wisteria with my family.

San Francisco has been my home since I started at Stanford, but Lake Wisteria has my heart…and Julian along with it.

But after spending years of my life catering to someone else's needs, I'm afraid of repeating the same mistake.

Jamie rattles on. "Things are going to move pretty fast because Archer wants to start interviewing potential home-owners after Christmas."

"Huh?" I shake my head. "That's in a month."

"I know. It's a lot to take in, but they're so excited about collaborating with you."

"Great." I try my hardest to muster up a cheery voice.

"They want to meet with us as soon as possible."

"I'm pretty flexible, so I can meet as early as next week."

"Perfect. My assistant can reach out once I nail down a date."

"Sounds like a plan. Thanks, Jamie."

She hangs up, and I turn toward Julian. He is quick to school his features, but it doesn't stop me from sensing the weird energy brewing between us.

"Julian."

"Congratulations," he says with a tight smile. "I knew it would be only a matter of time before you'd get another offer."

Oh God. He's already starting to pull away. "But—"

He silences me with a kiss. This one is fueled by a new kind of desperation that has my toes curling and my chest tightening all at the same time.

I'm hit with a wave of different emotions. Happiness. Sadness. Fear and uncertainty.

I might not have it all figured out, but I do know one thing: Lily was right. My biggest issue isn't that I don't trust Julian, but that I don't trust *myself*.

CHAPTER FORTY-TWO

Julian

I do my best to hide my true feelings about Dahlia's news as we head toward town in my truck. She deserves my support, no matter how much I dislike the idea of her leaving again.

I ask all the right questions and politely listen to all her answers, but her lack of enthusiasm worries me, and I wonder if I'm failing at my attempt to play it cool.

Don't ruin her moment with your bullshit.

Easier said than done, especially once she asks me an impossible question after I park in the half-empty lot behind the diner.

"What about us?" She assesses me from the corner of her eye.

I bite down on the inside of my cheek.

Say something.

As much as I *want* to, I know I shouldn't. She worked hard

for her recognition, and the last thing she needs is me tainting tonight with my insecurities.

So, instead, I undo her seat belt and pull her across the bench.

She places her hand against my chest to stop me. "What—"

I kiss her next question away while lifting her so she can straddle my thighs. She matches my punishing pace, bruising my lips in the process as she seals her mouth against mine.

I worship her body with my mouth. Tongue. Hands. Not a single spot within reach remains untouched, and she mirrors my desperation with her own.

Her fingers embed themselves into my shoulders as she grinds against me until the front of my pants is soaked with her need. I dig my fingers into her hips and lift her back and forth, earning a hiss and a tug on my hair as she presses on my straining cock.

"Julian." She tugs my head to the side by pulling on my hair. "We need to talk."

"Let's talk after? *Please*." I throw her back on the bench.

She parts her thighs. "Okay, fine, but what if someone sees us?"

"No one is around." I tuck my legs in the cramped spot between the gas pedal and the bench before lining my face up with her pussy.

She rises onto her elbows and scans the parking lot. "*Yet*."

I slap her pussy hard enough to knock the air from her lungs. "Focus on me, sweetheart."

Dahlia wants to know what will happen to us once she accepts the offer, and I want to make my intentions obvious.

Words were never my strong suit, so I would rather show her instead.

She cuts me a look as I lift the hem of her skirt toward her stomach. I lean forward, drag my nose over her underwear, and take a deep breath, making her blown-out eyes go wider.

I nip at the material, and her head drops back with a sigh as I slide her soaked undergarment down her legs. Goose bumps cover her skin, and I trace my way back toward her dripping center with my calloused hands.

Her legs drop to the side as I crawl between them and kiss her.

She slides her fingers into my hair and tugs. "We need to make this fast."

"Why?"

She answers by pulling me toward her. I quickly become distracted by her pussy and pleasuring her with my tongue. Her moans of encouragement fuel me, driving me closer to the edge of insanity.

I thrust my tongue, and she jolts with a gasp. My fingers soon replace my tongue, turning her into a writhing mess beneath me as they work in tandem.

Every time she gets close to the edge, I pull back, wanting to prolong the moment.

"Julian," she whispers with a harsh breath.

I suck on her clit and curl my fingers inside her.

She shakes her head. "It's too much."

There's no such thing wherever she is concerned.

"You can take it." I tease the sensitive spot inside her, earning another sharp inhale.

She claws at my hand. "Please let me come."

"Such good manners." I press my thumb against her clit.

Her thighs stick to the leather bench beneath her—both from her arousal and the sweat clinging to her skin. She shakes as I tease that spot again until she erupts on my fingers. I sit back up and tug my pants down far enough to get on a condom.

Dahlia trembles as she begins to come down from her high, although I don't let her fully return to reality as I have her straddle me again.

"Remember how I won the competition at the Harvest Festival?"

A moment of clarity passes over her. "Yes."

"You promised me anything I wanted."

"Did you finally decide?" Confusion bleeds into her voice.

My grip on her hips tightens. "Yes. I want you to answer one question honestly."

"That's it?"

I nod.

"What do you want to know?"

"Are you falling in love with me?"

No hesitating. No deep breaths. No questioning myself or whether asking her was a mistake.

Tell me this isn't all in my head.

Give me something to hold on to before I lose hope of us getting a real chance.

Show me that we can survive anything, your long-distance job and trust issues included.

The whooshing sound of my heart pounding fills my ears, so I nearly miss her answer.

"Yes."

All my thoughts scatter as warmth radiates through my chest, burning a path from my heart to my lower half.

With a full-body tremble, she rises to her knees and slides down my cock until she is fully seated. My thighs shake beneath her as I fight the pleasure threatening to consume every rational thought.

Dahlia was made for me, and I won't let another day go by where she doesn't know it.

"I want to hear it." My nails bite into her skin.

"Yes, I'm falling in love with you, but I don't know how I will ever get over—"

I lift her and slam her back down, cutting her off midsentence. "We'll figure the rest out."

"But—"

I repeat the same action while switching angles, earning a spine-tingling rush as she takes every inch.

Dahlia holds on to my shoulders while she follows the pace I set. My pleasure climbs as she glides up and down my cock, working herself to my groans of appreciation.

Her tempo changes, desperation biting at our heels as Dahlia chases her release. I'm not too far off, although I refuse to let go until she does.

At one point, I take over, holding her down by the shoulders as I pump into her from below. A galaxy of stars explodes behind my eyes as she clenches around my cock with the sweetest moan.

The angle sets her off, and it only takes a few thrusts for her to shatter around me with a cry. I don't stop moving as I fuck her through her orgasm. My fingers dig into her shoulder as I hold her in place, her pussy clenching around me like a vise custom-made to drive me wild.

She bites into my shoulder to muffle her cry, and my cock drips in response. I find my pace again, her pussy making it impossible to think as I slide in and out.

She kisses my forehead. My cheeks. The slope of my neck and the spot right below my ear that makes me shiver.

Sex with her has always felt incredible, but this…this is fucking phenomenal.

I'm falling in love with you. Her soft confession replays in my head.

I grip her hips as I come harder than ever before. My mind goes blank, and my vision turns dark as every nerve in my body goes haywire.

My orgasm was a life-altering event, and I'm afraid I'll never be the same again.

"Fuck." I smack the back of my head against the seat.

She gently holds my head between her hands and kisses me.

It takes every ounce of willpower to pull away. "About what happened earlier—"

A hard knock against the glass has our eyes widening. Dahlia turns and shrieks at Deputy Roberts, the thirty-five-year-old man-child, pointing a flashlight directly at us.

Mierda. Of all the people in town to find us, it had to be him.

Good luck talking your way out of this one.

"Put your clothes on and step out of the vehicle with your hands in the air." He turns around to give us some privacy.

"Oh fuck."

CHAPTER FORTY-THREE

Dahlia

My limbs are useless, so Julian carefully removes me from his lap and places me on the bench seat before taking care of the used condom. The rapid thump of my heart gets stronger as I consider the deputy standing outside the truck. I don't recognize him as the guy Lily and I met up with to discuss the prank, which only makes the acid churning in my stomach worse.

"What do we do?" I'm not sure how I manage to formulate a full sentence, but I do.

Julian shakes his head. "I don't know."

"Awesome." Panic bubbles inside me, the pressure becoming unbearable with every shallow breath. "Is he going to arrest us?"

Blue and red lights flash over his face. "I wouldn't put it past him."

"That's reassuring."

"Everything will be fine."

"Fine?" My pitch rises. "How is any of this *fine*?" I reach out for the dashboard as a wave of dizziness consumes me. "He's going to recognize me, and then this is going to make it onto the news, and everyone I know will find out, and I will lose the Archer deal only thirty minutes after receiving it."

Julian interlocks our fingers and tucks my hand against his chest. "Breathe." He demonstrates, and I follow along.

"Everything will be fine because you have me, and I'm not going to let anything bad happen to you," he responds between deep inhales. "This isn't going to make it onto the news, and Archer isn't going to find out about a silly misunderstanding."

Julian's confidence eases some of my panic, along with his forcing me to take big gulps of air. He helps fix my clothes, which I'm grateful for given how hard my hands are shaking.

"Dahlia." He lifts my chin up, but I avoid meeting his gaze.

He sighs. "About what you said earlier—"

"I don't want to talk about it." Not now, and maybe not ever.

I hadn't meant to confess my feelings when I barely understand them myself, but Julian didn't give me much of an option.

Now look at the mess you got yourself into.

"Do you plan on acting like you didn't admit that you're falling in love with me?"

"Seems on brand for me."

"Seems like bullshit."

I flinch. He reaches out for my trembling hand again and gives it a reassuring squeeze I don't entirely deserve.

Which is exactly why you're going to pack your bags and go back to San Francisco before either one of you gets hurt.

Except my plan quickly falls apart when my chest aches at pushing Julian away like he did to me all those years ago.

He deserves better than that from you.

I jolt at the deputy knocking on the window with his flashlight. "As entertaining as this show is, wrap it up. It's cold out here, and I'm losing my patience."

My nails bite into my thighs. "God. I hate this man, and I don't even know him."

"Consider that a blessing."

I hop out of the truck on shaky legs. The brisk December breeze hits me, making me shiver.

"Dahlia Muñoz?" A deputy I don't recognize calls my name. "Surprised to see you here."

"Um, where's Ben?" I scan the police cruiser parked beside Julian's truck for the man I planned the prank with.

He shoots me a confused look. "Last I heard, he was answering another call."

"Oh. Does he plan on coming here to back you up?" Maybe Lily changed the plan at the last minute so I wouldn't give anything away.

That little shit. I wouldn't put it past her.

"I think I can handle this civil disturbance on my own."

My stomach churns. "Civil disturbance?"

"Someone called to report two people having sex in a public parking lot."

Despite the chilly temperature outside, I break out into a sweat.

Julian walks around the back of the truck and stands beside me without touching me. "Deputy Roberts."

"Julian," the deputy sneers. "I thought it was you, but I wasn't sure with the dark tints."

Uh-oh.

I can tell based on Julian's rigid posture and the way Deputy Roberts reaches for his taser that these two have history.

The really, *really* bad kind.

"What can we do for you?" Julian grazes his pinky against mine.

I'm here, he silently says.

The gesture only seems to make the tightness in my chest worse.

"I received a complaint about inappropriate conduct and public nudity."

Julian rubs the back of his neck. "Right."

"You are aware that it's illegal to have sex in a public location, correct?"

"I am aware, yes."

"Julian!" I shout. Rule number one of dealing with cops: never admit guilt.

He realizes his mistake too late.

Deputy Roberts reaches for his cuffs. "Turn around, Lopez."

"Excuse me?"

"I've been waiting for this moment."

What?

Julian doesn't follow the deputy's instructions. "You're seriously going to arrest me for this?"

"I was thinking about detaining you, but keep running your mouth, and I'll be tempted to charge you."

Julian doesn't blink. "How much will it cost to make this all go away?"

I drag my hand across my throat in desperation. *Shut up! Shut up! Shut up!* I mouth.

"Add bribing an officer to your list of crimes tonight. Now, turn around and put your hands behind your back." He motions with the cuffs.

"This is ridiculous," Julian says.

"Do what he says," I whisper.

He spins around and locks his hands together.

Deputy Roberts makes quick work of the cuffs before turning to me. "Your turn."

"Me?" My pitch rises.

"Mr. Lopez wasn't having sex alone, was he?"

I blush from my head to my toes.

He gestures with his cuffs. "Turn around and put your hands behind your back like Mr. Lopez so kindly demonstrated."

"Leave her out of this." Julian's lethal tone draws a shiver from me.

"And miss out on an opportunity to piss you off? I don't think so."

My eyes widen at the deputy. "Why do you hate him so much?"

"Ask him that." He points the handcuffs in Julian's direction.

Julian locks eyes on Deputy Roberts. "My mom set me up on a few dates with Roberts's ex."

Roberts takes great pleasure in cuffing me, although Julian seems about one second away from having an aneurism.

"I'm sorry," he says as soon as we are placed in the back of the cruiser.

I remain quiet as I consider where everything went wrong in the last ten minutes. Julian checks in with me multiple times during the car ride, but my anxiety has officially taken over, and I see no end in sight.

🏆

Getting thrown in a holding cell because of a personal vendetta against Julian isn't doing wonders for my mood. Whatever bliss I felt in the truck has long since disappeared, leaving me antsy and irritable as I pace the perimeter.

Roberts didn't charge us with anything, although the photo he took of us in the holding cell is damning enough. I pray it doesn't make it on the internet.

I wrap my hands around the metal bars and shout, "This is unconstitutional!"

Julian takes a seat on the most uncomfortable-looking metal bench. "Welcome to Lake Wisteria."

I grip the bars and attempt to shake them to no avail. "Roberts! What about our right to a phone call or bail?"

No one answers my shout.

Asshole.

I press my forehead against the cold metal. "So, what? He's going to leave us here to rot because he hates you?"

"Eh. I give him a few hours before he calls our mothers to come pick us up."

"Our mothers?" I turn on my heels with a screech.

"I overheard him telling one of the other deputies about it while you were busy having a private conversation with yourself." His shy smile doesn't ease my anxiety.

My makeup might melt away from how hot my skin gets. "My mom is going to kill me when she finds out why we're here."

"Consider yourself lucky. Mine is going to start planning our wedding and invite the whole town."

God help me get through tonight without ending up disowned or deceased.

CHAPTER FORTY-FOUR

Julian

Despite my best attempts at distracting Dahlia from our current situation, I find her getting lost in her thoughts numerous times throughout the night. I hate to see her spiraling, but there isn't a lot I can do while trapped in a jail cell.

I know she regrets admitting she is falling in love with me. Just like I know she plans on fighting me every step of the way until either she accepts the truth or I give up.

Words will only get me so far, so instead of making her a promise she won't believe anyway, I keep quiet and hold her tight against me until Roberts returns.

The deputy takes his sweet time walking over to us, only to stop in front of the door and turn toward Dahlia. "Ben told me about the prank you had planned. Sorry I ruined it."

The asshole doesn't sound the least bit sorry.

"What prank is he talking about?" I ask her.

She rises from the bench and stretches her legs. "A stupid one."

Roberts leans against the bars. "Dahlia here planned on having you thrown in the back of a cruiser and dropped off at your mother's house with the sirens on so all the neighbors would make a fuss."

Although my mother would have happily filmed the whole thing, I would have died of embarrassment before making it up the driveway.

He shrugs. "Too bad I ruined Strawberry Sweetheart's plan."

Dahlia's cheeks flush.

"Don't call her that," I snap.

His lips curl. "Did I strike a chord?"

I force my mouth shut.

Dahlia stares at me for a solid ten seconds without blinking. "Strawberry Sweetheart?"

My hands curl by my sides.

She frowns. "My contact name on your phone doesn't stand for Satan's Spawn, does it?"

Mierda. No wonder she is hesitant about falling in love with me if she thinks her contact information on my phone means *that.*

Roberts unlocks the door with a special sparkle in his eyes. "You're both free to go, although I'm not sure you will feel that way once you see your mothers."

"*Gracias por eso, pendejo,*" I mutter under my breath.

Dahlia drags her feet behind me as Roberts leads us

Gracias por eso, pendejo: Thanks for that, dick.

413

through the station. She prolongs the inevitable by asking to use the restroom and grabbing a drink of water, which only excites Roberts more.

"Good luck." He walks back to his desk, where he can watch our mothers' reactions with glee.

Dahlia cringes at the expression on her mother's face as we walk up to them. *"Mami."*

"Not here," she hisses before walking outside. It's still dark, which means we couldn't have spent too long in the cell, although it sure felt like forever.

Dahlia follows behind her mother with slumped shoulders while mine locks elbows with me and whistles.

"¿En la camioneta de tu papá? ¿En serio?"

"Ma."

"I didn't think you had something like that in you."

I trip over my feet.

She swats my arm with a laugh. "It's okay. That truck has seen a lot of miles over the years, so I'm not one to judge, although it's a good thing you redid the whole interior."

A full-body shudder rolls through me as we walk outside to find Rosa raising her arms in the air and whisper-shouting while Dahlia's eyes drop to her boots.

"I raised you better than that."

Dahlia flinches.

"I expect something like this from your sister, but you? *Nunca en mi vida.*"

"Perdón, Mami."

¿En la camioneta de tu papá? ¿En serio?: In your dad's truck? Seriously?

"The whole town is going to know about this by tomorrow morning."

Dahlia looks as excited about the idea as I probably do.

Rosa's arms flail. "What will I say when Father Anthony asks how I feel about my daughter going to hell for premarital sex?"

"Do me a favor and ask him if the weather is hot all year round so I can plan my outfits accordingly."

"Dahlia Isabella Muñoz! *¡No empieces conmigo!*"

My mom nudges me. "Let's go save Dahlia before she reconsiders moving back here."

A little too late for that after her call about Archer.

"Rosa!" My mom claps her hands together. "Let's relax. They're kids. It's not like we can expect them to know any better."

"Kids? I had Dahlia when I was her age."

"And you did such a good job raising her—this little incident with the truck aside." My mother wraps an arm around her childhood friend and steers her toward her car. I bet she will talk Rosa down from her tirade in two minutes flat.

I loop my arm around Dahlia's waist and lead her to the sidewalk instead of my mother's car. "What do you say we walk back to the truck instead?"

Her gaze swings from my mom's car to me a few times while she gnaws on the inside of her cheek. "Okay."

Dahlia remains quiet as we walk toward the diner. I only

Nunca en mi vida: Never in my life.

¡No empieces conmigo!: Don't start with me.

last sixty seconds before breaking the silence. "Did your mom actually believe you were saving yourself for marriage?"

"If she did—which I'm almost positive was the case—it's safe to say she doesn't anymore."

I flinch. "She's going to hate me."

"Probably. You are the man who stole her virgin daughter's ticket to heaven."

"Pretty sure you earned yourself a one-way trip to hell years ago, but fine, I'll take the blame for your fall from grace."

"This is so embarrassing," she groans. "What will everyone think?"

"That it's about goddamn time."

She stops midstride.

"We got caught having sex in a parking lot. It's not exactly the scandal of the year." I press my hand against the small of her back and give her a little push.

"No one knows we're together."

"They will now."

"Julian," she pleads, but for what, I'm not too sure. She wraps her arms around herself. "This isn't going to work between us."

"Because of the long distance or your trust issues?" The comment slips out before I have a chance to rein it in.

Her step falters, along with her breathing.

I rub my face with a curse. "We'll figure it out."

Neither one of us says anything else for the remainder of the walk, which gives me time to process our situation.

Did I expect Dahlia to push me away when she realized how she felt about me? Yes, I did, yet I'm still disappointed to think she would so easily give up on us because of a few logistical problems.

I'm not the same guy she expects me to be anymore. I've changed, and if I have to fight Dahlia every step of the way to prove it to her, then so be it.

By the time we make it to the diner's parking lot, a plan has already started forming in my head.

"Are you hungry?" I unlock the truck and open the passenger door.

"No." A condensation cloud forms from her long exhale.

I grab her by the hips and lift her into the cab before she has a chance to climb on the step bar.

Once the engine rumbles to life, I blast the heat. "You should eat something."

Her nose scrunches. "I will."

Message received loud and painfully clear.

"Is this your plan, then?" My question packs a bite.

Her brows scrunch. "What?"

"Push me away because you'd rather avoid your feelings about us."

"I—I don't know."

"I think you do."

Her nostrils flare. "Since you know everything, why don't you go ahead and say what I'm thinking?"

"I don't need to be a mind reader to know you're afraid."

"I'm not afraid, Julian. I'm fucking *terrified*."

My forehead creases from my furrowed brows.

"I don't want to fall in love with you."

My ragged breath matches hers.

"I don't want to fall in love with anyone. *Period*. It nearly destroyed me the last time, and I'm not sure I could survive that kind of pain again." Her voice cracks toward the end. "You deserve someone who trusts you, and I'm not sure I'll be able to do that when I can't trust myself."

The twinge in my chest morphs into full-blown heartache. "I can't take back the pain you went through, no matter how much I wish I could, but I can promise to never hurt you like he did."

"A little too late for that." She can't hold my gaze for more than a second.

"Dahlia." I cradle her chin despite the pain lacing through my chest. "I'm not going to give up because you expect me to."

"Because you like a challenge?"

"Because I like *you* enough to know you're worth fighting for."

She stares out the window. "I'm moving back to San Francisco in January for my new show."

I'm aware, seeing as I spent the last few hours in a jail cell processing the fact.

But what are you going to do about it?

Somehow, in a short span of time, I went from planning the rest of my life in Lake Wisteria to putting everything on the line for the woman beside me. Because if Dahlia wants to move back to San Francisco, then I plan on going with her, and no amount of cons in the world will stop me.

I reach for her clenched hand. "When we break the news to my mom about moving, do me a favor and tell her you're in love with me. It'll help soften the blow."

Her cloudy eyes tug at something in my chest. "You can't seriously be considering moving."

"I am."

"But what about your company?"

"Turns out I'd rather build a home with you than a thousand houses by myself."

She turns away with a sniffle.

I cup her chin and turn her head toward me. "What part of *I'm falling in love with you* are you not understanding?"

"The part where you give up your whole life here for me."

"Life without you is hardly considered a life at all, so I'm not giving up anything by following you to San Francisco."

"No, but by being with me, you'd be giving up the chance at having your own family." She stares at her lap like it holds the secrets of the world.

"Is that what this is really about?"

Her face remains blank, but the vein in her neck throbs.

Why didn't you consider that sooner?

"You think I'll regret being with you because you can't have kids of your own?"

"I *know* you will because it's already happened once before."

"I already told you I don't want to have kids that way."

She shakes her head. "This isn't the first time I've heard someone tell me that."

I could find a hundred different ways to tell her I care enough to choose her, but none of them matter unless I find a way to *show* her.

Pro: She could find my list romantic.

Con: She may reject me anyway after I reveal one of my biggest secrets.

Shut up and show her.

I pull out my phone and open the note-taking app. "Here."

She grabs it from me and reads over the first few lines of text. "You've been working on a pro-con list about *me*?"

I nod.

"*Pro: She sucks at chess.* Seriously?" Her nose scrunches.

"Not my fault you started every single game with the queen's pawn opening. Change it up every now and then."

She returns to the list. "*Pro: I like her enough to attend Stanford too.*" She looks at me for a few seconds without blinking. "You chose Stanford because of me?"

"Yes. You liked California, and I liked you, so it made sense."

She shakes her head in disbelief. "How long have you been working on this?"

"Since sometime after you started competing for the Strawberry Sweetheart pageant."

She blinks. "That was over a decade ago."

"I'm aware."

"But why?"

"Informed decision-making is my thing."

She scrolls through the list while mumbling to herself. "There are things listed here that I don't do anymore."

I know. Unfortunately, I inherited my appreciation for nostalgia from my mother, and I have never been able to outgrow it, which is the only reason why I could never delete the list no matter how many times I tried.

After a few more minutes, she reaches the bottom of the note. "You only have one negative."

Con: She may never love me back.

"Little by little, your cons annoyingly started making their way over to the pros column."

Her laugh comes out like a half sob. "That's ridiculous."

"No, Dahlia, that's *love*."

"You agreed to a casual relationship knowing your feelings might never be reciprocated?" Disbelief colors her voice.

"Yes."

"Why?"

"Some people are worth the risk."

Her bottom lip wobbles.

"Life without you was a series of pros and cons. Risks and rewards. Black and white with very few shades of gray. But then you came back and flipped a switch inside me, flooding my world with color after a ten-year blackout, and I don't plan on giving that up. Not now. Not ever."

Tears pool near her lash line.

"You might not believe my words now, but I won't stop until you do. So go ahead and try to push me away, but you already know based on our history that I will stop at nothing to prove you wrong."

CHAPTER FORTY-FIVE

Julian

The trip to Dahlia's is a quiet one. She spends most of it staring out the window, while I stay focused on the road. Despite the urge to check in with her, I hold back and stay silent, not wanting to add to her distress.

It's not until I pull up to her house that she finally speaks up, surprising me.

"I'm sorry."

I blink rapidly. "What are you—"

"I know you're a good guy—possibly the best guy I've ever met—even if you drive me crazy." She twists one of her rings. "Your list. God. I can't believe you spent over a decade working on that."

"Twelve years, but who's counting?"

Her chin quivers. "Maybe if things were different for me, we could—"

"Stop."

"But—"

"No. I don't want to hear whatever excuse you spent the whole drive coming up with."

Her muscles tighten. "You can't ignore the obvious."

"Glad we're finally on the same page."

She glances away.

"What do you need?" I ask.

"Time? Some food and a good night's rest? Honestly, I can barely think straight, let alone talk when I'm this exhausted."

"Okay." I can give her that…for a day at least.

Her shoulders fall from her heavy sigh.

I grab her hand and kiss the back of it. "Everything will be okay."

"So you say."

"Only because I won't stop until it is."

She spares me one last glance before hopping out of my truck and taking off for her front door.

I don't remember the drive to my house because I spent the entirety of it lost in my own thoughts, sorting through all the things I need to figure out.

Silence greets me like a funeral march as I enter my house and head toward my kitchen to heat up some food. I make it through a few bites before my phone buzzes against the marble counter with a new message from Lily in the Muñoz-Lopez group chat.

LILY

> From lovebirds to jailbirds
> in a single week.

She attaches a photo of Dahlia and me in the holding cell. Rosa sends a link to schedule a confession session with Father Anthony, while my mother follows up with a heart-eyed GIF and a text.

MA

> Like Bonnie and Clyde.

RAFA

> They both died in a shootout.

MA

> Together.

RAFA

> Remind me to never fall in love.

I reply, telling everyone to delete the photo from their phones and in the chat before taking off toward the station to pay Roberts a second visit tonight.

"Back so soon?" Roberts leans against the counter.

"How many people did you send the photo to?"

"Just Lily."

"Delete it from your phone."

"I plan on it once the reporter gets back to me with a price for the photo."

"How much are you asking for it?" I snap.

"Ten grand."

I rip a sticky note off the top of the pack and pass it to him. "Give me your number, and I'll have the money transferred in an hour."

His brows jump. "You're not going to bother negotiating?"

I tap on the sticky note. "Your number."

"Make it twelve thousand."

"I'll drop my offer to seven if you don't stop talking."

His smile falls as he scribbles across the paper before passing it to me.

I tuck his number into the inner pocket of my coat. "Delete it."

"Now?"

I tap my shoe against the floor. He sighs as he pulls out his phone and walks me through the process of deleting the evidence.

As soon as he is finished, I walk out of the station, text Dahlia about how I took care of the photo, and head back to my house. By the time I make it inside, Dahlia still hasn't answered the group chat or my single text, which is unlike her.

My dinner sits in my stomach like a boulder as I take a shower and climb into bed.

You're going to find a way to make everything work out, I chant to myself in the dark.

I just need to figure out how.

Dahlia spends most of the next morning hiding in her office, so I don't get a chance to see her until she shows up for the team meeting scheduled over a week ago.

Originally, I considered handling my affairs with my team in private, but Dahlia's lack of trust and attempts at avoiding me pose a unique challenge I need to overcome.

Showing Dahlia that I plan on sticking around will require a lot more than promising her I'll move to San Francisco. I need to make some necessary changes to my life, starting with the one thing I've been putting off for years.

Dahlia mentally checked out of the discussion twenty minutes ago, once Ryder, Mario, and I began reviewing logistical issues about the Lake Aurora remodel. She spends the time sketching designs for her décor line, and I find myself getting distracted a few times by her skills.

"Are we all good here?" Mario asks.

"Yeah." I glance at Ryder. "Can you stick around once Mario leaves?"

He nods.

Dahlia makes one last change to her design before she tucks her tablet beneath her arm and rises from her chair.

"I need you to stay," I tell her.

Her face pinches with confusion as she retakes her seat.

"See you all next week." Mario tips his chin before walking out of the conference room.

"What's up?" Ryder asks.

I sit back down. "I've been thinking..."

Dahlia's chair creaks as she places her elbows on the table and leans forward.

My project manager tucks a pencil behind his ear. "About?"

I clear my throat. "I need some help."

Her eyes widen.

"Whatever you need, I'm your man." He doesn't hesitate, which catches me by surprise.

"You don't know what I'm about to ask of you."

"Doesn't matter. You've done a lot for me, so I'm up for whatever."

I blink. Dahlia seems equally shocked as her gaze bounces between the two of us.

Ryder continues, "Before you hired me, I was struggling with returning to civilian life after my last tour. When I interviewed for the job, I was living out of my car and struggling with PTSD."

I hide my flinch. "I didn't realize it was that bad."

Dahlia reaches out to give his hand a squeeze before she sinks back into her chair.

"You're not the only proud man in town, boss," he says with a small smile.

"No, but he is the *proudest*," Dahlia says.

I shoot her a stern look.

Ryder's soft laugh doesn't match his harsh features. "I owe you a lot, so if you want my help, I'm more than happy to offer it."

Dahlia's bottom lip trembles.

Shit.

I battle between shyness and gratitude before landing somewhere in the middle. "You don't owe me anything."

"Do you want my help or not?" he asks.

"His asking is evidence enough." The expression on Dahlia's face is worth every ounce of pride I forfeit as I do the one thing I trained myself to avoid.

"Yeah, I want your help." My shoulders loosen as the tension drains from my body.

"Tell me what you need."

"Between us, something came up that requires me to move next month, so I need to restructure the company in a way that allows it to operate without me being present."

His brows rise while Dahlia's scrunch.

"You're moving?" Ryder asks.

"Yes. Even though I'll attend meetings virtually and fly back every two weeks to physically check on everything, I need your help with the day-to-day operations and keeping an eye on things."

Dahlia's lips part.

Ryder nods. "Of course."

"Great. Here's what I was thinking…" I review my idea with Ryder while Dahlia watches. He gives his input and offers plenty of useful advice, and I adjust my plan based on his expertise. Dahlia gives a few pointers I take into consideration.

After an hour of restructuring Lopez Luxury's operations, Ryder stands and claps me on the back. "I never thought I'd see the day you finally decided to do what was best for you rather than the company." He glances over at Dahlia. "And I probably have you to thank for the promotion and raise."

Her cheeks are tinged a soft shade of pink. "I didn't have anything to do with this."

"*Right*." Ryder nods.

Stubborn, I mouth.

Ryder gives me a thumbs-up.

We both know Dahlia is the only person who could convince me to change the entire structure of my company, yet she won't accept the possibility because it would only threaten her weak argument.

Ryder walks out of the conference room, and Dahlia gets up to follow him, but I cage her against the door before she has a chance to escape.

"I'm not done with you."

She makes a show of dragging her eyes up toward my face. "What do you want?"

"Your opinion is a good start."

She fidgets with one of her rings. "You're really thinking about moving to San Francisco?"

"Did the last hour give it away?"

She glares.

I sigh. "How long do you plan on fighting me on this?"

"For however long it takes to convince you that this is all a big mistake." Her glassy eyes are full of uncertainty, and it wrecks me to know how much she silently suffers from her anxiety.

"You want to talk about mistakes? Fine. Let's talk about them."

Surprise flashes across her face.

"There were a few reasons I pushed you away all those years ago. Grief. The stress of running a struggling company. My fear that we would never survive long distance and all the other obstacles standing in our way. But the biggest mistake I made was believing you were better off without me because I wasn't good enough. I let my low self-esteem and insecurities stand in the way of what I wanted with you, and I'll be damned if I let you make that same mistake. In fact, I forbid it, because I refuse to spend another ten years waiting for you to come to your senses."

She blinks a few times.

"I will always fight for what's in our best interest, even if it means fighting you in the process." I kiss the top of her head and exit the room before I find myself unable to, leaving the woman I love behind to come to terms with what I said.

CHAPTER FORTY-SIX

Julian

I decide to stay away from the office and the Founder's house, both because I want to give Ryder a chance to run Lopez Luxury's daily operations without me micromanaging, and so Dahlia sees I'm serious about taking a step back.

I try to burn some nervous energy off by working out, making a few playlists, and having lunch with my mom, but relief doesn't last long, especially after Dahlia sends me a message with her San Francisco travel itinerary.

Soon enough, I find myself pacing the long halls of my house while my thoughts spiral.

When I told Dahlia I would always fight for what's in our best interest, even if it means fighting her, I meant every word.

But first, I need to finish the fight against my past. I have been battling my insecurities for years, and it's time to face what I've put off for far too long...

Accepting that I *am* good enough—not only for Dahlia but, most importantly, for myself.

So tonight, I head over to the one place I never imagined entering again.

My dad's woodshop.

I've tried to return over the years, but the task seemed impossible every time, with me quickly fleeing the scene before ever walking inside the place he and I spent years working out of, carrying on the Lopez tradition that started with his great-great-grandfather.

There was one major reason I avoided it, and it has everything to do with the tools hanging on the back wall and all they signify.

My hand trembles as I slide the key into the lock and turn it. The click of the lock and the creak of the door sound far away due to the rushing blood pounding in my ears.

After five deep breaths, I reach for the light switch and flip it once I've taken a step inside. My feet remain glued to the concrete floor as I look around. Thanks to my mom's routine dusting, the shed appears clean enough to eat off every surface, including the floor.

My dad would *hate* it.

I take another step inside the shop despite my feet feeling as though they are attached to cinder blocks. Too many memories fill the space, making my heart heavy and my breathing laborious.

Te extraño, Papi.

Te extraño, Papi: I miss you, Dad.

I walk to the back wall where my dad's tools remain hung the way he liked it, making it seem like he might return at any moment.

God, I wish that were true.

A second set hangs beside his.

A Lopez family heirloom, he said with a small smile as he pointed out each tool that was passed down from generation to generation.

I grew up asking my dad when it would be my turn to receive the tools, and his answer never changed.

When you prove that you've earned them.

I might have missed out on my chance the day he died, but I've done everything possible to make him and the Lopez family proud as I took on the family business despite my lack of experience and college degree.

The dull ache in my chest intensifies, and I grip the counter with a chokehold. My itchy eyes have nothing to do with allergies or any lingering sawdust in the air. Neither does the tightness in my throat nor the pounding of my heart.

A drop slides down my cheek, and I swipe at it before staring up at the ceiling in search of a leak. Except my cloudy eyesight makes it impossible to see much past the tears clogging my vision.

They roll down my skin like raindrops, falling in quick succession. The last time I cried like this, my dad was being placed in the ground. While the hole in my chest has healed since then, the dull pain has never left, returning at the most inconvenient times.

My shoulders shake.

Take five. My dad would grip my shoulders and force me to copy his movements.

Again, he would say when the original five-count didn't work. The tears don't stop, but my panic lessens with each exaggerated breath.

At some point after breath number thirty-five, I pull myself together and reach for the first Lopez heirloom I see. My fingers tremble, but I'm quick to stop it by tightening my hold around the base of the hammer.

I step toward my old workstation. My mom might have accidentally placed a few tools in the wrong area, but everything else remains the same, down to the last project I was working on before I left for college.

The half-finished jewelry box was meant to be a special Christmas gift for Dahlia. Over the years, we mainly stuck to gag gifts or presents our mothers picked out, but the Christmas before everything went to shit was supposed to be different.

We were supposed to be different.

After the kiss we shared, I knew we couldn't go back to the way things were before, and I didn't want to. I wanted so much *more*.

But then my dad died, and my mom spiraled into another deep depression, which I felt responsible for helping her through. I shelved my own grief—a stupid decision in the long run—and pushed Dahlia away after calling her a distraction.

I let my insecurities get in the way of what I wanted, and my fears of not being good enough for her consumed me until I couldn't stand the idea of being with her. She had all these dreams, and I was a broken mess with the odds stacked against me.

Now is your chance to right your wrongs.

Pain blossoms in my chest as I hold up the incomplete jewelry box. I want to find that courage again, starting with facing my biggest obstacle to date.

Overcoming my past.

With shaky hands and a pounding heart, I grab a few more of the Lopez tools and get to work on finishing the jewelry box. I don't know how long I meticulously obsess over the project, but I'm addicted to the adrenaline pumping through my veins.

By the time I finish, I'm sweating all over and heaving like I ran a marathon. I use the hem of my shirt to wipe my damp forehead before checking out the final product.

One day, I plan on giving Dahlia the jewelry box. I'm just not sure when.

CHAPTER FORTY-SEVEN

Dahlia

Looks like the reality TV princess finally decided to return to her tequila throne." Lorenzo drops into the stool beside me and places his whiskey glass on the counter.

"Don't you have anything better to do with your time than hang out here?" I scan the relatively empty bar.

He shrugs. "Not really."

"You need a job."

His brow rises. "At eight p.m. on a Tuesday?"

"How about a hobby, then?"

"Does plotting against my enemies count?"

My brows rise. "You have enemies? In Lake Wisteria?"

He laughs into his glass, although the sound comes off as chilling and haunted rather than warm and hearty.

"What are *you* doing here?" he asks before I have a chance to follow up.

"Meeting up with my sister." I check my phone for the third time within the last ten minutes. When I called for an emergency girls' night, Lily suggested we meet at Last Call after she closed the shop for the night, claiming she was craving their curly fries.

"Lily, right?"

I turn to glare at him. "Why are you asking?"

He ignores my question and asks one of his own. "Is she single?"

My eyes narrow. "No."

"Hm. Who's the guy?"

"Jesus, so don't bother hitting on her."

"She wants to become a nun?"

"Close. Virgin until marriage." I swallow back a giggle before it gives me away.

Lorenzo's upper lip curls with disgust. "Great."

I wave Henry over and order two seltzers.

A few minutes later, the door to the bar slams open, and my sister barrels inside wearing my favorite winter coat and stolen designer boots. She shrugs it off with a shiver, revealing another one of my outfits.

"I could kill her."

Lorenzo's eyes darken as they trail down my sister's body.

I swat the back of his head. "Stop checking out my sister!"

He drains the rest of his whiskey before raising his hand to request another.

My eyes roll as I slide off the barstool and drag Lily to the other side of the bar, far away from Lorenzo's burning gaze.

"Since when are you friends with Lorenzo?" she asks with a frown.

"You know him?"

"Not really." Her nose twitches. "He passes by the shop every Friday to pick up two custom bouquets."

"And?"

She shrugs. "I don't have a good feeling about him."

Maybe Julian was right about Lorenzo after all, and it's best for us to stay far away.

At least Lily doesn't seem interested in him.

Lily shimmies into the booth across from me. "So, what was this emergency meeting for?"

I pass the unopened vodka seltzer can. "I'm having a dilemma."

She laughs to herself. "You're quite famous for them."

"I'm being serious."

My sister takes a sip of her drink after opening it. "All right. What's going on?"

"I got an offer for a new show I pitched."

"Congrats!" She taps her can against mine before locking eyes. "Or not?"

I slump against the table. "It's in San Francisco."

"That's far."

My shoulders slump. "Julian says he is willing to move…"

"But you don't believe him?"

I fidget with my jacket's zipper. "More like I'm afraid he will follow through with his promise."

Her head tilts. "Now I'm confused. Shouldn't that make you happy?"

"I don't want him to change his whole life for me." He could come to regret his decision and resent me in the process, and I don't know if I would overcome that kind of heartbreak a second time.

Lily reaches for my hand. "Have you considered that he might not only be doing this for you but also for himself?"

I stay quiet, and Lily fills the silence with another shocking revelation. "Julian has been saying he wants to scale back on his job for years, but he never made a move to do so, despite how obvious it was to everyone around him that he should."

I blink a few times. "Really?"

"Yes. So imagine how surprised we all were when he suddenly began working on a project with you, started visiting his construction sites more often, and can't stop smiling when he speaks about working on new houses with you—something he hasn't done in at least two years."

A lump forms in my tight throat. "He... I..."

Lily gives my hand a reassuring squeeze. "And don't get me started on the carpentry thing. Everyone in town won't stop talking about how he was so jealous that he gave a guy a promotion to keep him away from you."

We both break out into laughter.

"How did they find out?" I ask.

"That carpenter he promoted loves *chisme* more than Josefina."

I take a long sip from my seltzer can. "I didn't ask Julian to do all that."

"That's my point. He decided to do those things because they made *him* happy, so why are you going to start doubting him and his choices now?"

My gaze drops to the table. "Because I'm afraid he will come to regret them in the long run, once the honeymoon phase ends and reality comes knocking."

"What if he doesn't?" She leans back. "No offense, but I'm more concerned about *you* making the wrong one if you decide to push him away."

My brows rise. "What?"

"Men like Julian don't come often, so you should be thanking your lucky stars that he stayed in this small town, because if he had moved away, someone would have surely snatched him up by now. That much I know."

The idea of him being with someone else makes me physically ill.

That's because you love him.

But if my love wasn't enough to save a doomed relationship before, what makes this time any different?

Falling in love with Julian was easy, but forgiving myself and moving on from a past that still haunts me?

Damn near impossible.

Instead of going home, I drive over to Rafa's house. I'm not sure who is more surprised by my visit—me or him—although he welcomes me inside without making a big deal of it.

Nico and I spend five minutes catching up before Rafa orders him back to bed.

"Love you!" Nico throws his arms around me for one last hug before running to his room.

"I'm sorry to stop by unannounced like this," I blurt out as Rafa steers me toward the living room.

"It made Nico happy, so it's fine, but don't make a habit of it."

I laugh. "Wouldn't dare."

"Can I get you something to drink? We've got water, aguas frescas, and alcohol."

"I'm good."

"Suit yourself." He drops onto the comfy leather seat across from the couch and pulls out his phone for the second time tonight.

I take a seat, my posture stiff, while he taps at the screen before swapping it for a beer.

"Thanks again for not shooing me away or something."

"Not sure you would have left regardless." He lifts his beer in a mock toast. "So, what's going on?"

"I don't know how to ask this without being rude—"

"We're practically family, so I'm still obligated to forgive you regardless."

"Fair point."

"Does your visit have something to do with my cousin?" he asks.

I blink a few times. "Sort of."

"I thought as much."

"But it's also about…you know…the thing I told you…" I stammer.

"About not being able to have kids of your own?"

I let out a sigh of relief. "Yes."

"What about it?" His tone remains nonchalant.

"I've been struggling with the news."

"Understandable. I had trouble coming to terms with a similar thing when Nico was diagnosed with his eye condition."

"After finding out about Nico, did you…" I struggle to finish the sentence.

"Think about not wanting kids again?"

My shoulders slump. "Yes."

"Yup. It was impossible not to after learning my son is going blind because of a condition he inherited from my screwed-up family."

"There was no way you could have known about some uncle having the same condition."

He takes a long sip of his drink. "I *know* that, but parents have a tendency to feel guilty for whatever happens to their kids, whether it's our fault or not."

My gaze drops. "I can only imagine."

"But to answer your original question, I made the choice to get a vasectomy after I found out about Nico's condition."

My brows rise. "Really?"

"It felt like the responsible thing to do. If I ever want another child—big emphasis on the *if*—I'll pay it forward and adopt."

"That would make Josefina happy."

"She would be happy with *any* grandchild. She's been hounding me for years about giving Nico a sibling, and yes, before you ask, she knows about my inability to have kids of my own anymore." Rafa's piercing stare makes me feel like I'm being picked apart.

I gather some courage to ask my second question. "Do you

think Julian would care in the long run about not having his own child?"

He takes so long to speak that I worry he won't bother answering me.

I speak up again. "I'm not sure if he has talked to you about wanting kids of his own or if—"

"Isn't this something you should be asking him?"

"I have."

His eyes flicker over my face. "But you don't trust him?"

"I don't trust myself, so it's nothing personal."

His grip on the beer bottle tightens. "My cousin has his faults, but he is a man of his word, so if he told you he doesn't care about having biological kids, then he means it."

My throat dries up.

"But I do remember him mentioning something along those lines a few times over the years."

"He did?"

"Yeah. He and I don't open up about our feelings often, but I know enough about his life before I came along to be comfortable saying it was rough."

My fingers turn white from the way I clasp my hands together. "I was too young to understand how much everything impacted him."

"Julian is great at channeling his emotions into other things."

"So I'm learning," I mutter under my breath.

"I know you don't believe him, and I don't blame you. People like you and me...we're not the trusting type any-more, after being hurt the way we were." He stares off into the distance.

Watching him battle his demons is like staring at my reflection for the first time.

Goose bumps spread across my skin, and the hair on the back of my neck rises as I come to grips with my biggest fault.

I love Rafa, but I don't want to end up like him, blaming myself for a failed relationship years later while struggling with trust issues.

God no.

Heavy pounding in the distance startles me.

"Are you expecting someone else?"

Rafa stands. "No, but you are."

CHAPTER FORTY-EIGHT

Julian

When Rafa texted me ten minutes ago, letting me know that Dahlia stopped by his place, I headed straight over. Something about his cryptic message made me worry.

I lift my fist to slam it against the door again, only for it to swing open before my hand makes contact.

Dahlia steps outside and shuts the door behind her. "Rafa texted you?"

"Yes. Are you okay?" I scan her face for any telltale signs of distress.

"Umm…yeah?"

"He told me you were crying."

"Crying?" She sounds as confused as she looks.

"Or not?"

"He was goading you."

Damn him.

"You came all the way out here because you thought I was upset?"

I rub the back of my neck. "Yeah."

Her unreadable expression has me speaking up again. "So you're okay then?"

"Yeah. I had a couple of questions I wanted to ask him."

"About what?"

She tucks her hands in the pockets of her winter jacket. "Mind if we walk and talk for a bit?"

"Sure."

"Could we check out the animals? It's been a while since I've seen Penelope." Dahlia tilts her head in the direction of the barn.

The sound of our boots crushing the grass beneath our feet fills the quiet, although it only lasts a minute before I ruin it.

"Does he know about your test?"

"Yeah." She stares straight ahead.

"For how long?"

She doesn't miss a beat. "Since I came back."

While I respect him for keeping her news a secret, I selfishly wish he'd told me. "He never said anything."

She glances at me out of the corner of her eye. "I'm kind of surprised he didn't."

"He's trustworthy."

"Funny, seeing as he said something similar about you."

"Do you believe him?"

"I want to believe *you*."

I stay silent as we walk into the barn. Dahlia stops by the first stall and holds her hand out.

"Hey there, pretty girl."

Penelope, a retired racehorse Rafa saved a few years back, nuzzles her head against Dahlia's palm. I stand behind her, trapping her between my body and the gate to the stall.

"I don't want to end up like Rafa." Her whisper can barely be heard over the horse's heavy exhale.

I stop breathing.

"I don't want to spend the rest of my life bitter and questioning everything and everyone. I want to trust. I want to love. I want to live freely without worrying that I'll get hurt, left, or betrayed."

I turn her around. "My cousin will get better, and so will you."

She leans against the stall. "I'm scared."

I kiss the top of her head. "I know."

She wraps her arms around herself. "How can I be sure you will be happy adopting a child?"

"Because I always admired my parents for adopting Rafa."

Her sniffle is the only reply I get.

"They treated Rafa and me equally. Attention. Discipline. *Love*. Not once did they make either of us feel like we weren't both their kids. But deep down, I knew Rafa filled a void in my mom's life that I couldn't, no matter how hard I tried. Something inside her changed after years of struggling through miscarriages and a stillbirth, and Rafa became that missing piece in her life. In all our lives."

She blinks up at me with glassy eyes.

"Adoption will never be a second-best option for me. Never has been and never will be, because to feel that way would go against everything my parents believed in and what made our family whole."

The seconds tick by painfully slowly, and I nearly give in and say something to fill the dreadful silence until Dahlia stops me.

She places her palm against my cheek. "I believe you."

After last night's talk at Rafa's place, I know Dahlia and I are moving in the right direction, despite her flying back to San Francisco to meet with Archer Media later this week.

I have some pent-up energy to kill, so I head to my dad's woodshop to start working on a new project. My Saturday is nothing but a rush of cutting, shaping, and sanding different pieces of wood. My phone buzzes every now and then, but I ignore the incoming messages, knowing Ryder will handle whatever needs to be done come Monday.

I immerse myself in my task, easily losing track of time until loud banging against the door has me nearly slicing my finger open on the circular saw.

"Julian! Open up!" my mother yells before slamming her fist on the door again.

I rip off my safety goggles and mask before unlocking the door. "What are you doing here?"

She waltzes inside with a plastic container. "I brought you dinner."

I grab it from her. "How did you know where I was?"

"Got an alert from the driveway camera you installed a few

years ago." Her eyes shimmer from unshed tears as they flicker around the shop.

I brush my hand across my sawdust-covered shirt. "It's a bit of a mess."

She blinks a few times before turning to face me with a watery smile. "I was wondering when you would finally come back."

"I saw you kept it nice and clean for me over the years."

"Your dad would have hated it," she says.

"With every fiber of his being."

We both laugh.

"I knew it was only a matter of time before you returned, so I didn't want it to be a mess for you."

My chest swells with emotion. "You think of everything."

"Now come and eat before your food goes cold." Mom ushers me over to a stool and forces me to try some of her famous pozole.

I pause mid-bite. "You didn't pass by only to bring me food, did you?"

She swipes her finger across the table, collecting sawdust and debris. "I wanted to see what my felonious son was working on for Dahlia."

"I never said it was for her."

She snorts. "Right."

My mom can't sit still, so she shuffles through my plans and notes while I finish eating.

She holds up the paper marked with a bunch of measurements and notes. "You're building this?"

"Mm-hmm."

"For the Founder's house?"

"Yup."

Ma releases the happiest squeal. "She's going to love it."

"Don't mention anything to Dahlia."

She holds her hands up. "I wouldn't dare."

While I eat, she quickly becomes distracted by the shelf near the back of the shed.

"Oh Julian. This is beautiful!" She runs a hand across the top of the jewelry box I made before spinning the hand crank a few times. "You got it to play music!"

The first few chords of the song play, and her eyes widen. "It's perfect."

I rub the back of my neck. "You think so?"

"Of course." Mom places the finished jewelry box back on the shelf before kissing the top of my head. "I'll let you get to your secret project, then."

"Do you want to help me?" My question rushes out.

"You want my help?" She checks my forehead's temperature with the back of her hand. "Are you feeling okay?"

I push her hand away with a laugh. "Forget I said anything."

"No! I'd love to help you."

"Do you remember how to use a circular saw?" I hold up a piece of unfinished wood, only for her to steal it with a huff.

"Don't insult me like that in your father's place of worship."

My chest rumbles from my deep chuckle.

She points at me with the wooden post. "I helped your dad in the shop long before you were born, so it's best you remember that, *mijo*."

Mom and I work side by side for hours after I finish eating.

She corrects me a few times, reminding me of my dad when she reprimands me for my joinery technique and wood selection for the more intricate pieces.

Reluctantly, I call it a night once my mom is ready to fall over and I can no longer properly operate the saw without trembling.

"That was so much fun!" She wraps her sweaty, saw-dust-sprinkled arms around me. "Thank you for including me."

I hug her back, ignoring the slight twinge of guilt. "It was nice to have your help."

"You can ask me anytime." She looks up at me with glassy eyes. "If only your father were here with us. He would have loved nothing more than to help you create something special for Dahlia."

My lungs stall.

She untangles herself from my arms and reaches for one of my dad's old tools with a shaky hand.

"I'm glad you're using these."

I can't speak, let alone breathe.

"He would have wanted you to have them."

I clench my hands to stop them from trembling.

She follows the movement before glancing back at me. "He planned on passing them down to you once you graduated…"

But he never had a chance.

"I know he is watching us and wishing he wasn't the reason you never graduated from Stanford." Her breath catches. "But I also know he would have been so incredibly proud of you for stepping up and taking care of me and his business. You accomplished more than we ever dreamed of in such a short amount of time."

My heart lodges itself somewhere in my tight throat.

She unclenches my fist before wrapping my fingers around the handle of the hammer. "*Te quiero con todo, mi corazón.*"

After one last kiss on my cheek, my mom leaves the shed, giving me the space I desperately need.

I hold my father's hammer with misty eyes.

Te extraño *mucho, Papi.*

I head toward the back wall and return the hammer where it belongs. The lights above me flicker twice, and goose bumps spread across my arms.

Could it be...

No, Dahlia must have poisoned my mind with all her conversations about the Founder's house ghost.

Yet despite everything I believe in, I end up speaking aloud regardless.

"*Te quiero, Papi.*"

Te quiero con todo, mi corazón: I love you with everything, my heart.

Te extraño mucho, Papi: I miss you so much, Dad.

CHAPTER FORTY-NINE

Dahlia

What's up with you?" Lily plucks the remote from my hand and shuts off the TV mid-episode.

"Why did you do that?"

"Because you're not paying attention."

I cross my arms over my PJs. "Yes, I was."

"Yeah, right. You didn't even flinch when the capo decapitated that guy with a machete."

"So?"

She raises a brow. "So you *always* look away when they get to the gory parts."

I release a heavy sigh that has her snapping her fingers.

"There! That's the fifth time tonight you've done that."

My head drops back against the couch.

"Does this have to do with your trip to San Francisco tomorrow?" Lily sits sideways on the couch.

"Am I that obvious?"

"A little bit."

"I should be happy about how quickly everything is moving, but every time I think about leaving…"

"You wish you could stay?"

The pain in my chest intensifies. "Yeah, but then I feel torn between wanting my show and wishing I could live here."

As much as I love my show and expanding my brand, I love the idea of staying in Lake Wisteria more.

Lily tucks her legs beneath her. "Why not have both?"

My eyebrows knit together. "The production company is based out of California."

"So? Lots of shows are filmed in other states and countries. I'm sure they could make some changes to make both sides happy."

I scoff. "I'm not exactly in the position to be making demands." After my former production company pulled out of the deal, the last thing I want to do is upset Archer by making changes to the original plan.

"You could at least ask and see what they say."

"But—"

Lily doesn't let me finish my train of thought. "What's the worst that can happen?"

"They tell me to get lost?"

Her chin lifts as she tosses her hair over her shoulder. "Then they're not worth your time and energy." She grabs my phone off the coffee table and tosses it on my lap. "Call your agent."

I stare at the dark screen.

"Do it. Do it. Do it," Lily chants.

But what if Archer Media says no and pulls out of the project? The nagging voice in my head speaks up.

After everything Julian has done to show he cares about me, including offering to move to California, the least I can do is take a risk and ask a question.

I unlock my phone. "Screw it."

Lily watches as I pull up my agent's contact information and give her a call.

"Dahlia! What's going on?"

I clear my throat. "I've been thinking about something, and I wanted to run it by you before our meeting."

"What is it?"

My heart thumps wildly in my chest. "Do you think Archer would be willing to change filming locations?"

"To where?"

"Lake Wisteria."

Lily shoots me a thumbs-up.

I continue, "They have tons of historic houses here, so the content would be the same, but I would be able to move back home."

Jamie pauses for a moment, and my lungs stop working in anticipation.

"I don't know. That wasn't part of the original pitch, and they already have crews set up in San Francisco for their other shows, so there is a high chance they'll say no."

My excitement dies. "Oh. I understand."

"That being said, let me see what I can do."

"You'll ask?" My pitch rises.

"Yes, but I can't guarantee they will say yes."

Excitement replaces the dreadful worry that was choking me. "Would it help for me to take some videos of the properties around here? Maybe show them a few projects I've been working on? Lake Wisteria and the surrounding towns are full of houses begging to be restored, plus the locals would make for entertaining TV."

"I'll reach out to my contact and see what they have to say."

"Thanks, Jamie! You're the best."

Her laugh is the last thing I hear before she hangs up.

"You did it!" Lily throws her arms around me.

I return her hug with one of my own, pouring every ounce of love and admiration I have for my sister into it.

While I had considered asking about filming a show here, I may have never worked up the courage if it weren't for Lily pushing me to try.

Don't get your hopes up.

Too late.

CHAPTER FIFTY

Dahlia

The heaviness in my chest that has been present since I left Lake Wisteria gets progressively worse with every hour I spend in San Francisco. I should be happy to be back in my old stomping grounds, but not even a poke bowl from my favorite spot can save me from the oppressive sadness choking me.

I expected the feeling to lessen when I entered the Archer Media building, only to be disappointed when it didn't.

"So, what did you think?" my agent asks once the elevator doors shut. Her strawberry-blond curls frame her face like a halo, giving her a deceitfully sweet appearance that doesn't match the woman who spent the last hour playing hardball with the people from Archer Media.

"I'm not sure." I lean against the support bar as the car begins its descent toward the lobby.

Her brows rise. "About Archer or the show?"

"All of it?"

"I know you had your heart set on filming in Lake Wisteria, but their scouts agree San Francisco would be a great place to film the first season. After that, if the show is renewed for another season, which we both know it will be, then you'll get dibs on the next location."

The idea sounds great in theory, but every time I consider moving back to San Francisco, the pit in my stomach deepens, something I never thought would happen after living here for years.

My gut is telling me not to accept Archer Media's deal, and it's not only because of the man waiting for me in Lake Wisteria.

You still trust your intuition after everything you've been through?

No, but it's about time I started because I'm tired of doubting myself. I let Oliver and the Creswells' judgmental thoughts and opinions haunt me for far too long, and for what? To torture myself by doubting every decision I make?

I'm the one who built Designs by Dahlia from the ground up. Sure, Oliver encouraged me to post a photo, but I'm the one who put in the work to turn my name into a brand. And yes, the Creswells helped produce my show, but the fans stuck around for *me* and my work, not because of the people funding the project.

It's time to forgive yourself for your past mistakes and move on.

"What should I tell them?" Jamie taps away at her phone.

"I'd like to take some more time to think about it."

"How long are you thinking?"

"I'm not sure. Maybe a week?"

She whistles. "There might be some pushback about scheduling."

"I know. If I make up my mind sooner, I'll let you know, but I want to take my time and think this through."

Although I feel my decision has already been made.

Returning to my empty townhouse solidifies my growing concern about moving back to San Francisco. I distract myself by falling back into my old routine of cooking dinner, watching a rerun of one of my favorite shows, and showering until my fingers and toes turn wrinkly, but nothing seems to lessen the ache in my chest as I consider my situation.

I climb into bed and hope sleep takes me soon to save me from the nonstop thoughts running through my brain.

What's the point of moving back here for a show if you're going to be lonely and miserable?

Sometime in the last three months, Lake Wisteria started feeling more like my true home while San Francisco became more of a distant memory.

My phone pings with a new message. I grab it off the nightstand and check who texted me at this hour.

JULIAN

How did the meeting go?

My chest pinches. Although I changed his contact name recently, I'm still not fully convinced I love it.

I send a quick reply.

ME

Good.

I don't have a chance to type out a reply before a new message from him appears.

JULIAN

That bad?

ME

It wasn't bad per se...

My fingers fly across the screen.

ME

They shared their plans, and my agent asked all the right questions.

JULIAN

But...

I can't think of an appropriate response that won't automatically get his hopes up, so I don't answer.

My phone vibrates a minute later from an incoming call. I debate between picking up Julian's call and letting it go to voicemail before deciding to trust my gut and answering the damn phone. "Hey."

"Hey." The hint of surprise in his tone makes me feel shittier than usual.

"How did the meeting go?" he asks.

"Fine."

"What a glowing review."

I drop onto my bed with an *oomph*.

"Want to talk about it?"

"I don't know. I've spent all night thinking about it and have gotten nowhere closer to making a decision about the TV deal."

"You? Unsure about the future? I don't believe it."

I laugh again. "I swear I'm not usually this indecisive."

"I watched you spend an hour deciding if you wanted to paint a room eggshell white or eggshell off-white, which, by the way, are the same color."

"Not true. One had a satin finish and the other had a semi-matte finish, thank you very much."

His deep chuckle pulls at the cord wrapped around my lower half. "You overthink everything lately, which is fine."

"Aren't you the guy who hides pro-con lists all over his house?"

"You found those?"

I stare up at the ceiling. "Out of curiosity, did you come to a decision about which toilet paper brand was best?"

"I knew giving you a key was a mistake."

We both laugh this time.

"Dahlia?"

"Yeah?"

"*Te amo.*"

Everything stops. My heart. My lungs. My ability to speak.

"I don't expect you to say it back, but I didn't want another day to go by without you hearing it." His confession pulls at every single one of my heartstrings.

His selfless, understated kind of love is the one I spent years searching for but never found—until now.

Julian wasn't the only one living through a ten-year blackout. *I was too.*

I fight a battle against my tear ducts and lose with a sniffle.

"Don't cry."

"I'm not crying…" My voice wavers.

"It sounds like it to me."

"Shut up and say it again."

"It sounds like—"

"No. The other thing."

"Don't cry?"

If he were here, I'd kiss the smile right off his face.

"Forget it," I huff.

"I love you. Good night," he repeats before hanging up the phone.

After Julian's confession, I can't fall back asleep, so instead, I obsess over our conversation until I've gone over it a hundred times.

Te amo: I love you.

With every fiber of my being, I know he loves me, and it's time I showed him I feel the same way, even if it means putting my heart on the line once more. Experiencing Julian's love for a moment is far better than me spending a lifetime without it, wondering what might have happened had I given him a chance.

🏆

My phone pings the next day with a text from my agent asking if I am going to this Saturday's party.

ME

What party?

She attaches a photo of the Creswells' fifth annual post-production party.

JAMIE

I thought that's why you wanted to meet with Archer this week as opposed to next.

ME

My invitation must have gotten lost in the mail.

JAMIE

Shit. You're on the RSVP list.

My phone vibrates from an incoming call.

"Hey, Jamie."

"Fuck them!"

My eyes go wide as saucers.

"You didn't know about this?"

"I mean, I've been to them in the past, but I thought they wouldn't host one this year after everything."

"Those assholes." She seethes through the phone.

"It's okay."

"No, it's not okay! They did this on purpose to embarrass you."

"Only if I let them."

Her heels click against the floor from her pacing. "You're not thinking of going, are you?"

I stay quiet.

"Dahlia, you can't be serious. You've come so far since the first time we met. No need to threaten all that progress."

When I first met Jamie, I had a breakdown in her office after telling her the story of how my previous agent dropped me as a client. At the time, I was depressed without knowing it, and my lack of control over my emotions was at its all-time low.

But look at you now.

"I want to show them they didn't break me." They might have come close, but I'm still here, fighting for myself and the future I deserve.

"Do you want me to be your plus-one?"

I consider it for a moment before thinking better of it. "Actually, I already have a date."

"Is he hot?"

"Absolutely," I say before laughing.

"Smart?"

My nose wrinkles. "Annoyingly so."

"Please tell me he's rich."

"He makes Oliver's inheritance seem like play money."

Jamie whistles. "Good for you. He sounds like a keeper."

I know, and it's time I told him so.

CHAPTER FIFTY-ONE

Julian

My phone rings, interrupting me in the middle of slicing through a block of wood.

I answer. "Dahlia?"

"So, feel free to say no, but I have this crazy request—"

"Done."

Her laugh is the sweetest sound.

She composes herself before saying, "You haven't heard what it is."

"Do I need to?"

She grumbles something under her breath that I can't make out.

My brows pinch together. "What?"

"The Creswells are throwing their annual postseason wrap party, and I conveniently ended up on the RSVP list."

I'm not the slightest bit surprised. With the media rallying behind Dahlia after Oliver's Vegas drive-thru wedding and the disaster of their last season, the Creswells need some major damage control.

"When is it?" I toss the wood post to the side and start cleaning up my station.

"Tomorrow night."

"I'll be there first thing in the morning. Should I bring a tux or a suit?"

"*Julian.*"

"Good call. I'll pack both, and you can pick between the two." I wipe my sawdust-sprinkled hands down my shirt.

"You seriously want to go?"

"Do you plan on attending?"

She pauses for a moment. "Yes."

"Then, yeah, I want to go."

"Thank you," she whispers before hanging up.

Last time I was in San Francisco, I could barely afford an economy ticket to get home for the holidays, yet here I am now, parking my private jet on a secluded landing strip.

Sam earned himself a nice Christmas bonus for finding a pilot at the last minute and renting me a red Ferrari worth more than all my cars combined.

I park the car outside Dahlia's townhouse before killing the engine and stepping out. The Victorian style fits Dahlia to a T, with white wood trim, blue siding, and those bay windows she loves so much.

I climb the steps, step over the faded *mi casa es tu casa* doormat, and ring the bell.

"Coming!"

The door swings open a few minutes later.

Dahlia rubs the sleep from her eyes. "You're here."

"I told you I would be." I wrap my arm around her waist and crush my mouth against hers, kissing her like I've dreamed of doing since she left Lake Wisteria four days ago.

It quickly turns punishing as I take my frustration and worries out on her lips, sucking and biting them until she hisses.

I pull away and rest my forehead against hers. "I missed you."

"It hasn't been a week since I last saw you."

"Four days too long."

"You're needy."

"Tell me about it."

She yawns. "When you said you were coming in the morning, I assumed you meant later."

"I thought we could spend the day together."

"What did you have in mind?"

"Whatever you want."

"Breakfast for sure."

"Yes, please." My stomach grumbles on cue.

"Pedicures?"

I make a face. "Sure?"

She clasps her hands together. "Shopping?"

"I expected as much."

The pure happiness radiating off her makes today's early wake-up call worth it.

She grabs my hand and pulls me inside before shutting the door behind me. "Give me a few minutes to get dressed. Feel free to snoop around."

I plan on taking her up on the opportunity, but a sealed box beside the door stops me.

"I've been meaning to send his stuff back."

"You got his address wrong. Hell's zip code is 666."

She wraps her arms around my waist. "I feel better already about everything, and you've only been here for two minutes."

"Am I going to find anything else of Oliver's around here?"

"No. This has always been my place, though he hated the idea of us living separately."

"Remind me to thank your mother for pushing against you living with someone before marriage."

"I have a feeling you'll regret that statement one day."

"What—"

A phone ringing snags her attention, and she takes off up the stairs, leaving me alone. The warm color palette, hardwood floors, and mix of furniture and textures match Dahlia's style perfectly, although the cardboard moving boxes in every room seem out of place.

Natural light pours through the windows, highlighting the picture frames hung in a neat row. Each holds a different sketch.

Her mother's flower shop. The Founder's house. Her current living room featuring different items from her décor collection.

"Ready?"

I turn to find Dahlia dressed for the chilly weather outside. "Are you moving?" I point to a stack of boxes beside her.

"Yeah."

My stomach tightens. "Where to?"

"I'm not sure if you've heard of it, but there's this small town in Michigan called Lake Wisteria—"

"What?" I must have heard her wrong.

"I told you it was small."

"You're moving back home?"

"I am."

"Why?"

"I turned down the deal with Archer Media."

I blink a few times. "Why?"

"It didn't feel right."

"But what about your show?"

She shrugs. "When the right contract comes along, I'll know it."

"No second-guessing?"

"Nope. I've never felt more certain about anything."

I clamp my hands around her hips and drag her closer. "You don't need to move back to Lake Wisteria, though. We could still live here—"

She wraps her arms around the back of my neck and tugs me closer. "I don't want to live in San Francisco."

"But—"

"Julian?"

"Yes?"

"*Yo también te amo.*" She rises on the tips of her toes and seals her mouth over mine.

A shiver rushes down my spine as she deepens the kiss. Our tongues fuse together, teasing each other until we're both breathless.

She pulls away with a laugh. "What do you say about getting out of here?"

"Where do you want to go first?" I pull my keys from my back pocket.

"Our old stomping grounds."

"You lead the way." I motion toward the front door.

We step outside, and she pulls her keys out of her purse to lock up.

I hit the button on the fob, and the Ferrari beeps.

Dahlia's eyes go wide. "Can I drive it?"

"Go ahead." I toss the key fob in the air.

She nearly misses it before diving at the last second to grab it. "Seriously?"

I open the driver's door for her. "Sure. It's a rental."

Dahlia adjusts the seat to her height.

"Let's not get into any accidents today, though." I hop into the passenger seat and buckle my seat belt.

She tosses on a pair of sunglasses, realigns the rearview mirror, and takes off down the road, making the tires squeal and my heart lurch in the process.

"Is it as good as you remember?" Dahlia asks.

I take another sip of my iced coffee. "Not bad."

"Not bad? It's the best!" She grabs my straw and takes a sip. "That's delicious, and I refuse to accept any other answer."

"Nostalgia is making you think that." I wrap my arm around her and tug her against my side as I stare up at the

Hoover Tower. "It seemed so much larger when we were freshmen."

She laughs. "Everything about this campus seemed so big and scary."

"I was convinced you were going to transfer back to a local college with how homesick you got during the first year."

"I only survived because of you."

"We helped each other as freshmen, but you made it through the other three years on your own."

She lifts a shoulder. "San Francisco warmed up to me eventually."

"Speaking of San Francisco, where do you want to go next?"

"I remember someone mentioning shopping?"

I tug my wallet from my pocket and pull out my black card. "Buy whatever you want for tonight."

"I was going to use a dress I already had…" She plucks the card from my fingers. "But if you insist!"

Warmth spreads through my chest like an inferno, consuming me.

Funny how I spent ten years searching for someone to make me feel a fraction of the way Dahlia did, only to end up here, hoping I get to spend the rest of my days with her.

🏆

Despite footing the expensive boutique bill, Dahlia doesn't let me sneak a peek at her dress until it's time to head out for the event.

Her heels click against the stairs, but I don't turn until she stops at the landing.

My vision tunnels until I only see her. "*Preciosa*."

From her perfectly styled hair and makeup to her silk dress, Dahlia looks like a billion dollars. She does a little spin, and the fabric of her dress flutters around her, changing colors with the light.

"Remember that when you get your credit card statement at the end of the month."

I grab her hand and give her another twirl, earning the best laugh. "Who's the designer?"

"Why are you asking?"

"I want to buy one in every color, not complain about the cost." I hold out my elbow for her to take. "Are you sure you want to go to this?"

"Yeah." She locks her arm with mine, and we head toward the door.

"Just checking." I help her into the passenger's seat of the Ferrari before sliding behind the wheel.

"Will you play some music?"

"Are we feeling like the *Stressed and Depressed* playlist or the *Fuck Love Songs* playlist?"

"Definitely the latter."

I take off toward the Creswells' mansion with rap music pouring out of the speakers. Their property is in the nicest part of town, where the land costs almost as much as the people's souls who live there.

The valet team rushes to open our doors and help Dahlia out of the car. When I reach for her arm, she trembles.

"Still sure you want to do this?" I ask again.

A visible change happens as she rolls her shoulders back and holds her chin high. "Yes, I'm sure."

I steal a kiss before she shoves me away with a laugh and complains about her lipstick. "I'm here for you."

"Can you promise me one thing?" She holds up her index finger.

"What?"

"When you see Oliver, please don't punch him."

"Should I give you the honors?"

"No. One night with you in a jail cell was enough to last me a lifetime."

I lift her hand to my mouth and kiss it. "I promise not to punch him."

No matter how much I want to.

CHAPTER FIFTY-TWO
Dahlia

ahlia!" One of the crew members, Reina, calls my name, and I turn to find her, Hannah, and Arthur all waving at me.

"Who are they?" Julian's tux brushes against my back as he whispers in my ear.

"They're part of the behind-the-scenes crew."

"Do we like them?" His emphasis on the word *we* has my body tingling.

"Yes, we like them a lot." Although I haven't been a very good friend to them for the last six months. They tried, but it was easier for me to get a grip on my depression by cutting myself off from the life I had.

I tug on Julian's hand and lead him toward the old crew, where I'm quickly pulled away from him and into a group hug.

"We've missed you!" Hannah, my makeup artist with

purple highlights and a tongue ring, squeals before Reina, a real-life Malibu Barbie, pulls me into a second embrace. "You haven't answered many of our texts."

I blush. "I was…"

"Listening to country music?" Hannah's knowing eyes catch mine.

"Exactly."

"We get it. Boys suck." Arthur, the show's hairstylist, assesses my split ends. "You're due for a trim."

"I'm heading out tomorrow, or else I'd ask if you have time."

"We can stay for another few days if you want," Julian offers.

"And who is this handsome lad?" Arthur checks him out.

I don't blame him for being starstruck since I had the same reaction earlier when Julian stepped out of my guest bedroom wearing a custom tux.

"I'm her boyfriend, Julian." He holds out his hand, but Arthur bats it away and wraps his arms around him.

"Did you hear that?" He turns Julian around and shows him off like an auctioneer. "Dahlia has a boyfriend!"

"Would you like a microphone so everyone else at the party can know Dahlia has a boyfriend?" Hannah asks.

"Boyfriend?"

The hairs on my arms rise as I turn on my heels to find Oliver standing slack-jawed with a drink in his hand and a shiny wedding band on his left ring finger. Once upon a time, I thought he was handsome, but now I'm revolted by his presence.

I prefer nausea over heartache, so I'm going to take my reaction as a win.

Olivia, who stands beside my ex wearing a beautiful gossamer gown and a stunning diamond ring similar to the one I had before, remains silently poised, although I catch her tipping her chin in my direction in silent acknowledgment.

Julian hooks his arm around my waist, soothing the discomfort away with a brush of his thumb over my hip bone. Where he seeks to comfort me, Oliver would have never bothered, solely because my ex wouldn't have noticed my uneasiness in the first place. How could he when his focus was always on impressing everyone else in the room?

To think you once compared Julian to him...

I cover Julian's hand with my own and give it a squeeze.

Oliver gawks. "Julian?"

"Oliver."

My ex's sharp jaw clenches. "I had no clue you two were dating."

"I would have added him as a plus-one on my RSVP had I actually received an invitation."

His face loses that golden color. "About that...my mother—"

"Is right here!" Mrs. Creswell arrives with her blond hair perfectly coifed and her smile deceptively sweet, while her husband trails behind her, stuffing his mouth with appetizers while looking everywhere but at his wife.

"Dahlia." She holds out her arms, which I ignore.

Julian makes a soft noise that sounds an awful lot like a laugh.

Her arms drop to her sides. "I'm so glad you could make it."

"I'm sure you are since you accepted the invitation on my behalf."

Oliver's father chokes on a bite of his lamb lollipop.

Mrs. Creswell claps her hands together. "Well, we were so excited to have you here for the final season's postproduction party."

"Is that so?"

Her right eye twitches. "Of course. You're one of the reasons why the show was successful."

"She *was* the reason," Julian snaps.

Mrs. Creswell's long blink is so unlike her. "And you are?"

"Julian Lopez. My ex-roommate and Dahlia's new boyfriend." Oliver manages to keep his sneering to a minimum.

"A new boyfriend already? How fast."

"I'm sure Oliver can speak from firsthand experience on what it's like to meet your soulmate, seeing as he got engaged and married all in the same hour." Julian tucks me closer against him.

Most likely sensing the tension, Mrs. Creswell beckons a cameraman over in the worst attempt to diffuse it. "Oh, great. Let's take a photo for the papers. Everyone gather around."

Julian swoops me to the side before the flash goes off, leaving the Creswells gaping and gawking.

"Say the words and we're out of here." He cups my chin.

"Did you see the look on his face right now?"

He traces my bottom lip with his thumb. "I did."

"You're the best."

He returns my smile with one of his own. A flash goes off, capturing our intimate moment.

Julian peeks over my shoulder. "Oliver is hating every second of this."

"On a scale of one to ten?"

"At least a nine."

"Surely we can do better than that. I want him screaming, crying, and throwing up all at the same time."

"You're a vicious little thing, but I love you for it."

"I'll show you vicious." I grab him by his tux lapels and pull him down so I can kiss him.

Julian's palm finds the small of my back, and he holds me tight as he matches my brutal pace. His kiss is one of passion and possession, making my body tingle and my head spin as our mouths fuse together.

Julian pours everything into every single one of his kisses, making me feel loved, admired, and appreciated.

He is exactly what I want from a partner and more, and I can't wait to see where this next stage of our life takes us.

"Shit. Where can I find myself someone who kisses me like *that*?" Arthur asks with a shout, making my cheeks burn.

Julian tucks a strand of hair behind my ear. "I spent ten years searching, so best of luck to you."

Arthur fans himself. "If you don't marry Julian, I will."

"Talk about marrying him again and see what happens."

Arthur holds his hands up. "Okay, *vicious little thing*. Put those acrylic claws away before someone gets hurt."

CHAPTER FIFTY-THREE

Julian

The only time I leave Dahlia alone is to get us some drinks. Thankfully, she has a few good people in her corner, so I'm able to wait by the bar without worrying over her.

"Did Oliver get the house?" a woman asks beside me.

"He finally pushed the seller into a deal, and we're supposed to go under contract on Monday," says the dainty voice that I assume belongs to Olivia.

Oliver's name has my ears perking up. I'm careful to keep my back to the women as I listen in.

"How much are they selling it for?"

"Eight million."

"You lucky bitch!" the other woman cries.

Olivia laughs. "I never thought we could find a house for sale in Presidio Heights, but we drove by it one day, and I fell in love with the corner lot on Clay Street. Oliver promised it to me as my wedding gift."

"Where can I find someone like him?" The other woman gushes as I open the Dwelling app on my phone and log in using my admin credentials. While there aren't any listings currently available on Clay Street, there are only four corner lots.

"Is it the Edwardian one you mentioned before?" the other woman asks.

"No. That one ended up staying in the family. This one's got more of a European style to it."

It only takes me a few clicks to find the only house matching Olivia's description. I pull up my text thread with Rafa and shoot off a message asking him for a favor.

RAFA

What do you need?

I send him the Dwelling link and a request, to which he responds, *Give me twenty minutes.*

🏆

It doesn't take me long to find Dahlia and her friends, seeing as they're the loudest ones here. While I was away, someone dragged one of the outdoor heaters closer to a table, which casts a warm orange glow on the four of them.

"Thank God." Dahlia grabs the fancy mocktail I ordered and guzzles half of it.

"Thirsty?" I laugh before taking a pull from my beer bottle.

"I'm terribly dehydrated, thank you for asking." Dahlia taps her glass against mine. "Cheers." She takes a sip before shutting her eyes with a sigh.

"What are you doing?"

"Tricking my mind into believing this has liquor."

"If you want—"

"No. They're not worth screwing up my progress." She takes another sip of her drink while I drag a chair over and drape my arm across the back of hers.

Her friends continue chatting about the new shows they were hired to help with and how no one will ever compare to Dahlia. I sit back and enjoy their interactions, all of which end with Hannah, Reina, and Arthur arguing over something.

Dahlia's happiness radiates off her with every grin, laugh, and joke, and I'm honored she invited me here to watch her thrive in front of the family who tried so damn hard to destroy her.

After one of Arthur's jokes, Dahlia's head drops back from the intensity of her laugh, earning looks from everyone, including Oliver.

My grip on the back of her chair tightens as I glare back at him.

Our staring contest is interrupted by his pocket lighting up from his phone screen. He reaches inside and pulls it out, only to frown at the screen.

I lean closer to Dahlia and whisper, "How do you feel about us joining forces and pranking other people instead?"

Her eyes widen. "What did you do?"

"I overheard Olivia mentioning how Oliver had a house lined up to buy in Presidio Heights as a wedding gift." I tilt my chin in his direction.

Dahlia's head swivels toward him.

"What do you mean someone else bought the house?" Oliver shouts into the phone.

A few people glance over at him with a variety of confused expressions.

"You promised it was mine." He stomps off in the opposite direction, only to pause midstride. "Ten million dollars?"

Dahlia gasps. "Tell me you didn't."

I tuck a loose strand of hair behind her ear. "Out of curiosity, how do you feel about homes architecturally influenced by the Italian Renaissance?"

"Absolutely despise them with every fiber of my being."

"Perfect. Me too."

The laugh that pours out of her makes the house worth every penny.

She barely has a chance to catch her breath before she asks, "Did you really buy a random house we both hate because you're that petty?"

"No. I bought a random house we both hate because I'm that in love."

♛

At Dahlia's insistence, we drive the packed moving truck back to Lake Wisteria rather than hire a moving company for the job. She claims there are too many valuables, but I quickly catch on to her plan of wanting to extend our trip for as long as possible.

Three days later, I park the moving truck outside the Muñozes' house with a yawn. Dahlia and I both climb out, fighting drowsiness as we walk toward the front door.

I grab her hand and pull her against my side. "You could move into my house."

"Sorry, but my answer hasn't changed since you last asked me an hour ago."

"But I plan to decorate it for Christmas."

Her brows rise. "Really?"

"Yup. I'm hosting the *posada* this year, which means you're helping."

She laughs. "That's fair after all you did for me during Thanksgiving."

"Because of everything that needs to be done, it's probably best that you stay with me. *Indefinitely*."

She shakes her head.

"Fine." I sigh. "I'll respect your wish not to live together until marriage."

"Assuming we get married to begin with."

I tap her nose. "It's cute that you think you have a choice."

She lets out a half laugh, half scoff. "God. What will I do with you?"

"I have a few ideas." I kiss the back of her left hand.

"Dahlia!" Rosa runs out of the house in fuzzy slippers and a head full of Velcro rollers.

Posada: Mexican Christmas festival to commemorate the nativity story.

"*Mami.*"

Rosa pulls her daughter into a quick, crushing hug before throwing her arms around me and squeezing all the air from my lungs.

Guess she forgave you for the jail cell incident.

She pulls away. "You brought our girl back home."

"She made the choice all on her own. I was only there to drive the truck back."

Rosa stares up at me with shiny brown eyes that remind me so much of Dahlia's. "You did a lot more than that."

Dahlia turns away and swipes at her cheek.

"Are you crying?" I laugh.

She flips me off as she walks into her house. "I hate you."

Some things never change.

When I helped Callahan Kane remodel his house last summer within a nearly impossible time frame, I knew I'd call in the favor he owed me one day, but I hadn't planned on using it on Dahlia's behalf.

My plan could crash and burn, but if it means helping Dahlia get a TV deal that makes her one hundred percent happy, then I will reach out to a man who owes me a big favor.

Callahan Kane is a difficult man to get in touch with. All of my calls go to voicemail, which only makes my anxiety worse with each passing day.

During that time, I focus on my project and getting ready for the holidays. Dahlia helps me decorate my house, and I repay her by fucking her underneath the Christmas tree and watching a few episodes of her favorite telenovela.

Sam keeps his calls to a minimum, which gives me faith in Ryder's abilities to help me run Lopez Luxury. I know he won't let me down, and everyone's feedback about him supports that, so I'm feeling more confident about stepping back and starting a few private projects of my own with Dahlia.

I retry Callahan Kane's number for a second time today, and he picks up after the third ring.

Miracles do come true.

"Julian Lopez. To what do I owe this rare phone call?"

I clear my throat. "Remember that favor you owe me?"

"Straight to the point. I like it. Reminds me of my brother—"

I stop him before he starts rambling. "Do. You. Remember?"

"Why don't you refresh my memory?"

I tap my fingers against my workbench. "I fixed your house in exchange for a favor of my choosing."

"Ah, right. Do you want me to connect you with Declan or Rowan?"

"I want to speak with whoever runs the DreamStream part of the Kane Company."

"You'd like to meet with the television streaming division? What for?"

I stay quiet.

"Why would a developer like you—" He cuts himself off and makes a confirmatory noise. "Oh. I think I know why."

"Can you help me or not?"

"Sure, but you have to answer three questions of mine first."

"What?" I ask.

"Does this request to meet with our streaming department have something to do with Dahlia?"

"Yes."

"Are you in love with her?"

"What does that have to—"

"Answer the question so I understand the severity of the situation."

Este pendejo. "Yes, I'm in love with her."

"Great. That means you'll do anything to help her."

"What's your final question?"

"Are you available tonight?"

"Tonight?"

"Is that a problem?"

"No." Although I'll have to think up a good reason for canceling dinner plans with Dahlia.

"Great. Meet me at the private airport at seven."

I have no idea what I'm getting myself into, but I know Dahlia is worth all the trouble, including putting up with Callahan Kane and his annoyingly sunny disposition.

CHAPTER FIFTY-FOUR

Dahlia

My phone lights up as Ryder discusses the schedule for the Lake Aurora renovation project.

"Excuse me." I step out of the conference room and answer my agent's call.

"You're not going to believe who I just got off the phone with!" Jamie squeals.

I hold my phone at a distance to protect my eardrums from rupturing. "Who?"

"DreamStream!"

"The Kane Company subdivision?"

"Yes! You've heard of them?"

"Is there someone who hasn't?"

Jamie laughs. "True. Well, they reached out to me, asking if you were available for a show idea they have."

"They contacted you?"

"I know. I'm equally shocked. Not that you're not amazing, but DreamStream contracts are huge. You'd become a household name with a company like that producing your show."

I lean against the wall before my knees give out. "What kind of show are they thinking?"

"Well, that's the best part. They're willing to go along with whatever you want, wherever you want, so long as you let them produce and stream it."

"You're joking." A deal like this seems too good to be true.

Probably because it is.

No. I shut down the anxious thought before it has time to fester.

But still, something about this deal seems too convenient.

Who cares? If they're letting you take full creative control of the show, does it matter?

But I can't help wondering how a deal like this came about in the first place.

"Who reached out to you?" I ask.

Jamie doesn't miss a beat. "Declan and Callahan Kane."

"Both of them?"

"Yes. Callahan Kane is doing some consulting work with DreamStream. Said he found out you were pitching a show from a town local and knew his brother would want to get involved since his wife is a big fan."

A town local?

It doesn't take me more than a few seconds to piece everything together.

Holy shit. This is really happening.

I must have said the words aloud because Jamie laughs and says, "Yeah. It is."

I smack my chest to get my lungs working again. "How soon can we meet with them to go over everything?"

Jamie goes into greater detail about the offer, and I diligently listen, my excitement growing with every minute. She hangs up ten minutes later with a promise to send me the revised contract once it is ready.

Now I need to find the town local responsible for all this, and I have a strong feeling I know where he is.

When I decided to move back to Lake Wisteria, I expected Julian to resume his usual position in the business, but I was surprised when he kept true to his original plan. He only works out of his office three times a week now, while he spends the rest of his time managing builds and helping at the sites.

Plus, we're taking on the Lake Aurora house together as project co-leaders.

I haven't seen him look this happy since...well, *ever*.

I open our text thread and send Julian a message.

ME

Are you still in a meeting?

He responds only a few seconds later.

FIRST CHOICE

Nope.

I head to Julian's office, only stopping to greet Sam before walking inside the private suite and shutting the heavy door behind me.

Julian leans back in his chair. "I thought we agreed not to see each other until lunchtime."

It was a valiant effort so we could get some much-needed work done before Christmas break next week, but Julian blew that plan to hell the moment he intervened in my life.

I forgo the seat across from his desk and choose his lap instead. His arm hooks around me, and I curl mine around the back of his neck before crushing my mouth against his.

Julian groans as I glide my tongue across his, earning the slightest shiver as a reward. His fingers press into my hips as he deepens the kiss.

No matter how many times he claims my mouth, it always feels like the first time with the way my toes curl and my spine tingles.

He reluctantly pulls back after another minute. "As much as I love the unexpected visit, I have a call in ten minutes."

I clean the lipstick mark staining the corner of his mouth. "No problem. I only wanted to thank you."

"For what?"

"Whatever you did that landed me a deal with DreamStream."

His arms tighten. "I didn't—"

I press my finger against his mouth. "Don't lie to me or play the humble-boyfriend card." It's the first time I called him my boyfriend, and the shock on his face made it worth the wait.

"Boyfriend?"

"Don't let the title go to your head."

"A little too late for that. Does it come with a lifetime membership?"

I pinch him between the ribs, making him jolt. "Start talking or else." I reach to repeat the move, but he traps my hands against his thigh.

"I wanted you to make a decision that was best for you, not based on my influence in the process."

"So you admit you played a part?"

"If by *played a part*, you mean merely making sure the right person heard about your availability and interest in filming a new show, then yes. Guilty as charged."

I swat his shoulder. "I knew it!"

"How did you find out?"

"Well, it was solely based on a hunch, but a good one given your connection to Callahan Kane and you being the only person in town who knew about me pitching a new show."

The tips of his ears turn pink. "He owed me a favor."

"And you used it on me?"

"I know how much you loved having your own show."

The Kanes rarely owe any favors, so the fact that Julian used his to pitch my show means the world to me.

My chest squeezes. "I can't believe you got me a deal with DreamStream."

He cradles my head between his palms. "All I did was speak with Declan and tell him about your idea for a show. His company offering you a deal was all thanks to you and your years of hard work." He pauses. "And probably the fact that Declan Kane's wife might be your second biggest fan."

"Who's the first?"

"You're in love with him." He slides his fingers through my hair and steals another kiss.

The phone on his desk rings, and we break away with a groan.

"I should get that."

I brush my lips across his. "You should."

He sighs. "Don't make this harder for me."

I run my hand down the front of his pants. "Not sure that's possible."

"Dahlia," he groans as I trace the tip of his cock.

The phone rings again, and I slide off his lap. His dark gaze trails down my body as I walk toward the door, and I'm hit with the same rush of butterflies in my stomach that never seem to go away no matter what.

I glance over my shoulder. "See you in an hour."

"Make it thirty minutes. And ditch the underwear."

"Deal."

CHAPTER FIFTY-FIVE

Julian

For the first time, I hosted Christmas Eve with my mom's and Dahlia's help. The last time all of us were together at my house for the holidays was before my dad died, so I'm a bit overwhelmed when everyone floods my kitchen bright and early in the morning with supplies to make tamales.

Cooking is a whole-day production filled with music, laughter, and too many embarrassing stories from all of our childhoods. By the time we finish dinner and the clock hits midnight, an antsy Nico drags us all toward the living room to open presents.

My godson tears at the wrapping paper with more speed than a superhero, revealing his gift. He squeals before jumping into my arms. "You're the best *tío* ever!"

Dahlia plucks the Formula 1 VIP paddock passes from the floor. "Nice choice."

"You could have been the best *madrina* ever," I tease.

When I mentioned going fifty-fifty on Nico's gift this year, Dahlia scoffed and told me there was no way she would go cheap on her godson.

We may be dating now, but that doesn't mean I'm giving up our competition anytime soon, she said.

I should have expected a response like that from her after spending eight years trying to one-up each other with our presents, but I was still surprised.

She nudges me with her hip. "Don't count me out of the competition yet."

I don't know how she will top my gift. After spending a month hearing Nico talk about his favorite Mexican driver, Elías Cruz, I knew I had to get him a VIP behind-the-scenes pass for Christmas. Although he is a relatively new fan of Formula 1 thanks to his nanny, Ellie, who watches races religiously, he has quickly become a superfan.

"Good luck topping that." I kiss the top of Dahlia's head before taking a seat on the couch.

"I got one for you and Ellie too." I toss Rafa the gift I kept hidden behind the couch until Nico opened his.

"One for Ellie? Why?" Rafa scowls.

"Um...because Nico said she's going on the summer trip with you?"

The vein in my cousin's neck looks ready to burst as he stares at his son. "Is that right?"

"You said I could do whatever I wanted." Nico places the VIP lanyard around his neck.

"I said you could *do* whatever you wanted. Not *invite* whoever you wanted."

"I want to *do* cool stuff with Ellie, so she has to come. Duh!" Nico poses beside me while my mom snaps a photo of us.

Lily laughs. "He got you there."

Rafa's eye twitches as he pulls out two more paddock passes from the gift bag and grumbles a quick *thanks*. Everyone knows he will go along with whatever Nico wants so long as it makes his son happy, including taking his nanny on a summer-long trip around the world, even if he hates every second of it.

"You're welcome for the tickets. Be sure to send us photos and videos of Nico and Ellie freaking out." I wink.

He brushes his eyebrow with his middle finger.

"Please. No fighting on Christmas Eve." My mom tsks.

"Sorry, Ma," Rafa and I say at the same time.

"My turn," Dahlia announces as she passes Nico a small, wrapped box. "Here you go."

"Thank you!" He rips at the red-and-white striped paper with glee before screaming.

"What is it?" Rafa leans forward to check out the tickets Nico keeps clutched in his iron grip.

My godson throws his arms around Dahlia's neck and squeezes her until she is about to turn purple from lack of oxygen.

"Easy there." I pull him away. "What did she get you?"

"Tickets to see Duke Brass in concert!"

"What?" my mom gasps.

"Whoa." Lily gapes. "Way to make us all look bad."

Shit. Those tickets are impossible to find. I tried to score a pair for Nico myself without any success.

Rafa's eyes remain permanently wide. "How did you get those?"

Dahlia shrugs. "I know a guy."

"What organ did you sell?"

"A nonvital one."

I whisper in Dahlia's ear, "You better be fucking joking."

She doesn't bat an eyelash. "We were born with two kidneys for a reason, Julian."

"*Dahlia.*"

Her shoulders hike.

I glare at her.

She nudges me. "A light guy who worked on my show before is now part of the production crew for the tour, so I contacted him and begged for a pair."

"Best gift ever!" Nico jumps around and waves his arms in the air.

Dahlia bats her lashes at me. "Aw. You could have been the best *padrino* ever, but no. I didn't need your help."

I press my lips against her ear and whisper, "Keep talking like that and I'll make your ass match the wrapping paper you chose."

Her face turns beet red, catching my mom's attention as she snaps a photo of us.

"For the photo album!" My mom grins.

Everyone continues to open their presents. Each time I pass one of mine out, Dahlia perks up, only to deflate with poorly concealed disappointment as I hand it to someone else.

Padrino: Godfather.

It's not until most of the gifts have been opened that she reaches under the tree and grabs a box with my name written on the tag. "Here. This one's from me."

"You got me something?"

Her cheeks turn pink. "Yes."

I carefully undo the wrapping paper, taking my sweet time solely because I love Dahlia's rare display of shyness.

"It's not much," she rambles when I fold the wrapping paper into a perfect recyclable square.

"Can you hurry up already? Some of us want to get to bed before Santa gets here," Lily announces.

"Yeah!" Nico high-fives her. "What she said!"

"All right." I laugh as I flip the lid of the box open and reach inside. "What did you get…" My voice drifts off as I pull out her gift.

I spot two main differences between the *Second Best* trophy Dahlia gave me as a graduation gift and this one. The first is that this trophy is far larger, and the second is that the plaque has a different inscription.

First Choice.

Dahlia peeks over at me. "Do you like it?"

I fight the tightness in my throat as I say, "I love it."

"I know it's probably silly, but since you kept the last one…" Her voice trails off.

"It's *perfect*." I wrap my arm around her and kiss her, earning a retching noise from Nico, a round of *ooh*s and *ah*s from our mothers, a sigh from Lily, and Rafa grumbling something to himself.

She breaks the kiss first. "How long do you think it will take before they stop doing that every time we kiss?"

"They have nearly a decade to make up for, so I give it at least a few years before they settle down."

Dahlia groans. "God help us."

"This again?" She grabs the black eye mask from me.

I press my foot against the gas pedal and take off toward the Historic District. "I'd hate to ruin your Christmas surprise."

Her knee shakes as she places the mask over her eyes. I carefully navigate the icy roads leading toward the Founder's house with the truck, being mindful of the sharp turns and slick pavement.

Dahlia doesn't speak up until the next song finishes. "I should have known you had something else planned after I was left empty-handed."

"Did you think I wouldn't have gotten you something?"

"I don't know, but I wasn't about to complain after the whole DreamStream thing. That's worth like ten presents in one."

I park outside the Founder's house and turn the car off. "I already told you. The DreamStream deal was all because of you and your talent, not me."

I doubt she will believe me until she meets with the team herself after the holiday break, but it doesn't hurt to emphasize her success whenever her self-doubt comes creeping up again.

Dahlia waits inside the truck while I go around and open her passenger door. She shivers against me when I help her out into the chilly night.

I interlock our elbows and lead her toward the house.

She tucks her mittens into the front pockets of her coat. "Did you buy me another house?"

"Nope."

Her teeth chatter as we walk through the gate leading to the backyard. "A private jet?"

"Do you want one?"

She laughs. "No, but I bet you'd get me one if I asked."

I trace the tip of her reddening nose. "You're finally starting to catch on."

"The amount of money you have is sick."

"So is my love for you, but I don't hear you complaining."

"Nope."

I push against the small of her back. "Just a few more steps." I lead her toward the perfect spot and let go. "Now, stay right there and don't take your mask off."

"Okay?" She blows hot air while I rush to flip the outdoor switch. I return to find her right where I left her.

My fingers tremble as I slide the eye mask over her head.

She gasps. "Julian."

I tuck the eye mask into my jacket pocket. "What do you think?"

She takes a few steps toward the gazebo and pauses. "You made this?"

I slide my hands into the front pockets of my jeans. "Yup."

My team may have helped me put it all together, but I was present for the whole process.

"It's stunning." She reaches out to stroke the column.

"Glad you think so." I walk up the steps and stop in the center of the platform.

Dahlia follows while gawking at all the details. "It's exactly like the one Gerald designed for Francesca."

"I made a few modifications." I trace over a wood-carved dahlia that would have been a rose if I had stuck to Gerald's original design. Thankfully, my mom had a different idea, which added a personal touch to the piece.

Her eyes shimmer. "I love it for so many reasons, but most of all because you made it."

I pull her against me. She melts into my embrace, our bodies molding together as we get lost in another kiss.

At some point, snow begins to fall around the gazebo, covering the ground like powdered sugar.

"A white Christmas! It's been years since I had one!" She takes off running.

I stay under the gazebo, watching her spin in a circle while attempting to catch snowflakes with her tongue.

Nothing in the world is more beautiful than Dahlia laughing up at the sky, standing in front of the house I plan on turning into a home with her.

I let her have a few minutes of fun before I loop my arm around her waist and pull her toward the Founder's house.

"Where are we going?"

"Home."

"What? Why? We just got here!"

"We're not going anywhere." I open the back door and walk inside while dragging her behind me.

A sigh escapes us as our fingers and toes start thawing.

Dahlia pokes at my chest. "What did you mean when you said we were going home?"

I wave around the living room. "You're standing inside it."

She blinks.

And blinks some more.

"We're keeping the house?"

"I never planned on selling it." I bite down on my tongue.

"Ever?"

I shake my head.

Her gaze bounces around the room, probably mirroring her thoughts. "Why?"

"It's been mine for years."

"*Years?*"

"Yes."

Her mouth drops open, but no words make it out.

I take a deep breath. "Do you remember your answer during the Strawberry Sweetheart pageant? The one about if you had three wishes?"

Her eyes widen.

Catching Dahlia by surprise is easy, but making her speechless? A difficult feat I never thought I would accomplish.

And for my last wish, I'd want to own the blue Founder's house, she said in earnest, after wishing cancer never existed and being able to have one last conversation with her father.

Her eyes shine, not from the moonlight streaming through the wall of windows, but from the strong emotions threatening to consume her.

"I never forgot."

A single tear rolls down her cheek, and I kiss it away.

"You made my wish come true without me realizing it." Her voice cracks.

When the Founder's house was put on the market a few years ago, I purchased it without hesitating. At first, it was a stupid way of seeking revenge on a woman who had every right to move on with someone else. But every time I planned on tearing it down, I stopped myself and considered how hurt Dahlia would be if she returned to find it gone.

Thankfully, I never went through with the plan. I'm not sure Dahlia would have forgiven me for it, and the way everything worked out was so much better.

"But what about the *For Sale* sign we drove by after you helped get rid of my engagement ring?"

"I texted Sam about the favor while you were eating the *nieve* from Cisco's."

"You're joking." She pauses before speaking again. "And you asking me to help design it…"

"Was originally because my mom begged me to find you a job to help you through a tough time."

Her bottom lip trembles. "You could have picked any house for us to work on, but you chose this one."

"Yeah."

"Why?"

"I knew you wouldn't resist working on this house…even if it meant teaming up with me."

"Why didn't you tear it down years ago?"

"That was the original plan."

"What stopped you?" She wraps her arms around my neck.

"Angering Gerald?"

She laughs, and I swallow the sound with my lips. I kiss her forehead. Cheeks. The corner of her mouth and the curve of her neck. Everywhere my mouth can reach, I kiss, all while Dahlia does the same.

"What do you say about making this place ours?" I drop a kiss on the base of her neck.

"Tempting, but you know how my mom feels about living with someone before marriage."

"That can easily be arranged."

Her eyes roll. "Ask me again in a year."

"I'll hold you to that."

Until then, I plan on making this woman mine in every sense of the word.

Mine to love. Mine to marry. Mine to cherish for as long as we live.

The End

EPILOGUE

Dahlia

SIX MONTHS LATER

Warmth encapsulates me, and I sigh as I snuggle closer to the source. The band around my waist tightens, tugging me free from the fog of unconsciousness.

I jolt awake in the wrong bed. "Shit!"

For the third time this month, Julian and I failed to stay awake after staying up way too late doing things that would have my mother attending confession on my behalf for the next five to ten years.

Julian rubs the sleep from his eyes before sitting up against the headboard. I quickly become distracted by his chest and the toned muscles rippling as he readjusts the pillows behind him.

He cups my cheek. "Keep looking at me like that and you're never making it out of here before your mom wakes up."

My heart skips a beat or two as I lean into his touch. "I should go." Yet I can't muster up enough willpower to pull away from Julian's touch.

To most people, my mom's rule of not living with someone until marriage might sound archaic—and I wholeheartedly agree—but I don't plan on challenging her Old Testament beliefs anytime soon, especially when it won't matter a few months from now.

Julian reaches for my hand before I have a chance to slide off the bed. "We could solve this annoying problem by getting married today."

I burst into laughter, only to stop when he doesn't do the same.

"Wait. You're not joking?"

He traces my ring finger, making me shiver. "Definitely not."

"You want to get married *today*?"

"Last night's weather report said it should be a sunny day without any clouds or afternoon summer storms," he nonchalantly announces.

I blink a few times before speaking. "You checked the weather report last night?"

"And the day before that."

"How long have you been doing that?"

He doesn't blink as he says, "Ever since I bought your ring."

My eyes threaten to pop. "My ring?" I jump on top of him, trapping his body beneath mine. "You bought me a ring?"

His bright eyes could rival the sun streaming through the crack in the blinds beside us. "Yes, but you said you wanted to wait until next—"

"*¡Necesito verlo ahora mismo!*"

The best laugh pours out of him. "You'll have to find it first."

"You hid it?"

"Of course. I already caught you snooping around the bedroom last week, so I couldn't take any risks."

My cheeks burn. When I found a jewelry insurance receipt underneath the seat of his truck after he spent the weekend in Detroit with Rafa, I was curious about what Julian bought. While my mind immediately jumped to a ring, I talked myself into assuming he had purchased a classic pair of diamond studs for my upcoming birthday.

Still, I snooped around his room, although my search came up empty.

He kisses my forehead. "If you find it, it's all yours."

I jump off the bed with a squeal before searching Julian's bedroom from top to bottom.

The ensuing mess could compete with my sister's bedroom. "It's somewhere downsta—"

I take off for the stairs, leaving Julian behind to pick up after me, although based on his laughter, he doesn't seem to mind.

I check every square inch of Julian's house, including the inside of the grand piano, the cramped spot behind the toilets, and every pot, pan, and appliance big enough to hide a ring box.

¡Necesito verlo ahora mismo!: I need to see it right now.

Where is it?

Either he got smart after I found all his pro-con lists hidden throughout the house, or he never hid the ring here to begin with.

You should have known he would trick you.

My feet are heavy as I head toward the stairs, ready to admit defeat.

"Find it yet?" Julian's deep voice echoing off the high ceilings startles me.

I follow the sound of his voice into the living room, where I find him leaning against the shelf that displays a few of his prized trophies, including his *Little Prince* book collection and the two trophies I gave him.

Wait a minute…

I checked *behind* the trophies but never inside them.

Way to go, Dahlia.

I stand on the tips of my toes and grab the *Second Best* trophy off the shelf.

Empty.

I could have sworn—

He swaps the one in my hand for the *First Choice* trophy I gave him last Christmas.

My eyes widen at the wood box tucked inside. I fail to control the shakiness in my fingers as I reach inside for the custom-made jewelry box.

"Did you…" I choke on the rest of the sentence as Julian goes down on one knee.

He sets the trophy on the floor beside him before holding out his hand. I place the jewelry box in his open palm. At this angle, I can take in his craftsmanship, including the impeccable and intricately carved details.

He lifts the lid to reveal a beautiful diamond ring nestled in a velvet cushion. The vintage design resembles a flower, with a brilliant solitaire diamond surrounded by a circle of marquise-shaped diamonds that resemble petals.

My vision blurs, and I desperately blink away the tears, praying they don't fall before he has a chance to speak.

The ring is perfect.

He is perfect.

And both of them are all mine.

The box shakes in his hand. "I practiced my speech a hundred different times, but nothing felt right, so I'm going to wing it and hope you say yes."

I already said yes thirty minutes ago, during his spontaneous scavenger hunt, but he doesn't need to know that.

I'm not *that* generous.

"You told me you wanted to wait a year before we talked about marriage, but I don't think I can last another day, let alone one hundred and eighty-seven more, before asking you to be my wife."

My lungs stall as he spins the crank on the side of the box. The opening notes of my favorite song start playing as he plucks the ring from the box and raises it so I can get a better look at the exact one I would have chosen for myself.

"You may have started out as my rival, but you're so much more than that. You're my business partner and best friend. My greatest challenger and the biggest, brightest green flag there is...and hopefully, my future wife."

The tight ball in my throat disappears as I break into laughter. His hand holding the ring trembles as he stares up at me with sparkling eyes and the softest smile.

I drop to my knees and cradle his face between my palms. "Yes."

His lips crash against mine, the ring forgotten as he claims my mouth, sharing a thousand unspoken promises while he kisses me.

Julian was and always will be my first choice, and I plan on spending the rest of our lives showing him that.

He breaks away from the kiss, leaving me breathless as he slides the ring up my ring finger before kissing my knuckles right above it. "What do you say about getting married today?"

I gasp. "Without a dress?"

"Yes or no, Dahlia?"

"Shouldn't we discuss the pros and cons of not having a traditional wedding—"

He lets out a half groan, half growl that has me breaking out into a fit of giggles.

"Fine. Let's get married."

The Founder's house—now known as our *home*—is buzzing with activity as our families rush to prepare for a spontaneous wedding. None of them seem too surprised by the idea, which proves Julian had this whole thing planned all along. From my sister having the perfect bridal bouquet already prepared to Josefina being easily able to secure a wedding license on a Saturday of all days, every piece falls into place.

"Beautiful." My sister snaps a photo of me staring out the window at the gazebo.

Josefina and my mom have their arms wrapped around each other, dabbing at the corners of their eyes while staring at me.

"You all are going to ruin your makeup," Lily chides before taking another picture.

"*Que bella*." Josefina sniffles.

"*Mija*." My mom comes over and pulls me into a hug that Lily catches on camera.

I hold out my hands and motion toward Lily and Josefina, who both join our hug.

"Be careful with her hair."

"And her dress." Josefina watches out for the satin train.

My sister must have stalked my Pinterest account because every detail, from the lace veil to the white dress she *randomly* had in her closet, matches what I pictured for myself.

Piano music playing outside pulls us out of the moment.

Lily places the camera on a side table. "That's our cue! Julian should be walking out now."

I stay glued to the window, but Lily pulls me away before I get a chance to sneak a peek at my future husband.

My sister herds us outside the room and down the stairs before stopping in front of the double doors leading out to the deck and yard beyond.

Que bella: How beautiful

Flowers and candles line the pathway straight to the gazebo, which has been decorated like another one of my dream boards. Julian remains oblivious to my ogling as he stands beneath the dangling flowers hanging from the top of the gazebo, wearing a deep blue suit that blends into the lake behind him.

That's my future husband.

My vision turns misty, and Lily warns me about ruining my makeup for the tenth time tonight.

She reaches into the pocket of her dress and pulls out a yellow rosebud. "I thought your bouquet could use a little piece of Dad since he couldn't make it." She tucks the rosebud in the center.

My eyes itch. "I thought you didn't want me to cry."

"Sorry! Remember to take your time and walk slowly so you don't fall on your face and break another arm."

"Hilarious."

She straightens my veil with a giggle before heading outside to join the small crowd gathering around the gazebo. There are less than twenty people at our impromptu wedding, and I couldn't be happier.

All I need is Julian, an officiant, and a couple of witnesses for the paperwork, all of whom are from our family.

Rafa tips his chin in my godson's direction, and Nico runs his hands over the piano keys once before he hits the first few notes.

"Don't you dare cry," I chant as I step outside.

Everyone's heads turn in my direction. I can barely hear the music over the thumping of my heart, and the only thing keeping my feet moving is the man standing underneath the gazebo, staring at me like I hung the moon shining above us.

My heels click against the wood steps as I step underneath the gazebo Julian hand-carved, taking in the candles and flowers covering every surface.

Julian lifts my veil while Lily reaches for my bouquet, freeing my hands for him to grab.

He leans in and whispers against my ear, *"Eres la mujer más hermosa de todas."*

Goose bumps break out across my arms, and I lean back with a smile, taking him in.

I've seen Julian look happy, but right now, he practically glows from the emotions pouring out of him.

"Ready?" He gives my hand a squeeze.

I glance at Josefina, who must have gotten an officiant's license at some point, before tilting my head toward the mastermind behind this whole operation.

"You had all this planned out, didn't you?"

He lifts my hand and kisses it. *"Jaque mate, cariño."*

Butterflies scatter, making my stomach feel light and bubbly.

"We are gathered here today to witness the marriage of two soulmates destined for one another. And while some couldn't physically be here today with us, we know they're here in spirit." Josefina tips her head toward the side.

I follow her gaze to the table beside the gazebo, where

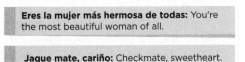

Eres la mujer más hermosa de todas: You're the most beautiful woman of all.

Jaque mate, cariño: Checkmate, sweetheart.

someone placed a photo of our fathers hugging in front of Lake Wisteria.

Since I don't want to put my waterproof mascara to the test, I blink a few times before I turn toward Julian again.

The world stops around us as we stare into each other's eyes. I barely pay attention to the speech Josefina recites, too caught up in our own moment to care about the traditional vows. Julian and I already shared our private promises hours ago after he made love to me following his proposal, so this display is more for our families than anything else.

I follow along and repeat after Josefina whenever Julian squeezes my hand.

She tucks her phone into the pocket of her dress and announces, "You may now kiss the bride."

My heart threatens to burst from the rush of emotions overwhelming me, but I'm not given a moment's reprieve before Julian loops his arm around me and claims his first kiss as my husband.

Best checkmate ever.

ALSO BY LAUREN ASHER...

LAKEFRONT BILLIONAIRES SERIES

A series of interconnected standalones

Love Redesigned

DREAMLAND BILLIONAIRES SERIES

A series of interconnected standalones

The Fine Print

Terms and Conditions

Final Offer

DIRTY AIR SERIES

A series of interconnected standalones

Throttled

Collided

Wrecked

Redeemed

Scan the code to read the books

What's next for the Lakefront Billionaires?

If you're obsessed with grumpy, single dads who will do anything to make their kid smile, then you will love Rafa Lopez's story releasing in 2024.

ACKNOWLEDGMENTS

There are a lot of people that help made this book possible, so this is my moment to say thank you.

To my readers—Because of you, this author dream is possible. Each of you taking a chance on my books means the world to me, and it's something I will never take for granted. Thank you from the bottom of my heart for your love and support. I hope you enjoyed *Love Redesigned*!

Kimberly Brower—Thank you for being the best agent an author could ask for. I'm so grateful that you've been a part of this process since the very first pitch idea, and I couldn't have done this without you.

And to the rest of the team at Brower Literary, including Joy—thank you so much for putting so much time and care into helping the Lakefront Billionaires (and the rest of my books) reach so many readers.

Christa, Letty, Gretchen, and the rest of the team at Bloom—Thank you for putting your absolute all into Julian and Dahlia's story from the very first developmental draft to the final draft. Pam, Katie, and Madison—Thank you for helping make the book launch such a success.

Dom—Thank you for welcoming me into the Bloom family and believing in my stories. I'm so grateful to be part of the incredible legacy you are creating with Sourcebooks.

To the team at Piatkus, including Ellie and Anna—Thank you for helping launch my books not only in the UK, but around the world. You've made so many dreams of mine possible, and I can't wait for this adventure with you.

Nina, Kim, and everyone at Valentine PR—I'm not sure where I would be without you all, but I'm glad I will never have to find out. You all are so dedicated to making each release a success, and I appreciate everything you do behind the scenes to make it possible.

Erica—I can't believe this is the eighth book we have worked on together. It's crazy to think I would most likely not be doing this if it weren't for Throttled, and it's something I will never forget. Love you (and M).

Becca—It's hard to fit my gratitude on a few lines, so I'll just have to send you a voice note. How does one say thank you for pushing me to be the best version of myself? It's impossible, but here's to me trying!

Sarah—Thank you from the bottom of my heart for all you do to help me with my stories. It's truly remarkable to think we have been working together for years with proofreading and editing, and I can't wait for the next book.

Mary—Tequeño mucho. Thank you for being the GOAT. The graphic design queen. The friend I can always count on, even when your social battery is critically low. You take everything I throw at you with a perfectly chosen WhatsApp sticker, and I seriously don't know what I would do without you.

Jos—I'm not sure I would have kept my head on straight during this process without you and our friendship. You're the best hype gal, alpha reader, motivational speaker, and genius problem-solver. And big thank you for saving me from The Secret Life of Love Redesigned.

Nura—It's hard to believe this is the fourth book you have alpha read for me, but here we are! Your excitement, buzz, and amazing suggestions helped bring this book to the next level, and I'm thankful you want to be part of my process.

To my incredible beta readers, Amy, Elizabeth, Fernanda, Jan, Kendra, Janelle, Isabella, Katelyn, and Mia—Thank you for rising to the challenge of beta reading for me. Each of you brought something unique to the process, and I'm grateful you shared your incredible skills and valuable time with me. Because of your feedback, this book was elevated to the next level for me, and I'll never forget that!

Leticia—Thank you for proofing this book. You're so talented and care so much about your work, and I'm lucky Elsie introduced us.

To my family—Thank you for embarking on this wild ride with me. Whether it's helping me with packages or listening to me ramble about plot ideas, you're always there to support me through it all.

To the future Mr. Asher—Thank you for making life, and this scary process, fun. Because of you, I remember to laugh more and stress a little less.

ABOUT THE AUTHOR

Plagued with an overactive imagination, Lauren spends her free time reading and writing. Her dream is to travel to all the places she writes about. She enjoys writing about flawed yet relatable characters you can't help loving. She likes sharing fast-paced stories with angst, steam, and the emotional spectrum.

Her extra-curricular activities include watching YouTube, binging old episodes of *Parks and Rec*, and searching Yelp for new restaurants before choosing her trusted favorite. She works best after her morning coffee and will never deny a nap.